For Carl Ragsdale
with best wishes

—Bill Mack

LIEUTENANT
CHRISTOPHER

LIEUTENANT
CHRISTOPHER

a novel of the sea

by
WILLIAM P. MACK

The Nautical & Aviation Publishing Company of America
Baltimore • Charleston

Library of Congress Catalog Card Number: 97-43810

ISBN: 1-877853-53-4

Printed in the United States of America

Library of Congress Cataloging-in-Publication Data

Mack, William P., 1915-
    Lieutenant Christopher / by William P. Mack.
        p.   cm.
    ISBN 1-877853-53-4
    1. United States—History—Revolution, 1775-1783—operations—Fiction.
I. Title.
PS3563.A3132L5   1998
813' .54—dc21

Front cover painting by William Gilkerson

Chapter 1

Matthew Christopher peered over the rail of the American privateer *Justice*. Low clouds scudded overhead, but the dark sea was quiet and only a few seagulls flew close to the ship in the dark, accompanying them on their swift run up the Delaware River. The speeding ship carried sixteen 9-pounders in a schooner-rigged hull that had been designed and built in Matthew's father's shipyard at Annapolis, Maryland. She was one of 2,000 ships that would be built in shipyards on the shores of the Chesapeake Bay in the next five years. Some were as large as frigates, and others as small as rowing galleys. All would receive letters from Congress authorizing them to prey on British commerce. Congress had begun this policy in March, 1775, and now, in the spring of that year, the *Justice* had already filled her holds with prize cargoes ranging from money to food.

Like most American built privateers, she owed much to French designers and shipbuilders. Her fore and aft schooner-rigged sails enabled her to sail twenty degrees closer to the wind than a square-rigged vessel.

Her forty tons were not much as warships went, but they were enough to carry her sixteen guns, their ammunition, and enough provisions and water to supply a crew of eighty-five sailors for three months. A crew this size could man one side of the battery at any one time, sail the ship, and still spare enough men for a small prize crew or two. Matthew knew that they had space in the hold for any valuable cargo brought aboard from British prize ships they couldn't sail to an American port and would have to destroy or sink. As the provisions were consumed, more of the hold became available for captured goods.

Matthew had watched his father spend countless nights thinking about the ship, planning her by drawing on plain brown wrapping paper, trying to remember the lines he had seen on the fast French ships that had sailed into Annapolis and Baltimore. Matthew knew that his father's two shipyards, one in Annapolis and the other in Chestertown on the Chester River across the bay, could build any ship his father could design. The men working in the yards were all skilled and dedicated workers, and the vessels they built were known throughout the colonies.

Matthew had worked after school and on holidays since his father had deemed he was old enough to swing an adze without hurting himself or endangering a nearby worker. At ten he had been as big as most other workmen. He was unusually tall and muscular for an Englishman, as were his father and mother. Age ten was also a year of change for Matthew. Until then his mother had ruled his education with an iron hand, insisting that he learn to read widely, write prose well, and that he spend his evenings reading from her extensive library brought from England by her father. Dickens, Montaigne, Shakespeare, and a host of other authors were his companions.

Her death from a mysterious fever left him and his older brother Michael in the care of his father and a black nurse named Mammy Sarah. Mammy was a name used in the south for all black women nursing or caring for children, and the two words, Mammy and Sarah, were used as one. Mammy Sarah had seen to the feeding of his growing young body, while his education took a new direction under his father.

Eric Christopher was at heart an engineer, concentrating on mathematics, engineering, and navigation. Social studies and literature simply did not interest him. Therefore, after his mother died, Matthew spent little time on social studies and let up on his reading. His father made sure he was proficient in mathematics, navigation, and engineering and subjects that contributed to those specialties, using textbooks he had imported from Scottish universities.

Matthew's school teacher, Elizabeth Cranston, tried with some success to counter Eric Christopher's aims, but the task was difficult. And while Matthew did become eligible for entry into King William College, the shipyard won out. Miss Cranston resignedly called Matthew in and gave him a collection of books. "Matthew, your mother would have wanted you to have these and to read them. If you want to discuss them at any time, please call on me."

As he left, she brushed her hand across his unruly hair. Matthew knew she liked him, and he returned her affection with a smile. Thereafter he tried to continue to read faithfully, and he remembered her over the years, as he grew into manhood.

Matthew kept his dark hair cropped short with his father's help and a set of English scissors. An English straight razor kept his growing beard under control with only an occasional shave. His father wore his hair equally short and kept his beard neatly trimmed while at sea.

In contrast, most other seamen wore their hair long and clubbed in a tail down their back, held in check with a dirty ribbon or a piece of hemp. Half of the crew wore beards. The younger ones, who could not as yet grow beards, let the other men think they simply did not like them.

Matthew sighed as he thought of all that had happened over the past eight years. Now, at eighteen, he was doing the job of an adult, and it was time for him to concentrate on the job at hand. He rubbed his tired eyes.

Matthew looked at the faint horizon, his brown eyes scanning it carefully with a battered brass long glass. It was still too dark on that early April 1775 morning to make out anything, save the occasional light ashore. About ten miles on the port bow loomed the city of Dover. It was not really a port, having no natural harbor, but merchants brought provisions and water to the beach by horse and wagons and then ferried them out by ship's boats.

Matthew remembered the configuration of the coast line from the battered chart he had studied the day before, and he knew they were on a safe course. There were only three watchstanders on the ship, himself, the boatswain, and the captain, and the boatswain's knowledge of navigation was rudimentary, but Matthew's father had taught him navigation and seamanship well.

Whenever they were on soundings his father was always on deck, and he watched now as his father leaned over the binnacle to check the course the helmsman was steering. The glow of the hooded lantern over the compass lit up his father's angular face and firm jaw. It reflected off his curly black hair and beard, catching the silver streaks just beginning to emerge. But his tanned face showed few signs or wrinkles of age, other than the lines around his eyes from squinting into the sun.

A few minutes passed and Matthew was sure there was a lightening in the sky toward the east and the open sea, and father and son stood by the bulwark anxiously searching the horizon. Matthew's young eyes were sharper, and his father let him use the long glass to sweep the horizon from astern. As he reached the starboard quarter, his heart nearly stopped. There was no doubt the white blur on the dark horizon was a sail. "Jesus!" he said, "A ship is back there, and she's a big one!"

"Give me the glass," the captain growled.

After a few seconds he swore. "It's a big one, all right. A three-masted frigate sailing along like she owns the bay, and she's a British man-of-war."

"Can't we come about and get to the open sea?"

"Hell, no. She'll see us in a few minutes, and in spite of our speed, she'll come left and cut us off. The shore is too close. I have learned my lesson. Next time I'll give myself more room and make an approach to port straight in the bay and turn toward the port after I have it abeam."

"Pa, give me the glass and I'll look up ahead."

The captain gave it to him and stood anxiously clenching his large horny hands as Matthew swept the glass slowly forward. Broad on the starboard bow his heart nearly stopped again. He gave a low whistle.

"Good God!" the captain groaned. "Don't tell me there's another ship up there."

Matthew cleared his throat nervously. "Yes, a second Brit, but not quite as big. Probably a brig or a sloop."

"Still bigger then we are. When it gets light, we're as good as sunk."

"Couldn't we reach Dover or Wilmington?"

"Too far. They'll cut us off ahead. We'll have to beach her at Bower's Beach and then fire her."

HMS *Barley*, a 36-gun British frigate, was standing up the reach of Dover bay to arrive off the Dover area looking for American privateers. The captain, the Marquis of Nottingham, had kept her well off the coast. A 12-gun sloop, the *Periwinkle*, also under the command of Nottingham, was ahead somewhere in the dark, acting as scout.

Captain Nottingham belched quietly. His digestive system was still trying to cope with the huge supper he had downed the evening before, washed down with a whole bottle of claret. He felt about his midriff, trying to locate the source of discomfort. For a moment he thought it might be a sign of serious illness, but he shrugged it off and resolved to change his eating habits. Perhaps more claret and less fatty meat.

Nottingham stopped his pacing, looked aloft, and shouted at the doubled lookouts at the forward cross trees. "Look sharp up there, or I'll keep you up there until noon!"

"Aye, aye, sir," chorused both seamen in loud tones. But under their breath they both muttered in unison, "Fall over the side, you old bastard!" The captain was not the most popular man on the ship.

Nottingham paced faster, feeling better now that he had eased the pressure on his stomach. Shouting at the lookouts had helped. On the next turn, as he passed the binnacle, he ordered, "Officer of the watch, search the horizon toward the shore again and do a better job of it!"

The lieutenant quickly raised his shiny long glass and braced it against a stay. After a few minutes, he paused. "Sir, I think I see a sail. It's against the land and doesn't stand out well." The lieutenant thought about the unfortunate lookouts aloft and realized what his report would mean for them. "Sir," he said, "I don't think the lookouts can see it without a long glass. The white sand of the beach is the same color as the sail in front of it."

Nottingham shouted, "No excuses! No excuses! If it happens again I'll send the lookouts to the gratings and you back to the midshipmen's mess where you came from!"

"Aye, aye, sir," the lieutenant said in his best quarterdeck voice, but then he muttered, "And I'll hope to see you in hell. I know you'll be there."

Nottingham grabbed the long glass from the young lieutenant and pointed it toward the sail. After a thorough examination, he snapped it closed and shoved it back at the lieutenant, bruising his breast bone. "Beat to quarters, and get word to the master to change course toward the sail and do it with all dispatch. I make her out to be a two-masted schooner-rigged American privateer. I mean to take her or destroy her. As soon as there's light, signal to the *Periwinkle* to close us for attack. Now get on with it."

The lieutenant turned forward and barked out a series of orders. Almost instantly the duty drummer began to beat to quarters. The boatswain's mate on watch scurried to the nearest hatch and shouted below, rousing out any of the crew still sleeping. The master came on deck, stretching his arms, and the lieutenant on watch gave him the captain's orders regarding the course change. The off-watch came scrambling on deck and headed for their guns.

Nottingham pointed imperiously toward the sail, now visible in the growing daylight, and shouted, "Head toward her!"

The ship's state of readiness increased, but not fast enough for the captain. He strode about, muttered threats, beat his hands on the seams of his white trousers, and tapped his foot impatiently on the deck. But there was nothing he could do but wait. He resolved to make a few changes when the emergency was over.

Nottingham's imperious manner was not matched by his physique. His white stockings failed to display his calves well and he occasionally wrapped several thicknesses of flannel around them to augment what little muscle he did have. His neck was equally scrawny, but strangely enough housed a deep, vibrant voice that welled out when he issued an order or voiced a complaint.

Searles, the first lieutenant, unable to explain this, said to himself, "The thing to do is listen to the bastard and never look at him."

Captain Nottingham pondered over the changes he wanted to make in his ship, but nothing seemed harsh enough to punish his errant crew. He resumed pacing the deck, being careful to avoid the scurrying seamen and speeding powder boys.

In what was only a few minutes, but seemed to Nottingham like hours, First Lieutenant Searles saluted and reported, "Sir, the ship is ready for battle."

Nottingham nodded. "It's about time."

Searles gritted his teeth, trying to swallow a sarcastic retort. Then he muttered, "Time for what, you bastard?"

Captain Nottingham turned a shade of red. "What was that, Lieutenant Searles?"

Searles rolled his eyes and avoided looking at the captain.

"Ah, sir, I said the American bastards are just in time for you to take them."

Nottingham sneered. "You don't make any sense. Lieutenant, try a little less grog next time and not before lunch."

On the fleeing *Justice*, the captain called out to the boatswain. "Boats, we're going to beach her at Bower's Beach. I'll run her in as far as she'll go. I figure it will be in about six feet of water and a hundred yards off shore. I'm heading for the mouth of the small creek below Bower's Beach. Then we'll fire her and set off the magazine."

Matthew bristled, "But, Pa, aren't we going to fight those bastards?"

"No, Son."

"You mean you'll just give up to them without firing a single shot?"

Eric Christopher sighed and said patiently, "Exactly that, Son. I don't want to see any of our men injured or killed."

"But I still don't understand."

"You saw this ship built, and you know we have two more building on our ways. On this cruise alone we've sent in prizes worth three times the value of this ship."

"I see what you mean all right, although I don't like it. You're going to write off the *Justice*? We worked so hard on her and now we have to go home and start a new ship."

"Yes. We'll find a lot of money waiting for all of us even after we pay for this ship. She's earned her keep. Now stop worrying."

"All right, Pa, I'm ready, but I don't like it. I think of this ship as part of our family and you treat her like a piece of property."

"I don't feel like that, Son. But this is life and it's war also. Now get the boats ready to lower as soon as we ground. We'll load them with about ten men each and the rest will have to swim ashore."

Matthew said, "But, Pa, the boats will take more men than that."

"No, they'll be loaded with the valuables we took from our prizes, as well as twenty muskets and ammunition. Load our navigation gear and any other valuable equipment you can think of."

"Why do we need that many muskets?"

"After we get ashore, they may try to land. I don't want to have to run from them. Losing the ship is bad enough, but running from a bunch of red-coated marines would be too much."

In the growing daylight it was obvious that both Royal Navy ships had sighted them and were closing rapidly. The frigate fired a ranging shot, but it fell far short.

Captain Christopher watched the single geyser of green sea water rise and fall into a puddle of foam. "Thirty-two pounder," he said. "Come left and head for the mouth of the creek. It's between the two rows of trees leading back from the beach. I'll take the deck. Go oversee the boatswain, and make sure those chests are hoisted and stowed in a single boat. Then take charge of that boat and put the boatswain in charge of the other with the muskets. Cast loose the metal plates securing the trunnions to the gun carriages and rouse out the anchor cable and pay it out after we go aground. Then throw over the side everything that will float."

"Pa, that's a large order. I don't have time to throw that much over the side."

"Use your own judgement Throw over some extra line attached to empty or half-filled butts and boxes. We'll want to gather it up on the beach before those bumpkins ashore try to steal it.

"We will also want to get as much cargo landed as possible before those bastards try to salvage it or destroy the ship. Then we'll help them if they find they can't get to her."

"What do you mean?"

"Get ready to fire the ship in a least three places. After that, rig a powder train to the magazine. Make sure it's long enough so I can get off safely."

The captain looked aft. The frigate was still firing ranging shots from her bow chasers, but they were even farther away, as the privateer's speed carried them toward the beach faster than the frigate could follow. "We'll have about ten minutes," he said. "Then all hell will break loose when they come within range. We want to be off and clear of the ship by then."

"Can the frigate board us?"

"No, not by coming alongside. It's too shallow where we are going. Their draft is far deeper than ours, by at least four feet, but they may lower boats and send them in to see if we've left anything of value aboard."

"And you expect to burn or blow up anything we don't throw over the side?"

The captain laughed. "Right. Now get on with it. Tell the men not going in the boats, and who can't swim, to take an empty butt or box or a plank of some sort. They'll only have to make their way a few feet to where its shallow enough to stand."

"But when will you leave the ship?"

"Last. I'll set the fires and light the powder train. Make it long enough to give me a few minutes to get well away from the ship. Our magazine is almost empty, but there's enough black powder down there to make a good explosion. I don't want to get any internal physical damage or be hit by flying debris."

Matthew nodded worriedly. "I think I know what you want, and I'll be off about my business." He stole a look at the smaller British ship, now heading toward them from the northeast. "Pa, that smaller ship won't get here in time."

Captain Christopher's neck bulged and his neck reddened. "Matthew, stop calling me 'Pa' when the crew can hear you. Call me 'Captain'."

Matthew laughed. "Yes, sir, but you ought to hear what the crew calls you when you are out of hearing."

The captain's redness began to subside. "Well?"

"They call you 'Pop'."

The captain grinned. "All right. I'm not that old. Just make sure I don't hear them."

"In a few minutes you'll no longer be captain of anything no matter what you're called."

"Maybe not, but the crew will still want to work in my ship-yard, and they'd better watch their mouths."

"I wouldn't worry what they call you as long as they like you and do the work."

"Stop chewing the fat and get on with your business. Time is getting short."

Matthew grinned. "Yes, sir."

Five minutes later all preparations had been made, and the entire crew came topside to stand by the after bulwark with the captain. The captain looked at them, one by one, with both affection and concern in his eyes. He had known most of them since they had been boys, except for a few men older than he was who were the petty officers and artisans. Some were from Delaware and Virginia, but most were from the villages near Annapolis and Chestertown. He knew why they were aboard. Unfortunately it wasn't patrio-tism and it wasn't loyalty to him. It was the prize money to be earned if the privateer did well, and they had done well.

The captain pointed to the chests in the bottom of one of the boats. "You all know what's in those chests. At least a million in English paper pounds. A lot of gold bullion, and several bags of valuable jewelry. You'll all be paid your proper share when we get it to Chestertown, so guard it carefully."

One of the younger seamen grinned. "What about your share, Captain?"

"As you know, the custom of prize division calls to pay for the ship first if we lose it, and we certainly will. Then I'm entitled to three-eighths share of the remainder as captain. Matthew and the boatswain get an officer's share. Then you divide up the rest. We never signed an agreement only because the custom is well known. Ask one of the older seamen to explain the details to you."

There was a cheer from the back.

"Well?" the captain asked.

"Nothing, Captain. I was just cheering for my share."

The captain laughed. "Men, we'll be there shortly. Now spread out and brace yourselves before we hit bottom. We'll slide up on it gradually, but if you're not holding on to something firmly, you can get banged up. Take your stations, and I'll see you on the beach."

Chapter 2

Captain Christopher stood by the binnacle, a wooden structure placed before the steering wheel, and fitted to hold a magnetic compass at waist level so the steersmen could see it well. At night a partial hood enclosed it, and a small lantern illuminated the face.

Occasionally the captain ordered small changes of course to compensate for the current and wind as the ship neared the point he had selected to ground her.

The morning weather was calm, and Matthew thought that the crew, even the poor swimmers, would have no trouble getting ashore in the calm seas and the low surf.

Matthew watched his father with pride, thinking how steady he was, and seemingly unconcerned about losing his ship and possibly his life.

Matthew looked at the dunes behind the small creek entrance. "Pa, er, Captain, there are a hundred men and women standing over there watching us."

The captain looked up at the group of people and laughed. "It'll be some show. I hope they like it." Then he raised his long glass and scanned the group. "I guess they heard the British guns banging away at us and came to the beach to see what it was all about."

Matthew could see them with his naked eye. "They're waving at us."

The captain, still looking through his long glass, said, "Yes, they're trying to warn us that we're standing into danger, but they don't know we're doing it deliberately. They'll be surprised when we ignore their warnings."

"Well, they'll find out soon enough."

The captain nodded. "There's old man Bowers standing in front of the group. He's the mayor of the village and has been for thirty years."

"You know him?"

"Bought some lumber from him one time when we used up all we could get in Maryland. Delaware is only a day's haul from our Chestertown yard. Some of it was put in this ship, mostly planking. Part of it may float ashore back to where it came from."

Matthew said, "I remember cutting the planking from the raw lumber before we put it in. It was good wood, but we didn't seem to age it enough."

Christopher shrugged. "We were in a war of sorts. We'll need hundreds of ships before it's over, and we'll have to use any lumber we can get, aged or not."

"I understand, but it will shrink like our decking did."

"Then we'll just have to pump the bilges more often. There's a price for everything."

The captain handed the long glass to Matthew. "Here, lad, put this and the compass in your boat together with all our navigational gear. Is everything ready to go? We're almost there."

Matthew said, "As ready as we'll ever be for something like this. It beats being sunk by gunfire. Fortunately we don't do it very often."

The next moment the captain could feel in the soles of his feet something others could not feel. He knew the keel was dragging over the ridges of the sand bottom. He shouted, "Hang on, there!"

Suddenly the keel ploughed into the solid sand. The ship listed slightly to port and stopped abruptly. Some of the men on deck who had not taken a firm enough grip on a nearby line or rail fell to the deck and slid forward. The masts and their sails heaved forward as well, and the rigging shuddered sickeningly. Two back stays snapped under the sudden strain.

They were firmly aground, and Christopher heaved a sigh of relief.

On the quarterdeck of the speeding British frigate, Captain Nottingham shouted at the top of his loud voice, "Fire a ranging shot from a bow chaser!"

"Aye, aye, sir," cried one of the young lieutenants as he scurried forward to carry out the order.

Nottingham watched him go and muttered, "Slow, demmit. I'll teach him to move faster."

The first lieutenant, studying the movements of the American ship, said, "I think the schooner has changed course away from us."

"Toward the beach?"

"Yes, sir."

"Then he can't go far in that direction. There's nothing over there but sand and a hell of a lot of it. A lot of this country is barren."

"I think he's going to beach the ship and then destroy her himself, sir."

"The cowardly bastard won't fight us?"

"I don't think so, sir, he couldn't even out-shoot the *Periwinkle*."

"That's got nothing to do with it. He'll never get to our cohort. Any sailor worthy of his name wouldn't destroy his ship without firing a shot."

The first lieutenant shrugged. "He may have a different point of view."

"Well, we'll have to kick him in the butt as he goes. Keep firing the ranging gun. As soon as we're in range, we'll change course to starboard to bring our port battery to bear and let the yellow cur have it."

The first lieutenant had had all he could take of Captain Nottingham, and he moved forward to oversee the young lieutenant now engaged in firing the bow chasers. The officer was doing well, but the first lieutenant needed an excuse to get away from the fussing captain. After six rounds, he came trotting aft. "Sir, we're in range."

Nottingham nodded, drew his sword, and turned to the master. "Master, change course four points to the north to unmask the port battery."

"Aye, aye, sir," the master answered. He turned and shouted the required orders.

Lieutenant Searles rolled his eyes and thought for a moment about drawing his sword, too, but he made up his mind not to copy the dramatics of the captain and left his sword in its scabbard. He mumbled to himself, "Now the ruddy bastards will catch it."

Captain Nottingham whirled. "What did you say? Have you been in the grog before lunch again?"

"Er, no, sir. I just said, 'The American bastards are about to catch it.'"

Nottingham shook his head, "I still think you were fogged up again."

On the slanting deck of the stricken *Justice* the captain shouted, "Look alive! Get the boats over the side and throw overboard everything that will float."

Matthew ran forward to see that the Captain's orders were carried out. The men were so well trained that there was little for him to do.

The captain watched his men running about the main deck carrying out his orders. Forward he could see the anchor cable being payed out over the side. Matthew and the boatswain lowered the boats as empty butts, boxes, and planks flew over the side. He was so preoccupied with the work on the deck that he momentarily forgot the British ships, but he was quickly reminded of them as a 32-pound ball flew over his head, carrying away the mainmast. Splinters flew around his head, and he tried to protect himself with his arms. When the last of the splinters had reached the deck and he found that none had injured him, he lowered his arms, "Damned lucky," he said. "Wood splinters do more damage than bullets."

Captain Christopher looked around, "Anybody hurt?" he asked anxiously.

A chorus of no's came back.

The captain looked back at the approaching frigate, gunsmoke wreathing her bow chasers and then passing downwind. Now that she was in range, a turn would unmask a broadside and send more

32-pound balls her way. "All hands over the side as fast as you can!" he shouted.

He ran to the first area where Matthew had assembled a pile of wood splinters and knelt down to set it on fire. The wood took fire and ran up a shroud and spread to the yards and their hanging sails. Two other piles flared up and ignited the deck planking. He ran over to the powder train leading to the magazine below. The frigate was rounding up to starboard, and the captain could see the muzzles of twelve threatening guns pointed at him by their laboring crews. He bent over, lit the powder train, and vaulted over the bulwark into the water. He came up rapidly and swam away as fast as he could.

When Captain Nottingham's ship had changed course so that all of the port battery would bear, he waved his sword. He ordered, "Prepare to fire!"

The gun captains, as soon as they had laid their guns on the target, reported "Ready."

At the port battery, Searles, the first lieutenant, shouted, "Commence firing!"

Captain Nottingham laughed, "That'll take care of the American bastards you were talking about."

Lieutenant Searles said, "Right, sir."

Nottingham snapped, "Don't use the word 'right' on the quarterdeck. It's 'starboard', not 'right', and we're already headed to starboard."

Searles shook his head and ran forward to get away from his exasperating captain.

The smoke of twelve 32-pounder guns boiled out and then downwind. The thunder of the explosions shook the heads of those standing on deck.

Captain Nottingham paced impatiently as the balls flew at the helpless American ship. The gun crews labored to reload and fire another broadside.

Nottingham waved his sword and watched the American privateer intently. As far as he was concerned, she was going to be destroyed, one way or the other. In either case, her captain was a poor sport, and was depriving him of the satisfaction of the chase. The Americans did not know how to play the game. "They were not officers and gentlemen," he muttered to himself. "I'll teach them a lesson."

In the *Justice*'s starboard boat Matthew heard the sound of the broadside and saw the splashes his father made as he swam toward the beach. When his father was about twenty yards from the ship with his feet on the bottom, Matthew could see the British broadside tear through the sails and hull of the stranded and helpless sloop. He shook his head. "The *Justice* won't last long one way or the other." He thought about all the hours of work he had put into that beautiful little ship. It was the first vessel he had worked on from the keel laying to launching, and he felt as if he had given her life. Now he watched as she died helplessly, and there was nothing he could do about it.

By the time the third broadside had torn her upper works, the burning powder train reached the magazine and exploded with an ear-shattering boom. He hoped his father was far enough away to escape injury from the underwater concussion spreading from the submerged magazine.

Pieces of planking, rigging, sails, and masts flew upwards and soared lazily, turned over slowly, and landed close to the laboring boats and even closer to his father. Matthew looked anxiously at his father, but he was now in shallow water, wading toward the beach.

Aboard the frigate, Lieutenant Searles, still carrying the long glass, trained it on the unfortunate target. "Sir, she's burning." he reported.

Nottingham's mouth flew open. "Burning? Demme! What do you mean? We just started our firing!"

"Sir, I think they've fired her."

Suddenly there was a huge explosion that shattered the relative quiet between broadsides.

Nottingham's neck turned red. "I'll teach those cowardly bastards a lesson! They're standing over there on the beach laughing at us. Master, strike your sails. First Lieutenant, lower two boats and load each with twenty armed marines. Dispatch them ashore under command of the marine officer. I want those yokels punished."

The first lieutenant started to protest the futility of the action, but thought better of it when he remembered the color of the captain's neck. This time he decided not to comment as he had probably reached the limit of Nottingham's patience. It was not the occasion to argue with him, but his emotional decision would undoubtedly cost lives when the boats reached the beach.

In the boat, Matthew stopped worrying about his father and concentrated on steering into the shallow creek. His four oarsmen pulled strongly.

A short distance up the creek, he found a place to moor the boat, secured it to two nearby tree trunks, and waved the boatswain to bring his boat alongside. When he was sure the boats were secure, he left the boatswain and two men armed with muskets to guard the boats and their contents. Scrambling up the bank, he made his way up the creek side where he joined the men and women standing on the dunes.

Below them, on the beach, the *Justice*'s crew stood in a group likewise watching the *Justice* burn. A few of them picked up debris that began floating ashore and put it in a pile.

Matthew saw his father wade ashore. The captain spoke briefly to the crew, and climbed up the dune behind the beach.

"Are you all right, Pa?" Matthew asked anxiously.

"Sure, Son, although that explosion knocked the wind out of me."

"I'm glad the magazines were nearly empty."

"Yes, it was bad enough as it was."

The captain went over to an elderly man standing in the center of the group and stuck out his hand. "Mayor Bower, I believe? Glad to see you again. My ship used to be the *Justice*. I also used to be Captain Christopher. Now I'm no longer in command of anything except a couple of shipyards."

Mayor Bower grinned and then quickly closed his mouth as cold air irritated his latest tooth cavity. "Welcome to Bower's Beach. I hope the British won't be coming ashore after you. I can see they've put their boats in the water."

Christopher looked at the British frigate offshore. "Looks like they thought about it but changed their minds. I think they hoped to salvage something from the ship, but there isn't anything left."

The mayor looked toward the frigate. "Looks to me like they've got their boats alongside and are getting ready to hoist them."

The captain shaded his eyes against the rising sun and looked at the frigate intently. "No, they aren't hoisting them. The boats are alongside loading marines. You can see their red coats as they climb down the ladders."

Bower frowned. "What's that all about?"

"I think they're going to come ashore and try to capture us. We can run away fast enough so they won't be able to catch us, but they'll take it out on you and will likely burn your houses. That's a typical British stunt."

Bower bristled, and his voice rose. "The hell they will! We'll fight them."

Captain Christopher laughed. "How many guns and swords can you muster?"

The mayor hesitated. "Maybe a dozen fowling pieces, some meat cleavers, and maybe an old sword or two. We'll use pitch forks and barrel staves if we have to."

"Well, you'd better start gathering them up. I count at least twenty marines in each boat, and the boats are rapidly heading this way."

Bower trotted away at top speed to rally his constituents.

Christopher cupped his hands and shouted at his men gathered on the beach. "Go to the boats on the double and bring back our twenty muskets and their ammunition and anything else you can find to fight with. Even the oars."

Matthew shouted back. "I'll bring back all fifty muskets."

"Damn!" the captain shouted back. "You've done it again. Even though I didn't tell you to do it, you've brought them all. And bring all our men up here behind the dune."

When the crew arrived, Christopher set them to work digging shallow gun pits behind the dune top, using their hands, pointed sticks, and meat cleavers. He distributed the muskets and spread the sailors out at three-yard intervals on each side of him. "We're ready," he said. "Let them come."

"Now what do we do?" Matthew asked.

Captain Christopher grinned, "It will come naturally, just wait and see."

A man lying prone in a shallow hole next to him said to Captain Christopher, "Captain, why are we making like a bunch of sand crabs? If we took off now we could easily outrun those clowns in their red suits."

Captain Christopher shook his head, "We've run far enough. We fight now when the odds are in our favor. Aim your guns at each one of those red suits, and try not to shoot the same man. Distribute your fire from right to left in the boat just like you are lying in the pits."

The man grinned and pursed his lips with a dour grin, "Well, I like that, too."

Captain Christopher, turning his attention toward the approaching boats, shook his head and said, "They'll be beaching in a few minutes."

He raised his voice so all the men could hear. "Now listen to me. I'll give orders to fire when the first boat beaches and before the marines can disembark. Only the men on my left will fire. We'll kill most of the men in the boat before they can get over the side and wade ashore. They don't know how well we are armed or how well you men can shoot. Some damned fool sent them in."

Matthew asked, "But what about the second boat and all the men on the right?"

Christopher raised his eyebrows patiently. "Don't worry about that. When the men in the second boat see what's happened to the men in the first boat, they'll either jump over the side or pull back."

"But don't you want to kill as many as we can? They won't be expecting our fire power."

"I don't want to kill them needlessly, and only if they become a threat. After all, you and I are English by descent. They may be our kin."

The British boats came on quickly, the oarsmen rowing steadily. The Americans picked individual targets in the left hand boat as Captain Christopher had told them to do. The left hand boat was now twenty yards ahead of the other.

One man grinned as he pulled the stock tight against his cheek. "It'll be like shooting quail in a barrel," he said to his neighbor.

The man next to him said, "I thought you said we should run away."

"Ah, no, just kidding. I wouldn't miss this for a useless American pound."

Just as the first boat grounded, Christopher shouted, "Commence firing on my left!"

Twenty-five muskets fired almost in unison, and most of the red-coated marines and some of the sailors in the first boat died quick deaths, but some were only wounded.

There was silence behind the dunes as the men from the *Justice* and the few townspeople who had joined them quickly reloaded their guns. The men on the right waited eagerly, their muskets pointed at the second boat.

Captain Christopher stood up and held up his hand. "Hold your fire on the right!" he shouted. "I don't think we will need to kill any more."

The British naval officer in the second boat held up both hands in a gesture of surrender. His oarsmen frantically backed water, and the boat stopped, still twenty yards off the beach. Those still alive in the first boat yelled frantically for help, and the officer in charge of the second boat, hoping that their lives would be spared, ordered his coxswain to take the stricken boat in tow.

But one man in the second boat had a different opinion. The marine officer was embarked in that boat. He stood up and began to argue with the young naval officer.

Christopher said, "The marine is trying to convince the naval officer to continue the attack."

"I don't believe it," Matthew said. "Couldn't he see what happened to the first boat?"

"Some marines are bull-headed. They never want to quit, no matter what the odds. Sometimes that's good. This time the marine is trying to set an impossible task."

The American seamen behind the dunes waited as the two officers argued. One or two hints were offered jokingly, but Captain Christopher silenced them. "Twenty men just died out there. Don't take it lightly."

Then the marine officer in the boat began to wave his sword angrily. Captain Christopher said, "This is enough. He might win the argument."

Christopher turned to a man he knew to be a good marksman. "Can you shoot that marine?"

The man laughed. "Certainly, sir. Exactly where do you want the bullet?"

Christopher looked at the marine again. "He's facing away from you. Can you hit him in the buttocks?"

The man grinned. "Right or left?"

"Left."

The young sailor drew the stock tightly to his cheek and peered over the sight as he steadied the barrel on the top of the dune. He squeezed the trigger slowly. The gun went off, and each man held his breath.

The marine staggered, turned to face the beach, dropped his sword, and fell over backwards, taking the naval officer to the bottom of the boat with him.

Christopher grinned with grim satisfaction. "Well, the naval officer ended up on the bottom, but he won the argument with a little help from us."

In the boat, the men paid no attention to the struggling naval officer or the wounded marine officer as they hurriedly tried to take the other boat in tow.

Christopher looked at the young marksman approvingly. "You were pretty good."

The sailor shrugged, "Captain, at this distance I can hit a squirrel in the head."

"Why would you want to hit him in the head?"

"Don't want to waste any meat. Captain, you should get out of your shipyard office more often. You'd learn a lot out in the woods."

One of the men near Christopher stood up. "Captain, you aren't going to let them go?"

Christopher nodded. "Yes. Maybe they'll remember us some day if we are ever taken prisoner. This will be a long and bloody war, and I hear they don't treat privateer prisoners very well."

On the quarterdeck of the *Artemis* Captain Nottingham swore softly. "Demme! Those upstarts have put another one over on us, but we'll get back at those hairy backwoodsmen."

A nearby midshipman smirked and inadvertently giggled.

The captain turned toward him and said, "Mister, you said something?"

"Er, no sir, I coughed. Powder smoke in my lungs."

The captain sneered and pointed upwards. "To the cross trees, and don't come down until sunset."

The captain turned to the first lieutenant. "Recall our boats."

The master, not as afraid of the captain as the first lieutenant, said, "I think they are already on the way back. They didn't like their welcome."

"Well, we'll leave a calling card. Fire a shot through that demmed outhouse."

When the boats came back, the captain looked over the side at the bloody dead, mostly marines, and the many wounded. He turned to the first lieutenant. "Get them aboard, send them below, and clean up the boat and set all sail. Then head out of this awful bay. I never want to see it again or the filthy backwoodsmen who live here. I'm going to my cabin."

The first lieutenant saluted and started to say something, but the captain was gone. Searles sneered, "You're the filthy one.

Won't even welcome all the men back who gave their lives for you."

Ashore, Captain Christopher heard a single shot fired by the frigate. A ball came flying at the dune, narrowly missing an outhouse. The house was used for swimmers living in the village during the summer. The ball bounced twice and rolled to a stop inland.

Christopher shrugged. "A goodbye present, I guess." He turned to the mayor. "Mayor, as soon as I've mustered and instructed my crew I'd like to do some business with you."

The mayor nodded. "I'll be pleased to talk to you about anything. As I remember it, our previous lumber dealings were very satisfactory."

"Satisfactory for both of us. Some of the lumber is lying down there on the beach now."

Christopher turned to his son and led him away from the mayor. "Matthew, let's go down to the boats and talk over what we are going to do. Stop by the beach and detail some men to stay there and pick up anything more that floats ashore before the townspeople steal it. Then join me at the boats."

Matthew asked, "Shall I arm them with muskets?"

Eric Christopher laughed, "I don't think you need to bother, Son. I haven't seen any one here yet who couldn't be scared off by a couple of growls from any one of our men. I think they're on our side."

"Yeah. This is a little too far south for Tories."

"I agree."

"Then why did you ask?"

"Just asking, Pa. I'll see you there."

Chapter 3

Fifteen minutes later most of the crew were gathered around Captain Christopher and the boats. Most of them were wet and covered with sand.

Christopher, himself still wet, said, "This June weather will dry us off soon. I'll make arrangements with the mayor to house and feed you while we do some salvage work off the beach. The boats can leave in a day or two and sail south around into Chesapeake Bay and up to our shipyard in Chestertown. Shouldn't take more than a week to make the three hundred miles."

Matthew asked, "Do you think we will run into small British sloops patrolling the coast?"

Captain Christopher pursed his lips. "Maybe, but not many. They can't afford to patrol all of the coast. I'd look for the small ships to be at the key points. Maybe as you round the point and head south. Also if you decide to take the route through Chincoteague Bay at Ocean City."

"Ocean City?"

Christopher laughed. "They think they're a city. Some day they may be. Now they're just a small settlement."

"Shall we take that route?"

"Make up your mind when you get there. If you can get into the sound, the weather and seas will be much better."

Matthew grinned. "I thought that's what you'd say, and I'll be doing the same."

Christopher continued, "Let's get back to the first subject. We're going to salvage everything we can and take it to Chestertown by wagon. I think the mayor will help."

Matthew was puzzled. "How're we going to salvage anything? The ship burned and exploded. I can't see anything out there."

His father replied, "Believe me, there are still twelve valuable guns out there. I didn't see any of them go up in the air when the ship exploded. There's plenty of daylight left. We'll unload the boats down here and keep the valuables and muskets under guard.

You and I will take ten good swimmers and enough small line to make slings to pass around the trunnions of the guns. Since you loosened their securing plates, they should have separated from their heavy wooden carriages."

"But, Captain, don't we want the carriages? They were well made and fitted the guns."

"Too clumsy. They're just wood. We can easily make new ones. Guns are expensive and hard to get, although our gun makers are getting better all the time."

"While you're getting the boats ready, I'll go up on the dunes and make arrangements with the mayor to house our crew for the night and to buy some more food for the next few days. Then I'll arrange for some teams of oxen or horses to drag the guns ashore."

"Then what will we do with them?"

"Use your head. I'll have a heavy wagon and four horses or oxen for each two guns we salvage, and some more for our valuables and food. The boatswain can rig some heavy shears to hoist the guns into the wagons."

The boatswain grinned. "Easy," he said. "With the yards and pieces of mast floating ashore I can do it in a hurry. If I have to, we'll cut down some trees."

Captain Christopher cleared his throat. "Well, time is valuable. We want to get home and put our next privateer to sea. Do whichever is faster, but remember the mayor will be watching us. If we want to cut down trees, he'll want our hide in pounds for them."

The captain walked over to the mayor standing atop the dunes, where he was still being congratulated by his constituents.

The mayor shrugged his shoulders expansively. "In the end, I didn't do much. The sailors here did it all, but I think if we'd had to do it all by ourselves, we'd have put up a good fight."

One man laughed. "The axes and cleavers wouldn't have gone far."

The mayor bristled. "We aren't hicks. We had a few fowling pieces, too."

Christopher interrupted. "Mister Mayor, can we do a little business?"

"Certainly, Captain, I will try to get anything I can for you after that magnificent bit of work you did this morning. The British got a bloody nose. Let's hope they won't be in a mood to visit us for a while."

The man who had been heckling the mayor spoke up. "Mayor, give him your shirt, too, it's a little ragged."

Christopher said to the mayor, "You really mean *anything*?"

"Well, short of my home and my wife."

"Let's get back to serious business. You may change your mind after I've finished asking you."

The mayor pulled at his chin. "Well, as I said, *almost* anything. I might have to charge you a little. We're just a bunch of poor farmers, you know."

Christopher kept a straight face. "The first request will be easy and won't cost much. Just the use of some hay and a couple of barns for my men to sleep in tonight. I'll pay for any food you may be able to give them. Tomorrow I'd like to buy as many loaves of bread as your citizens can bake. Also as many hams as you can spare and any other food we can take with us. The ladies around here are famous for their baking."

The mayor's eyes widened. "I agree with you. Just how much would you want?"

"Enough to feed my sixty-five men for two days here and two more days on the road to Chestertown. Maybe three if it rains and muddies up the road."

The mayor looked relieved. "I thought you was going to spend the summer here or something. I am sure we can do that. Might have to send to Dover for help, though."

Christopher cleared his throat. "Now for the hard part. I want to hire eight heavy wagons and four draft horses or oxen for each wagon."

The mayor looked puzzled. "I thought your men were going to walk."

"They are, but our guns have to ride."

"What guns? I don't see any guns."

Christopher laughed. "They're a hundred yards out in the sand. I expect to drag them ashore."

"What with?"

"There is an anchor cable lying out there as well. I expect to use some of my men and a few of the horses or oxen we spoke about to drag them ashore."

The mayor grinned. "Sure and I'll be damned! This I've got to see."

"That you will. We'll be taking our boats out soon and our men will dive for the guns. I'd appreciate it if you'd have at least six horses ready by noon."

"They'll be ready, and the owners will be down here to see the show."

Captain Christopher went down to the boats. "Let's go! The shore side will be ready."

Christopher jumped into the outboard boat. "Shove off," he said to the coxswain. He turned to the other boat. "Matthew, follow me."

When the boats reached the location, Captain Christopher found the area using carefully memorized landmarks ashore. He directed both boats to anchor near each other. He peeled off his shirt and looked at Matthew. "Let's you and me go down there first to see what we can locate."

Matthew took off his shirt, and together they jumped over the side. The water was fairly clear, and when the sun was out, the bottom could be seen faintly in the six feet of water. The Captain soon located the first gun. "Make me a sling," he said to the men in the boats, "and pass it down here. A couple of you come on down and stand by to help me."

Almost at the same time, Matthew said, "I'm standing on the pile of cable."

Christopher said, "Pull one end over here, and we'll attach it to the sling around the gun's trunnions. Now look for the other end."

Finding the other end buried under several bights of cable was difficult, but after a few dives, Matthew managed to drag it loose

and bring it up. He called one of the boats over. The end was secured to the stern of the boat and Christopher said to the coxswain, "Now get the cable ashore. The boatswain will know what
to do with it. We'll be ready with another gun when you get back."

Back on the beach the boatswain and the mayor waited anxiously
as the boat slowly stretched out the length of the anchor cable as
the oarsmen pulled steadily on their oars.

"Look at that! I never would have figured it out myself." the
mayor said.

The boat beached, and the boatswain directed a large group of
men to wade out into the water, cast loose the end of the cable,
and walk it up the beach to the edge of the dune where the horses
were waiting. The mayor told the farmer who owned the horses to
hitch them to the end of the cable using a set of whiffle trees usually used to hitch horses to wagons. Then all was in readiness.

"I'll have to see this to believe it," the major said, scratching his
two day beard.

The farmer replied, "These horses could pull almost anything,
but I've never tried fishing for no guns before."

The mayor nodded. "Neither have I. Let's start 'em up, and see
what we can get without bait."

The farmer cracked his whip and made some noises intelligible
only to his horses. The cable strained as they started forward. First,
it formed an inverted arc, and then it began to stretch. Water
drops squeezed out of the wet hemp, shone in the sun, and then
fell to the sand.

The farmer cracked his whip again, while twenty men grabbed
the line to add their strength.

The boatswain yelled. "Lay on it! Don't let them horses outdo
you!"

The anchor cable gradually moved forward, and soon picked up
speed. The team and the men were a hundred yards inland when
the black form of the gun broke the surface of the water.

The men cheered wildly as the gun slid right up to the top of
the dune. "Avast heaving!" the boatswain shouted. "Disconnect

and walk the cable down to the beach and secure both ends to the stern of the boat."

The mayor laughed, "Well, by Jesus! They did it just like they said they would."

The boat carried both ends out to where the other boat was anchored. Captain Christopher had discovered another gun, and the process was repeated seven times more until eight black, dripping forms lay on the dunes like big black slugs.

Christopher realized the remainder of the guns rested under heavy pieces of hull and wreckage and could not easily be salvaged. Christopher said to the mayor, "You can have the rest. If you can ever get them up, I'll buy them back from you for a good price."

The mayor grinned. "We'll give it a try. Plenty of long summers here."

∽

When the boats returned to the creek, Captain Christopher called Matthew over. "Son, we no longer need the boats. The boatswain and I can load the wagons tomorrow using shears. Now the next task is to get these boats home. They are well built and worth a lot of money and we'll want to keep them for our next ship. I reckon they'll sail at about six knots. If the wind dies, four oarsmen can make about three knots. The trip around the cape, into Chesapeake Bay, and up to Chestertown should be about three hundred miles. If the wind holds, I figure about four days. If it doesn't, maybe six."

Matthew nodded. "About right."

"Take nine men in each boat. That's two sets of oarsmen and a coxswain. Pick a man to put in charge of the other boat, and don't lose sight of it once you get to sea. You'll have to do the navigation for both boats because there isn't enough equipment for both. You won't need to use the quadrant as long as you keep the shore in sight, but you'll have it in case a storm blows you to sea. The chart you'll have is a little battered, but it's accurate."

"Can I take some muskets?"

"Sure. I won't need many. Take one for each man, but do your best to avoid a fight."

Matthew laughed. "The people in Delaware are mostly friendly. You won't need many guns going over land."

"Make the trip as soon as possible."

Matthew grinned. "Don't worry. I will, and I'll see you in Chestertown as soon as I can. My men won't want to get too far away from that prize money, and I think the married ones would like to get home."

Christopher raised an eyebrow, "In that case sail directly for our Annapolis yard. I'll be over there with the prize money by the time you get there."

Matthew called out eighteen younger men he knew well and gathered them by the boat. The captain and the other men returned to the guns.

Matthew looked carefully at the group and picked out one man. "Scotty, come over here."

The young man was about Matthew's size, but not quite as husky or broad in the shoulders. He was blond, fair haired, and unmistakably a Scot. They were out of hearing distance of the other men standing by the boat.

Matthew had gone to school with Scotty MacIntosh and knew him well. "Scotty," he said, "I deliberately picked these men because they're all our age and I know I can lick them all if they give me trouble. Can you?"

MacIntosh laughed. "If you can, I can. We used to be pretty even."

"You're to be in charge of the second boat. Take any eight men you want and get her ready. You'll have four oars, nine muskets, and a good set of sails. I know because I made them myself."

"Aye, I know, and we sailed many a day with them."

"I'm going to take the compass, chart, and quadrant with me. That means you'll have to keep me in sight if we get blown away from land."

MacIntosh shrugged. "I've no need for all that gear. I've got the chart in my head, and there's no way I can get lost as long as I can see the stars or the sun."

Matthew shook his head and laughed. "You've got it. You haven't changed. As long as we keep the land on our starboard beam, we'll eventually reach Annapolis."

"Aye, we'll know when to stop when we see all those spires. It won't be any place but Annapolis."

"Send some men up to the mayor to draw some food and fill all the water butts you can find on the beach if they aren't already full. I'll do the same, and we'll leave in an hour."

MacIntosh smiled widely. "Should be a pleasant cruise. Just like when we were kids."

Matthew nodded. "Do a good job and I'll ask the captain to put you on our next privateer as an officer under my brother. But you'll have to learn navigation."

"What makes you think I need to? I'm a quartermaster, you know, and I've steered the ship many a time when you and your father were taking and working out sights. I can do it all. Just try me."

Matthew nodded. "I will. We'll need you."

By the next morning, the boatswain had rigged a tall set of shears from yards and pieces of mast and two large blocks salvaged from the beach. The shears were just long spars set in a triangular arrangement. The tops were tightly lashed together. From the lashing hung a large block. Each gun in turn was dragged under the shears, hoisted, and loaded into a wagon pulled underneath. The eight guns filled four wagons, and Christopher rented two others to carry the food for the two-day trip along with the chests and other valuables. When all was ready, Christopher opened one of the chests, took out a double handful of English pounds, and counted out the agreed amount to the mayor.

The mayor grinned and counted the bills carefully. When he was satisfied, he held out his hand and said, "Thank you, Captain, it was nice doing business with you. Have a good trip. I don't think the natives will bother you. I think the ladies have enjoyed baking for you."

Christopher nodded. "I hope so, and at least I know the food will be good. I don't see any bad weather coming, and I've been over the road before. I hope to have your drivers, wagons, and horses back in four days."

The trip was pleasant. The crew walked behind the last wagon which carried the chests, making jokes about what they would do with their shares. The procession halted for meals, and for the one night the crew slept under the wagons. On the evening of the second day, the column of wagons pulled into Chestertown and drove down the main street to the shipyard. Christopher's older son, Kevin, met them and took over the unloading of the guns.

Christopher kept an eye on the wagon containing the chests and escorted it to a large vacant shed. The crew crowded around while Christopher had the chests unloaded. A shout went up from the men as the bank notes, gold sovereigns, and canvas bags of pearls and jewelry came into view. Christopher told three older men who could count to tally the money and inventory the other valuables.

As they started, Christopher turned to the men crowding around. "You men understand that right now all we can do is count. It must be turned over to a prize court in Annapolis before we actually share it."

There was a groan from some of the younger men, but the more experienced hands soon explained the laws of distribution of prizes to them.

Christopher said, "I'll advance to each of you a generous amount of money against your shares. How much depends on what the shipyard has in its cash box."

Kevin grinned. "They should do well. We've been taking in a lot of cash lately."

Christopher went on, "When I can get to the bank, I'll increase the amount. I will have to hire a boat to take it over to Annapolis tomorrow. I estimate the prize court will release it in about one week.

"After that, you are all guaranteed employment in either shipyard. My other privateer will be going to sea under my older son in about two months. All of you who want to go to sea are welcome to sign up."

Chapter 4

The boats left at dawn, just before the June sun came up over the eastern horizon. Matthew scanned the horizon carefully to make sure the British ships were gone. When both the jib and the mainsail were up and carefully set, Matthew estimated they were making six knots. Both sails were well-filled, and the wind was blowing from a favorable direction.

At noon, the sharp point of Cape Henlopen at the southern tip of Delaware Bay showed ahead to starboard. Shortly thereafter they rounded it and Matthew set course south for the day's long run down the Delaware coast. The wind was now from astern, and Matthew, carefully watching their wake, estimated they might be making seven knots.

The second boat rode easily on their quarter with MacIntosh firmly in command. Matthew had not really expected to run into the larger British ships; they would be farther south. More trouble would be caused by smaller ships lying in wait along the coastal waters to intercept coastal traffic even though his father had not expected it. Matthew kept a sharp lookout to the south along the flat coast, but all he could see was a succession of small farms ashore. The hours went by with a clear horizon to the east. Matthew expected to sight trouble somewhere to the east and felt increasingly apprehensive. A large ship could pin his two small but valuable boats against the coast, and he would have no alternative but to beach them and walk home. His men would probably escape, but the boats would be captured and burned by the relentless British. Like the *Justice* in the larger sense, they were expendable and could be replaced. Still Matthew felt a sense of attachment to them. He had constructed one and had watched the other being built by another crew of carpenters working nearby.

Just before dark, Matthew estimated they were leaving Delaware waters and entering Maryland territory. All of the coast looked the same, but he felt better knowing they were in the waters of his home state. About ten miles ahead, near the small coastal settlement called Ocean City, he hoped to turn inside the long, low piece of land stretching fifty miles or more to seaward of the mainland to form the eastern side of Chincoteague Bay. A small entrance would allow them to sail in protected waters for at least fifty miles. Weather would be milder with smaller seas and it was unlikely that British ships would enter the shallow, narrow waters. He felt safer, and he could see the end of the dangerous situation where he might be pinned against the shore by a British ship.

Matthew decided to shorten sail during the night so as to be off the entrance at dawn. They might well miss it in the dark. He called MacIntosh alongside and explained what he was going to do, and both boats shortened sail under the growing darkness. When he was satisfied MacIntosh knew what he wanted, he instructed the second boat to pull off astern.

In the three-quarter's moon, Matthew could see the loom of the white sails of their second boat just a short distance away, but the slight overcast was increasing and the moon no longer helped.

Matthew decided to catch up on his sleep while the boats were making slow way. He designated two men as lookouts and then set up a watch schedule to relieve them and the coxswain every two hours. Sleeping huddled on the bottom boards was difficult, but his young tired muscles soon relaxed, and he fell into a deep sleep, the dreamless state tired young men could achieve with little effort.

Just before dawn the coxswain nudged Matthew. Matthew sensed some uneasiness in the manner of the coxswain and said, "What's the trouble?"

The coxswain said, "I think there may be a sail out to sea, but I'm not sure. You ought to take a look through your long glass."

Matthew pulled out the old long glass, wrapped carefully in an old shirt and stowed under the after thwart. He pulled the sections out to full length and trained it in the direction the coxswain was pointing.

"Damn!" he said. "A sail it is, and I think it's a British sloop."

Matthew swung his long glass along the entire coast, looking for the entrance to Chincoteague Bay. It was forty-five degrees on the starboard bow and perhaps three miles away.

Matthew yelled at the crew, "Hoist all sail, and get out the oars! Hustle your bustles! We're in trouble, and we need to get to that entrance as soon as possible!"

The coxswain changed course toward the entrance. With full sails, the steady morning breeze, and four straining oars, Matthew estimated they were making seven knots. "Half an hour to safety," he yelled. "Give us all you've got, and when you get tired, we'll change oarsmen."

The oarsmen speeded up the stroke, and Matthew could feel the boat go faster. MacIntosh had seen the sail, too, and they were making the same speed fifty yards away on the starboard beam. It would be a close race.

But the patrolling sloop had seen them. She too, had hoisted all sail, and was headed for the entrance in an attempt to intercept them.

Matthew made some hasty calculations in his head. They would definitely get to the entrance before the sloop would. He bet that the sloop's captain would not follow them inside the narrow entrance. It would be as close as he first thought, and the sloop might begin firing at them any minute.

Matthew guessed they would start firing at about two thousand yards, but he did not think their accuracy would be good at that distance. Therefore their defense against the larger British ship would be to take advantage of their small size and their maneuverability. He would throw off the gunner's aim by changing course after every shot. There would be only one shot each time because the sloop was coming right at them and would have only one bow chaser in their narrow forecastle.

Matthew shouted orders. "You men not rowing, get the muskets out, check their loads, and be ready to fire at the quarterdeck of the sloop when she gets close enough! Aim at men on deck!"

One of the men protested. "But these things only have a very short range, and the balls wouldn't do much damage even if they do hit the ship."

Matthew shrugged. "They may be in range before we get away. At three hundred yards a ball can kill a man on the quarterdeck, and they won't be expecting it."

At a thousand yards the sloop opened fire with its single nine-pounder bow chaser. The ball fell short, but the sloop was closing fast. Fortunately, the boats were nearing the entrance to the sound.

The next nine-pounder round fell close. Then, as each succeeding shot was fired, Matthew changed course, the balls falling harmlessly in the wake. The sloop's gunners labored to readjust the positions of their guns each time, trying to anticipate where the small boats would be if they stayed on course.

Matthew anxiously took his eye off of the sloop and looked at the entrance. It was only a hundred yards away, and the sloop had closed to three hundred. Matthew yelled, "Let them have a volley of musket balls!"

The muskets went off, sounding like pop guns against the nine-pounders. The noise and smoke apparently took the sloop's captain by surprise, and he rounded up to a southerly course. The range began to open, but his six-gun broadside would now bear on the fleeing boats.

Just as the boats passed inside the entrance and changed course to the south, a broadside landed. Geysers of water flew up and soaked the crews.

"Anybody hurt?" Matthew shouted.

"No," said the coxswain, "and the other boat seems to be all right, too."

The sloop's gunners could no longer see the boats behind the dunes, and the firing stopped. Matthew breathed a sigh of relief. They were now safe for the passage south through the Bay, but they might have another problem when they had to pass out of it.

Matthew could see the sloop reverse course. "Must be patrolling the entrance," he decided. "She won't be in position to bother us off the exit well to the south."

They sailed south, relaxing from the strain of the morning, as the rising sun beat down on their shoulders. The day was unusually warm for June, and the men began to perspire and sought shade under the canvas sails.

One man, who had been scratching himself, spoke up. "Matthew, I'd sure like to take a swim. Even if I had to put my dirty clothes back on, I'd feel a lot better about meeting my family in a couple of days."

Matthew grinned. "I think they'd feel better, too. Coxswain, turn two points to port. We'll close the western shore of the outer bank and see if we can find a sheltered spot with a sandy bottom."

The boat, faithfully followed by the second boat, slowly closed the shore. Matthew carefully scanned it with his long glass. Finally he was satisfied. "Head for that sandy beach," he said to the coxswain.

The coxswain saw the patch he was talking about and headed for it. A few hundred yards away, Matthew ordered the sails doused, and the oarsmen slowly rowed toward the beach. When Matthew could see the sandy bottom clearly, he ordered, "Throw over the anchor and twenty fathoms of line."

Almost before the anchor found the bottom, two of the men hit the water fully clothed.

Matthew kept one man in the boat with a ready musket and an eye out for sharks and then jumped in, too. The water was cold but refreshing, and the men scrubbed themselves and their clothes as best they could with sand brought up from the bottom.

Soon the cold water drove them back into the boat. For the first time the men argued over who would row. "Gotta stay warm and dry off," one man said.

The wind held from the east as they sailed south. In the late afternoon the two boats sailed out of the southern entrance and into the open sea. Matthew anxiously searched the horizon, half expecting to see the sloop or another ship, but the sea was clear. The swells increased, but so did the wind, staying from the northeast. The boats made a full six knots to the south until dark.

Early the next morning, Matthew turned onto the waterways between the coastal islands and the coast and was able to sail in protected waters all the way to Cape Charles at the tip of the peninsula. The waters were too shallow to be used by ships of any great size, but the small boats had no trouble.

Sixty miles later, late in the afternoon, they reached South Bay, leaving just three more hours sailing to Cape Charles. Matthew decided to anchor overnight, rest the crews, and start for Cape Charles at dawn. They would be safe in the narrow waters overnight.

At 5 A.M. Matthew roused the men, hauled in the anchors, and started south. At about 8 A.M. they turned west for the passage between Fisherman's Island and Cape Charles. Matthew scanned the waters ahead anxiously, expecting British ships to be patrolling the waters around Cape Charles and the entrance to the Chesapeake Bay.

Twice his heart raced when they sighted sails ahead, but both proved to be fishing boats from Kiptopeake, a small village of fishermen nearby.

Well before noon, the two boats were on a northerly course, coasting along the inner arm of Chesapeake Bay. Matthew felt safe from British ships and began to relax.

As they headed north, Matthew, kept the battered chart open in the bottom of the boat to protect it from the wind. He calculated that they had 150 miles of open water to go. He would be able to see the shore of the outer arm of Chesapeake Bay to the east, but late in the afternoon he decided to take a short cut across Pocomoke Bay instead of following the shore. It was a bad mistake. About four o'clock a typical Chesapeake Bay summer thunderstorm built up to the west. There was nothing he could do but shorten sail and ride it out, making as much distance to the north as he could with reefed sails.

The sky blackened steadily, lightning flashed in the west, and the usual large clouds brought a curtain of stinging rain blown by high and unpredictable winds. Visibility was so low that Matthew nearly lost sight of the other boat. With great difficulty, his coxswain kept a steady course to the north, blown along by the heavy winds on the shortened sails. Fortunately the winds were from the south and there was clear water to the north instead of the shore they would have had if he had not decided to take a short cut.

After two hours the storm passed, leaving the crew soaked and bedraggled.

When the crew complained, Matthew said, "Quit squawking. Think of it this way. Now all the salt you had left from your swim has been washed out and you're completely clean." The sailors looked unconvinced, but seemed to cheer up.

The sky grew lighter, and the rain stopped. The wind shifted slightly, but was still from the south. Matthew looked around the horizon, but it was clear except for the retreating thunderstorm now distant in the east. He dragged the long glass out from under the stern thwart and scanned the horizon looking for the second boat. "Nothing," he said. "Scotty must have dropped back with his sails down or run before the wind."

"Shouldn't we go back and look for him? He may need help," the coxswain asked.

Matthew laughed. "No, he won't need help. He's a tough sailor. He'll catch up. We'll keep a reef in the mainsail to give him a chance."

Early the next morning, as daylight broke, the coxswain shouted, "There they are, coming up from astern!"

Matthew looked aft at the oncoming boat and grinned. "They'll be here soon."

Within one hour the second boat was almost alongside. Matthew looked at the boat carefully. There was a long patch in the mainsail. He shouted, "What happened?"

MacKenzie yelled back, "I was slow in getting my mainsail reefed. The wind ripped the hell out of it."

"How did you fix it? I don't think you had any needles aboard."

"I straightened out an old fish hook I found in the bilges and used if for a needle. I unlaid some line and used it for thread. Doesn't look very pretty, but it's holding."

"Yeah. All sailors carry knives."

MacIntosh laughed. "Sure, don't you?"

"I do. I'm glad you did."

Late the next day the spires of the churches in the city of Annapolis appeared on the distant horizon to port, and Matthew knew it was time to turn to port and go up the Severn River to the shipyard. It was well after dark when they arrived in the channel, but he knew the waters well.

After they had secured the boats in the shipyard, the crew scattered and left for home. Matthew walked in the dark through the muddy streets to his house near State Circle. He found the key where he knew it was kept and opened the door quietly. Before going in the front door he took off his muddy boots and left them on the steps outside. He walked upstairs in his socks and looked in his father's bedroom. His father was fast asleep, so he walked down to his own room and fell into bed fully clothed.

Chapter 5

The next morning Matthew was aware of a light knock on his door. It was different from the heavy masculine pounding he was used to hearing at sea. When he opened his eyes, a gentle-looking black woman stood at his open door looking at him.

"Mammy Sarah!" he said, "How are you?"

The woman beamed. She had most of her teeth left, and they were a brilliant white. When asked how old she was, she gave her age as anywhere from thirty to fifty depending on how she felt that day. Matthew judged she was probably fifty-five, but possibly younger.

Matthew looked at Mammy Sarah approvingly. "Mammy, you look almost like a teenager. No wonder Jebediah can't catch you. Limp a little or slow down."

"Aw, Matthew, you is a flatterer."

"Aren't you glad to see me?"

"Matthew," she said, "I'm glad to see you. You left your dirty boots outside the front door instead of wearing them inside just the way your mother used to tell you, but the rest of you is just plain dirty. You didn't even take your dirty old clothes off and your bed is a mess. Just look at the pigpen you been making with your clothes."

"Ah, Mammy, I did wash my clothes a few days ago."

"In salt water?"

"Yes, but with sand."

"Well, they's still sand in them."

"That's better than mud."

Mammy shrugged. "Not much."

Matthew grinned. "Sorry, Mammy, I was too tired last night to take these off. I haven't had a full night's sleep for at least four months."

Mammy scowled. "No excuse now."

"I'll get them off right away." He got up and started taking them off.

Mammy giggled. "You ain't going to shock me. I've seen you naked before. I used to scrub you when you was a squab. They's hot water in the wood tub in the bathroom for you. When you've washed the salt and dirt off of you, put on the clean clothes I've laid out in the bathroom and come down to the kitchen. I'll be waiting for you with breakfast, just like you remember."

Matthew grinned with pleasure and stretched his naked muscular arms over his head. "Thank, you, Mammy. I'll be there directly. Where's my father?"

"He be gone. Went to the shipyard. Wants to see you as soon as you kin get there."

"Do you know why?"

Mammy shrugged. "He don't tell me all those things."

"Now, Mammy, I know you hear everything around here."

"I don't. Now get on with it."

In the bathroom Matthew luxuriated in the hot water. It was the first hot fresh water he had felt in four months. On the ship they had only cold salt water baths.

After ten minutes Mammy burst in the door. "That's enough. Start dressing before my good breakfast gets cold."

Mammy did indeed have breakfast ready. She had looked after him and his older brother Kevin since their mother died eight years ago and she knew just what he liked. Matthew finished a large plate of scrambled eggs and his fifth biscuit and grinned slyly. "Mammy, are you still going steady with old Jebediah, or anyone else?"

Mammy Sarah bridled. "He ain't so old. He steady and slow, and he ain't any much older than I am. I think that man is so slow he'll never catch me. I don't hold with the other truck around here."

"Oh, he will, and I think I'll have to get married if I want to eat when you leave."

"No, he won't try too hard, because he know I probably won't have him."

"Why not?"

"He's tomcatting all over town. If he married me he wouldn't stop."

"I think you're woman enough to keep him at home for a long time."

"Stop talking like that. You got your own problems with the young ladies of the town. You still stuck on Miss Martha Juvenal?"

"Yes, if she'll have me."

"She's still working in her parents' restaurant. You better get with it. She getting too old."

"Too old? She's only eighteen."

Mammy Sarah raised her eyebrows. "And just how old are you, as if I didn't know, having been around when you were born eighteen years ago."

"Eighteen, but I feel a lot older this morning."

"Well, these days that too old for a man, too. I think you better talk to your pa."

Matthew picked up two biscuits, buttered them, put them in his pocket and stood up.

Mammy Sarah bridled. "Don't you spill crumbs on my clean floor. I can still paddle you."

Matthew laughed, "You could, too. I'll be careful. I'll be on my way now."

Matthew sat on the stoop outside the front door and pulled on his boots, now cleaned of Annapolis mud and set neatly on the top step. He got up, looked down and admired them, but after ten feet of slogging along the muddy street, they were as dirty as ever, even though he tried his best to avoid the muddiest puddles.

Matthew found his father bent over a huge table in the shipyard office. The office was piled high with drawings of ship views, manifests for materials, copies of contracts, and at least four dirty coffee and tea cups. "Hello, Pa," he called out. "I'm here. You wanted to see me?"

His father straightened up, looked at him, grinned, and put an arm around him. He squeezed him as if he had not seen him for months. "Good trip?"

"Well, a little trouble, but we made good time all the way here."

His father raised an eyebrow. "You're a little modest. Scotty MacKenzie has already been by. He says you two fought off a British sloop and then went through a pretty bad thunderstorm in the bay. They can be as bad as British ships."

Matthew shrugged. "Well, I guess so, but we didn't lose much time. I think my men wanted to get back here to that prize money."

"The local Maritime Court has it. Shouldn't be too long, although all lawyers like to fiddle around."

"I guess you need it for these ships of yours and the shipyard, too."

"Yes. Shipbuilding is booming, but I need money to buy materials and pay higher wages, and as always, the buyers never want to pay on time. Still, before the war is over the family will be rich. You can be glad you have a share in the shipyard."

"Aren't you afraid the higher costs will eat most of the profit?"

"That's why I'm putting all the family money I can save in land and gold. They'll be safe. The country's money won't be much good."

"I saw a big square-rigged brig on the main ways as I came in. Why did you want to build that heavy box? It will be slow as molasses in a Maryland winter."

"I don't want to sail it myself, but a large group of fat-bellied Maryland business men will pay me a small fortune to build her as fast as I can. They don't care how good she is, or how fast, but only how much she will carry and how soon can we get her to sea."

"I take it they want to get in the prize market or want to smuggle in cargo."

"Maybe a little of both, and they can hardly wait. They're down here every morning to see how we're doing and offering to pay me more if I'll hurry."

"Then what will you do when you get your main building way free?"

"That's why I was in such a hurry to see you. My scouts in the Maryland Legislature up on the hill tell me the Continental Congress is about to designate the yards to build some of the thirteen frigates that were authorized in December."

"And you want to get a contract for one?"

"Sure, but I don't think I'll get it, and I'm not sure I want it. The government isn't too good a task master to work for. They'll be very slow in paying and there'll be too many politicians hanging over our ways and wanting to cut a piece of the pie. I think I'd rather build for myself or for sale to a civilian. They'll pay on time."

"What are you going to do?"

"I want to lay down a very large topsail schooner. A hundred feet in length; twenty-foot beam; ten-foot draft; and displacing one hundred tons. She'll be fast and maneuverable. No British ship will be able to catch her, and she'll carry eighty men and sixteen 12-pounders. Your brother Kevin is going to take over the big schooner now building on the ways in Chestertown. These days a single voyage will pay for a ship. Even losing the *Justice* made us a lot of money before we had to burn her. I want all of us to collect some of this prize money. It's faster than just building ships."

"But Father, you still want to keep your hand in the large ship building business, don't you?"

"Of course. The present war and the prize-taking business won't last long. Shipbuilding will last forever, long after we're all gone."

"Well, what do the thirteen frigates authorized have to do with you?"

"We won't be assigned any of those, but the Congress may authorize some even bigger frigates, and I want you to find out how a good yard builds big frigates and bring the knowledge back here."

"Where do you want me to go to find out about that kind of knowledge?"

"Philadelphia. One of the thirteen frigates will be built at the Wheaton and Humphreys yard. It's now early April. It should be finished by July. If you go up there as soon as possible you will be able to work on her big hull timbers. You are good with an adze and an axe, but they will use timber three times the size you're used to. You'll have to get going soon before they finish this part."

Matthew frowned and shook his head.

His father noticed and said. "What's the matter? Don't you want to get rich?"

Matthew grinned. "Yes, but I also want to get married."

Eric Christopher scratched his head and laughed. "Well, lad, you aren't doing much about it. You ought to go and ask that girl."

"What girl?"

"Don't be silly. I know all about Martha Juvenal. You two walk all over the woods every night. I saw you with her many times before we left on our cruise."

"What do you mean?"

"You two took two-hour lunch hours. As soon as she sold all the lunches she had made and brought over here from her restaurant, you both disappeared. Can she cook?"

Matthew laughed. "Not quite as good as Mammy Sarah."

"We've got enough money to buy you a row house on Church Street as soon as you get back from Philadelphia."

"Can I take her with me?"

"If she'll go. The trip up should be a good honeymoon for you. Now go away and talk to her. You won't get anywhere just sitting here."

"But, Pa, I just got here."

"Stop complaining and go. She's probably waiting, and you ought to get your oar in the water."

Matthew walked out of the shipyard office and down the waterfront street to the restaurant run by the Juvenals. It was near the Middletown Tavern fronting on Market Square. He pushed open the door and went inside. Three young waitresses were setting up tables for the forthcoming lunch hour. "Good day," Matthew said, "Is Martha here?"

One of the girls looked up and smiled. "Hello, Matthew, where have you been?"

"Out to sea for a long time, and I'm glad to be back. I am anxious to see Martha."

"I'll bet you are. She's in the office."

Matthew hurried back to the rear of the building where the office was located and pushed open the door. Martha was bent over a desk, deep in some ledger. Matthew leaned over and kissed her ear. She gasped and turned around. When she realized it was Matthew, she smiled, sprang up, and threw her arms around him. Martha's blue eyes sparkled, as they always did. Though usually proper and restrained, Matthew remembered the walks in the countryside when Martha would raise her full skirts thigh high to cross a creek when it wasn't really necessary, and the sight always made his heart beat faster. He knew his emotions lay just beneath the surface.

Matthew kissed her passionately, as strongly as he felt he could get away with in the semi-privacy of the office. Her response was the same, and he was sure from the warmth of it that she loved him.

He released her reluctantly. "Will you marry me?" he burst out.

Martha laughed. "I didn't think you'd ever get around to it. The answer is yes. My only question is when."

She tried to rearrange her hair where he had nuzzled it, but with little success. Finally she pulled loose the ribbon, tossed her hair back, and re-tied it.

Matthew watched her, fascinated. "Beautiful hair," he said. "It matches the rest of you."

Martha looked at him coyly. "You haven't seen much of the rest of me yet. What was that you said about when?"

"As soon as possible. I want to take you to Philadelphia on a honeymoon."

"This is a little sudden. I thought about a week or two in some romantic place. Why there?"

"I know you'd like to go somewhere else but we can't. After we get married we'll have a week to ourselves. Then I have to go to work in a Philadelphia shipyard."

"You want to take the job?"

"No, but my father needs me."

"All right, I give in. Sounds like a good trade. I've always wanted to see Philadelphia."

Martha's parents, Christine and Ezra Juvenal, were unhappy about the shortness of time available for the preparations for the wedding and the couple's precipitous departure for Philadelphia.

Mrs. Juvenal fussed, "All my friends will think you're pregnant and have to get married in a hurry."

Martha ignored her mother's petulant expression. "No, Mother, I don't think they will, and if they know me, they won't. If they do, they're not really my friends."

Ezra Juvenal took a different view. "Well, Christine, I'm glad there's not a lot of time. If there were, we'd need to spend a lot of money on social affairs, and a lot more clothes would be bought. Remember, we don't have much money."

Mrs. Juvenal bristled. "This is your oldest daughter. She should have our best."

Martha sighed. "Mother, don't talk like that. I'm very happy, and I don't need all that."

In spite of the lack of time, the preparations went ahead. For Martha's dress committee Mrs. Juvenal gathered her younger daughter, and drafted the town's leading dressmaker, Madame de Paris. Matthew had no close female relatives, so he asked Mammy Sarah to take on the task of representing him.

Mammy Sarah frowned. "She ain't going to like a black woman on the team."

Matthew shook his head. "Let her grouse for a while. Don't sass her. She knows you are the best seamstress in town, including Madame de Paris, who thinks she's right out of Paris, but who has never been east of Chestertown."

"Isn't she from Paris?"

Matthew laughed. "She can hardly spell the word. Just listen to her and nod wisely. After the first day and when Mrs. Juvenal asks her friends around town about your work, you'll become the head rag-picker."

Mammy Sarah laughed. "There won't be any old rags used. We'll use new silk."

At the first meeting of the group, Martha let her views about expensive silk be known. When her Mother proposed, "Silk dress, four silk petticoats, and silk undergarments," Martha pursed her lips firmly. "Matthew gave me a small bolt of French silk his ship captured. It is very beautiful and is enough for a dress. I want the rest of what I wear to be cotton."

Mrs. Juvenal shook her head. "You should have the best."

Finally Mammy Sarah could no longer stay out of the argument. "Mrs. Juvenal, I sewed many a wedding dress for some of the richest ladies in town. I tried to persuade them to wear cotton underwear in the summer heat. One of them was so overcome with the heat she flopped on the floor, her silk petticoats flying in all directions."

Martha laughed, "I don't want to do that. I want a silk dress, two cotton petticoats, and cotton undergarments, and I don't mean pantaloons. Just short drawers."

Mrs. Juvenal gasped and fanned herself vigorously. "Such talk in front of strangers."

"They aren't strangers," Martha answered.

Mammy Sarah shrugged. "Then that settles it Madame de Paris will make the silk dress. I'll make the cotton petticoats, and the, er, drawers. I'll put two rows of ruffles on the under petticoat to make them look exactly like four, and they will give her some ventilation."

Before Mrs. Juvenal could object, Martha said, "Just exactly that."

Mrs. Juvenal would not subside. "But won't Matthew expect you to be wearing silk underwear?"

Martha sighed. "Mother, he'll never see any of it."

"Maybe a silk night dress?"

"If you wish, but if I know him, he won't see much of that either."

Mammy Sarah cackled. "Oh, girl, you know my boy all right."

Eric Christopher insisted that he take over the preparations for the actual wedding. Although custom called for Mrs. Juvenal to take on the chore, Mr. Juvenal tried to keep his wife out of it, pointing out that Christopher, a wealthy shipbuilder, could better afford to pay for the arrangements.

They were simple enough. Eric Christopher found out that Saint Anne's Church, located in the Church Circle, was being torn down to make room for a larger structure. In the meantime, the parishioners were worshipping at a nearby theater. The Episcopal minister proposed to hold the marriage ceremony in the theater.

A florist was hired to decorate the usually plebeian inside of the theater, and it rapidly took on the aspects of a church.

Handwritten invitations were delivered by messengers to the expected guests, and Eric Christopher's large house was prepared for a reception by a corps of maids supervised by Mammy Sarah in her spare time.

On the morning of the ceremony, Eric Christopher jumped out of bed, drew back the drapes, opened the swinging windows, and sniffed the morning. "Damn!" he mumbled. "As usual, a hot summer day. I hope Martha doesn't get overheated. But I know she's sensible. I've got to make sure Matthew doesn't wear an undershirt and puts on a loose collar."

He bustled down the hall to Matthew's door and knocked loudly. "Get up, Son, there's a lot to do."

A muffled groan inside indicated Matthew had survived the rigors of last night's bachelor party.

Eric Christopher left to get on with the rest of the arrangements.

The ceremony was as brief as Eric Christopher could persuade the Episcopal minister to settle for. "Please be kind to the children. I've sat through some of your long Episcopal services before. After all, this is going to be a ninety degree day."

The minister growled, but the ceremony was brief and appropriate, and soon Martha and Matthew walked out of the theater under a cloud of rice.

Eric Christopher grimaced and shouted. "Good old North Carolina rice! May you prosper and have many children!"

Martha blushed, but Matthew said comfortingly, "Just an old European custom. There'll be more of it at the reception."

In front of the theater entrance sat a long black carriage, usually used for funerals. The windows were still framed with black drapes, now diplomatically drawn back with garlands of flowers. It was the best Eric could do on such short notice.

On the carriage's box was Big Jebediah, togged out in a high hat, red jacket, and glistening boots. Jebediah raised his whip in salute. "Ready, Mister Christopher."

Eric Christopher handed the bride up the steps into the carriage and closed them after his son. He looked up at the driver. "Jebediah, if you hear any commotion in the cabin, bang on the roof with your whip handle."

Martha's head popped out of a window, dislodging a garland. "Don't you dare, Jebediah. Nothing is going to go on in here. I want to get to the reception with my hair arrangement intact and all my flowers in place. Please drive on."

She frowned at Eric Christopher, but she could not remain mad at him for long. As Jebediah cracked his whip and drove off, Martha waved her ring-finger at her new father-in-law and grinned at him. "Thank you for everything."

Eric Christopher sighed. "I should have known better. I think that girl is firmly in charge of the quarterdeck."

The reception was attended by the mayor, other government officials, and many leading citizens. His son and daughter-in-law received the guests gracefully in the lavishly decorated garden.

Dancing had been vetoed by Martha because of the weather. The cake was cut with a cutlass, and after tossing the bridal bouquet to Martha's younger sister, the couple withdrew upstairs. Mammy Sarah positioned herself as a guard at the top of the stairs and would not allow them to be disturbed except for the meals she occasionally served herself.

Two days later, Matthew and Martha prepared for the trip to Philadelphia. When they were ready, Matthew's father and brother and Mammy Sarah gathered to see them off. Mammy said,

"There's enough food under the wagon seat to take you clear to New York if you miss Philadelphia."

They had piled all of their meager possessions and wedding presents in a light wagon with Jebediah's help. The bed of the wagon held a new double bed and feather mattress given to them by Matthew's father.

Their trip was leisurely and pleasant, with early stops at roadside inns and picnic stops for lunch. On the seventh day, Matthew and Martha unloaded their wagon at a small house that Matthew's father had arranged for them to rent through his brother. Matthew put the wagon in a lean-to in the garden and stabled the horse at a nearby livery stable. He planned to ride the horse to the shipyard every day, occasionally leaving it to be hitched to the wagon so Martha could go shopping. On those days he would have to walk.

Their house was one of a row of a dozen hastily erected by a speculator trying to take advantage of the shipbuilding boom he was expecting. The windows leaked cold air, but the roof kept out the rain. The feather bed and the quilts they had brought for the purpose served them well. Huddled in the warmth of these reminders of home, they enjoyed together many a wonderful night.

Chapter 6

Matthew and Martha spent their first full day in their new home settling their possessions and distributing their wedding gifts throughout the rooms. The large double bedstead and feather mattress that had occupied a good portion of the wagon bed now filled most of the tiny bedroom.

After their first night, Martha rolled out of the bed carefully to avoid hitting the nearby wall and laughed, "We got a full year's use of it last night."

Matthew poked her playfully in the ribs. "I hope you can still cook breakfast. Tomorrow I have to find work at the shipyard."

"Will you have any trouble?" Martha asked.

Matthew laughed. "Are you serious? If I can walk in, they will give me a job. Workers of any kind in this country are hard to find, and shipyard workers are even harder to get. We pay double wages to our carpenters at home."

"You haven't told me why you're really up here. I judged there was a very important reason. At first I did not question you. All I thought about was getting married and visiting a new city. Now I want to know more."

Matthew shrugged. "Frankly, it's all very simple. My father wanted me to come up to this shipyard to learn how they build ships far bigger than the ones we build."

"Why do you need to know that?"

"My father plans to build big ships as soon as he can get a contract. By then we'll be ready."

"So we'll be returning to Annapolis in a few months?"

"Oh, yes."

Martha sighed and looked around the interior of the small house. "I can take this for a short time, but I'll be glad to be in a larger house of our own."

～

The next morning, after an early breakfast of four fried eggs for him and a full ration of hay for the horse, Matthew saddled the rested horse and set off at a fast trot for the shipyard a mile away.

Matthew carried his tools in two canvas bags secured across the horse's back. On arrival, he made arrangements with a livery stable nearby to keep his horse during the day and then walked to the shipyard. He asked an old man sitting next to the entrance gate under a large sign reading "Wharton and Humphreys" for permission to enter.

The old man replied, "Sonny, you can come in as long as you ain't got no British accent."

Matthew asked, "Where can I find either Mister Wharton or Mister Humphreys?"

The old man said, "You must be wanting to see Mister Humphreys if you want a job. First building on the right and don't fall over the piles of lumber."

"Do you think he might have a job for me?"

The old man laughed. "He will if you kin walk that fer without fallin' over that lumber."

Matthew walked over to the building and put his tools down just outside a door bearing a sign "Mister Joshua Humphreys."

Matthew opened the door and walked in. The office was occupied by three female clerks at small desks and a man at a larger desk in the back corner. The man was sitting behind another sign on the desk again lettered "Mister Joshua Humphreys," and he was studying a large sketch. He was about fifty, gray-haired and slim, but Matthew thought he might grow a lot fatter some day. Matthew cleared his throat loudly, shattering the quiet in the office. Mister Humphreys looked up and put down his sketch. "Yes?" he asked querulously.

Matthew took a deep breath. "Sir, I'm Matthew Christopher of the Christopher shipyard in Annapolis."

Humphreys raised his eyebrows and interrupted. "Ah, yes, I've heard of it. Do you work there?"

"Well, I do in a way. Lately I've been at sea as a lieutenant on my father's privateer. When we're in port, I do all sorts of work in the yard. Mostly in heavy carpentry, including ship framing."

Humphreys tried to act restrained when faced with the possibility of hiring such a prospect in the slim labor market. Shipwrights were very scarce. Humphreys looked at the ceiling briefly, trying not to show interest. "I take it you want a job?" he asked.

"Yes, sir."

Humphreys was puzzled. This was going to be too easy. He tried another tack to make sure Christopher wasn't trying to put something over on him. "But why do you want to work here? I can't see why you'd want to leave your father's shipyard."

Matthew nodded. "Quite simply, sir, I'm here to learn how your shipyard designs and builds large ships. My father wants to be able to do the same later in the war."

"Well, that's honest enough, and I'll be glad to take you on at top wages. Go down to the ways and find the tool shed, draw your tools, and tell the foreman, Forester, to take you on as a rough carpenter."

"But, I have my own tools, sir."

Humphreys laughed. "Maybe so, but they'll not be of any use to you in dressing the large rough forms. You'll be forming orlop deck timbers first. Twelve inches by twelve inches. You'll need a much bigger adze than you're used to."

Matthew said, "I see that, sir. That is one of the reasons I wanted to work here."

Humphreys looked more closely at Matthew's muscular arms. "Obviously you've got enough strength for the job. You just need the right tools."

Matthew thanked Mister Humphreys, picked up his toolbags, and walked down inside the huge yard to the tool shack. Inside, an old black man was sharpening a very large, heavy adze on a big grindstone, which he kept spinning with his feet on a treadle. Without stopping the spinning wheel, the old man asked, "What can I do for you, young man? You look like you wants some work."

Matthew said, "Mister Humphreys said I was to see you to sign out for some heavy tools."

Without stopping the wheel, the man said, "Let me see the adze you got in that bag."

Matthew lifted his adze out of the bag and held it up. The black man chuckled and finally let the wheel stop. He held out the newly sharpened adze. "Here, take this one. Bring it back when it begins to lose its edge. You got a good adze here, but it ain't heavy enough."

Matthew added the heavy adze to his toolbags and walked toward the waterfront.

Nearer the building ways was a larger shack. A sign on the door said "Forester, Foreman."

Matthew looked in the open door. On a large trestle table were several sheets of fine paper containing ship's plans. Matthew went inside and looked them over carefully. He whistled. The paper was of good quality and the plans were drawn skillfully in black India ink. When compared with the plans at his home yard, his father's work seemed mere scribblings. Matthew made a mental note that his first recommendation would be to upgrade their planning system. A large, complicated ship needed detailed, drawn plans to guide the workmen. His fathers amateurish efforts would not do.

Matthew was startled by a deep voice. "Yes?"

A grizzled, middle-aged man came forward from a back room. He wiped the saw dust from his calloused hands.

Matthew held out his hand. "I'm Matthew Christopher of Annapolis. Mister Humphreys says I'm to report to you as a rough carpenter."

The foreman looked Matthew over carefully and held out his hand. "I'm Forester. Glad to have you aboard. We need carpenters, but Mister Humphreys wouldn't have signed you up if you didn't know your business. Come with me and we'll get you started. Leave your toolbags just outside the door. They'll be safe there."

Matthew immediately liked Forester, and followed him out the door.

As they walked along the ways, Forester pointed out the huge ribs, called futtocks, now standing unconnected to each other, but attached to the keel on the bottom and the keelson above it. "This is what will someday be the *Randolph*. As you can see, we've got the keel laid and the beginning of the framework. Some other work is done. There's where the orlop deck will be. We need some skilled hands to adze large vertical timbers for that part of the structure."

Matthew looked at the giant futtocks in amazement. "Those are twice as large as the ones we use."

Forester nodded. "And hard to find, too. We have agents searching forests for trees with bent trunks and for large bent limbs that can be used naturally for these key pieces. There aren't many left, so we are beginning to make futtocks out of pieces put together."

"I can see that many of them are of pieces carefully fastened together."

"Yes, that way we can use many shorter, naturally bent pieces, but soon we will run out of those, too."

"I take it you can't bend pieces of this size."

"We probably could, but the process would be very costly, both in manpower and steaming machinery. A good fastening job does the trick. Take a look at this one."

Matthew bent over a futtock, lying flat before being put in place with the keel. "I can hardly see the joints. I'm already learning."

"Why do you want to learn?"

"One of the reasons I'm here is to learn to build large ships for my father, but I'll do a good job." he assured the foreman.

Forester pulled at his grizzled chin. "Well, I'm sure Mister Humphreys will be sure to get his money's worth out of you."

Matthew looked at the pile of white oak logs nearby. They were at least eighteen inches in diameter. "You use mostly white oak?" he asked.

Forester nodded. "When we can get it. If we can't, we have to make do with substitutes. Maple and the like. We only use live oak for the masts and spars. We've got a shipload on the way north now from North Carolina."

Forester stopped by the pile of logs. Four men hacked clumsily away with adzes at eight foot lengths of the huge logs. Forester grinned. "As you can see, I need better men. If you prove yourself, I'll put you in charge of this gang and double your pay."

Matthew grinned. "Come back here in an hour and see what we have done."

By nightfall Matthew was firmly in charge of the gang, and each man was laboring away with purpose, if not with superior strength or skill, on uprights for the orlop, or lowest deck. The six foot logs were quickly becoming twelve by twelve roughly squared beams for verticals.

Forester came by just before the end of the workday. Matthew looked up and nodded toward the workmen. "We're doing well. I expect to have all the orlop verticals finished and in place by tomorrow."

Forester grinned. "That's the best news I've had in weeks. You are not only in charge of this gang, but also my assistant foreman."

Matthew put down his heavy adze and wiped his brow. "I take it the owners of this yard are in a big hurry to finish this ship."

"Yes, they want to get it launched by early July so they can start another ship on these building ways."

Matthew whistled. "I think we can make it. May I see the plans in your office?"

"Sure. Now that you are my assistant you should see them every day."

Matthew went into the office, wiping his hands and shaking the sawdust off of his heavy boots. He looked around the office carefully and then bent over a long table on which were spread a series of plans. He looked through them, whistling excitedly at the quality of the drawings. They were a whole new world to him compared with his father's planning system. He looked at them with more understanding than he had the first time he saw them.

Looking at the various views, it was easy to visualize the finished ship. He realized how they would speed up the making and finishing of the individual parts of the framing. With this system, many parts could be made simultaneously instead of the system in his father's yard, where each part had to be finished and fitted before the dependent parts could be started.

Matthew left the office shaking his head. This day alone made his trip worthwhile.

After every workday, Matthew rode home and stabled his horse nearby.

Martha would see him ride by the house, and by the time he came in the door, she had a wooden tub of hot water waiting for him. Most of the time she gave him a huge supper after his bath, but sometimes they slipped into bed first and ate later.

Martha laughed at him. "I don't want you to fall asleep before we've had a chance to make love."

Matthew grinned mischievously. "A massage will keep me awake much longer."

"Well, last night a massage put you right to sleep."

"Then wake me up earlier."

On weekends Martha packed a picnic lunch, and they took the horse and wagon and drove to the suburbs of Philadelphia to look at the bigger houses and discuss plans for the house they hoped to build soon on a large lot south of the State House in Annapolis. Matthew brought home a used piece of expensive drafting paper from the shipyard, and they began the plans on the back of the paper. Martha held it up to the light and laughed. "If we build our house from the wrong side of this paper, we'll have a mast sticking out of the roof."

When they had had enough of driving around the city on their outings, they would find the nearest park, spread a blanket, and have a picnic lunch that Martha had packed.

"This is good," Matthew commented.

"I should hope so. I used to do this all day long in my parents' restaurant."

In the afternoons they would visit museums and public buildings. By evening after supper they were in bed again. "To save candles," Martha said.

By the tenth of July the frigate was ready to launch. Matthew brought Martha to the yard to attend the brief ceremony and for the free French champagne afterwards. "Funny," she said, "You used to launch ships all the time in Annapolis and nobody ever did anything like this."

"This is different. We were all civilians down there. Here, the Continental Navy is in charge, and tomorrow the new commanding officer, Captain Nicholas Biddle, will arrive. I suppose there will be a naval ceremony."

Martha asked, "Do you mean your job is finished and we can go home?"

"Not exactly. There is a lot of carpentry to be done and miles of rigging, and I think the new captain will want me to stay on as long as I can."

The next morning, as Matthew was collecting his tools and looking over the ship, now riding gently in her fitting out berth, a messenger came looking for him. "Mister Humphreys would like to see you in his office right away."

Matthew put his tools down by the side of the office door as he had done months before, and entered the same marked door, this time without knocking.

Humphreys was seated at his desk talking animatedly with a dark-visaged man wearing the uniform of a captain in the Continental Navy. The uniform seemed to be patterned after the uniforms of the British Navy. Matthew judged the man was about forty and noticed that his face was strong, but kind. Matthew liked him right away.

Humphreys looked up. "Oh, Christopher, come over here."

Humphreys and the captain stood up. Humphreys introduced Matthew. "Captain Biddle, this is the young man I was talking about. Christopher, this is Captain Nicholas Biddle of the Continental Navy. He is to assume command of the *Randolph* later today. He would like to talk to you about your future. Please sit down."

After they were all seated, Captain Biddle cleared his throat and looked intently at Matthew. "Christopher, I understand there is still a great deal of carpentry to do and much rigging to complete on the ship. After that will come the hard part, finding and training a crew. Mister Humphreys, here, tells me you have been to sea as a lieutenant on a privateeer and that you also understand ship construction."

"My officers, to be frank, don't know a damned thing about anything but politics. My first lieutenant has had some limited experience in the British Navy some three years ago, but he won't be much help, either. I need someone I can count on. If you are willing, I will arrange a lieutenant's commission in the Continental Navy for you and make you my third lieutenant. Unfortunately the other lieutenants will out-rank you by a few days, but you will be the one I depend on.

"If the other two junior lieutenants give you any trouble, I expect you will take them down below in a vacant compartment and straighten them out. I will support you as long as you don't mark them up too much. If you meet my expectations I will see that you are promoted as soon as possible. Will you accept?"

Matthew was taken by surprise, and hesitated for a moment. He looked at Humphreys. "Mister Humphreys, I understand you will be finishing the rigging for another month. I am not an expert on the rigging of this type of ship. Could I be spared for a month to take my wife back home and let my father know about this? He is expecting me back at work in the shipyard in Annapolis, but I think he will let me go for something as important as this."

Humphreys smiled and cleared his throat. "I think that will be a satisfactory arrangement. Captain Biddle, do you agree?"

Biddle was not entirely pleased by the way Humphreys had made the decision, but he finally nodded in agreement.

Humphreys rose, extended his hand to Matthew, and said, "Congratulations on your forthcoming lieutenancy. I wish you every success. You will be missed."

Chapter 7

Matthew burst through the door to their small house. "Guess what! We're going home tomorrow!"

Martha stood in front of him, clearly taken aback, and Matthew looked at her closely. Though new to the ways of young women, he sensed a subtle difference in her. In the weeks past she had occasionlly complained about the smallness of the house, but when he had questioned her about the details, she usually laughed and said, "I'll be happy anywhere with you, even in a hammock in a barn." Now there was something different. Yes, subtle, but different. She did not appear to be unhappy, rather there was a happy glow about her.

Again Matthew looked at her closely. Then she asked, "Back to your father's house?"

"For a few days. We're going back to Annapolis and buy our own house."

Martha became pensive. Now Matthew was sure there was something wrong. He had anticipated that she would be enthusiastic at the prospect of returning to her relatives and friends. He had brought up the new house and still she did not react as he had expected.

Then she said, "I don't know if I can travel."

"What! You had no trouble coming up here."

She sighed, "But I think I'm pregnant now."

Matthew's face clouded, but now at least he knew what the problem was. He asked. "How do you know?"

"Silly. How does any woman know? Besides, our next door neighbor, Mrs. Moriarity, used to be a midwife. She says I'm due in December or January."

"You mean you have to stay here?"

Martha laughed. "I don't think so. I'll go with you. I think we can put our bed in the wagon so that I can take short naps along the way. That way I can rest when I don't feel up to sitting on that hard wooden seat. Mostly in the mornings, I think."

"Mornings?"

"Yes. Pregnant women usually have what is called morning sickness."

"My God! I've got a lot to learn about this baby business."

"Babies? You don't even know much about women yet."

Matthew colored. "You mean I'm not a very good husband?"

"Oh, no. You're wonderful. But you still don't understand women very well."

"No?"

"No, you don't. I don't think many men in this age of science know much about women. Women don't tell you anything. Men just tell crude jokes about sex. They are usually afraid of discussing the subject frankly."

"Then you've just got to talk to me plainly. I do want to learn."

Martha sighed. "That tool you have isn't an axe. Treat it and me more gently."

"But I thought you liked, er, vigorous action."

"Just more of your crude jokes."

Martha took him in her arms and ran her fingers through his hair. "Oh, yes, my love, there is a time for everything. Just try a litle more tenderness first."

Matthew looked into her eyes and then held her tightly. "What about making love? Do you have to sleep apart from me for the next six months?"

Martha shook her head. "Mrs. Moriarity says you just have to be careful. As I said, don't be so wild when you make love. Be gentle." Then she giggled. "I'm pretty tough, and she says you can't hurt anything."

"I can't help it. You are very atractive to me."

"Just calm down about it. We can manage. You'll have to stop acting like a sailor."

"But I am a sailor."

Martha took him in her arms again. "Just stop charging at me like you were using your adze."

Matthew tried to object but Martha put a finger on his lips. "I didn't mean to upset you. I've never seen a sailor blush."

Matthew shook his head. "But I don't know how to discuss things like this with a lady."

"You used to talk to the waterfront girls and the waitresses in the restaurant."

"Well, yes, but...."

"Stop. I've been on the waterfront for years, you know."

"Yes, but you're different."

"I hope so, but I understand the language. After all, I've heard plenty of it in our restaurant."

Matthew shook his head and grinned. "I give up. Tell me what to do."

Martha took him by the hand. "Come with me now and I'll begin your education."

The next morning, Martha cooked all the eggs they could eat and hard-boiled the rest in an effort to use up the food they could not carry with them. Pickles and tomatoes went into a large jar, flour was made into biscuits and cookies, ground corn became corn bread.

Matthew watched her preparations with interest. Then he said, "I'll go see our landlord and settle our rent."

"And I'll go see Mrs. Moriarity, give her anything we can't fit in the wagon, and get some last minute advice."

By the time the wagon was packed so that the double bed was available for Martha, she decided to sit on the spring seat instead. After a few miles she changed her mind and decided to take a mid-morning nap.

The trip was slow but pleasant, and Matthew adjusted the pace to Martha's condition. She got stronger each day, and on the eighth day Matthew drove the wagon around State Circle and to the family home.

Matthew looked closely at the new State House. "Look at that scaffolding. They're still working on it."

"I don't think they will ever finish it," Martha said. "Only a few men are working today."

Matthew nodded. "Workmen who do even simple carpentry are hard to get with the war on. They're all building ships for higher wages. Some of my father's workers left the State House job to come to us, thinking themselves superior carpenters."

"Are they?"

"No. They have a lot to learn, and are still relatively unskilled."

Matthew guided the tired horse to the Church Circle and started down Church Street. "They ought to change the name of this street to Main Street. After all, most of the main business buildings are on it and only one church."

"Be patient. It will happen one day."

A few minutes later Matthew stopped the horse in front of the family home. Before he could get out of the wagon to help Martha down, the front door flew open and Mammy Sarah raised her skirt and ran down the stairs. "Hello, Miss Martha, I'm glad you be back!"

After she had put her arms around Martha, she said to Matthew, "Any news?"

Martha laughed. "I take it you mean am I expecting."

"'Course. What else is important?"

"You're right. I'm due about January."

Mammy Sarah ignored Matthew, turned Martha around, and guided her up the stairs. "Come with Mammy. We get a cup of tea and talk about this. There ain't be a little one in this house or in my arms for a long time."

Matthew was a little irked at being ignored as the two women left him. "Mammy, if you want to hold a baby, why don't you take on Jebediah?"

Mammy shook her head. "Mind your own business. Besides, I'm too old for that sort of thing. You done your bit already. Now leave us women alone. Bring the baggage in. That's what men are for."

Martha stopped and turned to Matthew. "Just bring the small things in. Tomorrow we'll go and rent our own house."

Mammy chuckled. "Woman, you don't need to rent a house. He can buy any house in this town."

Martha was puzzled. "I don't understand. We don't have that much money now. Just Matthew's wages, although they've been good."

Mammy laughed and slapped her leg. "The prize money has been released. His father has it, and it's a lot. Your husband's share would choke a horse. I've got just the house for you. Two doors up the street."

"Why, is it for sale?"

"Mr. Fairfax was killed two weeks ago and his widow wants to go back home to Virginia."

Martha shook her head. "We don't want to take advantage of her. We'll make a fair offer."

"Sure, and you'll have the house in a day or two. We'll put the wagon in the shed out back and leave the furniture and most of the baggage in it."

Minutes later Martha sat in the kitchen at the huge work table, cup of hot tea in her hands. "Mammy," she said, "Aren't you going to leave this house and marry Jebediah?"

Mammy laughed. "What for? Jebediah can come up the back stairs any night he want to. Mister Christopher don't care. I'll be around next January to take care of you."

"But you have this house to run."

Mammy shrugged. "Easy. I'll make Jebediah do all our heavy work and he'll do the same for you. My sister has a sixteen-year-old girl who ought to get some work. She'll be a maid to your family and a nurse to your baby when it comes, that is, if she can get the child away from me."

"But we can't pay enough."

"Sure you can."

"How much should we pay her?"

"Pay her well. She'll make a good one."

"All right."

Mammy laughed. "I don't think you know how rich your husband is. Get him to put his prize money in the new Annapolis Bank instead of under his Pa's mattress and it will earn enough to take care of all of you."

"Do you think he will listen?"

Mammy cackled. "Easy. Just don't let him back into that big feather bed until he promises you."

"And that's the way you control Jebediah?"

Mammy Sarah blushed slightly, but the change was barely visible in her mahogany cheeks. "No, child. I don't have to do that. Jebediah is so crazy for me I just have to crook my little finger."

Martha sighed. "Can I learn to do that with Matthew?"

"Honey, you ain't had time to know him yet. Soon you won't have to bother to crook your little finger. He'll just do what you want him to do."

Martha grinned. "There's something in what you say. I do seem to have better control these days."

"When that young baby comes along, you'll rule the roost all the way."

"Mammy, I wish you wouldn't think of me like a chicken."

"Why not? We eat chickens, we eat eggs, we sleep on feather beds and we depend on them all the time. They not very smart, but they get treated mighty fine."

Matthew's father came home that night to find his son and daughter-in-law well established in his house. He greeted them warmly. "Son," he said exuberantly, "tonight is for celebrating. Tomorrow we'll get down to work in the shipyard. You and I will be a great team."

Matthew was somber, and his father took notice, "Son, is there something wrong?"

"Pa, it won't be like you want it. Tonight enjoy your daughter-in-law, and tomorrow we'll talk."

His father raised his eyebrows, cleared his throat, and started to say something.

Matthew stopped him. "Pa, not until tomorrow."

The next morning Matthew ate breakfast while Martha slept and then walked down to the shipyard. His father was hard at work. He looked up as Matthew walked in. He pushed an empty coffee cup to one side. "Well, what's wrong?"

Matthew looked at the sloppy plans lying on the big table. "You need to use better paper and good India ink, and you need to find a draftsman. It will pay off in the end. First, your workmen can do better, faster, and more accurate work when they can easily read your plans and know what to do before the piece they are working on is finished. That way a lot of men can be working on a lot of pieces at the same time. Second, prospective buyers can visualize the ship more easily and will pay more. You can make more than enough money to pay for the paper, ink, and draftsman."

"Good advice. I'll take it. What else did you learn?"

"As you said, a lot about big timbers. Now I'm as good as any of their carpenters. I'll pass the knowledge along to your men. But there's something else we have to talk about."

"Let's have it then. From your face, I don't think I'll like it."

"One of the owners of the yard, Mister Humphreys, and the newly appointed commanding officer, Captain Biddle, both want me to take a commission in the Continental Navy as a lieutenant and join *Randolph's* crew."

"But as a lieutenant your pay will be a pittance! Why do you want to do that? You'll be paid ten times that here, and nobody will be shooting at you."

"I guess this is a matter of what our country needs from us now. The captain is in serious trouble. His officers are unqualified. They're just a bunch of politicians foisted on him by congressmen and other lubberly shore officials.

"But I thought we were fighting in a real revolution against practices like that. I never knew it was that bad."

"Maybe worse. Worms got into our system early on. It may be a long time before they're flushed out."

"Well, what are his other problems?"

"He has no crew as yet, and his ship needs a lot of work before she can become an effective warship."

"So? That's not your job."

"I think it is. No one else can do it, or the ship won't sail for months, if ever."

Eric Christopher sighed. "I see your point. MacIntosh will have to take your place until you get back."

Matthew shook his head. "It may be a year or two. This war will get worse."

Eric was quiet. Then he said, "I guess this will be our contribution to our new country. It will only be as good as we make it."

Matthew sighed. "I'm not one for talking about patriotism. I guess the best way to talk about something is to do it."

Chapter 8

That night Matthew did not sleep well. The next morning Martha said, "You tossed and turned all night. The next time when you have a problem tell me all about it so we can both get some sleep."

"Come down to breakfast and I'll tell you all about it," Matthew said.

Martha shuddered, "I can't eat breakfast yet. I know you have bad news. Tell me now."

Matthew slid back into bed. "I might as well come right out with it. I've decided to take a commission as a lieutenant in the Continental Navy and go to sea on the *Randolph*."

Martha sighed. "I could see you were closely attached to that ship, and I was afraid this would happen. I felt it coming."

"Yes, but there is more to it than that. The ship is not finished, and her captain is new and doesn't know a thing about the Continental Navy. The crew has not even been recruited yet."

"And you are the only one in the whole country who can solve their problems?"

Matthew shook his head slowly. "I'm afraid so."

"Not only that, but you think that our new country and its Navy are in trouble as well."

"Yes, and if all of us don't do our part, the country will fall apart and we'll be back under the British, only this time it will be worse."

Martha sighed. "For a moment I thought your objectives were selfish and that you just wanted to be away from me."

Matthew interrupted. "That's not true. I'll miss you terribly, but I must think about our new country, also."

"I'm willing to do my share if you can convince me that this is really necessary."

Matthew shrugged. "I think I'm right, but if I find it is a challenge I can't handle, I'll quit and come right back."

Martha sighed and held him tightly. "The British were bad enough when they had us under tight control. If we lose now I hate to think about it."

"You're right. They will take it out on us, both the sea-side citizens and the ship's crews. Even now they are treating our prisoners very badly, trying to discourage us."

"What about prisoners taken from privateers?"

"They treat them terribly. They take the position that these men aren't entitled to the same treatment given to members of the armed forces and they see them as traitors."

"Well, at least that won't be a problem for you. You'll be in the Continental Navy."

"Yes, but my brother Kevin will have to face it. He'll be the captain of a privateer. They might even hang him. Fighting the British will help all of us, and I'd like to do something to stop the British from mistreating our prisoners."

After Matthew went downstairs, Martha cried into her pillow. Then she got up, washed her face vigorously, and combed her beautiful brown hair. She went down to the dining room.

As she entered, Matthew looked up and took her hand. "You are a remarkable woman and leaving you is one of the hardest things I've ever had to do. But when I come back, I promise to never leave you again."

Martha smiled. "And our son?"

"Him, too."

Martha sighed. "I won't hold you to your promise. I suppose I have to make some sacrifices, too, but there is a limit to what I will do. After all, Mrs. Fairfax who would like to sell us her house, lost her husband early in the war. I can't eat any breakfast, but if you'll buy that house for me, I'll let you go to sea as soon as it's furnished."

Matthew sighed with relief. "Let's go to see the real estate man. We'll buy it today."

Mammy came in with a plate of biscuits. "I heard what you said. It's a nice house. Wait until you see the garden. Your child will be playing in it next summer."

Mammy looked at Martha's dress and said to Matthew, "And you got to buy her some better clothes. She's sitting there in the same plain cotton dress she wore to wait on tables. If she's your wife, she should be wearing silk."

Martha interrupted. "Oh, Mammy, this is good enough to wear in the house."

"You got plenty just like it. I've seed them. They won't do for the lady you is now."

"But I'll just get silk soiled."

"Oh, no, you won't. Your days of that are over."

"But after the baby comes?"

Mammy laughed. "You won't get near it. It'll never soil your silks."

Martha laughed. "I like those words 'soil your silks.'"

Mammy bristled. "You think it's funny. but you got to think about it from now on."

Mammy turned to Matthew. "You got plenty of money. You will be a leading citizen of Annapolis when you get back. She will be a leading lady of society, and I'll see that she dresses that way if you'll let her have the money. If we can't buy them, we'll hire a seamstress to make them."

"All right, Mammy, I'll do it. Just leave the biscuits here. We'll be back for a big lunch."

Martha grinned. "Oh, yes, I'll be hungry by then."

The house was all that Martha wanted. Matthew took her home, went down to the shipyard to see his father, and together they went to the real estate lawyer's downtown office. The deal was closed just before lunch. "My client will be very happy. She will leave for her hometown in Virginia this afternoon," the lawyer had said.

Late that day Jebediah finished unloading the wagon. The first item to be put in place was the large feather bed. A week of shopping quickly furnished the house to Martha's taste with the enthusiastic help of Mammy Sarah. "Just like the governor's house," she said. "We'll make it even better if you'll send for a few things from New York."

Martha laughed. "Not quite as big," she said, "but I like it better small."

Matthew grinned. "The one we build will be bigger and better than this."

Early the next morning Matthew caught the fast packet for Philadelphia from the waterfront in front of the marketplace. The fast packet was actually one of three ships plying a regular route between Philadelphia and Annapolis. Packet was a name for any ship used for fast and scheduled transport. The ships carried passengers, mail, and light freight. Most were small, two masted schooners, and very fast.

Matthew carried an extra seabag that was filled with the tailored uniforms of a lieutenant in the Continental Navy that a local tailor had made for him. He had decided to make the three hundred mile trip by fast packet rather than by the bumpy one hundred and fifty mile trip by coach. Even the six horses hitched to the sturdy coach could not negotiate the rough roads in better time. He figured the longer distance would be quicker by a day.

The packet would sail night and day at an average of eight knots and would arrive in two days. Matthew could sleep peacefully even if the weather was bad. The coach would poke along at five knots, stopping each of five nights. Matthew was also sure he would pick up some unwelcome passengers of his own, a load of bed bugs from the unkempt tavern beds.

Later the second day, the packet sailed smoothly into the public piers on the waterfront, and Matthew took a hansom cab to the shipyard.

Mister Humphreys greeted him cordially and asked him to sit down. Matthew eased into a mahogany chair tentatively.

"Well, my lad, what have you decided?"

Matthew said without hesitation, "I've decided to join the Continental Navy and to take a lieutenant's commission. Where can I find Captain Biddle, sir?"

Humphreys grinned. "Go aboard and you'll find him nervously pacing his quarterdeck or sitting uncomfortably in his unfinished cabin. In either case, he'll be glad to see you. He needs help badly."

Matthew found Captain Biddle slumped in a rickety chair in his cabin. Matthew knocked. Captain Biddle looked up through the unfinished door. "Come in, Matthew, I've been hoping to see you."

Matthew went in and shook hands with the captain. "Sir, I've decided to accept your offer. I'd like to join the Continental Navy and you can swear me in if you'll keep me with the ship."

Captain Biddle rubbed his hands. "Oh, yes, you'll stay aboard as long as I do. I'd hoped you'd be back, and I have your commission here. Sign on this line, raise your right hand, and I'll swear you in."

Matthew was now a lieutenant in the new navy. "Sir, I have my uniform in a seabag. Shall I put it on?"

Biddle laughed, "As soon as you can, but let's talk first. Then I want to take you on a tour of the ship and show you what has to be done. As you can see, I'm living rather sparsely here. I can not even offer you a chair to sit in or a cup of coffee."

Matthew looked around the cabin and grinned. "Sir, this is worse than sparsely. I'll pick up a couple of my men who came with me from our shipyard and have this in shape in a day. I suggest you stay home tomorrow while we finish it. Now, sir, you talked about walking about the ship. I'm anxious to see it."

"Ah, let's go. This chair is killing my back."

Captain Biddle led the way to the quarterdeck and began to walk up the starboard side. As they passed the after, or mizzen mast, Matthew stopped and dug his fingernail into the finish of the mast and smelled it. "Sir," he said, "this is white oak. The masts should be made of live oak."

"I can't tell the difference just by looking at it."

"You can't unless you examine it carefully as I did. The British use only live oak for masts. It is thirty percent stronger than white oak. White oak is really only suitable for framing and planking."

"Well, I did bring it up with the shipyard owners. They said they couldn't get any more live oak with the war on."

"Sir, I think we'd better talk with Mister Humphreys."

"All right. Let's go."

Captain Biddle walked over to the gangway cut in the bulwark. A petty officer, supposedly on watch, lounged near it. He raised his right hand to his cap diffidently and said, "How are you, Cap?"

Captain Biddle turned to Matthew. "This certainly isn't the British Navy. I'll correct him."

Matthew nodded. "It certainly isn't. Let me take care of this, sir." He turned to the petty officer. "What is your name?"

"Carrick, sir."

"Well, Carrick, I'm Lieutenant Christopher. Send a messenger to notify the first lieutenant that the captain is leaving the ship to visit the shipyard office. Next time he leaves, have the officer of the watch up here, and if you are ever on watch again, say to the captain, 'Good day, sir.' I'll teach you to salute later."

Carrick flushed, but made a better salute, and said, "Aye, aye, sir."

The captain grinned. "Good job, Christopher. I feel better already having you aboard."

Matthew followed the captain down the brow. He felt there was something salvageable in Carrick, but he hoped there were other men better trained than Carrick in the crew.

Captain Biddle said over his shoulder, "I know what you're thinking, but he's one of the better men. We don't have many yet of any kind, and not many as good as he is."

"Captain, we'll find a way. Let's make sure the yard is on the right track to finish the ship first."

Captain Biddle knocked on Humphreys' door and pushed it open without waiting for an invitation. Humphreys was seated before his desk, deep in thought. His eyes came up and fixed on Biddle. "Ah, Captain, come on in and sit down. I see your new lieutenant is with you. I'm looking forward to seeing him in uniform."

Biddle nodded. "He will be as soon as he finds suitable quarters on the ship in which to change. In the meantime I want to talk to you about the masts. They seem to be white oak instead of live oak."

Humphreys cleared his throat and colored. "Ah, yes, so they are. We'd like to use live oak and we always used to, but now it's not available. Not from Europe, Great Britain, or South Carolina."

Matthew said, "We have some in our shipyard. It's the only kind my father will use."

"We'd like to, I assure you. Our last shipment from South Carolina was lost at sea. There isn't any growing near here any more. We've substituted white oak masts of fifteen percent greater diameter than normal. That should do it."

Matthew shook his head doubtfully. "I don't think so."

Biddle had a resigned look. Obviously the war was only one of the problems he had been fighting. He sighed. "I guess we'll have to make it do."

"Yes," Humphreys said with relief. "The war is closing in on us. We can't get a lot of other materials either, and you'll find it even worse when you try to round up a crew."

Matthew interrupted him. "I noted there are no lightning rods installed on the tops of the masts."

Humphreys glared, but recovered. "There aren't any. We can't get enough copper to cover her bottom completely, so there's none to spare for lightning rods."

"I understand," Christopher said, "But this is very important to the safety of the ship."

Humphrey nodded. "I agree. I'll make every effort to provide it before you sail."

Biddle shrugged, now completely beaten. "Well, I guess we'll have to put our first effort on staying afloat. Lightning will have to get in line. Let's go back aboard, Matthew, and discuss the personnel problems."

They walked slowly through the shipyard. The captain was clearly depressed, but by the time they reached the bottom of the brow, he had cheered up. The spring weather helped. He took a deep breath. "Don't feel down, eh, Christopher. No lightning in the air today."

"No, sir. If you don't mind, sir, I suggest you go on home and have dinner with your family and then take tomorrow off. The next day your cabin will be finished, and we can work better on the personnel problem. In the meantime I'll find out what the first lieutenant is doing about finding some men. We need to get on with it."

"Very well. That sounds good to me. I am tired of that uncomfortable chair in that terrible cabin. I'll see you the day after tomorrow."

Matthew nodded. "I suppose captains in the Royal Navy live in better surroundings."

"Oh, yes. The captain's cabin always comes first and is royally equipped. A British captain wouldn't even stable his livestock in mine."

"Well, sir, you'll find it suitable if not royal by tomorrow."

Chapter 9

Matthew went back aboard the *Randolph* looking for the first lieutenant. The watch reported that he was in town. "Looking for men for the crew, I think, but I don't know why he's gone to the city prison and the prisoner of war stockade."

Matthew grinned. "Well, I'll find out tomorrow."

The petty officer of the watch shook his head. "But, sir, I don't see what men he could find worth anything in those two places. They're a bunch of losers."

Matthew pursed his lips. "Don't be too sure. There are a lot of good men in jail, too. Many are debtors who couldn't find a legal way to support their families. If they join the Navy they will at least have some income and won't be a burden on the city any longer. The trick is to carefully evaluate each man. Many of them may be better than our volunteers."

"But, sir, what about the prisoners-of-war? They are our enemies. They'll all try to escape or kill our men."

"Again, don't jump to conclusions. Each man will be considered carefully. Very few of the British enlisted men were true volunteers for the Royal Navy. Most are pressed men who now hate their old country and would like to make a fresh start in a new country."

"Many of the men are Americans and of other than British nationalities. Many are already trained and will make good sailors."

"Well, sir, you sold me, but if any of them come aboard I'll always watch my back."

Matthew nodded. "You ought to do the same now. We already have some questionable men. Many of them came to this country years ago to avoid trouble at home, and they have made a lot of trouble here."

Matthew found two of the men who had come to the ship with him from the shipyard. They were good carpenters. He took them back to the captain's cabin. They both shook their heads when they walked in. "Awful!" one said. "Looks like an empty cheese box and smells even worse. No self-respecting mouse would live in here."

Matthew nodded. "Let's get on with it. Put in a solid door, some cabinets, and better finishing for the wood that's already there. I'll go to see Forester and tell him he owes us the best finishing wood he can find. Then clean up what's left to get the smell out of here. We can build a swinging cot and a commode. The captain shouldn't have to walk the length of the ship to get to the head."

Matthew went ashore and cornered Forester in his shack. Forester was obviously ashamed when Matthew described the condition of the captain's cabin. Forester rolled his eyes. "Sorry, I guess it got away from me. I had too many other problems to solve. Come with me, and we'll do something about it."

Matthew followed him to a locked store room. Inside, Forester found a handsome dining table, four more or less matching chairs, a padded lounge chair, a small desk and chair, and a large folding cot that could be fitted to hang from the overhead. Matthew looked carefully at the other pieces of furniture in the storerooom but rejected them. Forester had already pointed out the best and Matthew gratefullly accepted them.

Matthew said. "Where did all this furniture come from?"

Forester laughed. "Most of it came from prizes. You can see some of the British merchant captains lived pretty well. We bought it at prize auctions, and then we forgot we had them. I kept it under lock and key so nobody would know we had them stored away."

Matthew said, "A little cleaning and some varnish will make them do very handsomely, and anything is better than nothing at all. I'm in your debt."

Forester laughed. "The other way around. Without you the ship might still be on the ways."

A day of cleaning and carpentering by the two men selected by Matthew, and the captain's cabin became serviceable. The furniture and wood trim varnish dried quickly, and the pieces were put in the cabin and neatly arranged.

The next morning Captain Biddle, ceremoniously saluted and welcomed aboard by the first lieutenant and the petty officer of the watch, went to his cabin and found Matthew and his men putting the finishing touches on the woodwork and furniture.

"My God!" the captain said. "You've made a silk purse out of a sow's ear. I'll never forget it. My compliments to both of your men. As far as I'm concerned, they're now both promoted to petty officers."

Both men beamed and Matthew grinned. "Thank you, sir. A good example of what Christopher's shipyard can do with little time and less money."

The captain said with relish, "I feel I can do better work now that I can spread my lists on this fine table, and we can all sit down. Now I'd like to get at this personnel problem. It bothers me a great deal."

Matthew sat down with Captain Biddle and the first lieutenant, Francis Forsyth, who had been summoned by the Captain. Biddle said, "Now, Forsyth, I want a complete summary of the crew recruitment program. We've put this off much too long. We're due to go to sea in January, and we have to fill out and train the crew before that."

Captain Biddle looked around the room. "I'm going to organize the ship somewhat like the British do it. We now have a first lieutenant and three junior lieutenants. I must admit that Christopher, here, even if he is junior in date of rank, is more skilled in seamanship than the others and I'll have to depend on him. The others are political appointees and have never been to sea."

Forsyth, who had served a cruise in the British Navy as a midshipman, looked up eagerly. "Yes, sir, I can help with the problem."

Biddle was not satisfed. "Lieutenant Forsyth, you don't just help with the problem. It is your problem. Solve it. I'll give you any authority you need."

Forsyth colored. "Uh, yes, sir. I'll get on with it."

The captain went on. "We won't use the master system like the Royal Navy does where the master handles the navigation of the ship and gives all orders regarding the setting and trimming of the sails. The captain gives general orders. I just won't be able to find one in this country and I expect to handle the ship myself. The watch officers will take over as soon as I can train them to handle the ship on their watch. Since I won't be able to find a master, I'll also have to retain responsibility for navigating the ship. Also, if we are ever fortunate enough to be assigned any midshipmen, I'll have to train them."

Forsyth said, "Captain, you won't have a spare moment for anything else."

Biddle looked at him sharply. "Don't worry. I'll always know what is going on. I'll depend on you very heavily to train the crew in sailing and gunnery. Lieutenant Christopher will navigate for me, and I already know he is well qualified. Still, I will have to take sights and check his navigation.

"Until the two lieutenants are qualified to stand watch, this means you, me, and Lieutenant Christopher will stand watch in three."

The captain got his second wind. "We'll need a boatswain, a surgeon, a carpenter, a gunner, and a purser as soon as possible."

Forsyth, fresh from his fruitless search for warrant and petty officers, cleared his throat nervously. "Er, Captain, this will be very difficult. I don't think we'll find there are many qualified warrant officers and men in this country, let alone in this state. We'll have to train our own."

Matthew spoke up. "Sir, I think Lieutenant Forsyth and I should go back into town to visit the prisoner-of-war stockade. It must be full of experienced talent. Perhaps the city prisoner debtors might be acceptable."

Forsyth bridled. "Talent be damned! It's all British! The bloody bastards will go right over the other side if we bring them aboard the ship."

The captain rubbed his chin thoughtfully. "I'm familiar with the British. After all, I commanded one of their ships and hundreds of their men. Seems to me many of the prisoners we have must have been pressed into service by the Royal Navy in the first place. Maybe some of them are of other nationalities. I don't think they want to go back to Great Britain. After all, we are fighting a revolutuion to make this country a decent and fair place for all men to live. After you've served in a British ship, you'll realize they can be worse than prisons. Half of the men would desert if they could. I think we can convince them not only to enjoy their independence, but to fight for it."

Matthew had been quiet, letting the Captain make the case. Now he spoke up. "Well said, sir. Now we have to administer this ship and the crew so we can get rid of the bad practices the British sailors hated: flogging, disrespectful treatment of the common sailors, and unfairness when it comes to recognizing performance. None of this should be used or allowed in this navy."

Forsyth, obviously thinking back to his midshipman days when he was treated sternly, began to mellow. "Well, Captain, my treatment may not have been as bad as yours, but it wasn't good. Maybe we can make this work."

Captain Biddle nodded vigorously. "We must. There is no other course."

The next morning Lieutenant Forsyth and Matthew borrowed a carriage from the shipyard and drove to town toward the prisoner-of-war stockade. Forsyth said, "We'll go there directly and maybe to the city prison tomorrow. I called on the mayor yesterday and got permission to have the warden send down to the ship any men we choose. I think the mayor wants to get rid of as many men as he can so he won't have to feed them. I told the warden I might be back."

Christopher raised his eyebrows, but said nothing.

In half an hour the carriage drew up to a large brick building with small windows covered with bars, used as a stockade to house several hundred prisoners-of-war. Forsyth and Christopher went into the the warden's office. "Well, well," the warden said, "I really didn't expect you back today. You weren't very happy when you were here last."

Forsyth frowned. "I changed my mind. May we see some of your healthiest prisoners again?"

"Come with me. I'll bring in about a hundred and more if you want to see them."

Forsyth and Christopher waited in a large room, and soon a group of men began to trickle in until a hundred stood before the two officers. Most of them were dressed in rags that had once been British Navy uniforms. Most wore beards, all were thin and undernourished, and showed marks of abuse. Miraculously none showed signs of scurvy. Matthew put this down to the the British efficiency of administering lime juice, and made a mental note to include the custom in their ship's routine.

Six, standing together, were a little cleaner and stood straighter. Forsyth poked Christopher. "Marines," he said.

Matthew looked at them carefully. "Let's take all of that group over there. We will need them for the nucleus of a marine company."

Forsyth pointed at the men and said to the warden, "We'd like those men."

The warden waved at a guard, nodded toward the men, and they were herded out. He pointed at a man a little older than the others. "He says he was a boatswain."

Matthew walked over to the man and put out his hand. "I'm Lieutenant Christopher. May I ask your name?"

The prisoner was surprised, but shook hands. "Well, mate," he said in a strong accent, "ye're a cool one."

"I'm not a mate," Christopher said, "I'm a lieutenant. Your name?"

The prisoner looked carefully at Christopher, taking in his determined face and bulging muscles, and said, "Boatswain Raster, of HMS *Bronson*, sir."

"That's more like it, Raster. Would you like to be boatswain of the USS *Randolph*, an American frigate now building here?"

"Depending on what would happen to me after the war, sir. My country would consider me a traitor."

"Your old country would consider you a traitor, but you'll be an American patriot if you come with us. When you are discharged from the American Continental Navy after the war you will be made a citizen. Land will be made available for you to settle on. Our country is vast and is growing rapidly."

Raster grinned. "I'm your man, sir. I can bring twenty men with me if you'll give them the same deal. We'd all like to become Americans."

Matthew smiled. "I'll guarantee it. My captain will re-affirm what I have said in writing before he swears you into the Navy. Now, are there any other men in the group standing over there who might be gunners, gun captains, gun crew members, or even a cook?"

Raster laughed. "That tough looking old bastard over there is the best seagoing cook I know. Not much with the fancy stuff ashore, but he can make the best plum duff I've ever tasted. No one seems to remember his name. He's just called Cookie. The next man over there was our warrant gunner. His name is Airlie. Three of the men were gun captains and some were artisans, carpenters, and the like."

Matthew called Airlie over and made him the same offer he had just given Raster. Airlie agreed to join the ship. Matthew went over to Lieutenant Forsyth who had been chatting animatedly with the warden.

"Sir, we've got about fifty men who will sign up. A boatswain, a gunner, a cook, three gun captains, and two full gun crews. They'll make a good nucleus."

The warden said, "Good, I'll send them over to your ship tomorrow."

Forsyth was exhilirated. "Maybe we should go ahead and take twice as many."

Matthew shook his head. "This is a pretty big bite we're taking already. Maybe we should try this out first and see how they mix with the Americans in the crew until we're sure they'll accept the Englishmen."

Forsyth shrugged, "All right with me."

The next day after Lieutenant Forsyth and Matthew had briefed the captain, several wagons loaded with prisoners appeared at the brow. They were a scruffy looking lot, and the Captain screwed his nose up at the stink.

Forsyth said, "I'll get them cleaned up, Captain, and give them some uniforms. They'll look better."

Matthew said, "But, Lieutenant, that's my job. How would you like me to do it?"

Forsyth shrugged. "Put them in a group on the forecastle, and then order them to scrub each other with soft soap. Use sand on the worst cases. They'll lose some skin, but also a lot of dirt, lice, and hair, too."

Matthew pursed his lips. "Yes, sir, I'll take charge of it."

As they scrubbed each other, a new atmosphere emerged. The sullen group became happy and then downright enthusiastic, shouting at each other as they rinsed off the soapy water and all that came away with it floating down the scuppers.

After they were cleaned up and dressed in new clothes, Matthew assigned them to billets. As they moved about the ship, it was clear they knew their business. At first the Americans kept their distance, turned off as much as anything by the peculiar accents of the Englishmen. They seemed to have forgotten that two generations ago they had sounded much the same.

Matthew circulated among the Americans, encouraging them to talk to the English. Soon the common language of the sea did the trick. A bowline was the same in both navies, and much of the jargon was also the same.

The boatswain was a forceful disciplinarian. The captain demanded perfection from him, but treated him with respect. His countrymen noted this, and morale began to build. They soon found out he had been a post captain in the British Navy. While captains in general were not popular with British seamen, those skilled in their profession and fair to their men were held in esteem and even liked. The crew came to see Captain Biddle as a knowledgeable naval officer and a compassionate captain who was interested in his ship and also in his men.

The cook, too, was a stabilizing influence. It took him some time to get used to the good, fresh groceries Matthew had brought aboard, but soon the crew was being reasonably well fed and therefore happy.

Matthew realized he could not devote so much time to the personal welfare of the crew nor the ordering and loading of provisions and supplies. The ship needed a purser and a surgeon to carry out these responsibilities. He went to see the captain to talk about the problem.

Captain Biddle heard him out. "You're right. I see what you mean. Finding a purser and a surgeon is my job. I'll go ashore and see what I can do about it."

A day later he came back with two young men in tow. The captain called all the lieutenants into his cabin. The captain pointed at a black-haired, gaunt young man. "Gentlemen, this is Benjamin Stein, our purser. He's looking forward to running his father's store some day, but his older brother is in line ahead of him. Stein wants to take a chance and go to sea. He thinks he might make a little prize money, too."

Stein laughed. "Not really, sir. Money is not what motivates me."

The captain interrupted. "And what *does* motivate you then?"

Stein became serious. "Sir, I suppose doing a decent job for a good cause. I think this will be such a career."

Biddle nodded. "Welcome aboard. It is."

"Thank you, sir."

Forsyth spoke up. "You'll have to get with it right away. We need to load the ship. When we go to sea we'll be eating differently, too. I suggest that you talk to the cook and the boatswain and learn what will keep at sea. He'll know all about that even though he'll eventually have to use all that dried and salted stuff. The British seamen are used to salted meat and canned biscuits, but if you can find something better, they'll eat it. Our American crew will eat anything if it's prepared decently."

"Good idea," Captain Biddle said. "Now this is the Surgeon, Doctor Little."

The young man next in line colored, his fair complexion turning pink. "Oh, sir, I'm not a full-fledged doctor yet. I was only a

medical student. I won't be a doctor for another year. I'm here because I ran put of money and couldn't stay in medical school."

Captain Biddle started to say something, but Lieutenant Forsyth
got him off the hook. "Never mind, Little, we'll call you Doc. The
crew will call you Sawbones anyway. Many of the British surgeons
are not as qualified as you are. I'll help you get a sick bay set up."

Captain Biddle knew when he was ahead. "Well, gentlemen,
let's get to work."

The weeks rolled by. Gradually a few more men were added to the
crew, but it was still dangerously low in numbers. Matthew wondered how they could man even one broadside and still tend the
sails. It would be difficult, and the captain was getting nervous.
Forsyth added a dozen prisoners of war, but they were not as good
as the first group. Matthew even scoured the countryside and
added a few farm boys looking to leave the farm. He was careful to
be honest in describing life at sea, but the boys he found needed
little urging.

Matthew kept counting the days on his fingers, wondering how
Martha was getting along. Finally, on the first day of January, a
note came on the fast packet. Martha had written it the day after
their baby was born. "It's a boy," she wrote. "A little early, but
healthy. His name is Matthew Junior. Six pounds."

Martha used the other pages describing the appearance and
abilities of their new son. "Eats all the time, too," she wrote, "and
a beautiful face," she added.

Matthew discounted the description written by a proud mother, but still he felt his son was superior.

Matthew walked up and down the deck all night, alternately
happy about the successful birth, but then sad because he could
not be home.

Finally he went in to see the captain. "Sir, may I have ten days
leave? I want to go to Annapolis to see my wife and our new son. I
may not have a chance to see him for many months."

Biddle beamed. "Of course you should go. I remember the
birth of my first child. It is a wonderful event, and you should

share it with your wife. Go by fast packet. You'll have a week there."

"But, sir, can you spare me?"

Biddle laughed. "While you're gone I'll crack the whip on those two useless lieutenants, Ambrose and Fitzgerald. I'll have them in shape when you get back."

Chapter 10

Two days later Matthew stood on the deck of the fast packet as it eased into a berth at the foot of Market Square in Annapolis. Looking beyond the square, he could see several streets radiating from it. The city design had been the brain child of Francis Nicholson in 1710. The principal street was Church Street, starting northeast of Market Square, and continuing to Church Circle.

Matthew's house was on the right of Church Street about half way up the gentle slope. Matthew could see that several more houses on the lower end of the street had been converted to stores or offices. He made a mental note to speed up their plans to build a new house south of State Circle and back from the waterfront and commercial district.

He looked up the street, trying to pick out his front door. It was difficult this morning because two inches of snow had covered the street and sidewalks. Then he realized something was different. Usually an hour after any snowfall, wagons and horses churned the white snow and the mud under it into a light yellow slurry. This morning there were horse and wagon tracks, but no mud. Matthew grinned. He said to a passenger standing next to him, "Great! The streets are bricked. No more mud."

The passenger replied, "You mean you used to have mud streets?"

"Yes, until now."

The passenger raised his eyebrows. "In Philadelphia we paved all our streets years ago."

"Well, your town council has a lot more money to spend than ours does."

"Yours probably taxes you less."

"They do. The shipyards support it, and our yard is at the top of the list of taxpayers."

As the passengers watched, two men ashore took the packet's mooring lines, put them on bollards, and pushed over a brow to the packet's deck. Matthew, the first over, trotted over the light snow, being careful not to fall.

At his door, he knocked impatiently. It was opened by a young black girl wearing an apron who looked at him strangely. "Yes?" she asked.

"My God! You're Elmira. Don't you remember me?"

Elmira looked at him carefully, and then recognition came. She giggled, covered her face in embarrassment, and said, "Sorry, Mister Matthew, I wasn't expecting you."

Matthew asked, "What are you doing here, Elmira?"

"Don't you know? I'm your maid."

"Mammy Sarah said she'd get some help, but I didn't know it would be a lady."

Elmira giggled again and smiled with pleasure. "I ain't no lady. Give me your coat and hat, Mister Matthew, and go back to the bedroom. Miss Martha is about done feeding the baby."

Matthew finished taking off his heavy coat, knit hat, and boots, handed them to Elmira, and headed for the bedroom. He could hear the angry cry of a small baby. He stopped at the door and looked in. Martha was bent over a crib with her hand on the flannel-clad chest of a squalling baby.

The baby stopped crying and started to gurgle quietly. Martha staightened and laughed. "That was what you wanted. You men are all the same."

She turned around toward the door. Her eyes widened. "Thank God! You're here!"

Martha held out her arms, and he ran to her. It was one of the best feelings he had ever experienced, holding his wife in his arms and looking at his new son.

After he had kissed her deeply, she pushed him away. "Come meet your son."

Matthew said, "Is he always noisy?"

"No, silly, he's a very well behaved young man."

With his arm around her waist, he walked over to the crib and looked down. Matthew Junior looked back.

Matthew grinned. "He doesn't know me yet, but he seems to like me," he said.

"Pick him up."

Matthew picked up his son and held him gingerly at arms length.

Martha laughed. "He isn't that delicate. He's going to be as tough as you are. You can throw him around a little. He'll like it."

Matthew refused to put his son down until Martha insisted and took him away. "He's hungry again," she said.

"How do you know?"

"Easy. He's dry, and he's always hungry."

"Is he healthy?"

"Like you. When he cries he's either hungry or wet."

The next morning Matthew went down to the shipyard. When he went into the office his father looked up and smiled. "I didn't think you'd be back before you sailed."

"I didn't either, but I asked for ten days leave and the captain gave it to me. So here I am."

"Since you are here, sit down and tell me some of what you have learned."

Matthew looked around the office. "First, Pa, I see you're using better paper and ink, but still no one can read your plans very well."

Eric Christopher shrugged. "That's the best I can do. At least the ships I build are the fastest around."

"Do you remember my old high school mathematics teacher, Miss Scranton?"

"Yes. So?"

"She could draw a beautiful freehand ship."

"But plans are mostly straight line and drawn carefully to scale."

"Also some curves. You could teach her to draw to scale. Every one could follow what she would draw."

"But she's a woman. If I brought her in here as a draftsman, the old boys out back would fall on their adzes."

"Might sharpen them up a bit to have a woman about who would know what she was doing."

"They're used to the old routine."

"Time for change. If she can teach mathematics to me, she can teach you that women can be more than just secretaries."

"How can I handle this?" he objected skeptically, pulling on his ear.

"Start by taking your sketches, some good paper and ink, and some drafting instruments and drop them by her house on your way home. Take a little time with her. Show her what you want done and exactly how you want it. On your way to work the next morning, just pick them up."

Eric lighted up. "The old boys will think I'm doing the drawing at home."

"At first. After they're used to seeing good work, tell them who's doing it. Then bring her into the office. They'll accept her in the office once they see what she can do and how much easier the work is without trying to follow your scribbles."

"All right. I'll try it." Then he grinned. "If it doesn't work I'll blame it on you."

Matthew spread out his arms and replied, "All right with me."

"Now what else did you learn?"

"Be careful what wood you use. The yard up there is taking a big chance. White oak for masts. Maple for planking."

"Good God! That is taking chances."

"We're going to have to travel to the South and bring back our own supply of live oak. Hoard live oak and copper. They will be almost as valuable as gold."

"Anything else?"

"No. That's it for now. I'll think over what I saw and tell you more later."

"Bring Martha to dinner tonight and we'll talk some more about this. Mammy Sarah will have all your favorite dishes."

"All right, Pa, with pleasure, but don't try to exclude Martha when we talk business. She knows almost as much as we do. She spent years listening to the shipyard workers talk at the tables as she served them."

Eric bristled. "You mean bad language?"

Mathew laughed. "Well, maybe a little, but she's used to it. I mean talk about shortages, substituting materials, and manufacturing processes. I'll bet she could even use an adze pretty well. I've seen her split wood. She has great pectorals."

Eric's mouth opened. "Now, Son, don't talk like that."

"Aw, Dad, you taught me to read and learn. Of course I know the names of muscles and what they do . . . Pectorals hold up her . . . ."

"That's enough, Son. I know what they do."

"Well, she might be able to help. Don't ignore what women can do, especially in this time of labor shortages. Some day they'll be in offices and even on ships."

Eric snorted, "Not in mine."

"Oh, yes, in yours, too."

Eric sensed he was losing the argument and changed the subject. "When do you have to go back?"

"In four more days."

"I'll have some of Miss Scranton's work for you to see before you go."

"Thanks. I guarantee I'll like it. So will you."

Two days before Matthew was to leave on the fast packet, his father stopped by for breakfast on his way to work. On the breakfast table, between the biscuits and scrambled eggs, he unrolled two sheets of drafting paper. Matthew studied them, ignoring the buttered biscuit in his hand. He let out a low whistle. "Better than the stuff at the Humphreys' yard," he said. "I like it. How about you, Pa?"

"Almost enough to ask her to marry me."

Matthew laughed. "Don't go overboard. Just make her your draftsman."

"All in good time. When are you leaving?"

"Day after tomorrow on the fast packet, and remember what I said about women."

That morning Martha bundled herself up against the late January cold, left Elmira in charge, and walked down Church Street arm in arm with Matthew. She kissed him good bye, holding back the tears, until she was back in the bedroom with Matthew Junior. He was sleeping, peacefuly, not knowing that his father had gone to war and might not come back.

Martha sat in a chair next to the crib and cried into a diaper. When Matthew Junior woke up, the diaper she was crying into was as wet as the one her son was wearing.

Chapter 11

On the deck of the fast packet as it left Annapolis, Matthew stood by the taffrail watching Martha's figure grow smaller and smaller in the distance. Long after he could no longer recognize her he watched the church spires behind her, and he grew more morose. He wondered if he would ever come back.

Then he noticed Little Jebediah, one of Big Jebediah's sons, standing next to him. Although he was called Little Jebediah, he was as big as Matthew, and probably stronger. Matthew said, "Jebediah, what are you doing aboard?"

Little Jebediah shrugged. "Please don't call me that any more. My name is now Johnson. That's my mother's name. My father may be Big Jebediah, but he wants me to use the name Johnson. He also wants me to leave town before Mammy Sarah discovers I'm one of his sons."

"Well, I'll be damned. Seems to me like he's got a lot of sons."

"All over town and also some daughters."

"Well, he must be faster than he looks."

Johnson laughed. "That man is surprising. Mammy Sarah don't really know much about him. She thinks she has first call on his services."

"Well, Johnson, assuming you had to get out of town, where are you going?"

"Philadelphia, of course. That's where the packet is bound, and I have a ticket that says Philadelphia."

"And what for?"

"Don't you know? Big Jebediah wants me to join the navy, go to sea, and look after you."

"Don't you cook? I think I remember that you cooked at the Middleton Tavern?"

"I spent three years cooking at the Middleton Tavern, and I think I was pretty good."

"But aren't you used to cooking small portions?"

"Sure. But if you can make it good small you can make it good big. I can cook good for you."

"Well, I may be able to make some arrangements. I eat with the other officers, except for the captain, in a place called the ward room. We eat food we get from the galley prepared by the ship's cook."

"What about the captain? He must not eat that stuff. Where does he eat?"

"He eats in his cabin, and a steward is supposed to fix and serve his food."

"I wouldn't mind doing that."

"That's a very good idea. How'd you like to be the captain's steward?"

Johnson pursed his lips. "Could I do that and still slip some of that good stuff to you sometimes?"

Matthew laughed. "I suppose so. You'll also have to take care of the captain's quarters."

Johnson shrugged. "Sounds like what I used to do upstairs at the Middleton Tavern. Only they was a bunch of women running around there too because they was a lot more rooms and beds. If I take the captain, he got only one bunk."

"Well, yes, I guess you wouldn't have any trouble."

"I could take care of one bunk in five minutes."

Matthew said, "I guess you could do that easily."

Johnson shrugged. "Sign me up."

Matthew thought for a minute. "There is only one thing you will need to do for me. The ship's cook runs the galley. He cooks for the whole crew. He has the only cooking fire, made on a bed of rocks and gravel. You will have to get your small pans in there somehow."

Johnson shrugged. "No trouble. I guess I could charm the bastard. After all, I'm the son of the greatest charmer of all time, at least in these parts. What kind of a man is this ship's cook?"

"The cook's an Englishman. Not at all like Jebediah. Very quiet. Large. Bull-necked."

Johnson sneered. "That don't mean nothin'. I'll twist it off if need be."

Matthew grinned. "He's used to cooking beans, oatmeal, sauerkraut, salt beef, and pork, and something the Englishmen really love, plum duff."

Johnson shuddered. "I've heard about that stuff, but can Americans eat it?"

"They'll have to."

"They might mutiny."

"Don't even say that word."

"I'm hearing you."

"We can criticize the cook all we want, but the fact is that after a ship is at sea for over a month all the crew has left to eat is mouldy cheese, oatmeal, molasses, salt meat, and boxes of biscuits full of weevils."

Johnson groaned. "Maybe that plum duff might go over after all. I think I'll take a few lessons from him about how to survive."

Matthew laughed. "I've heard a lot about the bad food on British ships from Lieutenant Forsyth, our first lieutenant."

"What does he know about it?"

"He was a midshipman for four years."

"He liked the chow?"

"Oh, no, he hated it. That's one reason why he left the Royal Navy and joined ours."

"What did he say it was like?"

"Said when the ship had been out to sea for two months everything got bad at once. The water butts got slimy inside. The biscuits got weevily, and . . . ."

"Whoa, what's this weevily?"

"The biscuits are really a hard bread baked in a shipyard and supposedly sealed tightly in a wooden box."

"Well, how did the weevils get in there?"

"They were born in there."

"Don't fun me."

"That's right. The flour the biscuits were made of had weevil eggs in it. They got sealed inside, too. Heat and a little moisture made the eggs hatch. Then the weevils grew and ate up a lot of the biscuit."

"Why didn't the cook throw it overboard?"

"It was all they had to eat, and we'll be in the same position."

Johnson shuddered. I don't like that. What did they do with the weevils?"

"Some ate them in the biscuit. Said they liked the flavor. Some dug them out and traded them to those who liked them, and ate what was left."

Johnson shook his head. I don't think I'm going to like them. Maybe Big Jebediah will take me back."

"Cheer up. You like crawfish, don't you?"

Johnson smiled, "Oh, yes."

"And you used to eat a lot of them."

"A lot."

"Well, just imagine the weevils are small craw fish."

Johnson shook his head. "You is worse when you toy with me than Big Jebediah. Ain't there any good food on that ship of yours?"

"There is an enclosure up forward on the forecastle of the ship called the manger. It has a few animals housed in it when we sail. Sheep, chickens, pigs. Maybe a heifer or two, but they don't last very long."

Johnson shuddered. "I can see why."

Matthew laughed. "It won't be that bad."

"Can I get some supplies to put aside for the captain?"

"Sure. Cheese. Wine. Canned fancy biscuits. Canned meat. The purser will get it for you."

"I can do all that." Johnson said. "I'll get enough for you and me, too. Just drop by the captain's cabin now and then when he ain't there."

"There's one other thing would help me. From time to time I may call on you to help the cook make something that will please the American sailors."

"You mean I got to make something good out of all that bad stuff?"

"You got it. Now, where's your gear?"

"You mean my clothes?"

"Yes."

"Boss, I'm wearing them."

Matthew laughed. "We'll stop at the ship's chandlery on the way to the ship and outfit you."

"Can I wear a sailor suit?"

"Sure. At inspection and when you go ashore, if you ever do. For most of the time you'll only need to have a couple of white jackets."

Johnson shrugged. "Used to wear them at Middleton Tavern. That isn't what I had in mind, but I'll get by."

Two mornings later Matthew and Johnson walked down the brow in Philadelphia. Matthew hired a hansom cab and took Johnson to a ship's chandlery where he had him outfitted him with a seabag, two hammocks, two seaman's uniforms, and two white jackets.

"Why I'm getting two of each of these things?"

"You have to have two to be able to wash them."

Johnson looked dubiously at the jackets. "I'm going to look like a damned fool if the captain don't want me and I have to climb the rigging in these."

Matthew laughed. "No, you wouldn't. Then you'd wear your sailor suit."

At the ship, Johnson shouldered his hammock and sea bag and followed Matthew up the brow, a big doubled plank fitted with horizontal pieces of thin wood every foot for traction. At the gangway, an opening in the bulwark through which the brow passed, Lieutenant Ambrose, a slightly overweight Yankee, with an accent to match, looked closely at Johnson. "What's this?" he asked.

Matthew looked at him sternly. "Not just 'this.' He's Mister Johnson of Annapolis. He's coming aboard to be sworn in as a seaman, and if the captain approves, he'll soon be the captain's steward."

Ambrose shrugged. "Whatever you say. The captain is in his cabin."

Matthew told Johnson to wait outside the captain's cabin and knocked on the door.

"Come in."

Matthew took off his hat and stepped inside. "Good morning, Captain. I report my return aboard."

"Good to see you back. How's the young son?"

"Great. Sir, he's growing very fast. I have a surprise for you. I've brought back a man I think will make a fine steward for you."

Captain Biddle laughed. "If I take him on, I'll be able to offer you a cup of coffee on your next visit to my cabin. Bring him in."

Matthew went to the door, opened it, and beckoned to Johnson. When Johnson entered Matthew said, "Sir, this is Mister Johnson. I recommend to you that you swear him in and assign him as your steward."

The captain looked him over. "Johnson, do you have a first name? I need it for swearing you in."

Johnson started to say he didn't have any, but Matthew interrupted him. "You can use Jebediah," he said. "That's close enough."

Johnson grinned. "Yes, sir, as you say, sir, that's close enough."

Johnson adjusted to his new station in life, as he had always done before. The captain treated him well, and appreciated his efforts to set a good table.

The captain sent Johnson ashore with the purser to buy fancy biscuits and tinned meats for his table. Johnson also brought back as much fresh fruit and vegetables as he thought the captain could eat before they spoiled.

Johnson managed to slip an occasional treat such as a fresh pear to Lieutenant Christopher, who appreciated it and looked after Johnson in return.

The ship's cook presented a problem that Johnson took some time to solve. On the few occasions that the cook said anything, his London accent made it hard for Johnson to understand him, although he had heard a lot of British accents at the tables at Middleton Tavern before the war had started. Gradually Johnson learned the cook's sign language and his likes and dislikes. He catered to the one and avoided the other. In spite of the cook's initial coldness, he thawed, and even spoke to Johnson occasionally.

One day the cook was amused by one of Johnson's antics and from then on Johnson was allowed to slip the small pots and pans he used to cook the captain's meals in among the cook's mammoth ones. Johnson was an expert mimic and could imitate Lieutenant Forsyth's walk and speech so closely that even the cook guffawed.

After days spent smelling Johnson's cooking, the cook became addicted to Johnson's exotic dishes and the spices Johnson added to the standard oatmeal, salt horse, and biscuits to made them palatable, if not always good. The salt horse was really salted pork and beef, but was always called salt horse by the crew, who claimed that in old times a sailor had actually found a harness buckle his portion.

Now that the problem of preparing food was solved, another load was lifted off of Lieutenant Christopher's broad shoulders.

The gunner, however, continued to worry Matthew. As a child, Matthew had stood too close to a gun powder experiment conducted by a friend. He still bore the small scars on his face caused by the explosion and the flying pieces of the container. When Matthew talked to Gunner Waugh, he remembered the flash and the searing pain following the explosion, and he resolved to make sure the ship's magazine was as safe as possible. At first his advice was ignored, so he took the problem to Lieutenant Forsyth, whose problem it was rightly, since he was ultimately in charge of the magazines and the guns.

Forsyth shook his head after he had heard Matthew's complaint. "Lieutenant Christopher, you worry too much. Waugh is an experienced gunner."

Matthew cleared his throat nervously. "Sir, maybe he is, but he's also lazy and I hope he doesn't take too many short cuts in safety precautions down there."

"How so?"

"I don't think he uses enough flannel to deaden footsteps, and the screens used to separate powder stages are too flimsy to be safe."

Forsyth promised to look into the situation and two days later ran into Matthew on deck. "Lieutenant Christopher, I've looked into this. I think the gunner has a few good excuses. He says a British ship has at least two powder boys in the magazine to load cartridges from the powder barrels and at least one powder boy for each two guns. We have only two powder boys total. That means he has to load several cartridges in advance to have enough ready when firing starts."

Matthew shook his head. "There will be powder cartridges lying all over the magazine. Sooner or later something serious will happen with all that loose powder, and by serious I mean the whole ship could go up."

Forsyth shrugged. "If you can recruit some more powder boys you'll help to solve the gunner's problem."

The gunner was a big, burly Scot, who had somehow acquired a German name, and who was good at training the gun crews. But Matthew guessed that the safety of the magazine was far down on Waugh's list of priorities, mainly because it was out of sight and rarely visited by the captain.

He tried to get the captain to inspect the magazine.

"Too far down on my list of priorities. I'll get to it when I can," he said.

Matthew talked to Mister Humphreys about the problem.

Humphreys smiled. "Don't worry, Lieutenant Christopher, we'll build the magazines to the King's specifications."

Matthew went over the construction carefully, but he did not know what the King's specifications were. The felt curtains and carpeting seemed capable of preventing sparks, and the horn windows in front of the illuminating lanterns seemed safe. He stopped worrying about the magazine, but it remained in the back of his mind. Gradually other problems pushed it aside, and he forgot about it. He hoped it would not return. Magazine explosions were pretty final.

As the days went by, Forsyth, the first lieutenant, made almost daily trips to the prisoner-of-war stockade and then to the city prison. Sometimes he brought back a seaman or two, although of decreasing quality. Gradually the crew grew to a point where the captain felt ready to go to sea, even though the crew was at an absolute minimum, both in numbers and quality. Even worse, the English prisoners were now in the majority. Matthew protested to Forsyth that this might lead to a mutiny if conditions got bad at sea.

Forsyth dismissed his concern. "It won't happen. Besides, I keep the keys to the armory."

The officers labored to organize and train the gun crews. Each gun was two men short of what Gunner Waugh said would be needed to keep up continuous fire, and Lieutenant Forsyth struggled to think of a solution to bridge the gap. Eventually Matthew designed a plan to use idlers, cooks, artisans, and the sail trimming crew to fill in the gun crews. Even Johnson joined up at the captain's insistence.

The first lieutenant ran some sail trimmers up and down the ratlines to exercise them at changing the trim and direction of the large sails. They became reasonably competent, although it pained the boatswain to watch the exercises. Matthew wondered how they would fare when the ship was laboring in large seas with the wind and rain up or they were in a prolonged engagement where the sails would need to be tended while the ship was firng.

In early February the preparations stopped, not because the ship and its crew were ready, but because a messenger arrived with urgent orders from the Secretary of the Navy.

The petty officer of the watch escorted the messenger to the captain's cabin and soon rumors spread through the lower decks at the speed of sound.

Captain Biddle read his orders in the privacy of his cabin, then called a conference of all officers. When they had crowded into his cabin, he held up the dispatch. "Gentlemen, we leave the shipyard tomorrow morning on the first favorable tide, ready or not."

Forsyth's face clouded. "But, sir . . . ."

Biddle looked at him patiently. "Don't interrupt, Forsyth. We'd never be more ready if we stayed here for another month. Now make all preparations for going to sea."

Forsyth recovered. "But, sir, I was just going to ask what our mission would be."

Biddle held the dispatch up. "Right now this is secret. I'll tell you more about it when we stand down the river."

Chapter 12

The next morning, the 3rd of February, Captain Biddle ordered Lieutenant Forsyth to call the crew to quarters at 8 A.M. Most of the men were expectant, some were unhappy.

The captain addresssed his crew with great confidence. "Men, we'll get underway at 10 A.M. The wind is fair and should carry us off the pier as soon as we take in our mooring lines and sail is made. We will not require a pilot or any other help."

"We will leave the pier with the main courses up, the jib and flying jib and the staysails up, and the spanker up aft. That will give you an easy break-in by using sails that can be rigged and tended from the deck. After we are fair in the channel and making way, we will hoist the topsails and give those of you who are detailed to them some time aloft. Later, we may add other staysails and maybe additional sails."

He turned to Lieutenant Forsyth. "Dismiss the crew and start preparations."

Captain Biddle turned on his heel and strode to the door of his cabin.

Matthew watched him go, and thought he could detect a new aura of confidence in Biddle's manner. There was no doubt that Captain Biddle was an experienced and competent sea captain. He had proved it in the Royal Navy and on a smaller Continental Navy sloop. This was not only a matter of Captain Biddle's confidence in himself, but a matter of the confidence of the crew in Captain Biddle as well.

Christopher shrugged. He knew that Captain Biddle was as concerned as he was, but he knew that a captain could not show it to the crew. Matthew thought there should be a new relationship between himself and the captain now that they were at sea, and he resolved to avoid seeing and trying to advise the captain from now on, and to wait to speak until the captain summoned him.

~

Until 10 A.M., the crew scurried about, making last minute arrangements and inspections. Then promptly at 10 A.M., the captain came on deck, looked at the ship traffic on the Delaware River, tested the direction of the wind with a wettened finger, and guessed at its velocity. He nodded confidently at Lieutenant Forsyth, who waited expectantly. "Get the ship underway, sir," the captain ordered.

Biddle turned to one of the quartermasters stationed at the wheel. "When we have way, steer course south." Then he stood back and watched his orders being carried out.

Lieutenant Forsyth relayed the orders to the boatswain, and the boatswain translated the general orders into detailed orders to the petty offciers and groups of the crew charged with the responsibility for casting loose, setting, and trimming each sail. The men scurried about making sure they had the proper sheets, halliards, and rigging in hand. The process was every bit as slow and confused as Biddle expected it to be, but he was patient, and soon the men began to sort out themselves and their equipment, and the sails slowly rose.

Matthew ran forward and supervised the raising of the jibs and fore staysails. They were all triangular sails, much the same kind of sail he had been familiar with on the schooner. He knew little about the large square sails, and he resolved to watch the boatswain carefully until he could learn about them and their rigging and trimming.

With the forward sails up and drawing to Christopher's satifaction, and the ship well off the pier with way on, Matthew trotted aft to the binnacle. Captain Biddle saw him coming. "Lieutenant Christopher, take your station by the binnacle and navigate for me while we are still in the river channel. I think you are the only man on board who has travelled on it."

"Yes, sir, I think so. I'm familiar with it and its navigational aids. If the compass is working, I'll get a fix and keep a course line running on the chart."

"Oh, yes, it's working now. At first it was off about ten degrees, but I discovered that that fat oaf, Lieutenant Ambrose, had been standing next to it while carrying a long steel knife. I threatened to cut off his head with it, and I don't think he will carry one again."

Matthew pursed his lips. To his relief, the captain had shown unexpected toughness, and it would be needed. Both Lieutenant Ambrose and the long, lanky southerner, Lieutenant Fitzgerald, needed to realize that their political sponsors were no longer available for them to hide behind nor to communicate with. They would not be able to get mail off for months, and during that period they would have to fend for themselves.

He thought about the captain's announcement last month that he would not use a master to do the ship-handling for him. Then he realized that there was a good reason for that decision. Senior British officers had little training in handling ships and therefore depended on masters. On this side of the Atlantic, there were few masters. The captain most certainly knew that he could not find one, and since his days with the Royal Navy this was the first time he would have to do without one.

The *Randolph* slowly spread her wings for the first time. Matthew took time off from navigating to watch the crew move about. Lieutenant Forsyth still had to issue general orders that depended very heavily on the detailed expertise of the boatswain. Matthew also noted that orders seemed to get lost. The British boatswain sometimes could not understand Forsyth's American brand of English and some of the American petty officers looked at the boatswain as if he were speaking a strange language. Fortunately the American and English names of most of the sails, rigging, and equipment were the same. As the day wore on, communication improved when the men realized they were really speaking the same language.

The ship started logging three knots, but by noon the main courses had been rigged and set, and the log readings rose to five knots. They passed Wilmington, twenty-five miles downriver, before dark, and the Delaware River broadened as they continued down the channel.

At dusk the captain ordered the running lights lit for the first time. The quartermasters had a litle trouble with the wicks of the lanterns but soon got the hang of it.

Matthew had come up the Delaware River at night on the fast packet that tried to arrive at Philadelphia at dawn, so he was familiar with that part of the river at night. Nevertheless, the night was long, and at dawn Matthew was glad to hear the captain order a quartermaster to relieve him for breakfast.

After breakfast, the captain ordered all officers, except for the boatswain left on watch, into his cabin for a conference. After they had all been served coffee by Johnson, resplendent in his white jacket, Captain Biddle pulled a sheet of white paper out of his pocket and said, "My orders, here, provide that we arrive at Henlopen Point at the mouth of Delaware Bay at dawn on the sixth. There are six merchant ships coming down the Delaware River somewhere behind us, and they will all rendezvous with us there at dawn. We will patrol Delaware Bay until we meet the merchantmen and ensure that there are no British ships lying in wait at the mouth of Delaware Bay. Is that clear?"

Matthew expected Lieutenant Forsyth to have something to say, but he was quiet.

Christopher said nothing.

Biddle looked satisfied, if not happy. "Back to work," he said.

The next two days provided a welcome period for working up. Biddle exercised the crew at changing, adjusting, and trimming the sails, and several times he ordered "Beat to Quarters!" The crew rushed to their battle stations, steadily cutting the time it took to run the guns out and be ready to fire them. As a final graduation exercise, the captain ordered the carpenter to rig a floating target out of empty barrels and had it thrown over the side. He brought the ship around and passed the floating target abeam to starboard at about a thousand yards. When he ordered "Commence firing!" the starboard battery fired, and powder smoke passed down the side for the first time.

Matthew rolled his eyes. "Thank God! We didn't explode then. Maybe Gunner Waugh really knows what he is doing."

For some of the young American sailors, it was the first time they had heard a large gun fired. None of the balls fell anywhere near the bobbing target, but by the fifth salvo the rate of fire was noticeably increasing and one ball even hit the mark. The boatswain, a veteran of hundreds of such firings, sneered, "It was sheer bloody luck!"

The captain nodded in agreement, but he seemed pleased nonetheless at the progress they had made. "Secure from battle stations and set course for Cape Henlopen," he ordered. "I'll be in my cabin. Call me if you need me."

At dawn the next morning the *Randolph* was cruising off Cape Henlopen. At daylight the captain swept the horizon with his long glass. "I make out six ships. That's all of us. The largest ship over there has been designated by the Secretary of the Navy to be in charge of the convoy."

Biddle turned to the first lieutenant. "Lieutenant Forsyth, lower the starboard cutter immediately. Send Lieutenant Ambrose to me."

Ambrose came lumbering up, halted, and saluted. He was pale and sweating, obviously in the beginning throes of seasickness. "Yes, sir," he said.

"Lieutenant Ambrose, take the cutter and make the *Marigold* over there. Give my compliments to the master and ask him if he understands his written instructions. If so, we will depart immediately and will proceed due east. Two hundred miles east of Cape Henlopen, we will release the convoy to proceed directly to France or to the West Indies according to their individual orders. Do you understand?"

Ambrose swallowed hard, "Yes, sir."

"Very well. Carry out your orders."

Biddle watched him trot slowly over to the gangway. He was not sure that Ambrose would make it, but he climbed over the side without heaving.

Biddle turned his attention amidships where a group of seamen were hoisting out the starboard boat. The way on the ship was so slow the boat could be safely lowered without reducing sail. Biddle groaned when he saw two American sailors trip over each other and lose their grips on the falls. The boat was about to run loose when the boatswain let loose a string of oaths and bellowed orders to the crew. He grabbed the falls, his muscles and neck bulging as he held them fast. The falls stopped running out until the two men could get up and grab them again and relieve the boatswain.

The boat descended slowly, and Biddle made a note to drill the crew in handling their boats. In company with more experienced ships, the *Randolph* would look like a beginner, but then she was just starting out and the green crew was learning. The only way to get better was to practice. Lieutenant Forsyth would have his ears burned when there was time for him to get to it.

Half an hour later the boat returned. Like the crew that had lowered it, the boat crew showed how inept it was, too. The coxswain and the after four oarsmen were ex-British prisoners-of-war, and their rowing was satisfactory. Their oars rose, swept, and fell approximately together. But the forward two oarsmen were American seamen, probably placed there by the coxswain to keep them out of major trouble. Their oars seemed to operate all by themselves, independent of the majority.

"My God!," Biddle said, "They must think they're paddling a canoe."

Forsyth turned to the captain and said seriously, "Sir, maybe we should carry a canoe for fast trips. It could go twice as fast as a cutter."

Biddle glowered at him. "Certainly it would, twice as fast straight down. A canoe wouldn't last twenty yards in these seas."

The boat was brought alongside the ship by the disgusted coxswain, and Lieutenant Ambrose crawled awkwardly up the sea ladder. On deck he took a deep breath, saluted the quarterdeck and the captain slowly, and said, "Sir, the master of the *Marigold* returns his compliments to you and says he will take course east right away. The others have orders to take position behind his ship, and he will await your direction."

Ambrose could hold himself in no longer, and he turned and rushed for the bulwark. He made it, heaved strongly, and then headed below.

Lieutenant Forsyth started to remind him to salute the captain, but Biddle shook his head. "Don't bother him. At least he got back and carried out his orders."

Matthew followed him below and found him on his knees with his head in a bucket. Matthew patted him on the shoulder. "Keep your courage up. You'll get better."

Ambrose raised his head. "I don't think so. I told my father not to send me out here. I used to get seasick crossing a bridge."

"Give yourself a little more time. At least this will take off some of that excess weight."

On the quarterdeck Captain Biddle anxiously watched the maneuver of hoisting the boat. Finally, he had all he could take for the day. He turned to the first lieutenant. "Forsyth, as soon as you're ready, take course east. Set as much sail as you think the watch can tend."

"Aye, aye, sir. Are you going to your cabin?"

Biddle nodded wearily. "I've had all I can take. Do what you can to get these clowns in shape."

"Don't you think the boat crews improved?"

"No. They didn't. You just substituted experienced men for the clowns. Now start work on the clowns. We need all of them."

Chapter 13

By early afternoon the captain's spirits had risen, mostly because of an excellent lunch prepared by Johnson accompanied by a glass of Madeira wine. The captain sauntered out onto the quarterdeck, belching quietly.

The wind was still blowing from the west, and the *Randolph* could sail before it, making the sail tending and trimming easy chores for the afternoon watch.

Biddle paced up and down the lee side of the quarterdeck, watching the crew being herded from job to job by the boatswain. Most of the signs of shore life were beginning to disappear as brooms, swabs, scrub rags, and scrapers dislodged and flushed over the side on strong streams from salt water hoses four months of dirt, debris, and saw dust that had been tracked aboard by yard workmen. Now it was slowly disappearing, and Biddle was enjoying the view of the clean decks.

Biddle rubbed his hands together. Lieutenant Forsyth had the afternoon watch, and Biddle was planning to take the dog watches coming up. The captain stopped his pacing to talk to Forsyth, who stood by the binnacle watching the cleaning of the quarterdeck. "I see you have young Lieutenant Fitzgerald up here in training as officer of the watch."

"Yes, sir, he's doing well. Lieutenant Christopher took a noon sun line, and I had Fitzgerald take one, too, and work it out and plot it."

"How did they make out?"

"The weather was good, and they were both able to take sights of the sun."

"And the results?"

"Lieutenant Christopher is an experienced navigator. His line, crossed with an earlier line, showed we were making four knots, which checks with the log readings."

"Are the quartermasters getting better with the log?"

"Yes, sir, they are doing well."

"And all of them are ex-British quartermaster mates?"

"No, the best one is an ex-American merchant mariner."

"Well, I'll be damned. That's good."

Biddle persisted. "So much for the log readings and Lieutenant Fitzgerald's line of position. Stop stalling and tell me how it was."

Forsyth laughed. "I think it's the first one he's ever taken."

"Well?"

"It showed we were cruising down the Mississippi."

Biddle roared. "Tell him to keep at it until he gets it right."

For the next two days the wind held steady, but on the following day it veered to north by northeast. The best the square-rigged ship could do was tack back and forth, never very close to the wind, and progress was slow.

Matthew, on watch, muttered, "Damned square-rigged ships! Regular cheese boxes. A schooner could sail twenty degrees closer to the wind."

The remainder of the voyage was also slow, but on the fifteenth day the captain ordered the quartermaster to hoist a prearranged signal meaning detached, and the *Marigold*, dipping her flag in salute, took course north along with three others. The rest of the fleet turned south for the Caribbean.

Biddle and Forsyth watched them go. Forsyth said, "Wouldn't mind going to the Caribbean."

Biddle shook his head. "Have you ever been there?"

"Well, no, sir, but the climate is supposed to be wonderful down there."

"It is. The yellow fever mosquitoes just love it. They really thrive."

"I don't understand."

"Half the poor devils in those ships will never come back, not even in boxes."

"Yellow fever?"

"We know what yellow fever is. There is no doubt about that. The mosquitoes are something else. Some doctors think they carry it, but others are not sure. Some day a medical genius will figure this out and do mankind a good turn if he can also find a way to prevent it."

Forsyth shuddered. "You've convinced me."

"I'd rather be with the ships going north; I'll take my chances with pneumonia."

"The weather?"

"Cold up there. By the way, the people down south call their tropical storms hurricanes. A lot worse there than the storms we get up here."

"How bad?"

"Sometimes you'll get winds of a hundred and fifty miles an hour. Sometimes worse, but the weather instruments blow away at one hundred and fifty."

"My God! What could survive?"

"Not much does. The only defense if you're ashore is to dig a large hole and get in it or if you're on a ship take the right course to get away from it."

In a few hours the *Randolph* was alone, and Biddle changed course to the north. He called the officers to a conference in his cabin, leaving the boatswain again on watch.

The captain looked closely at his officers. "Gentlemen, the Secretary of the Navy has furnished me with some intelligence. I am not privy to the source of it, but I'm told that the British frigate Tilford has been preying on our shipping off New England. Our mission is to find and destroy her. The first step we'll take is to double the lookouts. I want the guns to stay loaded at all times and to have their touch holes carefully covered so that moisture can't get into the ignition powder trains and prevent the guns from firing."

Christopher said, "I hope the second step will be to inspect the magazine."

The captain seemed puzzled. "Christopher, are you worried about the magazines?"

"Yes, sir. You will remember we were very short-handed when the gunner was supervising the construction of the magazines and the safety features included in them."

"Such as?"

"Canvas drapes over the windows in the interior magazines. Flannel coverings over the decks where the powder monkeys were to move about carrying powder bags. These are only a few of the safety precautions a ship should take."

"And are you thinking our gunner didn't?"

Christopher shrugged. "Well, I know he didn't do well with some of them. He was pressed for time and lacked manpower."

"And now?"

"He's still short-handed. Too few men are assigned to loading powder from the kegs to the bags. A British man-of-war would assign twice as many as we do."

"And if we don't do all these things properly?"

"We may have a terrible casualty."

The captain pulled at his chin. "Forsyth, conduct a thorough inspection of the magazines as soon as possible."

Forsyth was a little taken aback, but he came up with a good answer. "Of course, and Christopher can accompany me."

For two days the *Randolph* sailed north, the lookouts carefully scanning the horizon. It was empty except for marching lines of green Atlantic rollers.

On the morning of the third day after the breakup of the convoy the lookouts shouted, "Sail Ho! Dead ahead!"

After Biddle sent Lieutenant Christopher scurrying aloft to the mizzen cross trees, Matthew pulled the long glass out, steadied it on a shroud, and focused it on the distant sail. For two full minutes he studied it as both ships rolled and heaved. Then he went below, sliding down a stay.

"Well?" the captain asked impatiently.

"Sir, it's a two-masted brig flying French colors. She's on a course toward France. Her sails are lighter in color than the usual British sail or ours and are of French cut. Her hull lines are French, and I'm sure she *is* French. However, she is two-masted like the *Tilford*."

Biddle was disappointed, but he refused to deny his expectations. He wanted the ship to be the *Tilford*, and he expected it to be in in spite of Matthew's report. After all, she was spotted several times in this area, and no French ship had been mentioned. He decided to believe the intelligence report and not his eyes or Christopher's observation. He cleared his throat. "We'll close her and take a closer look. Beat to Quarters!"

Matthew could hear the warrant officers and petty officers opening the gun ports, rigging the guns for firing, and taking down the doors and partitions of the captain's cabin and the officer's staterooms and storing them below in order to reduce the possibility of flying splinters. He shook his head, thinking that it was going to be a useless exercise, but he gritted his teeth and kept quiet.

In half an hour the ship ahead was in range of the *Randolph*'s guns. The *Randolph* was on a course to intercept it, and the stranger made no attempt to evade. Matthew could see that she was not running out any of her twelve starboard guns, and the French flag continued to fly defiantly.

Matthew could hold himself in no longer, and he moved up abreast of Lieutenant Forsyth, who was intensely studying the ship ahead. "Sir, I think the captain is in trouble. That probably is a French ship."

Forsyth shrugged. "How do we know for sure? If it was British it might be flying a French flag anyway. We have to treat her like an enemy until we're sure just who she is. The captain is right."

Matthew stood silent and kept his counsel, watching the ship sail along seemingly unperturbed. When she was two thousand yards ahead, Captain Biddle shouted, "Hoist a signal 'Lie to,' and get ready to fire a shot across her bow." Biddle seemed to be sure of himself.

The quartermaster leaped to hoist the signal from the mizzen mast and it fluttered up.

For several minutes nothing happened, the ship apparently refusing to answer the signal.

Biddle cursed, "That does it! The bastard won't answer our signals. We'll send him a stronger one. Put a round across her bows and make it close."

One of the bow chasers boomed. The ball, under the gunner's eye, flew to the right of the ship's bow and landed a hundred yards ahead.

After a few minutes, with the captain watching through his long glass, saw the strange ship alter course and come into the wind.

The captain said, "She's lying to. Forsyth, get ready to lower a boat. Do you speak French, Forsyth?"

"No, sir, but Lieutenant Fitzgerald speaks a little."

"Then he'll board her with a squad of marines. We won't take any more sass from him. Tell Lieutenant Fitzgerald to take charge."

After the *Randolph* had also come into the wind, the boat was lowered without incident. As the crew rowed the cutter across the water between the ships, Biddle beamed. "Look at those oarsmen. A credit to us, and the starboard cutter is now to be used as my gig. But I won't put any fancy uniforms on the gig crew like the British captains do. Mine will be just plain American sailors."

"And ex-British," Forsyth said.

"How did you teach the American sailors to row?"

"I didn't. I took them out of the boat and searched the whole crew for men who had rowed before."

"Well done! You seem to have fixed this problem."

Half an hour later the boat fairly danced as the crew pulled strongly on their way back to the *Randolph*. Fitzgerald climbed to the quarterdeck, followed by the squad of marines he had taken with him. He was not used to wearing his sword and almost tripped over it as he passed through the gangway. On the quarter-deck, he saluted the captain.

"Well," the captain asked. "Was she French?"

"Oh, yes, sir. They all spoke French very well. Better than I did. Their papers seemed to be in order. Their log showed they left Boston a few days ago. The captain was mad as hell. Kept going on about you were a, ah, er, a *cochon*. I don't know that word in French."

Forsyth choked back a laugh, but the captain roared with anger. "It means pig, and the same to him."

Fitzgerald colored with embarrassment. "Sir, he says if you do it again, he'll sink you."

Biddle laughed, this time more under control. "I don't think so. We out-gun her."

Matthew looked at the French ship, now coming out of the wind to resume her voyage. The captain was right. She had only half the guns the *Randolph* carried, and he was sure that the *Randolph*, poorly trained as she was, would have had no trouble with the Frenchman.

As soon as the starboard cutter was secured, Captain Biddle gave orders to bring the ship about and take course south. He bent over the chart on which Matthew was plotting the ship's position. "We're two hundred miles off the coast, and that is where the Secretary of the Navy said his intelligence showed the British frigate *Tilford* was operating. We'll search along that line to the south.

The next morning, ominous oily swells built up from the east, and the wind increased steadily. Matthew kept his eye on the barometer's mercury column and noted that it was decreasing steadily. Although the captain did not say anything, Matthew thought it was time he said something himself. "Sir, the barometer is 29.50 and dropping."

"Yes, I know, it feels like a major storm brewing, and I don't like it. We can't do much but reef sails and secure the topside. I think this will turn out to be a big one."

It was, and the winds increased steadily to sixty knots. Biddle kept the ship on a course to the south even though the high winds and swells were on the port beam. The ship rolled frequently to forty-five degrees, forcing the boatswain to secure all guns with double lashings.

Matthew did not think the ship was in danger of rolling over, but the rigging began to creak alarmingly, and the masts and shrouds vibrated. He knew the new rigging was stretching and the masts were probably shrinking. He and the boatswain made the rounds of the topside with a gang of seamen, taking the slack out of the shrouds. When they had finished their rounds the boatswain shrugged. "That's all we can do unless the captain gives up this bloody chase and changes course down wind. I'm going below to find the carpenter and have a look at the mast butts along the keel."

"Good idea. I'll stay up here and try to change the captain's mind."

"Why are we staying on this bloody dangerous course?"

Matthew shrugged. "Apparently the captain interprets the Secretary of the Navy's orders as requiring him to stay on a north-south search line as long as he can, looking for that damned British frigate."

The rigging began to thrum loudly, the sound increasing in pitch.

"Sounds like a damned wild piano," the quartermaster on watch said.

The helmsman was increasingly apprehensive, nervously spinning the wheel, trying to stay on course. "Damn!" he said, "this thing is going to come apart soon."

After an hour of the increasing noise in the masts and rigging, the boatswain and carpenter burst out of the hatch from below and ran over to the aperture in the main deck where the foremast passed through. The carpenter was carrying a wooden mallet he was using to tighten the loosening wedges. The boatswain looked at the wedges between the mast and the deck. "Jesus! We're too late! They're going!" Then some of the wedges popped upward, with a sound like a gun, one narrowly missing the carpenter's face.

The carpenter started back to avoid the flying splinters. "Jesus!" he shouted. "That was close!"

The mast shuddered and there were loud cracking sounds. The weather shrouds holding up the mast against the wind popped loudly, one after the other. The mast cracked just above the deck like a gigantic chicken bone. Splinters flew in all directions, and the carpenter and the boatswain turned their backs to the rain of small pieces of white oak.

Then the whole mast and its ratlines fell slowly over the starboard side. The wind caught the sails dragging from the yards and the whole mass of wreckage dropped over the side and floated aft, trailing broken yards and pieces of rigging lines.

The captain, standing on the quarterdeck, was speechless. The boatswain, the wind tearing at his beard, looked at him. "Damn, Captain!" he yelled over the wind, "if you don't change course downwind, you'll lose the other masts, too."

The main mast was now making the same noises the foremast had made, and the carpenter, who had gone below, came topside again, frantically waving his hands. "The wedges in the butt area of the main mast are gone, and the butt is loose down there. Stand clear!"

He was too late. The mainmast went over the side more quickly than the foremast, and two men who had been standing next to it pounding replacement wedges in the space between the mast and the main deck were entangled in the shrouds and carried overboard.

The captain knew trying to rescue them was hopeless. He could not maneuver the ship because two of the masts were gone. All he could do was change course to downwind to save the mizzenmast. He gave the orders to let the ship fall off the wind, and she slowly eased to downwind.

With the top hamper of the masts gone, the *Randolph* ran comfortably, with staysails rigged from the mizzenmast, and a spanker, a large trysail, flying aft from the mizzenmast.

The captain called the boatswain up to the quarterdeck. When he came up, he yelled over the howling wind. "Boatswain, do you think we should rig a sea anchor?"

The boatswain looked over the side to see how the seas were passing the side, and walked over to the helm for a few minutes to see how she was steering. Then he yelled back, "Captain, I think we are all right just as we are. The ship is steering well. As long as we keep heading downwind, the remnants of the sails dragging over the side will serve the same purpose as a sea anchor."

"Thank you, boatswain, keep an eye on her."

"Aye, aye, sir."

The heavy rain that usually followed the high winds in tropical storms came with a fury. The officers and men topside stoically turned their backs to it, trying to keep their slickers made of oiled light canvas tightly closed against its penetrating fingers. For hours it pounded the deck and surface of the sea, and then slowly began to relent. The wind and seas abated while the barometer crept up under the watchful eye of the quartermaster.

The next morning it was over. The frigate rode to twenty knot winds over decreasing swells under a blue sky.

The boatswain and carpenter did their best to jury rig a mast forward in the area of the departed foremast with spare yards lashed together. They were able to rig one high enough to fly two jibs from it and eventually a fore course and a spare large course from the mizzenmast. These sails gave the ship steerageway down wind, but no ability to sail into or across the wind. South was the only course he could take, the direction of the wind following the storm. The Captain wisely chose to head for the Charleston shipyard, the only port he could reach except Norfolk. He knew the entrance to Chesapeake Bay was controlled by the British and trying to pass their blockade with a ship that could not manuever would surely deliver him into their hands.

On the second day on the leg south, the surgeon came to the captain's cabin. When the captain called to him to enter, he came in with a worried look on his young face. The captain looked closely at him and said, "Somebody injured?"

The surgeon shook his head. "No, sir. More than that. We've got a plague of some sort on board."

"What?"

"Yes, sir. I have ten men down with high fevers. I expect we'll lose some of them."

"What the hell is this?"

"Whatever it is, it's not in my medical books, and I never got to the part of my medical education covering plagues."

"What can we do?"

"Warn the men to stay away from each other. I recommend that all sick men stay below and the others bring their bedding on deck. They should rig hammocks where they can and the rest can sleep on deck. The boatswain can rig awnings out of spare sails. The weather is mild."

"Where did this come from?"

The surgeon said, "The only men exposed to other people after we left Philadelphia were the marines who went over to the French ship with Lieutenant Fitzgerald. Most of the men who made the trip circulated in the ship searching it and almost all of them are part of our sick list, as well as a few men who slept near them. That includes Lieutenant Fitzgerald. I think they gave it to us."

The captain slammed his fist against the arm of his chair. "That's it! Those dirty, unsanitary Frenchmen, and they called me a *cochon*. They're worse than pigs. Keep me informed."

But the young, inexperienced surgeon was not fully aware of naval etiquette. Instead of retreating below, he persisted. "But, Captain, why did you send those men over there to that ship? Everyone knew it was French."

Biddle's face got red and he fumed. "What do you mean, everyone knows?"

"I was standing on deck, and the former British sailors, who had seen many French ships, all were sure it was French. French design, French sails, and it just loooked like a French ship, they all said."

Biddle calmed down, but he was still mad. "Young man, next time think before you criticize your elders. You are now a naval officer as well as a surgeon. Now go below, and think over your sins."

The surgeon started to say something, but he had learned this last lesson well, so he turned on his heel and left the cabin to the still indigant captain.

The surgeon made regular trips to the captain's cabin, each report worse than the last. After two days there were thirty patients down, and eight had died. The surgeon insisted that the bodies be buried as soon as possible and that all men involved in handling the bodies and tending the patients wear vinegar-soaked masks over their faces. Strangely enough, the surgeon had recommended well. Those stringent steps stopped the infection.

On his last trip, Captain Biddle grinned at him bleakly. "You seem to be learning fast, Surgeon. Well done."

Chapter 14

A day after the surgeon declared the infection under control, the boatswain came to see Matthew. Raster's face was clouded, and he avoided meeting Matthew's eyes.

"What's the matter?" Matthew asked.

"I don't know how to bring this up, but I want to talk to you first before I go to see the old man."

"This sounds bad."

"The worst. It may end in a mutiny."

Matthew's jaw dropped. "My God! I can't believe it. What is happening?"

"You can guess most of it."

"You'd better tell me."

Raster sighed. "I'll do the best I can."

"Start at the beginning."

"A lot of bloody things came together. I have about thirty Englishmen up forward in the cable tier who are damned mad, but not at anybody in particular. They think the ship is jinxed. First we don't have a full crew, then the fiasco of the French ship. The storm was bad, and the plague came along without warning. They want to go into Chesapeake Bay so they can get off this ship."

"Do they realize what will happen to them if they try to do that?"

"I doubt it."

"Do they know the entrance to the Chesapeake Bay is blockaded by British ships and our lack of maneuverability is such that this ship is sure to be captured?"

"Probably they do in the backs of their minds, but they don't think about things like that."

"If the British Navy takes the ship, I'll be just a prisoner-of-war, but all of you will be tried for treason because you joined the American Navy while still a member of the British Navy. You'll be court-martialled and hung from yardarms all over the British ships in the Chesapeake Bay within twenty-four hours."

The boatswain sighed. "I don't want that to happen to me or my countrymen. Will you come forward with me and try to talk some sense into them? They haven't been listening to me."

"Of course. Let's go."

The boatswain led the way forward, feeling his way carefully in the moonlight on the forecastle. They started down the forward ladder.

As they approached the cable tier, a large compartment in which the ship's anchor cables were stowed in huge coils, Matthew could hear a loud and angry mumbling. At the access ladder, the boatswain led the way down, and Matthew followed. When the group saw the boatswain set foot on the deck and recognized him, a man named McCarthy said, "It's about time. Where was you? All the time we thought you had turned us in to the captain."

The boatswain ignored him and motioned to Matthew standing above.

Matthew climbed down and turned to the group. In the light of a single lantern were thirty men. Matthew looked around at them carefully. All were ex-British prisoners-of-war. Many of them were troublemakers, but some he had observed to be reliable, skilled men. They were sitting on small stools, bights of the cables, and some even sat on deck. There was no doubt they were serious and unhappy.

There was a rustle of whispered conversation, and the man who had spoken while Matthew was still top side, spoke again. The man said, "Damn! Why did you bring that bloody officer with you? Now we'll have to kill him instead of letting him go."

The boatswain held up his hand. "If you try it, MaCarthy, you bloody Irishman, you'll die first by my hands. Now all of you sit down and keep quiet. I want you to hear Lieutenant Christopher. You all know he's the only other seagoing officer aboard except for the captain. I respect his opinions."

Raster turned to Lieutenant Christopher. His full brown beard and hawk-like nose were highlighted by the lantern. "Go ahead," he said to Christopher. "Talk some sense into the bloody bastards before they get us all hung."

Matthew stepped forward into the lantern light, his heart beating rapidly and his throat dry. He cleared it.

McCarthy grinned. "Scared, ain't you? Lost your voice, haven't you?"

Matthew held his usual calm expression but inside he felt afraid of the consequences that might follow if he did not stop these men.

The boatswain glared at McCarthy. "I told you to shut up. This is the last time I'll tell you." He turned to Lieutenant Christopher. "Now, go ahead."

Matthew stole a look at Raster as he stepped forward. Minute beads of perspiration gleamed on the boatswain's forehead. Some ran down his face and into his beard, but there was no fear in his voice, and Matthew knew he was a brave man who could lick any man present. Still, Matthew would have to stand alone. Raster had already tried his best.

Matthew was buoyed by the appearance of Raster. The extra time provided by the boatswain's remarks to those present and the powerful appearance of Raster gave Matthew a second wind. He repeated the arguments he had given to the boatswain earlier, but he spent more time describing what would happen if the ship were taken by the British. His description of how the yardarms would look festooned with mutineers changed a lot of minds. There was a loud muttering as they talked to each other.

Matthew thought he had changed a good many minds. Yardarms were a powerful argument. When he finished there was more muttering among the men in the back row, but it was more subdued, and there were no outspoken questions.

Matthew's confidence built as he poured out his arguments, and the crew seemed to sense this. When he finshed there was a dead silence.

McCarthy rubbed his neck. "Well, I'll say I don't like the thought of my neck in a rope either, even if I don't buy your argument. and I never did want to end up swinging from a yardarm. I don't like heights."

The boatswain's dark face began to clear. He seemed to feel he was regaining control, and Matthew let out his breath as he watched the scene. The boatswain wiped the perspiration from his brow with an angry swipe of his forearm.

The boatswain said, "All right, you swabs, that's the truth. You all know that life in the best British man-of-war is worse than life aboard this ship. Maybe we have been jinxed, but the sickness is over, we'll get the ship refitted and remasted in Charleston, and there are still prizes out here. We ain't going to sea until the old man gets the ship fixed up right and finds some replacements. Maybe our luck will change. After all, the old man does know his stuff. He proved it as a post captain in the British Navy and in a good ship in the American Navy."

McCarthy sighed. "All right, I'm willing, but I'll be watching carefully." He got up and walked over to Lieutenant Christopher. "Will you keep quiet about this?"

"I will. All you did was ask about something, and as far as I am concerned it will be forgotten when we leave this compartment."

McCarthy nodded and turned to the other men. "Let's go, swabs. Forget this."

The men got up slowly, picked up their stools, and filed up the ladder from the cable tier.

Christopher and Raster watched them go up the ladder. When the cable tier was empty, the boatswain looked at Christopher and grinned. "Lieutenant Christopher, you'd make a good lawyer. You conned me, too."

Two days later Captain Biddle bent over the chart desk, looking carefully at the navigational plot Matthew kept on a plotting sheet. "I take it Charleston lies about fifty miles due west."

"Yes, sir. We should turn due west now. The wind is favorable and should stay that way. I figure we can be off the river bar to-morrow morning."

"Let's do it. I'm anxious to get into the shipyard and see if we can get repairs and replace the sailors we've lost."

"The surgeon says we do not have any more new cases and the other patients are up and around. That will help morale."

"Yes, sir, he did a good job of handling a very tough situation."

The captain went to his cabin, and Matthew stayed behind, working on his chart at a small portable table near the binnacle. The boatswain, who had been watching the captain and Lieutenant Christopher, came over to the binnacle. "Sir, can I speak to you privately?"

Matthew put down his pencil. "Certainly. Let's go over to the lee bulwark."

When they reached the bulwark, the boatswain looked around carefully. Matthew knew Raster as a stoic man able to conceal his emotions, but this time the boatswain seemed to be content and maybe even happy about something. There was a definite change in the manner of a man who had been so angry only two days before.

Matthew said, "Something's on your mind, but you feel better. Go ahead and say it."

The boatswain said, "Sir, I'm about to report to the first lieutenant that one of my men is missing."

"Since when?"

"Last night."

"Who is it?"

Raster cleared his throat nervously, "McCarthy, sir."

"Well, I'll be damned! What do you think might have happened to him?"

"I don't know. Maybe he was aloft and slipped. He wasn't very good up there. He was scared to death every time I sent him aloft."

"Could he have jumped over the side?"

Raster shook his head. "Not the type. It was probably an accident."

Matthew looked carefully at Raster who looked off in the distance. Matthew said, "Are you sure you don't know more than this about this accident, as you call it?"

The boatswain brought his eyes back to Matthew, but he could not hold his gaze steadily on him. He shrugged. "Whatever happened to him, he's not aboard any more, and a lot of our troubles are over."

"He was trouble. Not just for me and you, but a for lot of others, too. What really happened, Raster?"

The boatswain sighed. "Let it alone, sir. It's all over now."

Matthew nodded and looked out at the passing waves. "I'll take your word. Go ahead and report his absence to Lieutenant Forsyth."

As dusk approached, the captain came out on the quarterdeck. Matthew was plotting his evening position. Biddle asked, "How does our track look?"

"Good. The weather will be clear enough to let us get in a sight on Polaris tonight so we'll have a good latitude line and, using that, we'll be able to find the bar easily tomorrow morning."

"Looks good to me. By the way, I've noticed that some of the crew is looking at me strangely today. Are they telling you anything? The only untoward incident is McCarthy's unexplained absence, and I don't know anything about that."

Matthew shrugged. "Maybe they are just anxious to get into port."

"Maybe that's it."

Biddle shortened what was left of their sails on the midwatch. He did not want to get too close to the coast until after dawn so he could see the shore.

At dawn the sun coming up astern illuminated the near-tropical vegetation of the South Carolina coast dead ahead. In an hour they were close to the entrance to the river and the harbor. They had made a good land fall, and Matthew was happy with his navigation.

A small pilot boat was anchored off the entrance. Soon it hoisted its anchor, made sail, and came alongside the *Randolph*. A two-man crew skillfully lowered the sail and let the boat coast to a soft landing against the sea ladder. An old pilot climbed spryly aboard. He stopped and looked around at the jury rigging. "What the hell happened to you, Captain? I don't see no sign of gunfire."

"A storm, Captain, and a hell of one. We'll be indebted to you if you'll take us over the bar and on into the shipyard. We need a lot of repairs."

Chapter 15

The same pilot stayed aboard overnight waiting for a favorable wind and tide. The wind shifted to the south, and by noon the pilot had succeeded, by using the rowing tow boats, in getting them up the Ashley River to the shipyard. The yard master came aboard before the pilot left. The captain and the first lieutenant were busy with the pilot so Lieutenant Christopher escorted the yard master on a tour around the ship. When he went below and looked at the damaged sockets in the keel where the fore and mainmasts had been torn out, he shuddered. "A damned mess," he muttered. "We've got a lot of work to do."

Christopher said, "It was a bad time. We had the seas on the beam, and the wind literally tore the masts out. It was very sudden, but I think we could see it coming."

Then they looked at the damaged mizzenmast and its spread socket. "I can see why you lost the other two masts now. You were lucky not to have lost this one, too. Did the captain protest to the building yard about putting white oak in the ship for its masts?"

"Certainly, sir, I brought the use of white oak to the attention of the captain and went with him when he confronted the building yard head."

"And I take it he had no live oak available."

"No, sir, he didn't. I think the shipment that was on the way was sunk. We had to take oversize white oak or we'd never have left the yard."

"Let's go see the captain."

The two went up the ladders and aft to the captain's cabin. The first lieutenant had seen the pilot off, and the captain was standing on the quarterdeck looking over at the busy shipyard.

While he was looking at the scenery, he ran his hand over his dark, handsome face. Then he stopped. "My God!" he said to himself, "I'm getting fat. I can feel it on my face and chin." Then his other hand stole down to his midsection. He tentatively poked at it. Then he muttered again, "I'm getting fat here, too."

He paced up and down, thinking about his problem. Then he stopped. "It's the fault of that rascal Johnson. He's been feeding me too well with all kinds of fattening food. Bacon, puddings, cheese, cakes. I'll send him over to the market to buy fruit and vegetables for our next cruise. No more sweets and all that fattening food he puts together."

Biddle turned his attention to the yard master and Lieutenant Christopher as they approached him. "Ah, sir," he said, "welcome aboard. We really need your help. I'm Captain Nicholas Biddle, commanding."

The yard master held out his hand and said, "Ronald Chanson, at your service, sir, and I can see you really need it. I have never seen a ship suffer so much damage without having been in battle."

Biddle shrugged. "It was a hell of a storm, and, as you have seen, the substitute mast materials really did us in."

Chanson nodded in agreement. "Fortunately live oak still grows in North Carolina, although there is not much left. We have a small stock in the yard. I will make sure your replacement masts do the job."

"With your agreement and the approval of your navy and the promise to pay for it, we'll get to work. Tonight we'll draw up the plans, and early tomorrow we'll start the work."

The white oak mizzenmast was unceremoniously unshipped and lifted over the side by a masting hulk, a special ship fitted with heavy lift equipment. A week later the replacement masts, each in three sections, came alongside in a barge and were in turn lifted by the masting hulk.

The boatswain and sailmaker watched the installation impatiently, and when it was completed, the boatswain reported to the captain that the ship was ready to go to sea except for the loading of provisions.

The captain chuckled. "Maybe so in your department, but we need more men. We're still fifty men short of the number we left Philadelphia with, and even that wasn't enough. I'd like to find another twenty-five somewhere."

The boatswain said, "I saw a merchantman, the *Fair American*, come in this morning. There's something familiar about some of the seamen working around the topside. You might send some one over to pay her a visit."

The captain took the hint. Lieutenant Forsyth, accompanied by four marines, was rowed over to the merchant ship. Biddle watched him talking to the American captain on the quarterdeck while the marines disappeared below. Soon two seamen came to the quarterdeck, carrying their seabags, as the marines watched them carefully. Then the whole group embarked in the cutter, shoved off, and rowed back.

Forsyth climbed aboard the *Randolph* first and watched as the two seamen hoisted their seabags aboard.

Biddle, waiting on the quarterdeck, beckoned Forsyth over. Forsyth grinned as he saluted.

Biddle said, "Forsyth, I see you found something of interest over there."

Forsyth nodded. "Yes, sir, two men who had been impressed by the *Fair American*."

Biddle nodded understandingly. "Well, we're still fifty-eight short. We're going to have to try something else. I still want at least twenty-five."

Forsyth raised his eyebrows. "The navy authorizes the use of bounties if that's the last straw. That means paying them or the next of kin a sum of money for enlisting. Probably two hundred dollars in our new money."

"Yes, and it will be expensive to the navy. I don't like to have to buy men that way, but I see no other way. Go ashore and make arrangements with the mayor to print several hundred notices saying that we will pay bounties and post them around town."

In the last week of repair, the bounty offer began to work, although the men who came aboard and asked for it were not the most desirable. None seemed to have the slightest wish to be patriotic. Most just needed the money badly. Some were in debt, or were avoiding those trying to collect from them. Some were avoiding the consequences of fatherhood. A few were literally sold by their fathers.

Just as the ship appeared to be ready for sea with a full crew, disaster struck.

One evening, Matthew, having turned in to his hammock early, heard a heavy series of crashes, almost as loud as gunfire. He turned over and tried to go back to sleep, but the crashes persisted, getting louder. Suddenly he realized that he was hearing heavy thunder, and it was not far away.

Matthew rolled out of his hammock, put on his oil skins, and went up on deck. The petty officer of the watch was pacing back and forth nearby opposite the gangway. He was glad to see Lieutenant Christopher coming up.

"Jesus, Lieutenant, there's a hell of a storm coming along," he exclaimed. "You'd better get back below."

Lieutenant Forsyth came up on deck, fastening his oilskins, and looked at the lightning in the west. "My God! I've never seen the sky that black, even at night, and the lightning is fierce."

Christopher took a deep breath. "It's a bad one, and it's headed right for us. I'll time the interval between the lightning and the thunder so I can calculate the distance to it."

On the next flash, he counted to himself. Then he said, "Two seconds. It's coming toward us fast and it's close."

The interval decreased rapidly and Christopher said, "There's no question. It will pass right over us and very soon. Let's get below."

Forsyth said, "You, too, petty officer of the watch."

The three, plus the messenger, clattered down the ladder and stood just at the bottom of the companionway, looking up at the small patch of sky visible above.

The next two flashes were almost coincident with the claps of thunder. Christopher shook his head. "If those didn't hit us, the next ones will."

They did. Below the waiting men could hear the crashes on deck above and the loud noise of splitting wood. The acrid smell of ozone from the lightning and the odor of burning wood trickled down the hatch. Then the rain began to drum on the deck above and splashed down the open hatch.

Christopher moaned. "The masts are gone."

Forsyth shook his head. "We've had it."

The smell of burned wood turned to a different odor as the rain put the fires out. Then the clean, hard smell of burning oak changed to musty and ashy.

Christopher said, "At least the rain is preventing the fires from spreading."

Fifteen minutes later the lightning and thunder seemed to march off to the east, and Forsyth and Christopher went out on deck, but stayed near the hatch entry. The decks were dark, but in the flashes of the distant lightning they could see that the masts were completely riven from their tops to the deck. Large fire-burnt cracks snaked their way down the devastated wood.

Forsyth shook his head. "The petty officer and messenger can go back on deck. You and I might just as well turn in. There's nothing we can do until daylight."

"And not much then," Christopher said. "This means a complete replacement and a two week's delay."

"Yes, if only the lightning rod installation had been completed."

"Next time we'll have to insist that the lightning rods go on as soon as the masts are placed."

The next morning the storm had completely passed. Matthew knocked on the captain's cabin door. The captain's voice was melancholy. "Come in."

Matthew knew that the captain had guessed what had happened without opening his door. Captain Biddle said, "Christopher, let's go see the yard master."

Two weeks later the replacement masts were completely in place, including the lightning rod system. Chanson, looking up at the shining copper, said, "That stuff will be dark green in a couple of months."

Biddle shrugged. "It will do the job no matter what color it is. They still work on my father's barn after twenty years, and they're gray now."

Two weeks later the ship was moved out to the river mouth by the same pilot, and after waiting for a favorable wind, she slipped across the bar, dropped the pilot, and stood out to sea with all sails set.

Captain Biddle watched the sails being set quickly and correctly. He rubbed his hands together and turned to Lieutenant Forsyth. "Now we look like a man-of-war. Let's fight like one."

Chapter 16

For one day the *Randolph* stood east, making four knots into a ten knot wind from the northeast and moderate seas from the same direction. Biddle expected to have to move off the coast at least two hundred miles to intercept British merchantmen coming north from the Caribbean and enroute to Canada as well as Europe. However, about three hours before dusk on the third day, about one hundred and fifty miles east of Charleston, the lookouts shouted. "Sail ho! Broad on the starboard bow!"

Biddle, on deck, shouted back. "How many ships?"

"Four, I think, sir, maybe five."

Biddle was so excited he forgot about his rheumatism, and instead of sending Lieutenant Christopher aloft, stuffed his long glass down his trousers and began to climb the ratlines slowly and carefully. At the mizzen crosstrees, he stood up, grabbed a nearby shroud, breathed deeply, and waited a minute for his rapidly beating heart to slow down. Then he pulled his long glass out, narrowly missing his testicles, extending all its sections, and carefully steadied it on a shroud. He focused it on the distant sails. "Damn!" he said. "There are five. One warship and four merchant ships."

Without waiting to go below, he shouted down. "Make all sail! Head for the contact! Beat to quarters!"

As he climbed down slowly he was passed by young sailors headed aloft. Once he thought he might lose his grip, and he resolved never to go aloft again. It was a young man's territory.

Biddle shook his head, trying to clear it and to bring his blood pressure down. "It's worse," he muttered to himself. "I shouldn't even jump up on the bulwark. I'd better keep both feet on the damned deck."

~

On the quarterdeck, Matthew, who had the watch, watched the sailors and marines hurrying about the deck. Unlike British warships, quiet was not maintained, and Matthew thought the British system was better. On this, like other American ships, the sailors were shouting at each other. Most of it was exchanges of information or unimportant orders, but a lot of it was unnecessary epithets. Matthew resolved to take the problem up with the captain when he could. He knew that if he had to give an order it probably would not be heard, and there could be serious consequences.

In a record five minutes, Forsyth reported to the captain, "Crew at battle stations. All guns ready, sir. That's the best we've ever done." Forsyth was at his best school-teacherish manner, with his Franklin style glasses sparkling. Behind them his pride in his accomplishment showed.

Biddle nodded. "I'm heading for the warship. Lieutenant Christopher, go aloft and take a better look."

Christopher took the other long glass and ran to the ratlines. Biddle watched him climb up and said to Forsyth, who was also watching him in a fatherly manner, "Ah, youth, I couldn't do it any more." He scratched his graying head in an absent manner.

"He's better then a monkey," Biddle said, "and can hold the long glass in one hand. I put mine down in my trousers and damned near bollicked myself."

Forsyth heard him. "What was that, sir?"

Biddle shook his head. "Nothing important. Just an old man's musings."

Within a few minutes, Christopher was back on the quarterdeck, sliding nimbly down a shroud. "Sir, the warship has twenty guns. She's a schooner and is very narrow. Probably very fast, but she can't be carrying more than nine-pounders on that small hull. She doesn't have the gun port marks of a British man-of-war, so she must be a privateer. She's trying to stay between the other ships and us. There are two brigs, of good size, and probably ex-men-of-war being used as transports. The other two are smaller merchantmen. One slow, one fast. The latter is a small sloop. I think she is Chesapeake-built and therefore probably will be very fast and nimble. We'll never catch her if she doesn't want to be caught. She's in very light draft, and I think she is carrying people rather than cargo."

Forsyth nodded. "I agree. I can tell she's lightly loaded from here." Forsyth wiped his glasses carefully and took another look. "Yes, she's very lightly loaded."

Biddle pursed his lips. "To hell with the little fellow. We'll go for the warship first. Then we'll try to scare the other three into surrendering."

Biddle turned to Forsyth, standing nearby. "How far is it until we are in range?"

"About five minutes to maximum range. I'd like to try a ranging shot from one of the bow chasers then," Forsyth said eagerly, moving up and down on his toes.

"Of course."

Biddle paced up and down, anxious to close. He turned to the boatswain, "Boatswain, can we put on more canvas?"

"Yes, sir, but we will have to take men off the guns to do it. You know how short-handed we are." The boatswain was disturbed at the thought of taking men away from what he thought was their primary task, sailing the ship.

Biddle swore in frustration, taking into account the boatswain's feelings. "All right, adjust what we have. We may have to bend on more canvas after we take this first armed ship to catch the rest of them."

Forsyth nodded his head approvingly. "Good idea, Captain. I'll have the crew ready to go aloft."

Biddle shook his head, "This is a hell of a way to have to fight a ship. Do one thing or the other! We should be able to do it as well as the British do. They always have plenty of men available."

Forsyth remembered his old Royal Navy days. "Maybe they do, but remember all the pressing they did and still do. It was terrible. Many a man was literally torn away in sight of his family."

"Aye," Biddle agreed. "I remember, too, and I guess what we are going through, even though it might be difficult, is the price we are paying for independence."

Biddle sighed and turned his attention to the fleeing ships. The *Randolph* was getting closer.

The sea was relatively calm and the wind steady at about five knots. Occasional gusts predicted there would be an increase soon. For once Biddle wished for more wind to speed up the chase, but slowly the distance to the twenty-gun privateer ahead decreased. By now, he could see that the other ship mounted only smaller guns, as Lieutenant Christopher had estimated, and that the *Randolph*, if she shot well, could pound her to pieces before she came in range of the smaller guns.

Biddle thought about his Gunner, Waugh, who had worked so hard to train his gun crews. For a moment he was glad Waugh had spent so much time with the gun crews, but he remembered Lieutenant Christopher's complaints about Waugh's neglect of safety, particularly with the magazine. Biddle tried to put the negative thoughts out of his mind, and he was helped by Forsyth's suddenly bawled order forward to the gunner with the bow chasers. "Fire a ranging shot!"

Gunner Waugh repeated the order, and the bow chaser boomed.

Forsyth stepped over to the port bulwark and climbed a few feet up the ratlines to get a better view of the flying black ball.

Neither Captain Biddle nor Gunner Waugh could see from the deck level, but the captain was pleased when Forsyth yelled down to him. "In range, sir. If you'll turn three points to port, I'll have the whole starboard battery after her as soon as we are steady on course."

Biddle turned to the helmsman, gave the order, and the ship started swinging to port. No change was necessary in the sails, and Biddle noted that the new course would also bring them closer to the fleeing ships.

The gunner moved aft to the starboard battery. Lieutenant Fitzgerald was in charge of it, but the gunner knew that Lieutenant Fitzgerald had never been in battle before, and he wanted to be there to back him up.

But Fitzgerald, although inexperienced, was a typical southerner, and the prospect of battle made him more capable than usual.

Waugh looked at him expectantly. Fitzgerald was in turn watching the gun captains position their guns following the course change. When he was satisfied, he ordered, "Commence firing!" and Waugh stopped worrying. After a few encounters like this, he would become a good officer in battle.

The first salvo was fired raggedly. The gunner thought it would be unsatisfactory for a British man-of-war and a poor show, but for a raw American set of gunners, he thought it was satisfactory, and if he had his way they would get better. He made a mental note to speed up the aiming of the gun captains.

Then he was aware that Lieutenant Forsyth was cheering. Waugh didn't expect it, but when he took time away from watching the gun crews reload, he could see large tears in the sails of the enemy and one mast at an angle.

The enemy fired back, but the salvo fell far short. The gunner grinned. This was the way to fight. Shoot first, have bigger and more guns, and wait for time to win the battle. No boarding was going to be necessary. The only blood spilled on the *Randolph* would come from a pinched finger. "Come on! Come on! Load faster! Let's get this over!" he yelled. "We haven't got all day!"

Biddle was ecstatic, but he tried to calm himself so that his pounding heart would not give in before the apparent victory could be brought to completion. He knew he was old to be a captain during wartime, and he wanted to conserve his energy. If he were to die, he wanted to die in battle, not from his heart giving out as he lay somewhere in a bed.

Suddenly Lieutenant Christopher, intensely watching the enemy ship from the ratlines, yelled, "Captain, she's coming about and heading for us!"

"Damn her!" swore the captain. "She's not dead yet. Pour it on!"

The guns fired steadily, the gun crews loading as fast as they could.

Matthew exclaimed, "We're hitting her, but she won't give up! Her shots are getting closer!"

At that moment a ball hit the forecastle, caroming off a gun carriage, and bouncing off the opposite bulwark. Matthew looked at the gun crew. A man was down. The ball had splintered part of the gun carriage and the wood splinter had shattered the lower part of the man's leg. Matthew jumped down and ran forward. The gun crew was stunned by the sight of blood. One of the older hands, an ex-British prisoner-of-war, took charge and began to give orders. "Put a tourniquet on!" he yelled.

Matthew bent over the man's leg. Blood was spurting from a severed artery and the bone was shattered. The man was stunned, not yet feeling pain. One of the gun crew had torn a piece of his jersey and fashioned a crude tourniquet. As soon as the tourniquet was in place, Matthew helped him into a stretcher and sent him below, carried by his gun crew. Matthew made a mental note to talk to the surgeon about making up tourniquets and placing them near the guns. They weren't of any use stowed down in the cockpit.

Matthew trotted aft to report to the captain. Just as he arrived, another ball flew through the main course sail and fell into the sea aft, raising a white geyser.

Captain Biddle swore. "Damned pest! He can't last much longer!"

Matthew climbed the rigging again. Before he could get a good look at the oncoming enemy, Forsyth called out, "Captain, she has struck her colors and ceased firing."

Biddle heaved a sigh of relief. "Cease firing!" he ordered. "Let her lie there, and we'll chase the others."

Matthew climbed into the rigging to get a better view of the other ships. "I have a good view of them, Captain. We'll close to firing range in about five minutes."

"Shall we change course?"

"No, sir, we should continue on. It will be over soon."

Chapter 17

As the *Randolph* sailed past the battered ship, Matthew read the name on her counter. "*True Briton*," he said.

Biddle nodded. "One down," he said. "I don't think it's an apt name."

"Why not?"

"She isn't British and she's not true."

Forsyth came back from the starboard gun battery. "No casualties," he announced, "except for the man on the chaser who will lose a leg."

At first Biddle looked pleased, but then he thought about the man's leg, and he forced a smile. "Good. Give the starboard battery a rest and use the port battery to bend on some more canvas. They won't be needed because the next ships can't fire back. All we need now is more speed."

The young surgeon, Little, came on deck to report to the captain. His face was pale. The captain asked, "Are you all right, Surgeon?"

The surgeon took a deep breath, obviously glad to be up in the fresh air and out of the dank cockpit below. "I think I'm all right. That's the first leg I've ever taken off, and I've never seen the operation."

Biddle said, "Not a very pretty sight, son, but you'll get used to it. I'll come down to see your patient as soon as I can get away."

"Thank you. I know that will help him. A single casualty like that seems to make more of an impression than a whole cockpit of wounded."

"Of course. And if you were very busy you wouldn't notice it as much."

"I guess so, sir, but I'm grateful that there is only one casualty."

"Is he in great pain?"

"He would be, but I've given him a lot of laudanum."

"Thank you, Surgeon. Now get back to your patient. I'll be down soon."

The surgeon clattered down the ladder, obviously pleased that the captain had promised to join him.

Biddle paced up and down, watching the ships ahead frantically piling on more canvas. The small sloop was drawing away easily, and Biddle gave up on her. He wondered why the other three ships didn't separate. It would make his job harder to round them all up, but they huddled together as if to give each other moral support.

Fifteen minutes later, Biddle ordered Forsyth to try a ranging shot. It hit near the stern of the nearest ship, and that was all it took. Her colors fluttered down, and she turned into the wind. The other ships continued on for a few minutes, and then, one by one, they surrendered.

Biddle rubbed his hands with satisfaction, and the gun crews cheered.

The boatswain shook his head and muttered to Lieutenant Christopher, standing next to him, "Those bastards we talked to in the cable tier a few nights ago have short memories. I see some of them over there cheering like they thought this was their idea, too. Now they think the captain is wonderful and this is a charmed ship."

Matthew agreed with the irony of the outcome. "They'll get the same share of prize money as the others, and it will be a lot," he muttered.

The captain called his officers over to the quarterdeck as he watched the *Randolph* come up to the prizes wallowing in the small seas. "I have to keep Lieutenant Christopher aboard to navigate. Lieutenant Forsyth, select a squad of marines and ten men, and be ready to board the *True Briton* as soon as we return to her. We'll deal with these ships first."

He looked at his officers, standing next to him expectantly. "Gunner, you will take six men and we will send you to the nearest brig. Boatswain, you will take six men and go to the farthest brig. That's going to leave us shorthanded. But I must support you."

Biddle turned to Lieutenants Ambrose and Fitzgerald, standing slightly apart. He looked at Lieutenant Ambrose, shook his head slightly, and looked at Lieutenant Fitzgerald. "Lieutenant Fitzgerald, take six men and go to the merchant ship with the sloop rig."

Lieutenant Ambrose was in better shape than usual. He was twenty pounds lighter, and his color was good. "Sir," he said, "I know you think I can't do the job, but I request assignment to the merchant ship. I'll bring her in."

Biddle looked doubtful, but he decided to take a chance. "But if you get seasick?"

"No, sir. I've solved that problem. The surgeon gave me some medicine, and I only eat oatmeal. I'll take a bag with me in case the Brits have only salt horse and hard tack. I promise you I'll make it."

Biddle beamed. "I think you will, too. Good luck and go to it. Take Lieutenant Fitzgerald's place. He needs a little more time to recuperate from the fever."

The captain turned to Lieutenant Forsyth, who seemed to be eager to get off on his own command "I'm sending the carpenter and sailmaker with you to help with repairs. Hoist a signal when your prize is ready to proceed."

Forsyth said, "What do we do with the prizes after we follow you into port?"

"Anchor near me. I'll go to the shipyard and make arrangements with the yard master to send boats to all of you to take off your prisoners. I hope he will take you all into the yard soon to off-load your cargo so it can be processed and sold by the prize court. I will also ask him to send guards aboard each ship to protect the cargos until they can be off-loaded. I hope it won't be long."

Forsyth grinned. "I hope so, too."

"On the way in, examine the manifests and make a written inventory of your ship's cargo and any valuables. We don't want to waste any time turning the ships and their cargos over to the prize court. The sooner we do it, the sooner we'll all get paid our shares."

All the officers grinned. Fitzgerald said, "There should be more money for each of us than I've ever seen."

By now both boats were in the water, and the officers and men assigned were embarking. Matthew watched them go, realizing

that he and Lieutenant Fitzgerald would be left aboard alone to
stand watch unless the captain took pity on them and took a watch
with them. Fortunately, Charleston was not too far away, and
Lieutenant Fitzgerald was tough. He was learning rapidly.

When the boats were back and hoisted on board, the captain
sailed the ship slowly through the lying-to prizes, reading the
names on their counters. "*Severn*," he read. Then, "*The Charming
Peggy*," and, "*Assumption*." Then Biddle ordered all sail hoisted
and headed for the ship that had previously surrendered.

Matthew said, "Sir, the prizes are all low in the water. They will
be fully loaded."

Biddle beamed, so broadly that Matthew thought he might
break into a jig. He had been known to do that, according to Forsyth, who knew him from their days in the Royal Navy. But he was
older and somewhat rheumatic now. Biddle controlled himself and
said, "I'm going to need the prize money now to buy my wife
some clothes. She's been on short clothes rations since we've been
in this country."

Matthew nodded, wondering what a captain's pay might be. He
was sure that, whatever it might be, it was not much, and the Continental Navy's treasury was so bare he probably wasn't paid often.

Matthew looked at the captain's uniform. It had been kept clean
and well-brushed by Johnson, but it was threadbare and shiny.

"Sir," he said, "I've been to Charleston before, and there are
several good tailors there. May I suggest that you spend some of
your prize money on new uniforms?"

Biddle laughed. "I'll think about it. Right now I want to concentrate on herding these prizes in before we meet up with some
British men-of-war."

Matthew did not take the hint and kept on pressing the point.
"Sir, what percentage of the value of prizes do we get now?"

Biddle thought a while and then cleared his throat. "I wouldn't
say the Marine Committee of the Congress is very generous. Now
they give one-third of the value of merchant ships and one-half of
the value of men-of-war."

Matthew whistled. "We used to get all of it when I was sailing
in a privateer."

Biddle nodded soberly. "You might think about going back to the privateers some day. Promotion for those not politically connected in our Navy is almost nonexistent. Worse than in the Royal Navy." Then he brightened. "A young up and coming captain is about to change some of this. He has written a lot of letters pointing out the incompetency of many of the captains and even of the junior officers. He has also proposed that the percentages of prize money be changed from one-third to half for merchantmen, and all for men of war."

"Who is this captain to whom we may owe so much if he's successful?"

"Captain John Paul Jones, formerly of the Royal Navy. He's making a name for himself."

"But doesn't this forthrightness get him in trouble?"

Biddle laughed "It doesn't seem to. He's too good a captain at sea for them to fire."

When he was satisfied that the watch had settled down and the sails were drawing well, Biddle left Lieutenant Christopher in charge of the deck. "I'm going below to the cockpit to see our wounded man."

"Yes, sir. I'll send word down if it's necessary."

Biddle climbed slowly down the ladder to the orlop deck and then to the space called the cockpit. It was crowded with hammocks and cots for a dozen wounded. Today only one cot was occupied.

Biddle looked at the appointments of the cockpit and realized he had never been down in this particular space before. He had been to dozens of such spaces on British ships and he recognized the peculiar smells common to all cockpits of all navies. The odors of carbolic acid, vinegar, laudanum, and other medicines were overcome by the creeping smell wafting up from the bilges. Biddle wrinkled his nose.

The surgeon saw him and beamed. "Captain, thanks for coming down. Jeffers will be glad to see you, and I'd like to show you around."

Biddle cut him off. "Thank you, but I've seen many a cockpit. I'd just like to see your man."

The wounded man was still so sedated he could only mutter as the captain bent over him. Biddle patted his shoulder. "Jeffers, get well. We need you back on deck, and even with a wooden leg, you'll find plenty to do. How do you feel?"

The patient mumbled again. The surgeon said, "I think he was saying 'thank you.'"

Biddle nodded. "Well, I don't want to tire him. I'll be down again soon."

Biddle climbed carefully but quickly up the lower deck ladders as fast as he could to get back to the fresh air. A cockpit was not a pleasant place to be.

Soon the little flotilla was anchored off the Charleston shipyard, and Captain Biddle, after meeting with the officers commanding his prizes, had himself and the purser rowed to the shipyard in his gig to make arrangements with the yard master to take the prizes off his hands. He had in hand the inventories the prize captains had brought to him. As they rowed ashore he read the inventories aloud to the purser.

"Ha!" he said, "the *True Briton* was full of rum for the British troops in New York. This will be a cold winter for them now."

The purser said, "I'm a teetotaler, but I can sympathize with them."

"Well," Biddle said, "I'm not. At least when I'm ashore, and I feel for them, too."

He turned to the other inventories. "The *Severn* was full of sugar, rum, spices, and log wood." He slapped his knee and roared.

The purser was startled and asked, "What's wrong, sir?"

Biddle tried to stop laughing. "This is very funny. The *Severn* sounds like it was going to a Christmas party. Booze, sugar, spice. . . just what you'd like before a log fire, and they even had that."

Biddle roared again and tried to stop laughing.

Now the purser saw the point and joined him. "Sounds like Christmas."

Biddle wiped his eyes and went on. "The two brigs were loaded with salt. You can't drink the stuff, but it will sell well. So will the brigs."

"Sir, how about selling the ships?"

"Of course. You must be new to the prize business. The two brigs are undamaged, and even after the Continental Navy takes their cut, they alone will make our fortune."

The purser said, "I could learn to like this business. My brother can have the store."

Biddle shrugged. "Why? I thought you wanted to return to it some day."

"Well, I would. I like being home every night."

"And you don't like being at sea?"

"Well, sir, I've grown to like it, I guess. I was trying to say that we make a lot of money in just a few minutes. My brother will have to sell a lot of suits for that."

"You are right, but he won't stand a chance of losing a leg like poor Jeffers did."

The purser sighed. "I'll take the risk."

Chapter 18

Matthew watched Captain Biddle depart in his gig, leaving him in command. Lieutenant Forsyth had not yet returned, and the captain had sent Lieutenant Fitzgerald off on an errand. The port cutter had dropped him off and returned.

Matthew walked up and down the quarterdeck, enjoying his brief time in command. He thought about what Captain Biddle had said about the lack of promotion and command opportunity in the Continental Navy, and he thought about returning to privateering. Maybe he should. Life in the Continental Navy was very tough for everyone but the commanding oficer. Even then the responsibility of command was very heavy. As a privateer, he could just walk away whenever he wanted. But when he remembered his family he thought again about the navy. If he stayed in the navy, it would be a long time, if ever, before they could live well. As a privateer, he would have money early, but he might not make it through the war either way.

His wife had ben very patient and understanding about his long absences. She had to be considered in the near future, and he knew she would always stand by him. But he could not always call on her to sacrifice.

He resumed walking on the quarterdeck. Even though it was out in the open and exposed to the curious gaze of the men on the upper deck, there was also a certain amount of privacy that would help him to make a decision. Captains and other commanding officers were able to use this cloak while in public. He hoped he could use it when he was entitled to it.

Johnson brought him a cup of coffee. "Lieutenant Christopher, you look like you were made to be a captain. Maybe it will happen soon."

Matthew laughed. "I'm still pretty young. Some day, but not in this navy."

"Well, anyway, you look like you are pretty deep into something. Maybe this coffee will help."

Matthew took the mug amd lowered its level with a deep swig. "Thanks, Johnson. Your sympathy helps, although I can't talk about my problem."

The surgeon came on deck and approached Matthew. "Lieutenant Christopher, I understand you are now in command. I need to get something done. Can you help me?"

"Ask me."

"The man who lost his leg should be hospitalized. Can you send him over to the hospital?"

"Of course. I think you should go with him. I'll have the port cutter alongside in ten minutes."

"Thank you. I'd like to be able to go with him. There's no need for me to stay aboard."

"Yes, a doctor should always be with his patient when he can."

When the boat was ready, Matthew sent forward for the surgeon, and he appeared promptly followed by four men carrying his patient on a stretcher. Matthew went over to the gangway to supervise the lowering of the patient into the boat. The young seaman was alert and grinning.

Matthew asked, "How do you feel?"

"All right, I guess. My pain is gone. My shipmates tell me I'll get enough prize money some day to buy a small farm. Maybe even a big one."

"That's right. We should all do well from the proceeds of the prizes we brought in."

"I intend to try to ride a horse as soon as I can get a wooden leg."

Matthew grinned. "That's what makes life go on. A horse would help you run your farm. If you find you don't like farming, I guarantee you a job in the Christopher shipyard in Annapolis. Good luck."

Matthew watched the port cutter being rowed away. As it passed out of sight, he could see the young seaman wave. He marvelled at the resiliency of the young man, and suddenly he realized that he was no longer feeling young, even though he was still young in years. The war aged everyone quickly, and he could feel his years coming on.

Three hours later the captain returned. He climbed up the sea ladder, slowly passed through the gangway, and returned Matthew's salute. "Christopher, I want to see you in my cabin in ten minutes."

Matthew saluted him, wondering if he had done something wrong to irritate the captain. The captain did not appear to be mad, but rather just preoccupied.

Ten minutes later he was in the captain's cabin. "Sit down," Biddle said.

Biddle looked at him and cleared his throat.

Matthew asked, "Sir, is something wrong?"

Biddle sighed. "Yes and no. I have a set of orders for you from the Secretary of the Marine Committee. They were waiting for you in the shipyard." He tossed a letter over to Matthew. "Here, read this."

Matthew picked the letter up and started to read. "My God!" he said, "I don't understand this."

The captain said, "The yard master shed some light on it. He says Captain John Paul Jones is putting the frigate *Ranger* in commission in a Portsmouth shipyard. It seems Jones had a lot of pull with the Secretary of the Marine Committee and in addition has been a superb performer at sea, not only in the Continental Navy, but before that in the Royal Navy. Nevertheless, Captain Jones has failed to get all he wants. He was assigned a bunch of politicians for officers, and you and I know what that is like."

Matthew nodded. "Yes, sir."

"At any rate, he vented his unhappiness, and the Secretary of the Marine Committee has turned to you. Your orders call for you to be detached from the *Randolph* and to report to Captain Jones as his aide as soon as possible."

"But I can't leave you like this. The ship is just getting organized and beginning to succeed."

"I know, but I'm lucky to have had you this long. I understand I will get a relief for you before we leave port. Obviously he won't have your qualifications or experience, but I have to take what I get. A fast sloop leaves for Boston tomorrow. I think you will have time to pack up and say your good-byes tonight."

Matthew asked, "And what is this aide business? I'm just a sea-going lieutenant."

Biddle shrugged. "I don't exactly understand that either. Flag officers are generaly entitled to aides, but not captains. I suppose he will explain this to you when you arrive. I am sure he had something to do with it."

Matthew sighed, put the orders in his pocket, got up, and took his departure. As he walked down the deck to his stateroom, Johnson fell in beside him. "Sir, I heard that. I'm coming with you."

"Johnson, you can't. The captain needs you."

Johnson stopped, and Matthew, head down, walked on, trying to ignore Johnson.

By the next morning, Matthew had said good-bye to Captain Biddle and the other members of the crew. A seamen had volunteered to help him with his baggage to the fast packet landing. Just before he left, the ship was moved to the shipyard where he could walk to the landing instead of taking a boat ashore.

Just as he started to board the sloop, Johnson stepped out from behind a pile of cargo nearby. "Sir, I'm going with you, and please don't turn me in."

Matthew looked at him with surprise. "But, Johnson, you'd be deserting. That would mean you'd be picked up and tried by court martial."

"I don't care. I'll go by land if I have to."

"If you do, some of these slave owners down here might catch you."

"I'll make it somehow."

Matthew asked the man at the end of the brow when the ship was due to depart.

"Two hours," he said.

"Come with me, Johnson. I'll find a way to get the captain to let you come with me."

On the way back to the ship, Johnson was silent and glum, following behind Lieutenant Christopher. Matthew went aboard, followed closely by Johnson. He knocked on the captain's door.

"Come in."

Matthew thought the captain would turn him down, but Biddle was sympathetic. "You brought him to me in this ship in the first place. Now I owe you a favor. I'll write some orders for him. I'm sure Captain Jones will be glad to see him. I heard he had only half a crew so far."

The trip to Boston was quick in spite of the rough weather. As they passed the entrance to the Cheaspeake Bay, Matthew looked longingly to the west, knowing it might be another year before he'd see Martha. He wondered if he had become a father for a second time. Mail from Martha had not caught up with him in Charleston, and he resolved to write to her the day he arrived in Portsmouth. Mail could get there more easily than it could reach Charleston.

Johnson, watching him carefully, asked, "You think you a pappa again?"

Matthew laughed. "I hope so. Some day I want to stay home and enjoy my family."

Johnson was glum. "I ain't got none, and my pappy doesn't want me to come home neither."

Two days later the sloop arrived at a pier at Boston Harbor. Matthew hired a carriage to take himself, Johnson, and their baggage to Portsmouth.

As they bounced along the highway, Matthew wished they had been able to go by sea, but the packet system had not yet been expanded to include Portsmouth. The rolling of a ship and the spray were preferable to the roughness of the road and the roiling dust. The driver was an old gaffer who drove out of the limits of town in silence, and, after the carriage was safely on the highway in the countryside, he said in a peculiar accent, "Youse are sailor boys, I take it, bound for a ship in the Portsmouth shipyard."

Matthew said, "Right. The *Ranger*."

The old man spat to the down wind side of the carriage and said, "That Captain Jones must be a bad one. He's already killed two of his crew, one with a sword."

Johnson could barely make out the Yankee's accent, and he raised his eyebrows and looked at Matthew.

Matthew laughed. "Just gossip, Johnson, and if he did he had a good reason."

The driver slapped the reins on the horse, and they trotted a bit faster. "No, sir, it ain't gossip. More than that."

Matthew said, "If that's so, why has the Continental Navy made him a captain and then given him command of one of its best ships?"

"Can't rightly say why."

Matthew added, "Your accent seems to be a combination of English and Scottish."

"Right on, sailor boy, and I'm a Yankee now either way. I hate the English. I hope you and your Captain Jones kill a lot of them."

Johnson sat up straight, obviously reacting to each bounce of the carriage and also the driver's information. Matthew said, "Relax, Johnson, no matter how tough Captain Jones may be, it's rumored he treats colored people fairly. I'll guarantee that. Now sit back and rest. I want you to be in good shape and well rested when we go aboard the ship."

Johnson sighed, apparently satisfied, and leaned back against he meager cushions

Late that afternoon the carriage pulled up to the long brow leading up to the gangway cut in the bulwark. He brought the horses to a skidding stop with a flourish of his whip and a string of curses that excited the interest and envy of the seamen lolling above.

"This is it," the driver said. "Good luck."

Matthew got out of the carriage and stretched his legs. They were stiff from the long ride and the bouncing of the carriage. While he was stretching, he looked at his new ship. Although the masts were not completely rigged yet, he could tell that she was a square-rigged three-masted frigate. The lines of her hull were pedestrian. Typical New England bluff bows that would not give the ship any extra speed like the slim bows of French ships. Perhaps her hull was as sturdy as all New England, though, and that might pay off in battle or storm.

Johnson said, "Boss, let's get on with this getting aboard. I'm hungry."

Matthew and Johnson pulled the baggage out of the back of the carriage and walked up the brow carrying it over their shoulders. At the top of the brow, they put it down. Matthew saluted the quarterdeck and then saluted an officer standing nearby. Matthew said, "Lieutenant Matthew Christopher and Seaman Johnson reporting for duty in accordance with orders."

The officer returned the salute and said in a tone neither cordial nor questioning, "Please let me see them."

As Christopher took them out of his pocket, he looked at the officer carefully. He was as tall as Matthew, a little over six feet, but he was slim, only about one hundred and sixty pounds. The hair peeking out from under his cap was black and severely cut. He was well-shaved and neatly uniformed, but there was something distinctly unseamanlike about him. He seemed to be going through the motions of being a naval officer. Christopher resolved to find out what he was all about as soon as possible. His accent was definitely New England, and his voice was firm and not the reedy quality that might be expected from a man of slim build. It seemed to go with the stern face, penetrating eyes, and unfriendly expression.

The officer took Matthew's orders and unfolded them.

He read them carefully, and then his eyebrows went up. "Well, I'll be damned! I didn't know about this. These say you are to be Captain Jones' aide."

Matthew nodded. "That's right, sir, and Johnson here is to report for duty as a seaman."

Johnson poked him in the ribs. "I'm a cook, sir."

Matthew said in a low voice, "Certainly, but you are to be a seaman first."

The officer introduced himself as Lieutenant Simpson. "I'm the first lieutenant," he said. "Captain Jones will want to see you right away. Follow me."

Chapter 19

Matthew and Johnson followed Lieutenant Simpson to the door of Captain Jones' cabin. Simpson knocked on the door. A deep, resonant voice from the inside said, "Come in if it's you, Simpson. I've been waiting to see you."

Simpson said to Christopher and Johnson, "Wait here." He opened the door, took off his cap, and went in.

In a few minutes he came out, his face pale and unpleasant, and said, "Follow me in."

Matthew and Johnson stepped inside the cabin after Lieutenant Simpson, and Simpson said, "Captain, Lieutenant Christopher and Seaman Johnson reporting for duty in accordance with orders, sir."

A stern-looking man looked up under his dark eyebrows. Apparently he had reprimanded Lieutenant Simpson for something, but when he saw Christopher and Johnson, his face mellowed. "Welcome aboard. I'm Captain John Paul Jones. Please sit down," he said. He turned to Simpson. "Lieutenant Simpson, you may leave them here."

Jones got up and strode up and down, waiting for Simpson to leave. Christopher noted his wide-set eyes and large features. The combination gave him an intelligent look. Jones flexed his arms as he walked in the small area, also rising on his toes and simulating the sliding steps of a swordsman. His movements were ahtletic and at the same time graceful.

Christopher judged him to be a few inches short of six feet, but his body was well-knit, and his movements and bearing made him seem taller. His eyes were somewhere between blue and gray, and his hair was nondescript brown and short.

Jones voice was strong and well-modulated. Although Matthew knew he had been raised in Scotland to the age of ten, he had completed his early schooling in Virginia near Fredericksburg while living with his brother. It was evident that his Scottish burr had disappeared, and he spoke now with a faint Virginian accent.

Jones stopped pacing and turned to Johnson.

Johnson hesitated to sit down, and when Captain Jones noticed it, he gestured to him to take a seat. There was no doubt that Johnson was being ordered to sit down in the presence of his Captain. He sat down gingerly and eased to the back of the chair. His two hundred and twenty pounds caused the camp chair to creak loudly.

Jones looked over toward the sound of the creaking and grinned. "Johnson, take it easy on my chairs, I don't see many men in here larger than I am and both of you out-weigh me by twenty pounds."

Johnson grinned, now at ease. "Yes, sir. I think I got Lieutenant Christopher by about twenty pounds, and I'm way ahead of you."

Captain Jones turned to Christopher. "Lieutenant Christopher, I take it your former commanding officer, Captain Nicholas Biddle, understood why you are needed here. You will be the only officer, other than myself, who can navigate, and also the only other officer who has seen a gun fired in anger. Now you can see why I need you."

Matthew nodded. "I see, sir, but Captain Biddle faced the same situation, and we became a good ship."

Jones' dark face became even darker for a moment, and Matthew thought he had overstepped himself, but Jones face softened and he laughed, "Maybe Captain Bidddle is a better commanding officer than I am."

Matthew shook his head quickly. "He says you are the best commanding officer in the navy, and I am lucky to be going to sea with you."

Jones cleared his throat and grinned warmly. "Now that we have settled that, let's talk a bit. You will be what I call my *aide*. That's the only way I can see to put you over these clowns the Marine Commmittee has stuck me with. I know this is not strictly in accordance with navy protocol, but I don't care. You will find I do not always follow the so-called navy method. I believe in getting results so long as I do not hurt anyone in the process."

"Yes, sir, but how do I serve from day to day as what you call an *aide*?"

"You have authority to enter my cabin without knocking any time, regardless of who is in here. I will give you authority and responsibility that you won't believe, but carry out my orders as you get them and we will prosper together. Don't let any of these so-called lieutenants bother you. If necessary, you may take them below to inspect the bilges and straighten the matter out. I see you out-weigh them all by twenty pounds, and I think you can take care of yourself."

Johnson nodded and chuckled quietly.

Jones looked at him. "You said something?"

Johnson gulped. "Ah, nothing, sir, I must have swallowed something."

Matthew said. "I understand, sir, but just what do you want me to do? I am willing to try anything."

Jones looked at the overhead. "My God! So much! We have only fifty percent of our crew. We have very little aboard in the way of supplies and victuals. I'll put you to work on all these things, and when we go to sea you will have to help me navigate and stand most of the watches until I can qualify more officers. The lieutenants don't have the faintest idea of what to do. I ought to throw them all over the side, starting with Lieutenant Simpson, my first lieutenant."

Johnson's eyes opened wide. "Sir, did you really kill two of your men?"

Jones guffawed. "My God! Johnson, I like you. You speak right out. One I brought to mast, had him given a few lashes, and then had him transferred to another ship. He died there a good bit later of a fever. I never at any time touched him, and I certainly didn't kill him. The second man charged at me armed with a cutlass and was in the process of committing a mutinous act. I stepped back and tripped on a hatch coaming. He kept coming at me and impaled himself on my drawn sword. I guess you could say I touched him, but he did it himself. I was never charged with anything then or now."

Matthew laughed, "Yes, sir, that's what Captain Biddle told me."

"Biddle was really something in his youth. He started as a midshipman in the Royal Navy, worked up to Post Captain, and transferred to the Continental Navy about the same time I did. I don't suppose you know that he charged a bunch of armed mutineers and took the lot? A few were killed in the process, more than my two."

"I don't doubt that, sir, but he's a little long in the tooth these days."

"Maybe. He should keep himself in as good a shape as I do. I expect you to turn out early on occasion and do a little sword practice with me."

Matthew said eagerly. "I'm looking forward to it, sir."

Jones turned to Johnson, "Now, Johnson, let's settle you. What were you on the *Randolph?*"

Matthew interrupted. "Sir, he was the captain's steward and sometimes he stepped in to help the ship's cook. He was good at it, but we were shorthanded, and Johnson volunteered to be a part of a gun crew. He qualified as gun captain, and he was a very good one."

Johnson interrupted. "Sir, I'd like to do that for you."

Jones looked at him closely. "You shot before?"

"Yes, sir. Quail, and I cooked them, too. I can cook anything."

Jones shook his head and laughed. "Johnson, I still like you. You'll be assigned to a gun crew. If I like what I see, I'll promote you to gun captain. I believe you'll see that I want to help every colored person. I spent a cruise as an officer on a slave trader, and I hated it. I resolved to make up for it, and I'm working hard at it."

Jones looked up at the overhead, his handsome face thoughtful. "But, Johnson, I may need you as a steward in port for an important social affair from time to time. I may call on you for help."

Johnson grinned. "Yes, sir. I still have my two white jackets in my seabag. I can make fancy small food and I can serve it without spilling."

Jones said, "I'll always remember that you are a seaman and gunner first and foremost, just as I am. Other tasks I give you will not interfere with that."

Jones turned and looked at Matthew. "Lieutenant Christopher, I had a letter from Captain Biddle. He says he had some men desert when the *Randolph* entered Charleston just after being dismasted. Can you tell me why?"

"Yes, sir. They were all native Americans who had signed long term agreements to serve. Captain, under the Continental Navy regulations, he had no alternative but to offer them this version of a contract. On the other hand, the rest of our crew was over fifty percent ex-British prisoners-of-war. They didn't try to desert, but we had other troubles with them."

"Well, I'll not let those lubberly nincompoops in Philadelphia dictate to me. Write up a short enlistment contract to this effect, 'Twelve months and while absent from the eastern states.' Give it to Mister Simpson and tell him I said to explain it to each man he recruits."

Matthew said, "I think that would have gotten around Captain Biddle's problem. He had another problem he did not know of."

"What was that?"

"We had a near mutiny."

"What! On *his* ship?"

"It almost happened, as I said, but over half of the crew were ex-British prisoners-of-war. They weren't concerned with the length of the enlistment. They thought the ship was jinxed and wanted the ship to be sailed to Norfolk so they could get off before something else happened."

Jones snorted. "Damned fools! What did you do about it?"

"I talked some sense into them. I told them they might hang from the yardarm if the British captured our badly crippled ship."

"And they listened?"

"Yes, sir. No further trouble."

Jones thought for a momment, a succession of emotions passing across his strong face. "Well, that's just why you are here. You seem to know how to face any problem, no matter how complicated, and more importantly, how to solve it."

Jones turned to Johnson. "Johnson, I think we've got you straightened out. Go find Lieutenant Simpson, the officer who brought you in here, and tell him I said to put you in a gun crew."

Johnson grinned broadly. "Thank you, sir."

Jones waited until Johnson had departed. Then he said to Christopher. "I'm going to tell you some things about my officers. You need to know about them so you can serve me best. What I am going to say is not new. I have written it all to the Secretary of the Marine Committee and gotten no response, so I have to do the best I can and so do you."

Mathew shifted uncomfortably in his chair, but Jones paid no attention.

"First, my first lieutenant, the officer who met you and introduced you to me, I must admit, is socially an acceptable gentleman, but that is all he's got to offer as an officer. He's never been to sea and does not talk or understand the seagoing language, as you will find out. He has a strange New England accent that even we ex-Scots find hard to understand. I hope that you will teach him as much as you can, without letting him know that I have told you of his shortcomings."

"But, sir, how was he appointed?"

Jones laughed. "By now you must know that the Royal Navy is mainly officered by stupid, incompetent aristocrats, although there are a good many sons of parsons, doctors, and barristers as well. The American Continental Navy should have learned from them, but they are just as bad in other ways. Their officers are all political appointees. Lieutenant Simpson, for instance, is a brother-in-law of Langdon, the builder of this ship and a powerful politician in Portsmouth. Simpson is also a relative of Hancock and Wendell, two wealthy citizens of the city. Third Lieutenant Wendell is another political appointee of like incompetence. Unfortunately the custom is widespread."

"You are the only officer I asked for that I received, and the only one who has been to sea. You are sort of over allowance. Now you see what a tremendous job we have. I'll handle the politics, and you'll oversee Simpson and a warrant gunner named Dobie in recruiting the rest of the crew. Again, they should know it and be aware that you are reporting directly to me. They don't even know what an aide is and what one's duties are. Just keep them ignorant in that area for awhile. Is that enough for you to start on?"

"Yes, sir, but what about the procuremant of supplies and the completion of the ship?"

Jones laughed. "I know you were brought up in a shipyard, and as soon as you get a feel for personnel, I have other chores for you.

I want to keep a weather eye out for foul-ups on the part of ship-yard pesonnel. I will be walking on the weather decks of the ship every day and should catch most of the problems on the top side. I want you to find out what is going on below decks. Let me know what you see as soon as possible so we can correct it."

"Sir, there is one quick point. Are our masts live oak instead of white oak?"

Jones laughed. "Yes, you may be sure of that. I've tested them myself. They'll do."

Christopher grinned. "I feel better."

"You are particularly concerned?"

"Yes, sir, Captain Biddle lost two of his masts made of white oak in a storm."

Jones pulled at his long lower lip. "I feel sorry for him. You can be assured it will not happen to us."

Christopher said, "Thank you, sir."

Jones waved a hand airily. "Now get to work."

Chapter 20

Outside the captain's cabin, Matthew found the first lieutenant pacing up and down. Simpson stopped. "Christopher, I know your orders require you to report to the captain as his aide. Frankly, I don't know what an aide to a captain does, and I don't know what our relationship will be. Just exactly what duties has he given you?"

"The first thing I am to do is to give you all possible help in recruiting a crew. What can I do to help?"

Simpson seemed to light up. "Well, that's a step in the right direction. He's already got Gunner Dobie, Lieutenant Charrier, Lieutenant Hall, and the marine officers Captain Parker and Lieutenant Wallingford away beating the bushes, so to speak."

"Then I guess you don't need me to join them. By the way, the captain directed that I write up and give to you a paragraph to be inserted in the articles of enlistment that was used effectively by Captain Biddle. It will allow all men so enlisted to limit the period to one year."

"What! The Marine Committee won't like that."

"I strongly suggest we don't worry about that. I think Captain Jones can handle any complaints. How about using bounties?"

"We are now allowed to offer all able seamen forty dollars and landsmen twenty dollars."

"Good. Does the captain have anything else in mind with regard to new policies?"

Simpson chuckled. "You never know what he'll come up with next, but you can bet he will succeed."

Matthew changed the subject. "Could you tell me something of the other officers? I know about Gunner Dobie and the marine officers."

"Well, there's Lieutenant Charrier. I hardly know him myself. There are two other odd ones. One's a Swedish naval officer, here for instruction. He speaks fairly good English and will work hard at whatever task you give him. Then there is a young man named

Smith. I don't think that's his real name, and I don't know if he's commissioned. Not a lieutenant in any event. The captain seems to know about him and tells him what to do. I ignore him."

"And the working naval officers?"

Simpson laughed. "You know I'm the first lieutenant. The second lieutenant is Elijah Hall and the third lieutenant John Wendell. We have a midshipman named Hill and we may pick up some more. As you know, none of us except the captain can navigate. I understand that you can, and I'm counting on you to teach me before we get to France. I'm willing to start studying here in the yard."

Matthew raised his eyebrows. "I can navigate all right and I can teach you, but I've never been in the waters or harbors of Europe or particularly France or Great Britain."

"Captain Jones will take care of that. He's been everywhere. Went to sea at twelve. Born and raised in Scotland, and says he knows the Irish sea well."

Matthew was beginning to tire. "Can someone show me my quarters? I need to get settled and washed up, and maybe get a little rest."

"Certainly." Simpson stopped a passing seaman. "Young man, take Lieutenant Christopher to the ward room country. There's a vacant stateroom there."

Simpson turned to Christopher, "You'll be in time for supper if you don't rest too long. The food is good as long as we are in port."

A week later, after doing all he could to help with the recruiting problem, Matthew stopped by Captain Jones' cabin. Captain Jones called to him to enter when he knocked. Jones looked up. "Good morning, Christopher. Remember that you don't have to knock. I haven't seen enough of you. You should check in with me every day."

Matthew sat down, feeling that he had failed to do something Captain Jones had wanted done. "Sir, I haven't been up to see you because I didn't think I had learned enough about the personnel problem to take up your time."

"And now you're ready to talk about it?"

"Yes, sir. I've looked into all the steps you've taken. They are all working, but slowly. I suspect that the officers you sent out to recruit have not produced much in the way of results. I'm not blaming them."

Jones shrugged. "I didn't expect too much. I will have to get into that personally."

"Maybe not, sir. I think wider use of the bounty and the change in the length of enlistment will end the problem in a month. They did for Captain Biddle in Charleston. I predict the same results here."

"Do you want something else to do?"

"Yes, sir. I've looked over the construction of the ship. Inside, she's sound. She'll be slow as hell and slow to turn, but she is strong-hulled."

Jones slapped his leg angrily. "I knew it! I could tell just from looking at the hull and plans for the sails. And I never want anything but a fast ship. I'm hoping that when we get to France there'll be a larger, faster ship building in Amsterdam ready for us. I plan to keep the Ranger as a tender and consort."

Matthew pursued the subject of shipbuilding. "The rigging is way behind schedule. Unless somebody gets on the builder she will never be finished."

"You're right, and I think the builder, a bastard named Langdon, is deliberately trying to hold up the completion of the ship. I'll have to go over his head somehow and get the Marine Committee after him."

"Can I help?"

"Maybe you can drop a spar on him when he comes aboard."

Matthew laughed. "I'd like to."

Jones tired of the subject and handed some correspondence to Matthew. "You can read some of these letters I'm working on. Don't try to take any of the vitriol or sarcasm out. I mean it when I write it, and if I didn't put it in, none of the politicians or those damned congressmen would pay any attention to it."

"I'll take this with me and bring it back tomorrow."

"Yes, please do. I need a nap."

~

The next morning Matthew was back with the bulging portfolio of correspondence under his arm. Jones gave him a penetrating look and asked, "Well, what do you think? Speak frankly or your help won't mean anything."

Matthew took a deep breath. "Well, sir, the political stuff is deep water for me, but I like the way you have attacked it, and I hope it succeeds. I have a few suggestions, mostly about spelling and grammar."

Jones took them and leafed through the papers. Then he said, "Thank you. I see you've had more formal schooling than I've had, and that wasn't much. None after I was twelve except by my brother in Fredericksburg. I'm going to ask you to help me with my official reports from now on. They are very important, and are crucial to our success."

"Yes, sir."

"And now I want you to take on an investigation for me. Lieutenant Simpson is in charge of loading the ship with stores and victuals. We can't leave for sea until this is done completely. He is close to Mister Langdon, the builder, and I thought this would help, but it seems to hinder. I think Lieutenant Simpson is feeding information to Langdon who is using it against me to hold the ship in the yard while he collects more fees."

Jones flung some papers across his desk. "Look at this! Langdon has turned down a requisition for boatswain's pipes. He seems to think boatswains can give orders by whistling through their teeth. The dolt has never been to sea, yet he keeps telling me he knows more than I do about building ships, outfitting them, and even fighting them. He is the most overbearing, ignorant man I have ever met."

"Deliberately holding up the ship is too much. Are you serious, sir?"

"Yes, dammit. He has said as much in my hearing. Fortunately I didn't have my sword with me, or I would have run him through."

"I'll take care of the boatswain's pipes if I have to take it out of my pay."

Jones laughed. "Have you seen any pay yet since you've been in the Navy?"

"Well, no, sir, but I have money of my own. If I didn't, I could not have stayed in the navy."

"Too true, and I'm spending a lot of my own, as well. I resent having to buy rum for the ship, though. If you'll look at that other requisition, he's reduced it to thirty gallons for the whole ship for one cruise. Hardly enough for medicinal purposes. My God! There'll be a mutiny if the crew finds out that's all the rum we'll have. The British could run through thirty gallons a day and then some."

The next day Jones decided to bring the Langdon matter to a head. "I'm going to invite him down to the ship tomorrow to conduct an inspection with me."

The next morning Jones sent for Christopher. "I've decided to beard the lion in my den."

Christopher was puzzled. "I don't understand."

"Maybe I'm a little dense this morning. I spent last night thinking about Langdon." Jones handed Christopher an envelope. "Read this."

Christopher removed the contents of the envelope and read them. At first his face clouded, but as he read on, he began to smile.

Jones said, "As you can see, I'm inviting Mister Langdon aboard to inspect the ship with me to see how well he has done."

"Won't he find some excuse not to come? He will know from Simpson that you are very unhappy and will try to take it out on him."

"I thought about that. You will note that there is a lot of flattery in there and a lot of mention of the good features of the ship."

"I see."

"I think you do. No human being can resist a chance to be flattered in person. He'll be here. Now please hand this message to him personally."

The next morning, promptly at 9 A.M., a sleek carriage and four rolled up to the bottom of the brow. A man Christopher judged to be Langdon got out and started up the brow, carefully stepping on the small pieces of wood nailed to the large planks to provide traction. Christopher had never seen him, but the description given to him by Captain Jones matched the man laboring up the steep brow. Christopher noted that the man was not in particularly good physical condition. He was short, with proportionately even shorter legs. Altogether, he might weigh one hundred and fifty pounds. As he took his beaver hat off at the top of the brow in salute to the quarterdeck and the colors aft, a large bald spot was visible.

Christopher was more interested in his face. It was pinched. the eyes narrowly placed, and the lips thin and small. Langdon looked at Jones. Before he could say anything, Jones stepped forward and grasped him firmly by the hand and elbow. "Welcome aboard, Mister Langdon. I hope this morning will be pleasant and productive."

Langdon seemed to be taken aback by Jones' apparent hospitality. "Er, Captain, thank you. I'm glad to be aboard."

Jones turned toward Lieutenants Simpson and Christopher standing nearby. "These are Lieutenants Simpson and Christopher. You know Simpson, of course."

Simpson smiled and saluted.

Langdon grinned slightly. "Ah, yes, I do."

"You have not met Lieutenant Christopher. He is my aide and is an expert in shipbuilding. He was trained in his father's yard at Annapolis."

Langdon scowled and looked coldly at Christopher. Matthew was sure Lieutenant Simpson had been telling tales.

Jones went on, "You may have seen some of the Christopher-built ships around here. They are very fast."

Langdon scowled again. "Don't believe so. I doubt that yard has built many ships."

Christopher could not resist a dig. "About one hundred, sir. The Chesapeake Bay yards have built over five hundred since the start of the war."

"Haugh!" Langdon muttered.

Jones took his visitor by the elbow. "Come with me, sir. I'd like you to see the ship. The lieutenants will accompany us."

Jones began a clever manipulation of Langdon. Christopher grinned at his tactics while Simpson suffered. Jones began by praising some insignificant pieces of equipment. Then he complained bitterly about something else or a slowness in producing supplies.

Before Langdon could open his mouth to defend himself, Jones was off on another small Langdon triumph.

Christopher dug his elbow into Simpson's ribs on one such ploy.

Simpson glowered, "What's so funny?"

"I didn't think you'd like that one, but you must admit Jones is clever."

Simpson's lips compressed to a point they were almost as thin as Langdon's. "I think Jones is making a fool of himself," he said bitterly.

The tour was coming to a close, and Jones brought Langdon back to the quarterdeck. "Mister Langdon, I would be honored if you'd stay for lunch. My steward has prepared broiled Maryland crab cakes."

For a moment Christopher thought Jones had him as Langdon's face relaxed for a moment. Obviously Maryland crab cakes were a favorite.

Then Langdon recovered his dour countenance. "Sorry, Captain, I have a luncheon appointment with the mayor. Perhaps some other time. I thank you for the tour."

Jones got in one last dig as Langdon carefully made his way down the brow. "I hope you can remember all the points we discussed today."

Langdon, carefully watching his step, did not reply, but waved his ornate stick irritably.

Christopher moved over to Jones' side. "Captain, do you think you did any good?"

Jones laughed. "I doubt it, but I enjoyed watching him twist."

"Well, at least, now you can enjoy the Maryland crab cakes in peace."

Jones laughed, "There aren't any Maryland crab cakes within two hundred miles of here."

For two weeks Matthew ran down the requisitions for equipment and victuals that Captain Jones directed him to prepare. He became adept at circumventing Mister Langdon, skirting forgery and theft as closely as he could, and Captain Jones cheered him on, even suggesting new tactics. Simpson tried his best to find out what Matthew was doing, but Matthew kept the papers concealed under his mattress.

Slowly the holds and storerooms filled up, the rigging rose and was completed and tested, and new crew members clambered up the brow.

With a week to go before Captain Jones made final preparations to sail, the building yard had not completed a single set of sails. The captain grumbled, "Not only not a complete set of sails but no spares. Doesn't he think the wind can blow them out and British cannon balls can tear them up? The man is stupid."

Matthew laughed. "I hear you asked the ladies of Portsmouth to contribute all their extra petticoats to be made into spare sails."

Jones laughed. "Actually I've done something about those petticoats, and I'm not talking about extras. I mean the ones they are wearing, but they won't last long as sails. I think I'll give them back."

"Really?"

"Oh, yes, I'll enjoy giving them back as much as I did taking them off. Besides, I only wanted to embarrass Langdon by having the people of Portsmouth think he couldn't even provide the sails."

"You certainly hate Mister Langdon."

"Oh, yes. I've called him 'that stupid bastard' so often I'm beginning to think 'bastard' is his first name."

A week before Jones planned to sail, a northeasterly gale came up and blew steadily for five days. The ship rode to three cables and anchors. Jones ordered the top masts and rigging struck below, and the *Ranger* looked like a bare skeleton.

Jones spent the five days alternately cursing and pacing silently up and down the lonely quarterdeck in his oilskins. When he could stand it no longer, he went to his cabin. Then he sent for Lieutenant Christopher, who helped him prepare a series of caustic letters to members of the Congress and particularly to the members of the Marine Committee. Simpson tried to enter, but Jones threw him out.

"Wants to spy on me," he said. "Don't even hint as to what's in these letters. Take them ashore yourself as soon as the weather abates and post them."

On one occasion, Matthew looked up from an exceptional letter and said, "This doesn't sound like a sailor's writing. It is almost poetic."

Jones clouded up. "Dammit, Christopher, can't a sailor be something else, too? I think you should read more. That's where I got almost all of my education."

Jones pointed to a set of book cases, specially constructed so the books would stay on the shelves in a sea. "Take any of those you want. You will find much of the wisdom of the world in those books."

Matthew selected a half dozen, and as long as he was aboard, he read steadily, getting back into the habit his mother had insisted on.

On the 30th of October, 1777, Captain Jones called Matthew into his cabin. "I have here a will, duly signed and witnessed. Please go over and post it. In the second envelope is a bank check for a deposit on a small farm in Virginia. I hope I'll return to it some day."

"Sounds like we are preparing to leave, sir."

"Soon. Don't let any one know, but we are going to sail quietly on the first of November."

Chapter 21

Early the morning of the 1st of November, Jones came on deck, looked carefully at the weather in the east, and scanned the water over the side for signs of the current and tide.

He turned to Lieutenant Simpson, standing idly on the deck. "Mister Simpson, prepare the ship to get underway at 11 A.M. I'll conn us out. No pilot needed."

Simpson's jaw fell open. "But, sir, Mister Langdon doesn't even know about this!"

"And that is because you haven't had a chance to leak it to him. I don't want to see anyone leaving the ship before we sail either. Let me know when we are ready, and it had better be by 11 A.M."

Matthew stood on the quarterdeck, watching Captain Jones nonchalantly get the ship underway. Although the crew was unskilled and untried, the boatswain, a rough and burly Irishman named MacCarrick, roared at them and lashed the green hands into shape.

Jones watched the crew with interest, admiring the boatswain's performance and choice of salty and profane language, some of which he had never heard before. The boatswain alternated between deploring the mistakes of the green crewmen and questioning their ancestry.

Jones grinned at one involved epithet heavily laced with Gaelic. "Better than my own father could do after a horse had stepped on his foot," he said to Simpson.

Simpson blushed. "Well, at least I don't know exactly what he means."

When well clear of the harbor, Matthew, plotting on the chart, recommended a change to an easterly course. The captain followed his recommendation without question.

For two days Jones paced the deck impatiently, piling on all the canvas the ship would take.

Matthew, watching him, asked, "Sir, are we pushing this new canvas for some reason?"

"Ah, yes. I want to get to France as soon as possible to bring the news to the authorities of Europe of General Burgoyne's surrender. The news will be of great political significance and will help our country's fortunes in the courts of Europe. I'll only slow our crossing if we should chance upon a valuable prize.

"By the way, take time off from your navigating, go to my cabin, and look over my daily reports of our cruise. I want to keep the Marine Committee fully informed of what I am doing. They have given me a very open charter to do whatever I want to do in European waters, and I owe them a complete report. I will send them off at every opportunity."

Gradually the crew got better at changing and trimming sails, if not with skill, at least with celerity, because the boatswain drove them mercilessly. By now the crew had heard all his oaths, and he worked to dredge up fresh ones.

Jones, watching and listening to him admiringly, said, "He never fails to entertain me."

When the boatswain let them up, Gunner Dobie took over the gun crews, and the they ran the guns out, loaded, and fired, until they appeared to Matthew to know what they were doing.

Captain Jones, however, still was not satified, and hoped to have a few more days of drill before action might occur to test them. But it was not to be.

That morning the drill was interrupted by a report from the lookout, "Sail ho!"

Jones scampered up to the mizzen trees and was back in a minute. "Make all sail!" he shouted to the boatswain, who was on watch, "Beat to quarters!"

The crew reacted strongly to his enthusiasm, and the guns were readied in a record time. Matthew had never seen such speed on the *Randolph*.

Yet, Jones was still not satisfied, and his vitriolic tongue lashed those who were not fast enough. He even used a few oaths he had learned from the boatswain. Those who were slow tried to speed up, and the faster ones were even faster.

The *Ranger* bore down on the two hapless ships. Soon they were in range, and Jones ordered the gunner to try a shot. It was close, and the two ships ran down the British colors and came into the wind.

"Damn fools!" Jones said. "They should have separated to make it harder to take them both."

The whole procees was hardly a morning's work for Jones. He had two midshipmen and prize crews over in half an hour. Simpson was sent with them to make sure they put the arms of the ships under lock and gave them the order, "Proceed to French ports, either Brest or Nantes if you can get there, and the devil will take you if British ships capture you and retake our bloody prizes."

Matthew said, "They won't like a cruise in the British prisons, either."

Jones swore, using one of his new stock of oaths. "Right. I'm going to do something about that soon. Somehow I'll find a way to make the British pay."

When the boat was back and barely hoisted clear of the water, Captain Jones gave the order to resume all sail and head for France. "Give me a course," he said to Christopher.

Christopher looked quickly at the chart. "North by northeast," he said.

"Make it so," Jones said to the helmsman.

Simpson came up from the boat and reported, "Sir, the cargo was fruit. I brought some back."

"What kind?"

"Apples, pears, and oranges."

"Good." Jones acknowledged. "Send some to my cabin and I'll have pears for lunch."

Jones resumed his daily pacing, now satisfied that the crew was ready. He stopped by to look at Christopher's course line on the chart. "Not fast enough," he said. "Someone will beat us to Nantes."

~

On the 28th of November, as the great circle course took them near the Cape of Ushant, the lookouts sighted a convoy. Jones looked at it longingly, knowing that any long delay would put them in Nantes long after a fast sailing ship would be there with the news about Burgoyne.

Temptation overcame him. "Come about!" he shouted. "Beat to quarters!"

For a day he shadowed the large convoy, trying to cut out at least a slow merchantman, but every time he got in position, one or more large British frigates came after him, all sails set and their gun ports open for battle. "Damned British terriers!" he snarled. "I can't fight two of them before my gunners and sail trimmers are better trained."

"We can always get away from them."

"Not always. We're slower than Vermont syrup in the winter."

"But they cannot afford to leave the convoy for long."

"Yes. That would save us in a chase."

That night Captain Jones tried a new tack. "Get ready for night action," he said.

Simpson blanched. "But, Sir, we aren't trained enough to fight well in the daytime."

"Stop worrying," Jones said. "Let me know when you are ready, and send the gunner to me."

The gunner came trotting up and saluted. "You wanted to see me, sir?".

"Can we fight at night?"

The gunner shrugged. "Of course, sir, but our gunners are not very ready."

"We're going to try it. Now make all preparations."

The gunner grinned, saluted, and trotted off.

At dusk Captain Jones took a good bearing on the nearest merchantman in the convoy and estimated a course that would intercept it. He ordered the helmsman to come to that course.

Christopher pulled out his long glass and focused it on the hull of the merchantman.

"Can you still see her?" Jones asked.

"Yes, sir, but I can also see a frigate."

"Damn!" Jones said. "Keep on her and keep me informed as to her action."

The minutes went by. Just as Jones was about to order "Commence firing," Christopher sang out, "Sir, the frigate is headed for us. Her guns are run out, and she will soon be between us and the convoy."

Jones said, "Well, we'll leave a calling card. Fire a broadside."

Jones turned to the boatswain. "Wear ship!"

As the ship turned and the starboard battery opened up, Jones shouted, "Commence firing!"

The firing was erratic and ragged, but the projectiles fell in the path of the oncoming frigate.

Jones said, "So much for them. Now crack on all sail, and let's get out of here!"

The next morning Jones was still watching the convoy in the distance. He had not slept nor eaten for two days. Finally he said, "Damned ship! If it would only go two knots faster I could get around those damned frigates. I never wanted to sail a slow ship."

Matthew heard what he was saying, and he could not hold back. "Captain, if you'll let me make some drawings for you, I think we can add a knot or two to this ship."

"You don't think that that great seagoing shipbuilder Langdon built her right?"

"No, sir, I don't."

"I agree with you, and I complained daily about what he was doing, but I got nothing from the bullheaded bastard. Now I don't really care. I expect to be given a really fast ship now building in Holland."

"But if you don't get it?"

"Then we'll go on trying to fix this ship. I think we can do it together."

At the end of the second day Jones gave up. He had tried every possible tactic to get at the convoy, but the British frigates combined to anticipate his every move. He turned to Christopher. "Lieutenant Christopher, give the watch officer a course to Nantes. I must admit that those British frigate captains are the best in the world. I'll be in my cabin."

Matthew roamed the quarterdeck, thinking about the fact that they were getting farther and farther from Maryland and his family. He looked back over the boiling wake toward home, and wondered how long he could stay in the navy. There was no money in it and no future. Patriotism could carry him only so far, and he would have to make up his mind soon if something did not happen.

On the 2nd of December, the *Ranger* slipped quietly into the harbor of Nantes and anchored. Jones knew instinctively that he had failed to arrive first, and when his inquiries to the American authorities in Nantes revealed that a fast packet had preceded him by two days, he shut himself in his cabin with Christopher and began to compose a new series of letters to congressmen and government officials.

After a week he came out of his cabin, the letters in a portfolio, and went ashore.

Life aboard went on as usual without him. Simpson did his best to get the ship cleaned up, but the crew was surly and just went through the motions. Simpson asked Christopher, "What do you think is wrong with them?"

Matthew shrugged. "No pay. No rum. No time ashore. Any of them or all of them. The captain will make them look beyond all that when he comes back."

One week later the captain came back, said nothing, not even a greeting, and stomped into his cabin.

Matthew looked at Simpson and shrugged. "Let's just leave him alone. He will come out when he's ready."

Simpson sighed. "I can't figure him out."

Christopher looked at him searchingly. "You might try giving him what he wants."

Chapter 22

Two mornings later, Captain Jones burst out of his cabin, full of energy. He had a foil with him, and he rubbed his shoes on the clean deck and made several passes with it at an imaginary enemy. Having dispatched him with ease, he deposited the foil on the deck, and sought out the messenger, now cringing behind the binnacle. "Messenger, find Lieutenant Christopher for me."

The messenger burst into Christopher's stateroom without knocking. "Lieutenant, the captain wants to see you."

"All right. Be patient until I get my trousers on."

The messenger fidgeted. "Sir, I should tell you that the captain has his sword out."

Christopher came on the run. Jones said, "Come into my cabin."

Lieutenant Simpson, standing nearby, having witnessed the brief morning workout, asked, "Do you want to see me, too, sir?"

Jones laughed. "I don't think so. See what you can do to clean the ship up. It's still a mess, and looking at your muscles, or lack of same, I think you could use a little exercise with me in the mornings."

Christopher followed Jones into his cabin and watched as Jones wiped off his foil and put it away.

Jones said, "I want to go into the plans for upgrading the speed of this bucket. Did you complete the drawings you were talking about?"

"Yes, sir. They are over there in your book shelves. I'll get them out." He went over to one of several book shelves and began to rummage around.

Jones laughed. "What's the trouble? Can't find them in there?"

"No, sir. I put them on the shelf myself."

"Well, look some more. I do read the books, you know, and I may have moved them."

"Yes. sir."

"And Johnson does dust and straighten up."

Matthew sighed and bent over. "Here they are over there under your cot, sir."

"Oh. yes, I remember I was reading them last night just before I turned in. Very interesting stuff."

Matthew spread them out on the table.

Leaning over the drawings, Jones muttered loudly and tapped his forefinger on parts of the sketches. "This is good," he said at one point. "We won't have time to complete all of the others."

At the end of the hour, Jones sent for Lieutenant Simpson, the carpenter, and the boatswain. When they were assembled, he pointed to the drawings. "This is what I want. I'll be gone for a week. When I come back I hope to see this finished."

Followed by the other officers, Lieutenant Simpson took the drawings to the wardroom and spread them on the table. He studied the drawings, shaking his head frequently. Then he banged on the wardroom table. "The old man is crazy! This doesn't make sense. Langdon is one of the smartest ship builders in America. He didn't think these methods of building and rigging would work."

Matthew grinned. "But it will work. It has for the French and the Dutch and for ships built in our shipyard."

Simpson sighed, "I guess we will have to try it."

Matthew said, "I'll be glad to take charge of it."

Simpson nodded with relief. "You'll have to take responsibility for it when it's finished."

Matthew nodded. "The Captain takes chances. So will I. I will take full responsibility."

Simpson walked off, and the carpenter and boatswain crowded around to get better looks at the drawings. "Sir, explain this, please?" the boatswain asked.

Matthew said, "Very simple. We're going to shorten the lower sections of all the masts and shift the mainmast aft."

"You mean we can do this without the lifting of them by a sheer hulk?"

"Sure. I'll make it work. Obviously you will have to cut a new hole in the main deck and patch the old hole. Then you'll have to relocate the sockets in the keel."

"I've never done that," the carpenter said, pulling at his chin.

"I have," Matthew said. "I'll show you how."

"I don't know," the carpenter said, "it's a big job."

"It is, and shifting the ballast will be a dirty and smelly job, too, but all this will give us as much as two more knots. If we can make arrangements the captain wants us to careen the ship and clean the bottom, too."

"We've only been out of dock two months," the boatswain said.

"Yes, but a clean bottom will give us another knot."

"What's the point of all this?" the carpenter asked.

"You know Captain Jones. Speed is everything to him. It lets him catch another ship when he wants to, and it helps to get away when he needs to."

The boatswain laughed. "That ain't bad. I'm for getting at the work right away."

The carpenter began to grumble and shook his head. Matthew knew he would be a source of trouble with the crew, and he jumped on him. "Carpenter, after the captain gets back, he'll want to know how we made out. If I have to, I will tell him that you dragged your feet and the crew followed."

The carpenter's eyes widened.

But Matthew noticed that he did not deny that he had caused trouble. He would bear close watching. Matthew studied him more closely. His name was Cloughley, and his face always looked like he was beginning to grow a beard, but actually his facial hair was heavy and black and grew faster than he could keep it shaved. One morning Matthew had seen him taking a saltwater bath on the forecastle. Long black hair grew all over his arms, legs, and torso. He looked like a small black bear. The long hair on his head was clubbed with a piece of his carpenter's twine.

Somehow Matthew suspected that Cloughley's loyalty was not to Captain Jones, but rather to someone in the shipyard. Matthew decided not to trust him and to check everything he did.

The next morning Matthew decided to follow Captain Jones' example and got up early and exercised on deck using a foil. After a few minutes he found he was making imaginary thrusts at Lieutenant Simpson, Mister Langdon, the carpenter, and even the boatswain. He did not know the lieutenants well enough yet to know whether they were potential enemies.

He decided he had done enough with the foil and began to exercise his individual muscles. Then he stopped, breathed deeply, and thought about the boatswain. His name was MacCarrick, a second generation Irish-American. His accent was a mixture of Irish and New England. Unlike most red-haired Irishmen, he was not prone to bursts of temper, but was placid until aroused or until his duties called for a display of energy. Then his emotions came out in bursts of profanity that he seemed to think was usual language for talking to the crew. He appeared to be loyal to the captain, who in turn liked him. Captain Jones had never openly disagreed with him.

The boatswain was his only remaining choice to trust among the officers.

He picked up his foil and went below, ignoring the suppressed smiles of men about the deck. As the captain had predicted, the exercise made him feel better.

The next morning the captain appeared on the quarterdeck carrying a small bag. He turned to Lieutenant Simpson but made sure Lieutenant Christoper could hear him. "I'm going to Paris for about a week. I'm going to see Mister Franklin and others, and I hope to come back with good news. I want the changes in this ship to be made by the time I come back."

Simpson grimaced as he watched the captain climb down the sea ladder.

Mattthew said out of the side of his mouth, "Cheer up. We'll have it done."

Simpson turned to him. "Are you sure you can do it the way he wants it?"

"Certainly, but I'll need your help to keep the crew in line. The carpenter is trying to subvert them, and I may need to take him down in the bilges to straighten him out. If necessary, I will ask you to put him in his stateroom and I'll take over his tools and do the job."

"My God!" Simpson said, "The captain has infected you more than I thought!"

Matthew laughed, "That's possible."

One week later the Captain came back, as jaunty as ever, and ready to go. The moment his foot hit the deck, he said, "All officers to my cabin."

Simpson's expression was almost a sneer as he turned toward Christopher. "Now we'll find out if you are really responsible for what happened in his absence."

Chapter 23

Captain Jones could hardly stay seated. He was full of energy and ready to take on the world. As usual he clenched and unclenched his large sinewy hands. His feet and lower legs moved in coordination with his hands as if he were dancing. Under his white silk stockings and his tight white trousers, his long taut leg muscles alternately bunched and relaxed. Matthew had never seen him so emotionally and physically high.

Finally Jones could hold in his emotions in no longer. "I'm sure you all know I was to take over command of a larger, new ship building at Amsterdam, the *Indienne*. Big guns, lots of speed."

The officers looked at each other questioningly. Matthew said, "Captain, we've been shut up out here. They don't know you were to take over that ship."

Jones interrupted. "Well, no matter. It's off. The British got wind of it and started their usual machinations. Now she is to go to the French. I am to stay in command of the *Ranger*."

Matthew said, "Actually we are relieved. We would have missed you."

By now the captain seemed to be adjusting to the disappointment of not getting the large new ship. His muscles began to relax, and the tension went out of his face.

Jones went on, "I hope you've completed all the changes. I do not intend, as I've often said, to sail into harm's way on a slow ship."

Simpson started to say something, but Matthew beat him to it. "Yes, sir. It's all done. We'll add at least two knots, and the new position of the mast and the change of ballast will give the rudder more bite and we'll come about in two thirds of the usual time."

Jones' handsome face broke into a broad smile. "Good! Now that I'm no longer thinking of the disappointments of the past, I've got some plans for the future that will make you all happy. But first, let me give you a review of my trip. I had a conference with

Mister Franklin. He and the Secretary of the Marine Committee, Mister Morris, gave me direct authority to carry the naval war to Great Britain. This means entering the Irish Sea, going wherever I want to go, and doing whatever I want to do as long as I comply with international law."

Simpson, always more attentive to his personal financial future, asked, "What are the instructions regarding the disposition of prizes?"

Jones looked at him quizically. "Well, since you bring it up, we have orders to send all prizes into French and Spanish ports."

Matthew asked, "Are there any conditions under which we can send prizes to the United States?"

Jones laughed. "You always ask the right questions. I don't know the answer. But, I know you'll find a way to do what you want. The instructions have a clause that says prizes may be diverted to the United States in case of extended inclement weather or if the enemy is threatening. That should do it."

Matthew grinned. "Thank you, sir."

Captain Jones turned to another subject. "Mister Franklin, now our minister to France, has made available to me five hundred gold *louis d'ors*. I can do what I want with these, including giving the crew bonuses. For the moment you can hint to the crew that they will be getting a bonus of undetermined amount. Mister Franklin also gave me a letter to read to the crew complimenting them on their patriotism and spirit."

Christopher nodded. "That is a wonderful thing for him to do."

Jones smiled, remembering his visit with Benjamin Franklin. "He is a wonderful person. Sort of dumpy but underneath he is physically very strong. Wears some sort of double lensed spectacles he invented."

Matthew, always curious about engineering, asked, "How do they work?"

Jones shrugged. "I am no expert on the subject, but I think each half of the lenses is different. The lower half is for reading and the upper for seeing far off. Other than that, they are just like the ordinary spectacles others wear. I'm glad I don't need the damned things, anyway. Mister Franklin seems to be right at home with them. Said he could make out all the details of the ladies clear across the room."

Simpson cleared his throat, ignoring the conversation about Franklin's glasses. "I don't think that letter will have as great an effect as the gold."

Jones' lips curled and he said disgustedly, "Simpson, you certainly hoist your colors quickly. If you have nothing more important to say than that, you may go. Lieutenent Christopher, please stay behind."

After the other officers had departed, Jones turned to Christopher. "Did Simpson give you any trouble over the changes in the ship I asked you to supervise?"

"No, sir, but he didn't help either. In case you hear about it, I had to take a few chips out of the carpenter. Frankly, I think he is more loyal to Mister Langdon back in Portsmouth then he is to you."

Jones fingered his lip. "I agree. I've always suspected him. He's more out in the open than Simpson. I don't trust either one of them. I noted that the carpenter wasn't at our conference."

Matthew grinned. "He was, ah, nursing an illness. Maybe he ate something."

"Knuckle soup?"

"Something like that. He'll be all right in a few days, but I suspect you'll hear from Langdon about this some day."

Jones sighed. "I don't give a damn about anything he can do to me, but you'd better tell me all the details so I can protect you."

Matthew shook his head. "Well, it all started when I went down to the lower hold to look at the keel where I wanted to change the socket. The carpenter was down there on the deck above with six men. He was haranguing them about what a useless job this would be. Finally I came around the bottom of the ladder and confronted him. He sneered at me, and that was all it took. I rolled a couple of punches off the black mat on his chest and ended with another on his black chin. Then I inadvertently pushed him down the next ladder to the keel area. The men took off and ran topside. I went below to see how the carpenter had taken the fall. Fortunately for him he was unhurt, but when he got up and came after me, I laid a few right hands across his sneering face to make my point. I left him lying in the bilges and sent the surgeon down to bring him up. I told him I thought the carpenter might have slipped."

Jones slapped his thigh. "I wish I had been there."

Matthew said. "The surgeon says he'll be all right in a few days."

"Tell him to see me if he has any complaints and to put them in writing."

"I don't think you'll ever hear about this, and I'm not sure he can write."

"Who did the carpentering?"

"I did. I'm well experienced at this. I've done it before in my father's yard. I gave the carpenter back his tools a lot sharper and cleaner than when I borrowed them. I don't think he's much of a carpenter."

Jones got up and paced the deck in his small cabin. "Now that we've got that all settled, my next move will be to have our flag saluted by the French. I have made some preliminary arrangements, and we'll get underway soon."

Three days later, a messenger was rowed out to the ship with a dispatch box across his knees. He insisted on delivering it personally to Captain Jones.

Jones called Lieutenant Christopher into the cabin to help him sort out the papers in the box. "Here," he said, "is a copy of the recent treaty between the United States and France. With this in hand, I'll be free to attack the British in their home waters, even in the Irish Sea. All of the rumors I told you are true, and we will carry out my long anticipated plans for the welfare of our country and eventually for the prisoners-of-war."

"Yes, sir, but which comes first?"

"First, I intend to select an American merchant ship to convoy to Quiberon Bay. The large expanse of water of the bay occupied by many French ships with embarked French flag officers will be ideal as a stage for our first exchange of salutes. The shore is a busy place in close proximity to the anchorage, and will offer a good view of the ceremony. Word will be spread through Europe in a few days, and we will command its respect."

"Do you have a ship in mind you intend to convoy to Quiberon Bay?"

"Yes. The *Independence*. She's at anchor nearby. Take my gig and inform the commanding officer that he should be ready to leave on the 10th. We will arrive at Quiberon Bay about the 13th, wind permitting. Remind him to have his saluting battery ready, and, when I hoist the appropriate signal, make a salute of thirteen guns."

"I understand, sir."

"Then be off. This will be an historic occasion."

One hour later Christopher came back and climbed up the sea ladder. "All is arranged, sir. The captain of the *Independence* is honored to be selected to carry out your orders and to help you make history."

Chapter 24

On the 10th of February 1778, the *Ranger* got underway, her new rig enabling her to manuever out of the harbor quickly. Her increased speed was evident, although Christopher complained that there was not enough ballast in the hull to do the job he had in mind even after he had shifted all of it on board to new locations.

"Never mind," Jones said, slapping the bulwark ebulliently, "This will do for now. I shall purchase another fifteen tons of lead in Quiberon Bay or in Brest."

Christopher beamed. "Thank you, sir, I know we will then do better."

On the 13th Jones anchored the *Ranger* off the entrance to Quiberon Bay and sent Lieutenant Hall by longboat to call on Rear Admiral Picquet of the French Navy. As he watched the long boat disappear, the oarsmen pulling aganst a strong offshore wind, he said to Simpson and Christopher, "Clean up the ship. After an exchange of salutes, we will be visited by seniors who will be curious as to what kind of ship we Americans keep. We want to make a good impression."

Simpson asked, "Sir, why did you bother to send Lieutenant Hall all the way in there?"

"I wanted to assure myself that the Admiral would actually return my salute. If he did not plan to, we would both be embarrassed. Now we both know what to do, and we can both play our roles in history."

Simpson shrugged. "Sir, I don't see why we are making such a big thing out of this salute."

Jones bristled. "My God! Simpson, don't be such a dolt. This is an historic occasion. It will be fired to a foreign nation which will, by replying to it, acknowledge the existence of our fledgling country. It is the first salute to the American flag ordered by Congress."

"Wasn't there a salute of some sort fired in the Caribbean not long ago?"

"Yes, but not an official one ordered by our government. This one will be officially ordered and will be known throughout Europe. The work of our consular and Ambassadorial officials will become much easier."

"Then you think it is important."

"Oh, yes. We will make every effort to do it right and on time as well."

Simpson shrugged. "I'm not convinced, but I will do my best to have it done."

Jones glared at Simpson. "You will or I'll confine you to your quarters."

With the offshore wind holding its direction and intensity, the longboat had no trouble making the trip back. When it came alongside, Lieutenant Hall climbed the sea ladder, and greeted Captain Jones with a broad smile. "Good news, sir. The French Admiral will return your salute as you expected, and he thanks you for informing him of your plans."

Jones slapped his thigh enthusiastically. "Get underway immediately. Inform the *Independence* that she is to stay at anchor. I don't think she could make it to the anchorage before dark against this wind. Prepare the saluting battery. I am going below to change my uniform and put on my sword. You do the same, and pass the word that the crew is to be in full and complete uniform. I will throw any man over the side who doesn't look top hole."

Jones was on deck in minutes, resplendent in his dress uniform and sword. The captain had designed his own uniform, patterning it after the new Continental Navy uniform, but his version also owed much to the Royal Navy. Such as it was, it was well-tailored, clean, and the gold stripes glowed.

Simpson was still below, but the boatswain was on deck sweating in the heavy breeze to ready the ship for getting underway.

Jones fretted. "How long, Boatswain?"

"Two minutes, sir."

Jones opened his long glass and took a look at the *Independence* nearby, still at anchor. He shook his head. "I'm sorry to cut him out of this, but he'd never make it. I'll include her tomorrow in my plans for a second salute from both of us."

The boatswain shouted, "Ready, sir."

"Very well. Hoist the anchor and make sail."

Simpson came clattering up the ladder, his sword catching on the hatch coaming. Jones shot him a look that bordered on contempt. "Well, sir, you're a bit late." he said. "Fortunately your sword arrived at the same time you did."

Jones looked about the weather decks, surveying preparations. He noticed the perspiring boatswain. "Ah, Boatswain, I see you already have your dress uniform on. How were you able to do that?"

McCarrick stopped for a moment. "Sir, I sent a hand down below to fetch my kit. Then I changed into it in the manger when I was supervising the hoisting of the fore sails."

Jones laughed. "Aye, I knew you Irish could get your trews off in a hurry."

The boatswain grinned. "Sir, put a bonnie Irish or Scottish lass up here with me and I'll do it even quicker."

Jones nodded. "We Scots have always been good at that, and we don't want to be outdone by the Irish. Well done!"

The ship gathered way, and the sails bellied out in the strong wind. After one mile on the first tack, Jones ordered the boatswain to prepare to come about, and then gave the order to the helmsman to change course. The ship swung quickly and steadied on a new course.

Jones shook his head. "It will be dark when we get in position. Stand by to fire the salute at six bells no matter where we are at that time. Have all guns loaded with saluting charges."

The gunner scurried to load the guns with small charges, each with a lanyard rigged to it to permit withdrawing it if it was not fired.

Jones paced eagerly, hoping their new speed and the changes in the ship would help.

Promptly at six bells, with the ship in the middle of the channel, but still downstream from where Jones wanted her, Jones ordered, "Commence salute."

Gunner Dobie pointed at the forward starboard gun, and it went off promptly. Five seconds later the gunner pointed to the port forward gun. It fired, and then he pointed alternately to the other guns until the salute of thirteen guns had been fired. Each interval was exactly five seconds. Jones had the use of his pocket watch, and he marvelled at the gunner who had timed the explosions so exactly in his mind.

Jones was exultant. "Damned good!" he said. "Very seamanlike. I'll have to buy you a watch, or at least a sand glass, not that you need it!"

Then he put his long glass on Rear Admiral Picquet's flagship. The glass was not necessary because the flame and smoke of the return salute was plainly visible, but Jones wanted to watch the activity on the quarterdeck. "There's the Admiral walking about on his quarterdeck. He wouldn't miss this. I think he is as interested as we are."

Nine guns boomed, with Jones counting carefully. "That's it. Come about! We'll return to the outside anchorage. Tomorrow we will do it again with both ships and we'll move closer to the French ships so they can see better."

After the *Ranger* anchored, Jones sent Lieutenant Hall to call on Rear Admiral Picquet to tell him that he intended to enter the inner harbor tomorrow with the *Independence* accompanying him, and repeat the salute with both ships. He briefed Hall carefully.

An hour later Lieutenant Hall returned. "Sir, the Admiral was very complimentary and says he looks forward to tomorrow," Hall reported.

"How did he appear to be taking this?" Jones asked.

Hall said, "He was genuinely enthusiastic, and that is an understatement for a Frenchman. I think he really liked what was going on and realized he was being a part of history, as all of us were. He spoke mostly in English. He filled in with some French I could understand."

At 9 A.M. Jones got the two ships underway with a flurry of flag signals. The wind had abated, and the entry into the inner harbor was easy.

The salute went off with precision again, with the *Independence* joining in.

Jones ordered "Down sails. Anchor when our way is off. Send a signal to the *Independence* to follow our motions."

Jones turned to Simpson. "We'll be deluged with visitors this morning. Sweep down carefully and make sure the crew is in full uniform all the time they are topside. I'll throw any man overboard who does not comply."

For once, Simpson said, "I understand, sir."

Boats began lining up to come alongside within the hour, and Jones stood at the gangway receiving visitors. Matthew watched him. He turned to Lieutenant Hall standing near. "He really likes this sort of thing. I have never seen him happier."

On the 5th of April Jones received a communication from the Secretary of the Marine Committee. He called Christopher into his cabin and read the dispatch to him. "The *Randolph* blew up at sea while engaging the enemy. There were no survivors, and there is no known cause."

Christopher blanched. For a few seconds he could not speak. Then he said, "Poor ship. Poor Captain Biddle. They were just getting good."

Jones asked, "Do you think you know the cause?"

"Yes, sir. The gunner took too many chances. However, I will admit they were short-handed, and he did what he had to do to keep the captain happy."

Jones shuddered. "I'm going to inspect the magazines tomorrow."

"Yes, sir, I'd like to come with you."

Jones soon tired of life in Quiberon Bay and planned to move to Brest where he hoped to exchange another salute.

The results were disappointing. After the exchange of salutes, he said, "Damned country town! Nobody ashore paid any attention."

Christopher said, "But the ships in port saw it, and the word will be passed along."

Jones grumbled as he rubbed his carefully shaved chin, "We're just wasting powder. I think we should use it to shoot at somebody."

Matthew tried to keep from smiling. "Sir, you've changed your mind again. A few days ago gun salutes were at the front of your mind."

"Well, not anymore. Now we'll do the really important things."

When he had his attention, Matthew prevailed on him to buy another fifteen tons of lead ballast and have it loaded according to his theory.

Three weeks later Jones gave up, got the ship underway from Brest, and set a course for the Irish Sea. When the ship was settled on course and clear of the coast, he called a conference of the officers.

Chapter 25

Jones could hardly wait for the officers to assemble. He drummed nervously on his desk. "Come in! Come in!" he shouted. "I want to get started."

They crowded in and ranged around the bulkhead of his cabin. Jones turned to Christopher. "Lieutenant Christopher, the extra ballast worked fine. I had to give up some of Mister Franklin's *louis d'ors* to pay for the lead, but it was worth it."

Matthew beamed. "Yes, sir, and you won't be able to test our improved ability completely yet."

"How much additional speed do we have now since we made these changes?"

"About two knots, including the temporary increase from cleaning the bottom. This will last maybe six months until the hull is cleaned again."

"Well, we'll try to clean the bottom as often as possible. What about maneuverability?"

"We won't really know until we've had enough time at sea to test it out. I still expect to decrease the time to tack by one-third."

Jones beamed. "I'll take it all. Those sorts of things can win battles."

"That would help, sir."

"Yes, speed, dash, and victory go together."

"That's what you've been saying."

Jones laughed, "You learn fast."

Jones could wait no longer. Spread on his table was a chart covering Ireland, England, Scotland, and the Irish Sea between them. The officers leaned forward eagerly to see what he was doing.

Jones slammed his open hand on the area of the Isle of Man in the middle of the Irish Sea, just below Kirkcudbright peninsula. "This is where I was spawned and raised and went to school until I was almost twelve years old. I haven't been back since, except for a brief visit or two. Now I'm going to make a visit those English will never forget. First, I'll take every prize we meet on our way north through the Irish Sea."

Of all the officers looking on, only Simpson did not smile.

Christopher interrupted. "But you said that's not our objective."

Jones laughed. "Christopher, you always cut to the quick. Certainly it's not our primary objective. After taking prizes in the English backyard and making this seem routine, I want to make the English afraid that we and the other American ships will attack them on land, too."

"I have a third objective. The British have been mistreating their American prisoners for months. Hundreds have died and many hundreds more are malnourished. After the next phase of our campaign is completed, I intend to take a hostage of importance to the British and trade him to the King of England for our prisoners-of-war.

"But back to our second objective." Jones slapped the chart again, this time pointing to a small port named Whitestone. "This is where it will be."

Simpson, still unhappy, said, "That's not much of a port, Captain. Can't we do better?"

Jones shook his head. "Certainly it isn't very big as compared with the major British ports. The size of the port means nothing. Always strike where you can find the enemy concentrated and they cannot defend themselves very well. It has a high tidal range. When the tide is out, there will be one hundred and fifty warships and merchantmen sitting aground on the mud flats. Not many of their guns will bear, and I think the ship's crews will be ashore thinking they will be safe from attack. Actually, they will be at our mercy."

Simpson shook his head. "I prefer not to have anything to do with this operation. There's a chance the shore batteries will sink our boats no matter what we do there. There'll be no material gain for us."

Jones barked, "I knew what you'd think. I won't even let you go ashore, Simpson, and only those who go ashore will share in the reward from Mister Franklin's gold fund."

Lieutenant Hall spoke up. "I think the same way Lieutenant Simpson does. The chance is not worth the reward."

Christopher shook his head and thought to himself, "The poor bastard has been listening to Simpson. They're both going to end up swinging from the same yardarm."

Jones was exasperated. He looked at the two officers. "Dammit! I'll lead the party myself. There will be two boats, each loaded with fifteen men. Marine Captain Wallingford and Midshipman Hill will go in the boat to take the north wing of the harbor.

"I'll command the whole expedition and the first boat. Lieutenant Christopher, you will go with me. I'll leave you in charge of the second boat while I take a small party to spike the guns. Our Swedish Lieutenant will go with you to stay in the boat if you have to leave it for any reason. I don't trust the boat crews to be left by themselves. I've been smelling mutiny."

Jones looked sneeringly at Simpson and said, "Lieutenant Simpson, you will remain in commmand of the ship while I am away. If you move it so much as a fathom while I am gone, I'll have you drummed through the fleet."

Matthew said, "Sir, the fleet isn't within three thousand miles."

Jones grumbled, "Then I'll run him through several times with a dull sword."

The mysterious young man named Smith spoke up for what seemed to be the first time on the voyage. "Sir, I'd like to be in the northern boat."

Jones was hesitant, but finally he said, "All right. Just don't get in the way."

Jones looked around the cabin at each officer in succession. "Any other questions?"

There were none, and Jones said, "That's all. Let's make all preparations and make sure your lanterns and matches are ready and in good shape."

Early the next morning the lookouts sighted a sail. Jones watched it carefully as they closed on it. "Too small to bother with," he said. "We'll sink it and put her crew in her boats. We're close enough to let them get ashore. They'll spread the word around, and that will make the people put pressure on the politicians, who in turn will bother the Royal Navy, and that will get to the admirals ashore. Then all hell will break loose."

A second ship showed up before dark, but it was larger. Jones bore down on it and ordered it to surrender. Its colors came down promptly, and a midshipman and prize crew were put on board with orders to take it to Brest. Two of the crew who claimed to have special piloting knowledge of the area and didn't like the British were taken aboard. Jones said, "They'll be useful on this voyage."

As the *Ranger* drew off to the north, Jones said, "Enough of this. Tonight should see us off Whitehaven."

It did, and Jones conned the ship into the harbor entrance against a stiff wind and in the gathering darkness.

Simpson stood on the quarterdeck glowering. He muttered to Christopher, "Now see what will happen. We and our boats will be under fire before we can reach the shore."

Christopher shook his head. "You are imagining things that won't happen. The city is dark over there. I think the people who live there are asleep and the ship's crews are ashore in the grogshops or in bed."

At 11 P.M., after the boats were ready to lower and the crews were mustered on deck, Jones decided the wind was too high. He withdrew.

The wind increased rapidly, and Jones had to browbeat the boatswain and his men to get enough sail on in order to claw off the shore. The crew was unhappy about their mission and took every opportunity to show the captain their displeasure.

The next day, the *Ranger* encountered the fast revenue vessel *Hussar* and attempted to make her provide them with a pilot, but her captain refused, and Jones tried to sink her. Her speed and maneuverability enabled her to escape, followed by rising geysers of foam. Jones watched her go. "To hell with her! We'll go in without a pilot."

On the 22nd the wind was down, and Jones put the *Ranger* in position for an attack that night.

Jones again asked Simpson and Hall if they wanted to go ashore. Both claimed to be ill. "I think it was something we ate," Simpson said.

Jones sneered. "You ate something yellow."

Christopher stepped between Simpson and Jones, expecting a physical clash, but Simpson subsided and strode over to the lee side.

When he was sure Simpson could not hear him, Christopher said, "Captain, why do you continue to suffer the conduct of that mutinous bastard, I think you ought to order him before a court martial or at least get rid of him. I will be glad to testify against him, and Johnson has heard him preaching treachery and mutiny to the crew several times."

Jones put his hands behind his back and pursed his lips. "Ah, youngster, you have not experienced the depths of American politics. The bottom of the barrel is stinking."

"But it is clean and clear out at sea. Next time I will let him strike you and you can take action and see what he will do."

Jones grinned. "Yes, but he probably won't. He is too cowardly."

"But why does he continue to act like this?"

"He wants to command this ship. The easiest way is to get the politicians in Washington to throw me off and give her to him. You can bet he's taking every opportunity to write to his friends to accuse me basely and falsely."

"But if it doesn't work?"

"Then he hopes to incite a mutiny and have the crew get rid of you and me. Then they'll give the ship to him."

Christopher shuddered. "I'll throw the bastard over the side some night rather than let him have the ship."

Jones laughed. "Just be sure it's a dark night."

After sunset Jones gathered the two boat crews on deck. "Men, stay with me. The first ashore will be the first off, and you'll be rewarded that way."

Jones conned the ship in again against a lightening wind but an adverse tide. This time it was much easier. As before, the city was completely dark. Jones looked at the shore. "They'll not know we are here until it's too late for them."

He anchored the ship at about midnight, and the crews embarked in the lowered longboats.

Matthew made sure Johnson was one of the crew of the other boat. "Watch out for Smith, and let me know what happens when you get back."

The Swedish officer, Lieutenant Meier, was added as planned to the crew in Jones' boat, but since he was Swedish, Christopher would be in command when Jones was absent.

The oarsmen started out pulling eagerly, but the trip was longer then they expected, and their enthusiasm lagged. Jones watched them carefully, suspecting they had been subverted by Simpson and might be turning mutinous.

The dawn began to break, and Jones dispatched the second boat to the north as they entered the harbor. He had committed himself to this operation, even though it was no longer protected by the darkness. The port slumbered on. There was no reaction from the soldiers in the fort, the crews of the ships, or the townspeople, and he hoped for the best. He turned to Christopher, sitting beside him. "Nothing good happens unless you take a chance."

Chapter 26

The boat assigned to the north sector of the harbor disappeared slowly in the murkiness of the dawn. The oarsmen labored to make progress against the steady breeze and tide and tried to keep their oars rigged in muffled oarlocks to be as quiet as possible.

The boat quay ahead of the first boat was empty, and Jones ordered the coxswain to steer for it and go alongside. "Careful," he said, "The stone steps are wet from low tide and moss-covered."

Once alongside, Jones jumped out, sword in hand and walking carefully, but slipping slightly anyway, in spite of his own warning. He pointed with his sword to three men he had picked out. "Follow me," he said.

Christopher took all but Lieutenant Meier and the boat crew and left to start fires in the ships alongside the jetty. "Secure the boat," he said to Lieutenant Meier. "Don't let any of the crew disembark."

Matthew gestured to the eight men. "Follow me. Bring the matches and lanterns."

The men followed Lieutenant Christopher, moving carefully along the steps, and keeping a lookout for local citizens. No one stirred, and no dogs barked. They boarded the first ship stealthily, but there were no ship keepers in sight on their decks.

"My God!" Christopher said, "This place is like a graveyard. Bring forward the matches and lanterns, and let's get started before someone wakes up."

There was no trouble starting a fire in the first ship, but it spread slowly. The sailors were hesitant to move to a second ship. One man complained that his lantern was out, and another put his out.

Christopher shouted, "The next man who tries to sabotage this operation will feel the flat of this sword. Try it a second time, and you will feel the point!"

Matthew sent a man to find a barrel of tar to feed the flames, but he had no success in finding one or did not look very hard.

Jones soon came running back, followed by his men. "We're safe. We spiked all the guns." he said. "Why aren't there more fires?"

Matthew shook his head. "These men either are scared of the sleeping population," he said sarcastically, "or they have been subverted by Lieutenant Simpson. I haven't been able to do much by myself."

Jones looked toward the north. "Damn! I don't see a single fire up there and our boat is heading back. I also don't see many of the townspeople out there."

The noise and flames spread slowly on the ships near them. It woke the townspeople near the jetty, and perhaps one hundred men walked slowly down toward the boat, pulling on their clothes and rubbing their eyes.

Jones leaped out of the boat and walked toward them, brandishing his sword. They stopped fifty yards away. "Get the men in the boat," Jones shouted over his shoulder, still facing the gathering crowd with an apparent calmness that bordered on disdain.

The boat crew tried to shove off from the landing without Jones, and Matthew, who had boarded it with his men, had to strike two of the crew with the flat of his sword to keep them from throwing off the mooring lines. The Swedish lieutenant also yelled at the crew and felled one with a skilled blow of his hand.

Jones retreated slowly, watching calmly. Three hundred townspeople were now milling about but would not approach Jones. Jones turned on his heel and walked slowly toward the boat. "Let's go!" he said calmly, and he carefully walked down the green steps, avoiding the slippery parts. He stepped gingerly into the boat and stood in the stern sheets.

The boat crew now threw off the mooring lines, and rowed away as fast as they could under Captain Jones watchful eyes.

Jones said, "You didn't row that fast coming in. Stop worrying. Those people can't swim."

Just as both boats passed beyond the arms of the entrance to the harbor, two cannon balls flew by wildly, bouncing twice on the surface of the water and sinking at the end of their shallow trajectories.

In a few minutes the boats were out of range, and all the passengers relaxed.

Matthew said to a large marine sitting next to him in the bow, "I thought Captain Jones said you had spiked all the guns in the fort."

The marine shrugged. "They were all spiked by our party, and I saw it done myself. Those balls must have been from two guns that were lying on the jetty and not on carriages. I don't think they can do much with them because they can't aim them. We didn't bother to spike them."

As the firing from ashore fell off, Christopher sat back on his thwart forward where Jones had placed him. "Get up forward," he had said. "That way if any one of them starts anything we'll have them between us. I expect to keep my sword drawn. You do the same."

Now that he had time, Christopher said to the large marine sitting next to him, "You said you were with Captain Jones and the group spiking the guns?"

"Yes, sir. There were three of us."

"Tell me about it. It must have been hair-raising."

The huge marine grinned. "That it was. It was quite a trip, but in the end not very dangerous. I would go anywhere with Captain Jones now."

"Tell me what happened to you to make that decision."

"The captain led the three of us up the street at a run, and he was in pretty good shape. Never even breathed hard, although I was puffing halfway there."

"Nobody stopped you?"

"No, sir. There wasn't a sound in any house. Not even a dog barking." Then he grinned. "These English dogs are poor watch dogs. All they do is sleep."

"And so you got to the fort easily?"

"Yes, sir. We made a quiet pass around the walls that faced the harbor."

"Were they high?"

"About twelve feet. There were firing apertures every few feet, about three feet below the top of the walls. The captain had me hoist him on my back so he could peek in one. 'Nobody in sight,' he said."

Matthew was becoming interested in the marine's account and squirmed on the hard thwart despite the captivating words. "What happened then?"

"He says, 'Boost me up.' I stood up straight, and he could just reach the top of the wall. It was easy for him to pull himself the rest of the way up. The other two men followed him up, and he leaned over and looked down at me. It wasn't hard for him to figure out that I was too heavy to make it up there, as I was all alone with no one to boost me up. He said, 'Stay on watch down there and keep any of the townspeople who show up away. Yell to us if you need help with them.'"

"And you couldn't see any of the rest of it?"

"Hell, yes, sir. We marines never say no. I dragged a barrel over and got up on it. I could see it all through a firing aperture, as we marines call those holes in the walls. Actually they work both ways and I could see inside just as well as soldiers inside could see out."

"They must have spiked the guns in a hurry."

"Oh, yes, they did it quickly and as quietly as possible. The people must have heard the noise of the hammers on the spikes, though."

"How did they use the spikes? Did the marines know how to use them?"

"Not at first. It was the first time most of them had done it. Captain Jones did one to show them, and they did the rest of the guns. Just regular carpenter's spikes pounded into the touch holes. The regular gun crews could get them out, but only after a couple of hours of work, and two hours was what the captain wanted."

"Nobody showed up, not even the soldiers?"

"No one."

"That was it?"

"Just about. After they had pounded spikes in all the touch holes so the guns couldn't be fired, Captain Jones said, 'Leave the extra spikes and tools here. We can make better speed without them.'"

Christopher laughed. "He always wants to go fast. What did you do with the tools?"

"Just left them there as the captain said. Two large hammers and several spikes."

"Where did you get them from?"

"The captain said he got them from the carpenter, and he didn't care if he didn't get them back."

Christopher pounded on his knee. When he stopped laughing, he said, "The hairy bastard will be mad as hell when he finds out who took his tools."

"I don't think so. I heard the captain say he'd pay for them. Now the carpenter will have some new hammers."

Christopher shook his head, "It looks like everybody will be happy except Lieutenant Simpson."

The marine said, "I don't understand, sir."

"Nevermind. We're almost to the ship. You did a good day's work. Well done."

In one hour the boats were alongside the ship, and the crews were on deck. Jones strode up and down in front of them. "Not much of a show," he said. "We could have burned a hundred ships. The fire might have been seen in London, and we'd have made great history. I know you dolts don't care about history, only your own hides. Half of you should be put to the gratings, and the other half of you should be pushed over the side to join your English friends."

Jones turned to Lieutenant Wallingford. "What happened in the north, Wallingford? I didn't see any smoke from up there. Your matches wouldn't light?"

Lieutenant Wallinford shrugged. "I don't really know, sir. Our men couldn't seem to keep the lanterns lit, and then a lot of townspeople came out and gathered around us. It was evident that somebody had alerted them."

Jones asked, "Are you missing any men?"

"One, sir."

Johnson pulled Matthew aside. "That bastard Smith is responsible. He's a traitor. I saw him knocking on doors and yelling to the people who came out that the Americans were here and that the Irish would save them. If I'd had a gun, I'd have shot him right there on some bastard's doorstep."

"Tell me more about what you saw."

"I was surprised that the two officers did so little, and didn't take charge."

"What do you mean?"

"When we saw this Irishman run up the steet and knock on the first door, I offered to run after him and bring him back the hard way."

"Lieutenant Wallingford wouldn't let you do it?"

"No. He seemed scared as hell that a bunch of Brits would burst out of the doors and capture us."

"Did that bother you?"

"Hell, no. We had the boat close by. We were armed, and the Brits were sound asleep. They don't wake up very fast, and they wouldn't have reacted very quickly to a nut pounding on their door. As it was, he had a tough time just getting a few gents out in their nightgowns. Most of them took one look and slammed their doors in his face."

"And you couldn't get the marine officer to do anything more to carry out Captain Jones' orders?"

"No, sir. Every time I lit a lantern some son of a bitch put it out. I finally gave up and watched the show. I never saw so many men just giving up and quitting."

"Thanks, Johnson, I will take it up with Captain Jones as soon as I can."

The next morning Matthew went into Jones' cabin without knocking. Jones was busy writing his official report. He threw the finished pages across his desk to Matthew. "Look at this," he said.

Matthew read it rapidly. "Sir, you say you lost a man. You didn't name him."

Jones shrugged. "I don't think that's important."

"Sir, he was not named Smith. The crew knew his name was actually Freeman. He was an Irishman and a traitor to our country.

The crew knew all about him when he came aboard. I think Lieutenant Simpson should do a little investigating. There may be more like him aboard."

Jones pushed his chair back. "There's more to this. I have to tell the Secretary of the Marine Committee later about him, but I don't want to make this a matter of official record. Someone on the Marine Commmittee knows about him all right, and some congressmen are sponsoring him. There are many disloyal men masquerading as congressmen. Some of them support the Irish cause, too, and say helping it is a way of fighting the English. There are a lot of troubles and disagreements that will have to be straightened out one day before we are a unified country."

"Wouldn't Mister Franklin like to know about him?"

"Of course, and he'll set Congress on its ass over it, but you have no idea how difficult the practice of politics is in the Congress. Now let's drop this until I can see Mister Franklin. It has to remain in that channel."

"Captain, there wasn't much of a fire last night, but it will light up the world and particularly Great Britain. You have shown that we can attack them on land in their own country as well as at home. We have shown that we can go ashore wherever we want to."

"The Royal Navy will have to withdraw ships from other parts of the world in order to patrol their own waters. They'll never know now where American ships will turn up."

Jones laughed. "At least they will be afraid I will show up to tweek their mustaches or to kick their butts."

"Now what's next?"

"I'll tell you later." Jones pushed aside the remains of his breakfast. "I'm sorry you weren't with us spiking the guns. It was glorious. It seems the British soldiers had all gone inside the fort to keep warm while they slept. The British soldier is a good sleeper and apparently gets up late. I had to stand on the shoulders of one of our tallest men to get in the embrasure. Inside two of us quickly spiked thirty-one guns, and no one tried to stop us."

Matthew said, "Sorry I missed it, but one of your marines told me all about what happened. We had a near mutiny on the boat.

Some of the crew were on the verge of leaving without us. Lieutenant Meier took over and stopped them with a little help from
me. He deserves a lot of credit."

Jones shrugged. "I know the whole crew is right on the edge,
and Simpson keeps them there. I'll have to be strong with them. I
would by no means have retreated while I had a chance of even a
partial success."

"And now?"

"We're about to get underway to fulfill my next objective.
We're off for St. Mary's Isle, but before we go, we'll take a look to
see if the *Drake* has been flushed out or is still lying there waiting
for us to take her."

Chapter 27

After the boats were secured and the crew had finished its breakfast, Jones got the ship underway and headed directly for St. Mary's Isle, about two hours sailing from Whitestone. The island was small but seemingly spacious because it was sparsely populated. The small farms were beautifully kept, and the trees and bushes around the small houses of the village were neat and orderly.

The ship hove to off the entrance to Kirkcudbright Bay, and Jones assembled the party he wanted. When he called them to the quarterdeck, they fell in in two ranks standing quietly and admiring the scenery ashore, while Jones made last minute adjustments to his uniform and sword.

"Looks like a park in Portsmouth," one man said.

An answer came from the rear rank. "I haven't seen anything in Portsmouth like this, especially in the winter."

"You live on the wrong side of town."

Captain Jones, now ready to board the boat, barked, "Quiet in the ranks!"

This time Lieutenant Simpson volunteered to be a part of the early party. Jones said aside to Christopher as they stood on the quarterdeck, "Now he wants to get in on the action. He knows there'll be no fighting and maybe there'll be some loot and he wants some of that."

Jones took Lieutenant Simpson, Marine Lieutenant Wallingford, Lieutenant Christopher, and ten armed men, many of whom had been in the boat during the affair at Whitestone. As they were rowed in, Jones briefed them. "I want to kidnap, to use the word, Lord Selkirk. I aim to exchange him for American prisoners-of-war. No matter how many I can free, I hope also to embarrass the King and make him treat the American prisoners better. If he doesn't, he can expect a repeat of this operation somewhere else. I'll keep at it until he gives in, and I am deadly serious in this matter."

Matthew looked back at the ship. She was lying to, her gun ports covered so that she looked like a merchantman, and she flew a British flag.

Ahead lay the green island. The boat came to a landing, and the party disembarked, led by Captain Jones. A group of men stood nearby. Some were young, but most were old, and none of them seemed to have anything better to do.

Jones and Christopher approached them, while Lieutenant Simpson lined up the armed men in two ranks.

Jones said to one of the older men, "Are there any other merchantmen in port?"

The younger men eased away from Jones and ran away up the paths. Nobody answered Jones' question.

Jones laughed, "They think we're British and want to press them into the Royal Navy. I don't blame them. I would run away, too."

An old man stayed behind, leaning on a sturdy cane. Jones said, "Old man, you have nothing to fear. I don't think we want to press you."

The old man said, "Aye, and you bastards would feel my cane if you tried. What are you doing here and who are you?"

"We're from the American Navy."

The old man shook his head, "That do beat all. I heard of America, but I didn't know you had a navy. I thought you were British. That's what your flag says out there on your ship, although I don't see too well anymore."

Jones colored. "Well, sir, flying that flag is what's called a ruse."

"Russians, are you? I thought you said you were Americans a minute ago."

"No, sir. I meant we are Americans and are temporarily flying the British flag, a procedure that is considered legal. The British Navy does it, too. Before we fight we will show our true colors."

"Well. I don't recollect I have ever seen an American flag. What does it look like?"

By now Jones was losing his patience, "Sir, I'll show you one sometime, but now I have to get on with my business. We're getting late."

"Business? You're a bunch of damned merchants. Thought you said you were from the American Navy?"

Jones rolled his eyes patiently. "I came to capture Lord Selkirk and to trade him to the King of England for American prisoners."

The old man cackled and seemed to be slightly confused. "What do you want with him?"

"As I said, I expect to trade him to the King."

"What? You really are Americans?"

"Yes."

"Well, don't that choke the horse. Lord Selkirk ain't here right now. He's in London. Even if you took him prisoner, it wouldn't work."

"Why not?"

"The King hates him. He'd make you keep him."

"Damn!" Jones said. "This is a bad day."

Jones turned to Simpson. "We'll return to the ship. Enough of this."

Simpson scowled and said, "Sir, please reconsider. These men, most of whom were with you last night, need some kind of loot. So far they've got nothing but loss of sleep, and they aren't patriotic like you are. Can't we go to Lork Selkirk's castle and take something back? The British do that to us in our country all the time."

Jones pulled at his lip. "Well, I'll have nothing to do with this personally. You may take the men to the castle. Ask Lady Selkirk for the Selkirk silver plate. You are not to allow any of the men to go inside the castle. You, Wallingford, and Christopher may go inside the door. Get back as soon as you can. I'll wait by the boat."

Simpson led the group up one of the paths, following instructions from the old gaffer, who still didn't seem to realize just what was going on. As he limped off on his cane, he muttered, "Americans, Russians, they don't seem to know who they are, but I know they ain't English. Maybe Scots or Irish trying to make trouble. And as for the captain, he can't make up his mind. Came rushing in here, and now he's just pacing up and down, waiting for his men to go off somewhere and trample the grass. I think Americans are off it."

Jones took Christopher aside as the group departed. "Go with them. If Simpson gets out of hand and disobeys my instructions, take over. I'll back you up later. Don't let them chivvy Lady Selkirk or her house staff. I plan to purchase the silver myself later and to return it to the Selkirks."

Matthew strode up the path, following the Simpson group, and accompanied by a small boy who had been standing by listening to the proceedings. The urchin said, "Ain't this pretty. These trees are a hundred years old and the bushes are all newly trimmed."

Matthew grinned. "There are old trees in America, too, but we don't bother to trim the bushes. We just let them grow independently, just like our states."

The boy said, "Don't your states have to answer to a parliament?"

"Something like that. We call our legislative body a Congress."

The boy shrugged. "I guess no matter what you call it, you don't like it."

Matthew grinned. "Yes, you're right. All they do is tax us."

Soon Matthew caught up with Simpson and his group of armed men. He stayed close enough to see what went on but not so close as to interfere.

Simpson tramped up the path, ahead of his sweating men, his face grim and avaricious.

Matthew shook his head, expecting the worst, but Simpson stopped short of the castle door and lined up his men near the front entrance.

Some of the men asked to go in, but for once Simpson was firm. "You'll stay in ranks, or you'll see the gratings when we get back to the ship."

Simpson knocked on the door, Wallingford standing nearby to one side.

Lady Selkirk's butler opened the door. His eyes widened, but he retained his composure. "Yes, sir?"

Simpson said grumpily, "I want to see Lady Selkirk."

The butler bowed and said, "Please come in. She's upstairs, and I'll call her."

Matthew went in behind the other officers and moved to one side. Lady Selkirk came down the stairs, obviously pregnant, and said, "What can I do for you, gentlemen? I understand you want to press men, and I don't have anybody on my staff of the age you might want."

"We are from the American Navy and we don't want to press anyone, at least not openly." Simpson loked at the butler's fat figure with disdain. "We don't want any of your men."

Lady Selkirk bridled. "I'm sorry if you don't seem to like any of them, but they serve me faithfully."

Simpson frowned. "Never mind that, madam. I'd like for your butler to bag up your silver plate and give it to me."

Lady Selkirk raised her chin and turned to the butler. "James, please put all of my silver plate in bags and give it to this officer."

The butler put on a small pocketed apron and began to take the silver carefully out of a high cabinet.

Simpson said in his best sneering tone as he watched the butler's slow progress, "Please hurry it up. We haven't got much time for this sort of thing."

Christopher was amazed at Lady Selkirk's composure. She stood aloofly, her arms crossed in front of her. She watched all the proceedings carefully although she was seemingly unperturbed.

Matthew noted that the butler attempted to slide several pieces under his butler's apron and into the small pockets, but decided not to say anything.

Lady Selkirk saw him and said, "James, don't try to hide any. Give all of it to them."

Christopher could keep silent no longer. "Lady Selkirk, I admire your conduct in such a difficult situation. Captain Jones, in command of the ship to which we are attached, plans to buy the silver back and and will return it to you whan it has served its purpose."

"But why are you going through this charade, sir?"

"I am not at liberty to tell you why we are taking it, only to assure you that it will not be damaged and will be returned very soon."

Simpson said to Christopher in a low tone, "That's what you think. Something may happen to some of it."

Lady Selkirk said to Christopher. "You make me feel better about Americans. I have heard that they are generally boorish, but you and the marine lieutenant here appear to be quite gentlemanly."

It was obvious that she was not including Simpson in her remarks.

Simpson snorted, realizing he was not included in the exchange. He turned to the laboring butler, "Speed it up, fatty," he said in his usual tone.

Lady Selkirk raised her chin even higher and turned to the officers, "Gentlemen, would you like a glass of wine?"

Both Simpson and Wallingford acepted, but Christopher declined.

In a few minutes the silver was in bags. Lady Selkirk said, "Please sign a receipt."

Simpson shook his head and pointed to Wallingford. His embarrassment was so deep Matthew realized he could not read very well.

Wallingford stepped forward, read the paper briefly, and signed the receipt.

All the officers bowed to Lady Selkirk, following Christopher's example, and left the castle.

Matthew followed the group to make sure no one took any of the silver out of the bags, within half an hour the group was back at the boat landing.

Jones was still pacing up and down, obviously impatient and out of sorts. He looked inquiringly at Lieutenant Christopher. Matthew nodded in assent to indicate that all had gone well and the silver was safe.

Jones said, "Embark. I want to get on with flushing out the *Drake* from her snug harbor. I'm good at fighting them at sea, but I don't understand their damned English politics."

Christopher said, "There must be other ways you can think of to make the King treat our prisoners-of-war better."

Jones shrugged. "Let me know if you have any ideas. Right now I am tired."

"Sir, I assured Lady Selkirk, in your name, that you would purchase the silver in the near future and have it returned to her."

Jones shrugged and raised his shoulders, trying to ease the fatigue that seemed to be creeping over his usually vigorous body. "Of course I will."

Christopher kept talking, although Jones plainly wanted silence. "Sir, this was a useless exercise, and it will take a lot to undo it."

"I agree, and I would not do it again, but today is not the time to talk about it."

Christopher said, "I think you were pressured by Lieutenant Simpson."

"Of course."

"Sir, I admired Lady Selkirk. You would have liked her. She was a true lady in the English tradition."

"I am sure she was."

Christopher grinned, remembering the events. "I wish you could have seen her take Lieutenant Simpson down. It was worth the whole trip."

Jones came to life. "You mean he offended her?"

"Not on purpose. He was just his usual boorish self, to use her phrase."

"Then I'm sorry I missed it, but enough talking. I need to rest now."

Chapter 28

The next day the weather was blustery, and Jones took the ship to shelter under the lee of the Irish coast. For several hours the ship sailed at minimum speed as Jones was trying not to get too far downwind from Ireland. When the weather broke, Jones said, "We'll take a pass by Carrickfergus to see if the *Drake,* a British frigate, is there. I heard she might be there from a fisherman we captured and kept aboard."

Matthew said, "The crew is very restive. Can we take a chance on this?"

"I think so. They'd like to take a prize when we have an advantage of some sort and there is little personal danger to themselves."

"I don't understand."

"That's the situation I'm trying to set up. I expect to enter the harbor at night disguised as a Dutch merchantman. We'll destroy her topside by raking her from astern before she can get to quarters. The men will like that. Even old yellow Simpson will agree with that."

Christopher nodded. "I see what you mean."

Jones called Simpson over and outlined his plan. Simpson smiled for the first time in weeks. "I think the crew will understand this."

Jones said, "I thought you'd like it. Get busy disguising the ship. Put canvas over the gun ports. Have a Dutch merchant flag ready to hoist and an American flag to hoist before we open fire. Instruct the crew to stay out of sight and keep a minimum number of our men on the open deck at all times. I presume the British captain is smart enough to have lookouts on both headlands of Carrickfergus Roads. We want them to report us as a bumbling merchantman with just a small crew wandering about topside."

Simpson smiled enthusiastically. "It will be done right away, sir.

Jones nodded. "We will enter the harbor at midnight. Have the men on the forecastle ready to drop the anchor promptly at my order. We'll go right across her stern, and after we anchor we'll be in positon to rake her repeatedly. She won't be able to fire back except with her stern chasers even if the crew is partially alerted."

Christopher was less enthusiastic than Simpson had been. He muttered, "He'll have it all fouled up somehow."

Jones heard his muttering, "What was that?"

Christopher thought better of his judgement. "I think he'll get it done, sir."

As the ship approached the entrance to Carrickfergus Roads, the men took position for battle. Some behind the bulwarks were ready to climb to the foretops with arms and hand grenades, small cans of black powder fitted with fuses. The marines crouched below the bulwark. The members of the crew needed for manning the guns and trimming the sails stayed below at the bottom of the hatches.

Jones gave the order. "Clew up except for topsails and jibs. Stand by the port anchor. I want it let go the moment I give the order."

The ship sailed in slowly as Jones used the captured fisherman to help pilot her.

Just before the ship reached the position where Jones wanted to anchor her, a gust of wind came up and her forward progress increased moderately, but he thought she was still close enough to the position he wanted to anchor. "Let go!" he called.

Nothing happened up forward and the ship forged ahead. "Damn" he shouted. "Let go! Or I'll throw you all over the bow. The anchor was dropped a little later, and Jones could see that the ship had travelled too far past the stern of the *Drake* to be able to rake her. Now some of the broadside guns of the *Drake* would bear on the *Ranger* but the *Ranger*'s guns could not fire aft. Jones knew when to retreat. "Cut the cable!" he shouted, hoping the watch on the *Drake* would think they were just a clumsy merchantman trying to anchor.

The wind increase held, but with the anchor cable cut, Jones skilfully brought the ship around, narrowly missing going aground on the opposite side of the harbor entrance.

Still there was no reaction from the *Drake*, and Matthew let out his breath as the ship barely cleared the nearby harbor entrance arm.

"Jesus!" he said, "Simpson has done it again!"

"No, no! Not this time. The boatswain is in charge of operations up there."

"Dammit! What happened?" Jones demanded as the boatswain came running aft.

"Sir, my mate got a bottle or two from one of the fisherman prisoners. He was too drunk to carry out my orders on the anchor properly."

"I take it you took care of him."

"Yes, sir, he's lying in the cable tier. I don't think he'll be able to eat for a week, and he'll be lucky if his jaw isn't broken."

Jones shook his head. "If it isn't, I'll break the empty whiskey bottle over his head."

Testing the wind, Jones said, "This is over for tonight. The wind will increase. We'll have to shelter under the lee of Scotland."

For several hours the *Ranger* cruised with sails closely reefed near the lee shore of Scotland. Jones paced the quarterdeck, grimly swearing new oaths no one had ever heard him use. Nobody dared come near him except Christopher, but even he wisely stayed away.

Early on the morning of the 24th, Jones was ready to try again, but he realized that stealth might not work this time. He cruised by the entrance to the Road of Carrickfergus, and the *Drake* was still anchored there.

Jones called his officers to his cabin. When they were all there, he said, "I am going to lure her out of the harbor so I can take her."

Simpson was doubtful. "How so, sir?"

Jones looked at Simpson as if he did not understand the rules of the game. "Simpson, disguise us as a merchantman. He'll want to take us as a prize."

Simpson spoke up quickly. "Sir, the crew is nearly mutinous now."

Jones flushed, "If they show it openly I'll not hesitate to issue summary death sentences, and you can tell them that. I'll try to lure her out into the open sea and still maintain the weather gage. I'll guarantee we'll beat her with little loss. Now start preparations for battle. By the way, if there is a mutiny and I put it down, you will be one of those tried and hung from the yardarm."

Simpson blushed and had trouble talking. "No, sir, I won't be involved."

The officers left, and Simpson soon began his usual actions, talking subversively to small groups of the crew.

Johnson heard him and went to Christopher. "Sir, he's at it again."

Christopher sighed. "I heard him tell the captain he wouldn't be involved in this sort of thing."

Johnson shrugged. "Seems like he's lost his fear of the yardarm."

"Yes. I wish he'd show the same courage for a good cause or in battle."

One hour later Johnson came to Matthew again. "Sir, the crew is really restless. That bastard Simpson is still doing his thing. They threatened to throw the captain over the side and to turn the ship over to Simpson."

Matthew said, "Thank you. I'll tell the captain."

When Matthew repeated Johnson's information, Jones looked surprised but then guffawed. "Thank you, but I will handle this. I will be wearing my sword from now on, and my men won't face it. Keep your sword on, too, until the battle is over. Once we've won, they'll turn to something else. If we take the *Drake* with little loss, and I think we will, they'll forget all this. I hate to say it, but the prospect of prize money can change the feelings of American sailors overnight."

Matthew said, "There are times when I am ashamed to be an American. I don't think British sailors are like this, even though they have more provocation."

Jones nodded. "I agree with you, but these men of our crew aren't average Americans. Most of them came from jail or were lured into service by bonuses. You must remember that in the main all Americans are malcontents who fled Great Britain just a few years ago to get away from cruel indebtedness or crimnal charges of doubtful validity. Those aboard like you, Johnson, and Wallingford, are exceptions. Your kind must lead our country in the years to come and not the Simpsons."

At noon the *Drake* loosed her sails and appeared to be coming out. A barge from her rowed toward the *Ranger*, which was still disguised as a merchantman. Jones, looking through his long glass, could see his counterpart on the quarterdeck looking at him through his own long glass. The British captain seemed calm and apparently unaware that he was facing a warship.

Jones counted the guns on the British ship and estimated their size. "We'll outgun them," he said.

The barge came closer and the officer hailed the *Ranger*. The young midshipman appeared unconcerned, apparently believing he was approaching an innocent merchantman.

Jones ordered marines to rise from behind the bulwark and hold their guns on the barge.

The young officer was no fool, and he quickly surrendered, raising his hands over his head and giving the order to cease rowing.

Jones said, "Take him in tow."

Now Captain Burdon of the *Drake*, watching through his long glass, knew that something was awry. He began to pace his quarterdeck and shout orders.

Captain Jones remembered Burdon from the days they had served together in the Caribbean. Jones recognized his lanky, thin form, and when Burdon raised his hat to mop his brow, Jones could see his mostly bald pate. Still, Jones knew him to be a formidable opponent; good at seamanship and gunnery. Burdon's hawk-like nose and fierce close-set eyes could not be seen at this distance, but Jones remembered them and resolved to give him due respect.

Burdon was not the most intelligent commanding officer Jones had encountered, and he thought he could out-wit him. Burdon had already revealed his weakness by sending an unarmed boat after a large ship, even if it did appear to be a merchantman. This was a risk a good captain would not take.

Jones made sure there was no longer any doubt. "Hoist the American flag." He turned to the boatswain. "Use the speaking trumpet and tell him 'This is the American Continental Navy Ship *Ranger*. We are waiting for you. Come on out. The sun is setting, and it is time to begin our fight.'"

Jones could see the captain of the *Drake* become more animated, as he issued orders to his crew, but he did not answer the challenge by voice.

Jones said, "I'm sure he heard that. The boatswain could raise the dead. I think he's coming out and just hasn't gotten around to answering us."

For a few minutes the *Drake* pressed on, hoisting more sail and clearing away all of her guns.

"That does it!" Jones shouted exultantly. "We're about to do battle." He turned to the waiting helmsman, "Two points to port please."

The helmsman spun the wheel, and the ship quickly swung to port. When the broadside would bear, Jones shouted, "Commence firing!"

The battery fired as one. Gunsmoke swept to leeward, and Jones waited patiently for it to clear, but without waiting for the results, he ordered, "Four points to starboard, please."

Again the ship swung rapidly, this time to starboard.

Christopher noted that the ship was now swinging more rapidly with the changes he had made. He clenched his hands with satisfaction.

Jones looked at him as the ship swung and smiled, "You did this," he said. "Your work made it possible."

When the ship was steady, Jones shouted again. "Fire the port battery!"

This battery also fired in unison, spewing what looked like a single sheet of flame and a deadly hail of iron that tore the rigging of the British frigate. This time the smoke cleared more rapidly downwind while the guns rumbled across the deck in recoil.

Still the *Drake* had not returned fire. Jones looked at her decks. "They're not even completely at battle stations. I gave them plenty of warning. They're just slow."

Jones kept tacking back and forth to alternate his battery firings and to maintain the weather gage.

The *Drake* finally got off a few shots, less than a complete broadside, but the fire was ineffective.

Matthew, walking behind the gun crews, noticed that the crew had changed from being surly to embracing Jones' expertise. The whole atmosphere had changed in only a few minutes.

Jones continued to order alternate broadsides, on the seemingly helpless *Drake*. In a last gasp, she managed to put a single ball aboard the *Ranger*. The ball caromed from one bulwark to the other, finally hitting the gun carriage of one of the after guns. A few splinters wounded some of the gun crew, and one flew toward Jones. He staggered briefly but did not say anything.

Christopher ran over to him. "Are you hurt, sir?"

Jones shrugged. "Just a small wound, I think." He looked down at his hip. A three inch rip in his white trousers was soaking slowly with blood from a wound below it. Jones took a clean kerchief from his pocket and shoved it down inside his trouser waistband. "Not bad," he said. "I'll fix it later when I have time."

Christopher turned his attention to the sailors of the gun crew who had been hit. The men who had sustained wounds were being looked at by Lieutenant Wallingford and the gun crew. "How are they?" Christopher asked.

Wallingford said, "Nothing serious, but the surgeon will have a lot of work with his needles."

Suddenly it was over. The quartermaster shouted, "Sir, the enemy has struck her colors!"

Matthew could see that her topside was a wreck, but no shots appeared to have penetrated the hull. The masts were intact, but all of her spars lay crooked, and some were on deck, tangled in sails. Her rigging was almost completely parted and the sails were torn badly.

Jones looked at the *Drake* through his long glass. Then he irritably handed it to a quartermaster. "Here, I don't need this thing.

She is close enough to see clearly, and I don't see her captain. He must be down."

Christopher, who was also looking at the beaten ship, said, "I agree, sir, the quarterdeck is a shambles. I don't think anybody who was on it could have survived."

Jones nodded. "I'm going over to take the surrender."

"But, sir, you're wounded."

Jones looked down at his trousers. There was a trail of blood on one leg from hip down to knee. Jones shook his head. "A bit of blood, but no problem. I can go easily."

He turned to Simpson. "My gig, please, sir. Embark a squad of marines and let me know when its ready."

Jones sent for the boatswain. "Boatswain, bring her in the lee of the *Drake* and lie to. When I leave the ship, Lieutenant Simpson will be in command."

Ten minutes later Captain Jones gingerly climbed the sea ladder of the *Drake*. He favored his wounded leg slightly. At the gangway he paused and looked aft. There were no colors hoisted, so he saluted the quarterdeck.

Two officers and a small group of marines stood on the quarter-deck, obviously disorganized. The *Ranger* marines were then lined up in two ranks by the corporal in charge opposite the *Drake* men.

Jones said, "Where is your captain?"

The senior lieutenant stepped forward. "Sir, he was killed early in the engagement. So was the first lieutenant and forty-two men. The captain's body is in his cabin. I have his sword here." He held it out toward Jones.

Captain Jones took it, almost tenderly. "Thank you, young man. I regret the loss of your officers and men and of course your brave captain. My condolences to all. The prize master will be over as soon as I return to my ship. My marines will remain here tem-porarily."

Jones turned on his heel and carefully saluted the quarterdeck, again noting that there were no colors flying aloft or aft.

Five minutes later he climbed the sea ladder at the *Ranger* even more gingerly.

On the quarterdeck Lieutenants Simpson and Christopher were waiting for him.

Jones said, "The captain and the first lieutenant are dead. Also forty-two men. She's seaworthy, or will be after repair. Lieutenant Hall, take the carpenter and ten men and man her as a prize. Send fifty prisoners over here. You will keep me in sight at all times and we will head for Brest. Let me know when you are ready to proceed."

Christopher said, "Sir, your wound hasn't been attended to yet. Shall I send for the surgeon?"

"I think the surgeon will still be attending our wounded. I'll go to my cabin. Please join me and bring Johnson with you. I'll need you both."

Christopher sent for Johnson, and when the two entered the cabin they found Jones carefully peeling off his tight trousers to reveal the wound. When he took the kerchief off, he said, "Not bad, and the bleeding has already stopped. I think it should be sewn up. Johnson, please fetch my shaving things from that cabinet over there. Also bring some clean kerchieves, and my sewing kit. You'll find them back of that metal basin next to my shaving kit."

Christopher said, "We'll need a couple of buckets of clean salt water. I'll send for them."

While water was on the way, Jones sat in a camp chair and removed his shoes, trousers, and stockings. When the buckets of water arrived, Jones said, "Johnson, please put this clothing in one of the buckets. My mother taught me that cold salt water would remove blood. I got a lot of it on my clothes when I was a lad. I can use these garments again."

Jones grinned. "My mother also taught me to take care of my clothes. They were hard to come by when I was young, and these trousers can be mended."

Johnson said, "Sir, I'll do it for you."

Jones shook his head. "Thank you, but I'll do it myself. Something else my mother taught me."

Johnson took a closer look at the wound. "Not too bad. I've sewn up worse than this one on my pappy on after a big Saturday night."

Jones sighed. "I'm beginning to feel a little weak, or I'd do it myself. Use some of the clean thread from that sewing kit and cover it with a clean kerchief."

Johnson pulled out a splinter carefully, washed the wound out with clean salt water, and sewed up the open wound with quick overhand stitches. "Six stitches. They are not as fancy as the surgeon would put in, but they'll work just fine. I'll take them out in a week."

A messenger knocked on the door.

"Yes?" Jones asked.

"Sir, Lieutenant Simpson reports we are ready to proceed."

"Very well. Tell him to lie to until the prize is ready to get under way." Jones sighed. "I'll be here in my cot until we're ready to sail."

Johnson took the extra bucket of water out, and Christopher stayed behind. "Do you want anything, sir?"

Jones shook his head. "No thank you, but I've been wondering about that dead captain of the *Drake*. I shouldn't talk about him now that he is dead. After all, he gave his life for his country. Still, he didn't measure up to my expectations of most British frigate captains. They are noted for their dash, speed, and courage. I'll give the captain courage, but somehow the *Drake* wasn't handled very well, and certainly not with much speed or dash."

Christopher shrugged, "They can't all be like you."

Jones laughed. "I hope not. Otherwise I'd never win."

Christopher asked, "Why did he come out when he did? He wasn't ready."

"I don't think he had any respect for us. He wasn't quite sure what kind of ship we were."

"Was it because he didn't think any American ship would be a danger to him?"

"I think that was a good part of his miscalculation. Most British captains are good frigate captains, think they can beat any ship of any navy, and have no respect for American ships."

"I think they'll soon learn that the Americans are not to be tri-fled with."

Jones said quickly, "Oh, yes, they will when we win more bat-tles. This is just the start of a new era of increased respect for our new navy."

Chapter 29

As the two ships lay to the next morning, Jones, now rested and up at dawn, had himself rowed over to the *Drake*. When he returned, he called Lieutenant Simpson to his cabin. "Lieutenant, I have just made a careful inspection of the Drake in company with Lieutenant Hall and the carpenter. They've been working all night and haven't made much progress. I conclude that she could be put into shape for sailing by tomorrow with proper attention. All that is necessary is the replacement of some spars and the rigging. There are no major holes in her hull. I want you to take charge of four additional men and finish necessary repairs."

Simpson cleared his throat, and Jones knew what was coming. Simpson said, "Sir, I don't think it could be done short of a week or more."

"That's just what I thought you'd say. Send Boatswain MacCarrick to me."

The boatswain came in, and Jones repeated his assessment of the damage to the *Drake* to him. "Do you think you can make repairs by tomorrow?"

McCarrick shrugged. "Sir, I haven't seen her up close, but if you say it can be done, I'll do it. Certainly I could repair her enough to sail her."

Jones grinned. "That's more like it. Go to the *Drake* as prize master and take over from Lieutenant Hall. If you need help from Lieutenant Christopher to make additional repairs, send me a message."

The next morning Boatswain MacCarrick reported that he was ready to proceed, and Jones called Christopher to his cabin. He pointed to a chart lying on the table. "Here we are. I'm going north around Ireland instead of south. The British may be looking for us to the south now. Also, we'll pass Carrickfergus Roads, and

I want to put all of the fisherman off. They did me a good turn with their piloting advice."

When the ship was off Carrikfergus Roads, closely followed by the *Drake*, Jones came in close and sent the fishermen ashore. He gave them all the ready money he had in his pocket. "To compensate you for your lost time," he said. "I hope your fishing in the future will be better."

The captain of the fishermen grinned as he pocketed the money. "Good luck, sir, call on us at any time."

While the ships were lying off, waiting for the boats to return, Simpson ran up to the quarterdeck. His face was suffused and he was obviously disturbed. "Sir," he said without any preliminaries, "I think you have maligned and ignored me and my service. I believe I was responsible for the expert firing of the gun batteries, which were my responsibility, and which damaged the *Drake* so badly. I think I am deserving of receiving Captain Burford's sword."

Jones was astounded, but he held his composure. "Lieutenant Simpson. You surprise me, but at least you are now strong enough to speak out."

Jones sent to his cabin for the sword. When it was placed in his hands, he said, "The engagement with the *Drake* was one of the finest I have ever seen, and I'm proud of this sword. Nevertheless, I present it to you. I will also acknowledge your service by sending you to the *Drake* to take over from the boatswain as prize master."

Matthew, watching from nearby, expected Simpson to turn down the assigment, but then Simpson saluted and said, "Aye, aye, sir."

Jones went on, "Keep close company with me. We are bound for Brest, but you are not to enter before me if we are separated. Keep close to me on my starboard quarter and pay attention to my signals. Do you understand my orders?"

Simpson saluted, "Yes, sir."

On May 5th, The two ships arrived off Ushant, not far from Brest. The *Drake* was taking on water and was not handling very well.

The *Drake's* sails and rigging had been severely damaged in the fight, but the boatswain had made extensive repairs and had reported that the ship could be handled well if attention were paid to the various jury rigs. Jones did not expect Simpson to know what to do, so he closed the *Drake*.

Jones came under her quarter and tried to hail the quarterdeck, but Lieutenant Simpson was not in sight, and the watch on the quarterdeck did not hear him.

Jones said, "That's enough of this fiddling. Prepare to tow her."

Jones moved closer and hailed her again. Then Simpson came on deck, just having awakened.

Jones yelled at him, "Get ready to be towed."

Simpson nodded, and soon men on deck began to make preparations to take the towline.

Jones said, "Your command is poorly handled. You must do better next time."

Simpson's mouth flew open and he started to say something, but he soon realized Jones would not listen to him. He turned on his heel and stormed below.

Jones took her in tow with Simpson still below. He brought the *Ranger* upwind of the *Drake* and sent a messenger line to the *Drake* as the *Ranger* ranged alongside. A heaving line and then a light messenger were rapidly replaced by a heavier line and this was finally atached to the towing cable of the *Drake*. On the *Ranger* the towing cable was quickly secured to a set of bitts aft. The men on the *Drake* payed out the towing cable to a proper length for a long catenary as the *Ranger* drew ahead. When the towline was out to the proper length it was secured to a set of bitts on the *Drake's* forecastle. When all was in readiness, the *Ranger* hoisted more canvas to add speed.

On the second day of tow, the lookouts sighted a sail. Jones cast off the tow to give chase, but the *Drake*, instead of heading for Brest to the west, turned east and seemed to be heading for America.

In exasperation, Jones gave up the pursuit of the sail and went after the *Drake*. Darkness overtook them, but the next day the *Drake* appeared again, and Jones overtook her. When he was close enough, he ordered her to lie to and sent Lieutenant Hall with six marines over to the Drake to relieve Simpson. "If he won't consent to being relieved, tell the marines to take him into custody."

Jones paced angrily, watching the progress of the party on the Drake under Lieutenant Hall. He could tell that Simpson was angry with Hall, but the marines were more than Simpson could cope with. When they moved toward him, he shook his head and in a few minutes boarded the boat.

When the boat came alongside the *Ranger*, Jones watched in silence as Simpson climbed the sea ladder. Simpson saluted the colors and walked rapidly toward Captain Jones, his face clouded with anger. As he neared Jones, he began to talk rapidly.

Jones raised his hand imperiously and cut him off. He would not listen to him.

Jones said, "Your orders were clear and your intentions were just as clear. You are under arrest. Go below."

Simpson turned on his heel and stormed below.

Matthew said, "He is getting pretty good at that maneuver of storming below."

The two ships turned together toward Brest, but within the hour the lookouts reported a sail. Jones said, "I'm sure Lieutenant Hall will carry out my orders with no trouble. We'll see what this ship is. Hoist a British flag and head for her," he said to the master. He had finally decided to use a master and had found one in Brest. Now he was occasionaly allowing the master to handle the ship, and he had turned over Christopher's navigational duties to him.

In an hour the *Ranger* overtook the sail. Jones, looking at it through his long glass, said, "She's a two-masted brig, fairly good-sized. Probably not a very big crew, but low in the water. Probably with a cargo from the Indies. She seems to think we are British, although there isn't anything she could do no matter who we are."

The wind and seas were very light, so it took some time to overhaul the slower ship. When the *Ranger* was close enough, Jones didn't even bother to fire a gun. He ordered the British flag hauled down and the American flag hoisted.

The other ship simply gave up, lowered her colors, and came slowly into the light wind.

Jones decided to test the skills of his new master. "Master, bring her alongside."

The *Ranger* banged slightly as she came alongside the brig and Jones had lines thrown over.

Matthew could see the name *Mystery* on the counter. Two British officers were on deck, but the rest of the crew was black. Jones, sword in hand, swung aboard followed by the marine lieutenant and a squad of marines. Christopher followed, his sword at the ready. Jones sought out the captain, who identified himself as a British merchant captain.

Jones said, "What's your name, Captain?"

"Buchanan, sir," the captain replied.

"What's your cargo?"

"Barrels of rum, sir. Nothing else."

Jones laughed. "Just what we needed. I wish that bastard Langdon could see this."

"Sir?"

"Oh, nothing. Just a private joke."

Jones sent the marine lieutenant to search the ship and make certain everyone was on deck. Jones said to Christopher, "Come back to the ship with me. I want to talk privately with you in my cabin."

Matthew turned over in his mind his and Jones' words as they climbed back over the bulwarks, wondering if he had done something to displease him. In the cabin he soon found the answer.

Jones sat down. "Christopher, it is time for you to be rewarded. I am going to put you in this ship as prize master. I'll give you ten men and your friend, Johnson. Take the prize to Philadelphia."

"But, sir, I'm supposed by our instructions to take her to a French port."

Jones laughed. "We already talked about that. I expect you to follow me until dark and then encounter adverse weather during the night. Then proceed by great circle to Delaware Bay and up to Philadelphia. I want the Congress to see a real live prize I've captured. I think this ship is fast enough to evade most British ships except sloops. I'm counting on your ingenuity to take care of those who can catch you."

"And in Philadelphia, sir?"

"Before you turn her over to the prize court, engage a distiller to have enough rum taken out of the barrels to fill a gallon jug for each Congressman and each person on a list I'll give you. I'll write the names out along with some notes to accompany the jugs while we are transfering enough rum to last us for the cruise."

"I understand your orders, sir, but I don't want to leave you."

Jones sighed. "You will soon anyway. I don't think I will sail in this ship again after we reach Brest."

"But why, Sir?"

"Too many politicians are after me. At the same time they will have to give me a bigger and better ship."

"Who will take command of this ship?"

"Can't you guess? That bastard Simpson."

"But he can't command anything."

"Oh yes he can. The minute I am gone, his friends and the crew will come out of the sewer and take care of him. I wouldn't be surprised if they moved to have him take over command from me. That's why I want you to leave before this happens. I think you should resign your commission after you arrive in Philadelphia. Go home, see your wife, and when she's tired of you, go to sea as captain of a privateer. Make enough money to keep you in the style you deserve. Now get packed while I write some notes to go with the rum. As soon as we complete the transfer of it, I'm off." Jones laughed. "Wait a minute. I want you to send a jug to Langdon. Put a cup of pepper in it so no one can drink it except maybe a Texan. This is the note you will send with it." He had been writing it while he had been talking, and now he handed it to Christopher.

Christopher read the note. "Mister Langdon, I am returning to you the last gallon of the thirty gallons of rum you authorized for me. I didn't need it all."

When Christopher looked up Jones was gone.

An hour later, as the last barrel was swung over, Jones came on deck and handed Christopher a packet of letters. He grinned.

"Good luck, lad. I'll miss you, but I hope to see you again some time."

"In America?"

Jones said sadly. "I'm not sure I'll ever see my country again, at least not unless I am under arrest."

"Why would you be under arrest?"

Jones shrugged. "A lot of rascals are after me. Langdon would love to bring charges against me. Many others, too numerous to mention, would be delighted."

"If they do, I'll make it a point to find you, sir, and testify in your defense. Good luck."

Jones grinned. "I'll be moving fast."

Christopher laughed, "I don't think anyone will be able to out maneuver you, sir."

"And to you, bon voyage."

Christopher saluted and swung over to his new command. He looked back at the *Ranger*.

He could hear Jones giving orders to the master. "Master, take her out. Set course for Brest."

As the *Ranger* slowly separated from the *Mystery*, Jones took off his hat and waved.

Matthew returned the gesture, his eyes so misty he could hardly see.

Johnson, standing behind him, said, "He was a great man. We will miss him."

Chapter 30

As the *Ranger* faded over the horizon to the east, Matthew turned his attention to his new command. Johnson, a pistol in his belt, stood behind him. All of the other members of the prize crew were white sailors, but somehow Johnson exuded more authority. He had watched Captain Jones for months, and his stance and manners mimicked Jones exactly. If nothing else, the strong muscles rippling below his shirt intimidated the white sailors from the *Ranger* and kept them from challenging his authority. The black crew members of the prize seemed to be quite docile.

Matthew turned to him. "Johnson, you are my acting First Lieutenant. See if you can find a sword below. Lock up all the other arms you find and keep the key around your neck. Don't give it to anyone but me."

The former captain of the ship, a middle-aged Britisher, stood nearby, resigned to his fate.

Matthew beckoned him over and held out his hand. "What is your name, Captain?"

"Ryan Buchanan, sir."

"A Scot?"

"Irish."

"How long have you been at sea?"

"Since I was ten, except for some time working in a shipyard."

"And you have never been a prisoner before?"

"Luckily no, but I've come close."

"If you are given parole, will you serve as Lieutenant under my man, Johnson?"

Buchanan frowned. "Ordinarily, with the Haitian crew aboard, I'd think twice about serving under a black, but your man is unusual. I'll do it."

"What about your other officer?"

"I think you ought to lock him up while we are at sea. Keep the black third mate. He runs the crew well. They can man the sails, and another man can cook well."

Matthew said, "Johnson will keep an eye on him, and probably will cook for me as well."

Buchanan laughed. "That man has a lot of talents."

"You will find that he does."

"I recommend that you keep a good guard on the booze. The Haitians don't like it anyway, but your men will be after it."

"Thank you. I'll have a modest regular rum issue every day and tell them if they steal any, they'll go right over the side after it."

"Will they believe you?"

"Oh, yes. I'm tougher than I look, and I was brought up under the toughest officer I ever heard of, Captain John Paul Jones. My father was pretty tough, too."

Buchanan whistled softly. "Jones? Was that who took us? I've heard he has already killed two of his crew."

"Pure poppy cock, but he is tough enough to take on anyone, though he doesn't usually have to kill them."

As Matthew got used to the sails and the rigging of the brig, he made several changes that increased the speed. He had the black sailmaker alter the cut of the main courses, raise the trysails, and then moved the ballast aft.

He moved the projected great circle course one hundred miles to the west. It added a day to the trip, but there was little traffic on this course, and the increased speed made up for the added track change.

On the 10th day, a sail came over the horizon to the east. Matthew watched it, and changed course to the west to try to avoid it. The stranger did not change course and passed five miles away.

A second contact appeared the next day. Clearly it was a ship on patrol, and not one making a transit; she was on a westerly course, not headed for a port.

Matthew had done his best to disguise the merchantman as a small warship. On a calm day he had put men over the side to paint fake gun ports on the side. Both American and British flags were ready to fly, as was a Dutch flag.

This time he hoisted the Dutch flag and headed directly at the stranger, all canvas on.

The stranger also came on at full speed. At two miles Matthew ordered a change of course to bring what would have been his port battery to bear.

The strange ship did the same, but to her it was obvious that the *Mystery*, if she were actually a warship, was heavier than the stranger, and she should have carried guns of heavier calibre.

"She's wearing ship," Johnson cried. "I'd say she's had enough and is hauling ass."

"Shall we try to take her?"

Matthew laughed. "We can bluff her, but we can't make her strike her colors unless we can catch her and shoot at her. Since we have no guns, we may end up being taken by her if she finds out. I think we'll just let her go."

Two weeks later the *Mystery* stood into Delaware Bay. As they passed Bowen's Beach, Matthew looked at it through his long glass. "Looks the same," he said. "The old outhouse is still there, and the kids are on the beach."

As they sailed up the Bay, Matthew thought about what he would do with his prisoners. Most he could turn over to the Continental Navy, but Buchanan was different. He called Buchanan over. "Captain, I don't think you want to go to sea on an American navy ship, nor do I think you want to join me on a privateer because the British would be very hard on you if you were captured and might try you as a traitor. But would you want to work in a shipyard?"

Buchanan didn't hesitate. "I started out in one, and I'm good with new rigging. I'd like that."

"All right. I'll take you with me to Annapolis. There are a lot of English people there who settled generations ago and enough Irishmen to keep you company."

The next day the *Mystery* made her way up the Delaware River, passing close to Wilmington.

A few hours later the waterfront of Philadelphia came into view. Matthew searched it with a long glass. "There it is," he said, "Humphreys' shipyard. We will go in at a vacant berth. I'll pay old Humphreys with a little rum before I tell the prize court where to find the ship."

"Why are you doing that instead of going directly to the prize court?"

Christopher grinned. "Just a precaution. I want to get some rum off of the ship before the Continental Navy representatives here discover it."

"So?"

"They are just as bad as the British. They might try to confiscate it rather than pay for it as prize. This way my old friend Humphreys will protect me until I do what I want to do. He owes me something."

Chapter 31

As they approached the waterfront at Humphreys' shipyard, Matthew said, "I got a ship out of here without a pilot a year or so ago. I don't think I'll need a pilot to get this one moored at the same yard."

He eased the ship in carefully, not wanting to crack up his first command on her first landing. "I don't want to bang up Mister Humphreys' pier either," he said.

Humphreys was waiting on the pier, and as soon as the brow was over, he came aboard.

When he reached the quarterdeck, Matthew thought he was about to take him to task for landing at his pier without seeking permission. Then Humphreys recognized Matthew, "Ah, lad, good to see you again. But why are you here?"

"I'm prize master of the ship *Mystery*," he said. "The prize court will take her off your hands in a few days. In the meantime I hope you will accept a gift of part of our cargo, a barrel of fine rum."

Humphreys glowed. "Thanks. It's hard to find nowadays. The British sink all the ships carrying it or capture them. I've taken to drinking beer."

"This was a British ship that was trying to take a load of rum to England for the Royal Navy."

"And you borrowed it for the Continental Navy?"

"Something like that, sir, but only if they'll buy it from the prize court."

"You are just as smart as ever. She will be safe here for a few days."

"Not smart, just careful."

The next day Matthew hired the services of a liquor bottling firm and turned over a dozen barrels of rum to be rebottled in fancy jugs. He had filled the exact number Captain Jones specified, and on an impulse he added a few additonal. "Might run across a few friends of my own," he said to Johnson, who was watching the operation very carefully.

He affixed the notes prepared by Captain Jones to the jugs and hired a carriage to take them to the government buildings. With Johnson's help, he delivered a jug to each person on the list.

As he left one Congressman's office, he grinned. "He asked my name and how I came to be here. That won't hurt if I change my mind and decide to stay in the navy."

"Might you?" Johnson asked.

"Not a chance."

"Well maybe he'll remember you if you need some help with the shipyard."

Matthew shrugged. "I hate to admit it, but this seems to be the way the business world is going in this country, and I might as well be prepared to go with it."

He made a final stop at the stage office and put in their charge, the special jug with its pepper spiced rum, addressed to Mister Langdon.

Johnson asked, "Why did you do that? Nobody, not even a Texan like you said before, could drink that."

Christopher kept a straight face as he handed it to the stage office manager. "Special delivery from Captain Jones to ship builder Langdon in Portsmouth."

Johnson shrugged. "I don't think Captain Jones likes him."

This time Cristopher smiled. "You've got it."

With the job completed, Matthew had a few extra jugs delivered in his name to the Congressmen from Maryland. He then turned the ship over to the prize court and marched the prisoners off to the prisoner-of-war stockade, turning them over to the Continental Navy.

The *Ranger* prize crew reported to the same Continental Navy official and was given a few days leave before reporting for transportation back to their ship. Matthew gave them the last two jugs of rum and wished them well.

Matthew kept Ryan Buchanan out of sight. Then he submitted his resignation and helped Johnson present a written request for discharge from the navy to the senior officer of the Continental Navy in Philadelphia.

The next day he bought three tickets on the fast packet for Annapolis, and they boarded it just before it sailed.

Matthew asked the captain if they had had any trouble getting by the blockade.

The grizzled skipper said, "No, lad. We stay closer to the shore than the British care to go. We will get you there safely and on time unless the wind stops blowing altogether, and it never does in this country."

Two days later they watched the church steeples in Anapolis grow taller as the packet made her way up the Severn River and came alongside the pier.

"Home at last!" Johnson said.

Matthew laughed, "I thought big Jebediah threw you out some time ago?"

"He did, but I'm now bigger and meaner than he is. If we have an argument, he leaves and I stay. Johnson is going to be a bigger name than Jebediah in Annapolis."

Chapter 32

When the packet had moored to the pier, Matthew could hardly keep from going directly home, but he felt he had to take care of Ryan Buchanan and Johnson first and also see his father.

As they walked up the street toward the shipyard, Matthew asked Johnson, "What are you going to do now?"

"Go right to Middleton Tavern and go to work, I guess."

"Wouldn't you rather work in the shipyard? You are now a well qualified seaman."

"Yes, but I'm a better cook, and I want to set up my own restaurant someday."

"Why not now?"

"I've only got a little of my pay and prize money so far. When I get it all, I'll start up. Right now I've got a little of my crap winnings tied up in my shirt, and I want to put it in the bank."

"I didn't know you were a gambler."

Johnson shrugged. "Not much of one. None of the sailors had much money either."

"All right. If you want to borrow money let me know."

Johnson, dropped off at the bank, waved good-bye to the other two.

Matthew took Buchanan to the shipyard office. He asked him to wait outside. Inside his father was engrossed in studying a large drawing. He looked up when he heard Matthew coming. "I'd know your steps anywhere," he said, as he folded Matthew in his strong arms.

"Where's your beard?" Matthew asked.

"Well, I'm going to be married. The lady you will meet soon doesn't seem to like it."

"Anybody I know?"

"I'm not sure. Her name is Theresa Livingston. She is a wealthy widow. Lives on a large horse farm outside of town."

"Recently widowed?"

"About a year ago. Her husband was killed in the war. I think she is getting tired of running her estate by herself. She's pretty good with horses, though. Directs the stud operations of the biggest horse farm in the county and maybe the state."

"And with men?"

"I'll have to steer a straight course."

"I have somebody with me waiting outside who might free up some of your time, either by helping to manage your shipyard or by acting as overseer of your new farm."

"Sounds interesting."

"His name is Captain Ryan Buchanan. I took his ship as prize and put him out of business. He ran a good ship, and I think he was a good captain."

"Bring him in."

Matthew went to the door and beckoned to Buchanan. When he came in, Matthew introduced him. "Pa, this is Captain Ryan Buchanan."

Right away it was evident to Matthew that Christopher and Buchanan were going to get along.

Eric Christopher glowed. "Would you like to work for me in the shipyard?"

Buchanan nodded. "Yes, sir, very much, if you can stand an old Irishman."

"You don't look any older than I am. Do you have a place to stay?"

"No, sir, I've never been here before."

"Sit down and have a cup of coffee. Later I'll take you home with me. I've got lots of room."

Matthew said, "He lives by himself in a big house, and he has a good cook."

"Thank you both. I hope to repay you someday. Someday I would like to become an American."

Eric patted Matthew on the back. "Now go see your wonderful wife. By the way, on your way home, take a look at the sloop in the fitting out berth. She's the best thing I've ever done. She's yours if you want her. My new wife won't let me go to sea in her."

"But you haven't even married her yet."

"When you meet her you'll see why there won't be any doubt in my mind."

Matthew said, "I saw her on the way in. She looks French."

"Let's get this straight. My wife-to-be isn't French. She's English."

Mathew laughed. "I'll start again. I've never met your future wife. I have met your ship. I saw her on the way here, and I think she looks very French."

"I'll say she does. She'll be the fastest ship in the Atlantic. No British ship will ever take her unless you try to take on a first-rater close in. You can get away from any ship you don't like and sail rings around any ship you want to wear down. But enough. Let me know later."

Matthew walked rapidly up the brick sidewalks of Annapolis toward his house. He banged on the door until Mammy Sarah opened it.

"Quiet out there! I'm coming as fast as I can," she began. Then she opened the door. "Oh, Mister Matthew! I'm so happy to see you!" She took him in her arms. Then she stepped back, "Where's your navy suit?"

Matthew grinned. "I resigned two days ago. I'm not in the navy anymore."

Mammy Sarah said, "Stop just standing around here and talking to old Mammy. Your wife and children are in the garden."

"Children?"

"Yes. You didn't know? You also have a daughter."

"Well, I'll be damned! I haven't had a letter for at least six months."

"Your wife hasn't done much better. She thinks you are still in France. As a matter of fact, she thinks one of the senoritas has trapped you."

Matthew laughed. "There are no senoritas in France. They're called mademoiselles in France."

"Well, anyway, she's worried. Go see her."

Matthew trotted out the back door to the garden and ran the rest of the way to Martha's arms. He held her for five minutes, squeezing her as hard as he could. He only let go when his young son began pulling at his trouser legs. He leaned down and picked up his son.

"Do you remember him?" Martha asked.

"Of course, but he may not remember me."

"He knows all about you. We talk about you every day. Now come meet your daughter."

Matthew followed her to the baby carriage sitting in the shade. Matthew leaned in but the baby was asleep.

"She will wake up soon. Now let's sit and talk for a minute." Martha turned to Matthew Junior. "Junior, make a castle for your daddy in your sandbox."

Junior grinned and made a beeline for his objective, falling over his daddy's feet in the process.

Matthew asked, "What is our daughter's name?"

"Mary, of course, after your mother."

"Funny," he said, "that's the name of Pa's new ship, too."

"Just right, I think, and you don't have to ask me about taking her to sea. I know you want to command her. All I ask is that you come ashore for good after six months in command and take over the shipyard. I don't know if you know, but your father wants to give it up, get married to a very charming woman, and become a farmer."

"Yes, I stopped by on the way home. I left with him a man who may take over the shipyard until I get home. If he's as good as I think he is, he will make life a lot easier for both of us in the future."

Finally Martha could wait no longer. "The children are quiet. I'll call Mammy Sarah to sit and watch them."

"You have something in mind?"

"Of course. I can't wait until tonight and neither can you. You sailors are all alike."

Matthew, alone with Martha in the bedroom, folded her again in his arms. He kissed her so violently that he bruised her lips, but she did not object. She began to undress him, and she realized for the first time that he was not wearing a uniform.

"My God! You aren't a sailor any more!" she teased.

He laughed. "No. I resigned, but I still have the instincts of a sailor. Now stop talking. We'll talk later."

He lowered her gently onto the bed, and tried his best to caress her before he took her, but she was as ready as he was, and for an hour they made love, resting after each torrid meeting.

By suppertime, Martha said, "Enough for now. We're both going to have supper with our children, or they will think you've kidnapped me and taken me to sea."

Matthew laughed, stretching his arms over his head. "I think Mammy Sarah knows what happened. She'll have some story ready for the children. Little Mary doesn't even know to miss me yet."

Mammy was indeed ready for them. The children were in high chairs in the dining room, and a large plate of biscuits and another of fried chicken were in front of Matthew's place. Mammy Sarah giggled. "If you two hadn't showed up soon, I'd have knocked on your door anyway. Missy, I see you have your hair down. Anyone would know what you was doing."

Martha colored. "Well, I'm not a missy any more, and anything I do in my bedroom is all right."

Matthew laughed. "I'll say it is."

Chapter 33

For a month Matthew played with his children, made love to his wife, and walked about the city with them. It was the happiest time of his life.

Toward the end of the month the walks seemed to take them past the *Mary* more often. Her rigging was finished, and his father was loading her with stores and provisions and putting aboard her guns.

Martha knew she could not win, and thirty days after his homecoming she said. "I will keep my promise. You may take of her tomorrow, but remember you promised to stay out at sea not a day over six months."

Matthew laughed. "That's all the provisions she will carry, I'll be home in six months or the crew will starve."

The next day Matthew stopped by his father's office where he was looking at plans with Buchanan. Matthew said, "Those are beautifully drawn. I take it Miss Cranston has taken over in the drafting office?"

"She certainly has. She's in the next office. The only problem is that Buchanan, here, takes up all her time."

Buchanan blushed. "I try not to bother her during office hours. It just happens that she runs the office coffee and tea pots."

Eric Christopher guffawed. "You told me you never drank coffee before you joined us. Only tea."

"Well, that's all the damned Englishmen had. I'm going to be an American, and they drink coffee. So do most Irishmen."

"So does Miss Cranston."

Buchanan shrugged. "She's a wonderful woman, and she is always right."

Matthew laughed. "She always was when she was my school teacher. I wish you luck."

Matthew turned to his father. "Now, Pa, let's get down to business. I want to take up your offer to command the *Mary* when she's ready to go to sea."

Eric Christopher wiped his eyes. "You noted her name. Only you or I could ever have the honor of taking her to sea on her first cruise. Step aboard and from that day she's yours."

Matthew said, "I agree, but what about a crew?"

"The fact that you are going to command is all that's necessary. We only need a few more men, and your name will bring them in."

Matthew nodded. "I'll go to the *Mary* and step aboard right now."

"Let me know when you think she's ready to go, I figure about one week."

That night Matthew went home for supper early. He told Martha that he was now the captain of the *Mary.* As he watched her, he could tell that somewhere inside tears were forming, but she would not let him see them fall.

That night, after they had made love, she cried softly in his arms. He touched her lovingly. "Cry all you want. This is for both of us. You know I hate to leave my family."

"But you still go to sea."

"I think I should. You know we are reasonably well off, but in a six months' cruise I can take prizes enough to make us rich for the rest of our lives no matter what happens to the nation's economy."

"What do you mean by that?"

"I don't know how stable our currency will be or how secure our economy will be after the war is over."

"What can you do? Your money might be worthless after you have risked your life to earn it."

"I plan to buy land and gold. I will also invest in a variety of foreign bonds. All of them can't go bankrupt. With what I make in prize money to add to what we have, I can't fail. If I don't take the opportunity, we may never be well off."

Martha wiped her eyes. "I trust you, Matthew, but I will miss you.When you return I never want to have to miss you again."

"You won't. I don't want to leave again either. I've seen enough blood, salt water, storms, and treachery to last me for a lifetime. I just want peace and quiet."

Matthew spent hours going over the material condition of the *Mary* until he was satisfied.

Strangely enough, recruiting a crew was easy. The Continental Navy had trouble recruiting, but privateers did not. Life on a privateer was relatively easy. There was no enlistment period involved. A privateer could quit at his pleasure, though few did. And more importantly, the privateers got all the money produced by a prize. In the Continental Navy, long after Captain John Paul Jones' effort, the ships of the navy got only half of the value of a British man-of-war, although they got the full value of a merchantman.

After one week Matthew had a complete crew. Scott MacIntosh volunteered to be his First Lieutenant, and Johnson came aboard quickly and asked to be made ship's cook. "That damned new management don't appreciate my cooking. Can't cook what I want. Just what the menu says."

Matthew laughed. "On the *Mary* you can cook whatever you want. You are in charge. Now get aboard all the supplies you want for six months. The only thing is, I trust your helpful advice about seamanship and gunnery. I may have to call on you."

Johnson bristled. "Well, I expected to be a gun captain as well as the cook."

"You will be, but what was the reason why you didn't want to stay ashore?"

"Well, nothing serious. I had another run-in with my Pappy, Big Jebediah."

"What happened?"

"Well, he ain't never going to get old, at least he will never admit it."

"Fighting, or women?"

"Both. One worse than the other. I tried to reason with Big Jebediah and convince him to settle down with Mammy Sarah."

"Well, you'd be better off at sea for a while. When we get back, your pay and prize money ought to be ready. I'll make sure you have enough then to start your own restaurant even if I have to loan it to you myself."

Johnson sighed. "It will sure be peaceful at sea."

Chapter 34

A week later Martha, Eric Christopher, Ryan Buchanan, and Miss Cranston stood on the fitting out pier as the *Mary* slid quietly out of her slip.

Miss Cranston threw aboard a bouquet of Black-eyed Susans, and Matthew promptly had it hoisted from the main mast.

Scott McIntosh, watching from the quarterdeck, said, "My God! What an arm! That's some woman!"

Matthew nodded. "Yes, she is, and always has been. I think Captain Buchanan will be very lucky."

Matthew handled the ship expertly without a pilot. His father had asked him if he wanted one. Matthew had said, "Not unless you want to do it."

Eric Christopher shook his head. "You don't need me, and if what I hear up and down the coast is true, you've been learning from the best ship handler in the world, Captain John Paul Jones."

"He was good, and I miss him, but I'll have to command my own ship in my own style. Part of it will be yours, Pa. You were always very good."

"I have great faith in you, Son."

"And I in you. You taught me everything I know.

The *Mary* shook down quickly on her way south in the Chesapeake Bay. The men Matthew had recruited were all highly motivated and well qualified. Most had sailed in the Chesapeake for years, and many had been at sea before with either Matthew or his father.

The winds were light and favorable, and at times gusty enough so that Matthew could sense her potential speed and her ability to tack and turn. She was indeed fast and very maneuverable. Her schooner-rigged fore and aft sails could all be controlled and trimmed from the main deck. Furthermore, trimming and changing sails could be done in heavy weather from the deck. Only a few men were needed. Ten men could do what fifty men would be needed for on a square-rigger.

As he paced the quarterdeck, watching the slim hull slip easily through the water, he thought about Captain John Paul Jones and how he would have sailed and fought the *Mary*. The only penalty paid for her speed was the necessity of mounting lighter guns. Matthew had shrugged when this was discussed. "I'd rather have it like this. We have to get into position where we can rake the enemy with our broadside and the opponents can only bring the bow or stern chasers to bear. If we can do this, we can use lighter guns with long ranges. The weight of ball they can throw doesn't matter then."

"Captain Jones was an expert at this, and he did it using a square rigged ship. We'll be even better at it. I'm not concerned."

All the way down the bay Matthew conducted sail trimming exercises. On the second day he held gun firing exercises. At the end of the second day, he called MacIntosh, Enders the boatswain, and Farrell the gunner, to his cabin. "Well, gentlemen," he said, "are we ready to fight?"

Enders laughed. "The men who man and trim the sails have been ready for years. All we needed was a little warmup and we got it. We're ready."

Farrell hesitated. "My gunners are a little less experienced. I've got gun captains who have fired guns all right, but never have had what gunners need—experience with a particular gun. These are lighter and stronger than we are used to and they throw a smaller ball, but can withstand a heavier explosion internally and therefore have greater range than we are used to. The trajectory will be flatter, and we will need to experiment with them."

"I take it the guns we are getting from the new foundries in Philadelphia are stronger than the guns the British produce these days?"

"Much stronger. They can use fifty percent more powder without exploding."

"And we could throw a heavier ball with the same sized gun?"

"Yes, but we've made a decision to get more range instead. Your father made a wise decision as usual."

"He always does."

"I think we are almost ready to fight. After we get out in the bay in rougher weather, I'd like to do some more practice firing so the gun captains can get used to firing on various rolls."

Christopher said, "That's very important, and I want them trained to fire on either the up or down roll."

"Why both?" the gunner asked.

"Up roll when we want to spare hull and damage her masts and sails and capture the ship in condition so we can repair and sail her."

"Then why do we need the down roll?"

"Later on, when we are low on prize crews, we will want to unload the ship and then sink her."

"We'll be ready then."

"You may need to fire for real before that. We go through the Bay entrance either tonight or tomorrow morning. You can count on half a dozen British warships trying to blockade us and close the Bay entrance."

Farrell shrugged. "It's wide enough for us to get through if the wind is good."

"It always is," Matthew said. "But I haven't made up my mind yet whether to try a transit tonight or to do during the daylight tomorrow."

The next evening, as the *Mary* approached the Bay entrance, Matthew stood by the wheel talking with MacIntosh. "What's your guess, Scotty?"

MacIntosh shrugged. "Fifty-fifty."

Johnson brought up two cups of coffee. "You gentlemen look worried," he said.

Matthew shrugged. "Not really. I am trying to decide whether to go through the blockade late at night, or slow up and go through tomorrow morning."

Johnson laughed. "There ain't no real choice. Put on all sail and go right through as soon as you can at night."

"Why?"

"You ain't never been a gun captain at night like I have . You can't really see the target in the dark and you can only guess at the range. After the first shot, your eyes are blinded unless you can remember to close them just before you fire. Also you have to make sure to set the gun off first and that ain't easy either. You might miss the touch hole with your eyes closed."

"But Captain Jones never tried that."

"Well, he tried to attack the *Drake* at night and he couldn't even get the *Ranger* anchored accurately one hundred yards away. If he'd done that, he could have just let her have it. But he didn't, and he cut his cable and ran. He knew when not to try something that didn't have a payoff any more. I wouldn't want to be in a crap game with him."

"And you still think we should go through now?"

"Sure. Captain Jones would have, too. Just pick out a gap and run like a scalded dog. Nobody will get near you."

Matthew turned to MacIntosh and grinned. "Looks like John Paul Johnson made up our minds."

Johnson said, "Up to now I ain't never had a first name. Now I'll call myself Jones Johnson. After all, Captain John Paul took on the name Jones, too."

"He took it on as a last name."

Johnson shrugged. "I ain't proud. I figure it will look just as good on the front as on the back."

Chapter 35

Matthew called Boatswain Enders, a young man from Chestertown, and asked him to hoist an extra staysail and to trim the other sails for maximum speed.

"Yes, sir, I take it we are going to go right on through tonight."

"Right. The wind is up to twenty knots from the north. We'll have to tack against it to get out, but the British will have the same problem, and even worse. We'll do a lot better job of it than they will."

"I agree, sir."

The *Mary* was up to ten knots, which was pushing spray across her bows, and Matthew knew she could do more without having to reef her sails. He looked up against the fading daylight, admiring the cut and set of the sails. "She's a beauty," he said. "This is the best Pa has ever done."

About midnight the track on the chart showed that they were about to pass out the entrance to the bay, but no land was in sight.

"Keep a sharp lookout up there," he yelled to the lookouts aloft.

In an hour the lookouts shouted down, "Sail ho! Broad on the port bow!"

"Can you make her out?"

"Probably a brig. It's pretty dark out there."

MacIntosh said, "It is dark, and the moon won't be up for four hours."

Matthew scrambled up the ratlines. He was careful because he was not familiar with them yet. When he reached the cross trees, he pulled out his long glass and found the sail. He estimated he could pass safely ahead of the oncoming ship, and he went below.

Within ten minutes the lookouts reported another sail to the southeast. Matthew went aloft again, now feeling a little safer with the ratlines. It was a ship on a northerly course. He estimated she would pass just astern of the *Mary* if she held course. She was definitely a threat. Matthew went below. "Scott, change course one point to port."

MacIntosh said, "But won't that take us too close to the ship to the northeast?"

Matthew shrugged. "I think we'll be safe from her. A lot depends on the contact to the south. She is the most dangerous of the two."

Matthew paced nervously, watching the approach of both ships, still barely discernible in the dark. He realized he would be safe from the northern ship, but there was no way he could completely avoid the southern ship.

As a privateer, the *Mary* could not afford a boy who was just a drummer, but a lad who had come aboard as a cabin boy had said he could also drum a little. Matthew told him, "Beat to quarters."

The boy flailed away at his version of beat to quarters, and the crew, laughing at the odd collections of sounds, quickly turned out and manned their stations.

Soon all was ready, and the crew was at its stations. Matthew watched both ships carefully, still guessing that the southern ship posed the real threat.

The bearing was staying steady, and the range as he estimated it decreased slowly.

"Something will happen soon," MacIntosh said.

"Sure. The bastard will shoot at us."

"Yeah, that's what Johnson, er, Jones Johnson said would happen."

The ship to the south suddenly lit up.

"She's firing from her bow chasers only," MacIntosh said impatiently.

"We've crossed ahead of her, and our starboard battery bears," Matthew said, "but we don't want to fire and give the ship a point of aim."

"I agree."

Two geysers erupted in the gloom, barely visible in the distance.

Matthew laughed. "As Jones Johnson said, the gunners can't see a damned thing now. We're safe."

The firing continued, with the balls falling all over the horizon, and the bearing of the southern ship drew aft. Soon the enemy geysers drew farther away as the range increased.

"We've made it easily," MacIntosh said. "In the morning we'll be in business."

"No we won't. I don't want to take prizes this far south. The distance to a safe port is too great. We'll go farther north off the Delaware Bay, or as far north as Portsmouth. Then we can send a prize in without worrying that the British will re-take it before we can get rid of it."

"I don't see how you find time to think about all this stuff."

"Scotty, you will be a privateer captain soon, and your job will be to think for the whole ship."

Chapter 36

The next morning the *Mary* sailed north across broad Atlantic swells that lifted the ship bodily at the same time as they slowly rolled her.

"Is this the start of a large storm?" MacIntosh asked.

Matthew shrugged. "Don't think so. This isn't the season for them. Also the barometer is still up. Just a few rollers coming off a large storm thousands of miles to the south. This is just a left-over."

For two more days the *Mary* ran north at a steady ten knots in a twenty knot wind. Matthew had the new rigging tightened as it stretched.

Off the entrance to Delaware Bay, Matthew settled down to patrol east to west, hoping to intercept British traffic, either smaller men-of-war or merchantmen crossing from the Caribbean to Great Britain.

For one week nothing happened, and Matthew became impatient.

Johnson brought him an early morning mug of coffee. "Maybe we need a new worm on the hook," he said.

The next morning the lookouts reported a sail. Matthew watched it carefully, wanting it to be worthwhile, but not so strong that his crew would be tested too early.

Instead it was almost too easy. It turned to try to avoid them, but the *Mary* glided after her, easily and quickly overtaking her. She was a medium-sized merchantman, and she offered no opposition, quickly running down her colors and submissively turning into the wind. Matthew put aboard a prize crew and followed his first prize almost to the mouth of Delaware Bay to make sure the British did not re-take her.

They were not as fortunate two days later. The approaching ship was bow on, and Matthew could not tell what kind of ship she was. As they closed, he decided to take a chance. He could tell that she was square-rigged, but he could not tell whether she was two or three masted.

When they were in range of *Mary's* nine-pounders, Matthew shouted. "Four points to starboard, please. Commence firing as soon as possible."

When the ship steadied, Matthew hoped he had judged the range correctly.

They fired a broadside, and Matthew watched the flight of the shot anxiously. At least four or five of her rounds landed on board the target, some tearing holes in the sails. At least one holed the hull near the figurehead.

The gun crews cheered, although they had little opportunity to see much as they worked to reload, but the gun captains made some guesses and egged them on.

When the other ship turned to starboard, Matthew heaved a sigh of relief. She was two masted, and overall she was smaller than *Mary.*

The crew of the other ship, clearly distracted by the fire she had received, returned fire badly. The shots scattered around the *Mary* but none came aboard.

The *Mary's* second salvo was an improvement over the first, and the third salvo was even better. The sails of her target were in tatters now, and much of her rigging hung from the yardarms like spaghetti. Matthew wondered why she did not strike, but in a few minutes her colors came down.

"Cease firing! Prepare to lower a boat!" Matthew shouted.

Matthew brought the *Mary* up under the lee of the prize, ordered her sails lowered, and sent a five man prize crew over to the foundering ship.

It was over, and Matthew heaved a sigh of relief. The next one might not be that easy, and he resolved never again to get within range of an unidentified ship until he knew how strong she was. This might have been a disaster had it been a full-sized frigate.

For two more months the *Mary* cruised off Portsmouth, taking six merchantmen. Then provisions, and, more importantly, the men available for prize crews, began to run short. "We can hardly man a battery," MacIntosh complained.

"Then we will go back to the area off Delaware Bay for one last try," Matthew said.

They took a small sloop near the mouth of the Delaware, and Matthew put aboard a slim prize crew, only three men. He followed the ship into the Bay to watch over her as she sailed into Wimington.

The next morning at dawn, the lookouts reported, "Sail ho!"

Matthew felt apprehensize, so he quickly climbed aloft. To port, between them and the coast of Delaware Bay, sailed a British frigate, headed out of the bay. There was something familiar about the lines of the ship. Then he knew who she was, and he swore. It was the *Bailey*. He had learned later after their adventure at Bowers' Creek, that her captain was Lord Nottingham, not a very popular captain in the Royal Navy. Matthew climbed down. "Scotty, that's the same damned ship that drove us aground."

MacIntosh shrugged. "She's still a frigate, and we don't have any business messing with her. Those are our rules. If we take a chance, she'll probably take us."

Matthew gritted his teeth. "I know that is one of the rules we follow, but my father would never forgive me if we didn't try to take her."

"He won't forgive you if you lose his ship either."

"I think he would. He'd want me to go at that dog."

"All right. I'm game."

Matthew shouted, "Beat to quarters."

Matthew looked at the frigate again and held up his hand to test the wind. "Now we have the weather gage, and Captain Jones would say that's worth a dozen guns."

"Yes, and she's near the shore. She made the same mistake we did years ago. Now she can only sail upwind toward us or parallel to the shore. She can't sail more than sixty degrees into the wind. We can do forty-five with our rig, and we have at least three knots over her. We can maintain this position as long as we want to."

Matthew nodded, "And we can tack in half the time she can."

MacIntosh said, "We've talked ourselves right into the lion's den, and she's a big lion."

Matthew took a deep breath. "Head right for the frigate, Helmsman."

He turned to MacIntosh, "Ready all guns. We will fire to starboard first."

The range decreased with the frigate on a starboard tack, and apparently heading north.

When Matthew felt all was ready, he shouted, "Come to southwest. When you're steady on, steer a careful course. Commence firing as soon as you can see the target!"

On the quarterdeck of the *Bailey*, Captain Nottingham strode up and down, banging his sword against his leg. "What is that insolent bastard doing over there? She's not following the rules. She keeps changing her course, and our gunners can't get a bead on her. She can't shoot at us either. The ship looks like a Spanish woman twirling her skirts at the audience."

The first lieutenant mumbled, "I could use some of that."

"What was that?"

"I said, sir, her captain is a twit."

"And just what the hell is a twit? Some kind of bird?"

"No, sir, just an expression from the latest London musical stage review."

Nottingham sneered, "You haven't been to a play for years, and you aren't likely to see one for some time."

The first lieutenant sighed. "Maybe not, sir. I heard that from a sailor we pressed from a merchantman recently."

The captain chuckled. "Twits, twits indeed. You are going over the brink. Now we will see if she can really shoot when she has to settle down to a course."

The first lieutenant shrugged. "We'll soon see."

Just then the other ship let loose a salvo and a shot flew through the mainsail. Another passed down the port gun battery, knocking over a gun carriage and killing a dozen men.

The first lieutenant said, "I guess she can shoot on the fly. We've got to learn to do it."

The captain snorted. "That's assinine. Change course to south west to keep him out of our tail feathers."

Then more shots came aboard, tearing huge holes in the main courses. A fourth destroyed two more guns and their crews.

"Egad!" Nottingham said, "This ain't fair. I'll have the bastard at my yardarm when we take him."

The first lieutenant ran over. "Captain, the steering system has carried away."

"Well, don't just stand there. Fix it."

The *Mary* swung rapidly with full rudder and then steadied. Her guns boomed, and the frigate shot back. Nobody was hit, but the *Mary*'s shots were closer. The *Mary* fired again, and Matthew could see new holes in the sails of the frigate.

With the *Mary*'s superior maneuverability, she could change course frequently before the frigate's gunners could lay their guns on her. She could still keep the frigate in her sights.

MacIntosh said, "She seems to be in trouble. She's not steering well."

After firing two more salvos the *Mary* drew aft of the frigate, and MacIntosh said, "She seems to be having trouble steering again."

The frigate should have changed course to avoid the *Mary* getting in position to rake her from aft, but she couldn not.

"We've got her on the ropes!" Matthew shouted. "Fire at will!"

The gunners kept up a rapid fire at the stern of the British ship. Matthew didn't think she had enough maneuverability to come about but she made it slowly with several guns still able to fire.

Two shots came aboard, one passing through the mainsail, and the other bouncing over the lee bulwark. Another salvo crashed into the frigate. She seemed to shudder, and Matthew thought he could see her heel as her guns rumbled back in recoil and her gunners worked feverishly to reload. The end had to be getting close.

Matthew was puzzled. "She ought to strike soon."

Scotty nodded, "Her sails are luffing. I think she's lost steering control again."

"Yes, and not many of her guns are firing. Come to north by east, and let's foul up her gunners and get a close look at her damage."

On the decks of the *Bailey* the blood ran freely into the scuppers. Only two guns were still useable, and the temporary repairs to the steering system had given away. She sailed slowly in circles, her sails flapping sadly as the once proud *Bailey* slowly passed through the wind.

The captain, a cut on his forehead, was still conscious, but ready to quit. "Strike the colors," he said.

The first lieutenant could not hear him. He was dead. Another lieutenant tried to untangle the halliards to the colors, but they were hopelessly fouled. He slashed them with a sweep of his sword. The colors and the halliards fell across his head.

He shouted, "Down all remaining sails," and he moved over to see what he could do for the captain.

The captain refused to go below, and leaned against the binnacle, holding a cloth to his wound.

The young lieutenant said, "Captain, you should go below to the cockpit so the surgeon can take care of your wound. Can I help you down?"

The captain shook his head sadly. "Nothing can help me or this ship now. I'll wait here for the boarding party to arrive. I can't see much with this blood in my eyes. Let me know when they come aboard."

On the *Mary*, Christopher shouted "Come about!" The abrupt tack threw off the aim of the remaining gunners on the frigate, and the *Mary* sped by throwing a final salvo into her quarry. By the time she was abreast, the colors had come down.

"Close her," Mathew shouted. "Get ready to lower a boat, I'm going over to see how that bastard made out. Then I want you,

Scotty, to act as prize master. I'll give you all the men I can spare, and I'll guarantee your safe passage."

"Where do I take her?"

Matthew grinned. "Home, and I'll get you through the blockade somehow and escort you all the way. Anchor her off our shipyard."

Chapter 37

For four days the *Mary* cruised south, closely followed by the Bailey commanded by MacIntosh as prize master. Her captain was sulking, locked in his cabin, refusing to see even the surgeon. All of the crew were locked below in the living areas aft, except for the wounded who were allowed to go to the cockpit for treatment by the surgeon.

On the first day a brief burial ceremony had been conducted by MacIntosh and the captain of the *Bailey*, who had been brought on deck temporarily, grumbling and unhappy. Fifty-one men had been buried. Of the officers, only the captain and one lieutenant were still alive.

When the *Bailey* left Delaware Bay, she was marginally seaworthy and could only make half of her normal speed. Scotty MacIntosh had spent years in the Christopher shipyards, and most of the prize crew were yard workmen who had gone to sea to share in the profits of the privateer system. Given enough time, they could fix anything, and when limited in time they could perform near-miracles.

MacIntosh worked the crew of the *Bailey* hard, choosing the best artificers and petty officers from them. On the first day a jury-rigged steering system was completed. By the end of the second day, all of the holes in the hull were completely repaired, capable of withstanding the strongest seas that might be expected in this season. The temporary canvas patches put on the first day were replaced by semi-permanent wood patches made from spars, room partitions, cannibalized gun carriages, and spare canvas sails.

By the third day, MacIntosh's group was hard at work on the rigging, yards, and sails. Her speed increased proportionatly to the amount of canvas that could be spread. She would never match the *Mary* in speed, but for a British frigate, she was showing reasonable seaworthiness.

MacIntosh released the *Bailey* crew and sent them below, and gave the prize crew a whole afternoon off in which to sunbathe or sleep.

As they neared the entrance to Chesapeake Bay, Matthew decided to go through in the darkness. He had no doubt that the *Mary* could make it, but the challenge was to lure any British ships in to chasing the speedy *Mary* while the banged up *Bailey* could slip through. Late in the afternoon, Christopher brought the *Mary* under the *Bailey*'s quarter and he and MacIntosh exchanged information using speaking trumpets about the state of repairs on the *Bailey* and made plans for the evening. When he was satisfied, he pulled clear and headed south.

When he was sure they were far enough south to be abreast the middle of the Bay entrance, he slowed and turned west. About midnight he began the transit. Then he put on all sail. MacIntosh brought the *Bailey* men who had replaced her torn sails and damaged rigging back on deck to man and trim the sails. Matthew estimated she could make more than two-thirds of her normal speed and he hoped the jury rig for the steering system would hold up.

As they neared the blockade line, he climbed into the rigging and swept the horizon. There was no ship in sight to the north, but there was a ghostly sail to the southwest barely visible in the moonlight. He changed course to the northwest, and the *Bailey* followed, slowly dropping astern.

Now was the time to mislead the contact, and Matthew changed course to the southwest, right across the bow of the oncoming contact. The *Bailey* continued on for the entrance. The contact took the bait and followed the *Mary.*

Matthew could see the *Bailey* disappearing to the west, and he changed course slightly to encourage the pursuing ship to keep following him.

He watched the pursuing ship change course slightly to try to improve their chances. Then he laughed, "The poor sod never had a chance."

Johnson, standing by him, said, "Show her how the *Mary* can dance."

"Good idea, Johnson. Take the helm."

Johnson relieved the helmsman who stood aside and grinned in the semi-dark.

"Now, Captain?" Johnson asked.

"Yes. Bring her across the wind and head for the entrance."

Johnson spun the wheel with all of his strength. The *Mary* hesitated for just a second, and then began to wheel to starboard. She picked up turning speed as the bow neared the direction of the wind, then her slim bow headed into the wind. Her large sails lost the wind and the back edges began to luff, flopping slightly from side to side, at first delicately and then fully. The fluttering edges made a peculiar sound Matthew knew he would never forget. The wooden hoops holding the main sail to the main mast began to rattle.

Johnson grinned. "Sounds like castanets," he said.

The sail trimmers brought the huge main sail in and then began to let it out on the other side as the turn continued. The musical thrumming of the shrouds on the port side stopped and began to increase on the starboard side as they took the strain of the tall mast.

Then, as the bow passed the direction of the wind, quickly the luffing stopped when the wind began to fill the huge sail. As it bellied out, the thrumming got even louder in the weather shrouds.

Matthew estimated that the *Mary* was easily making twelve knots, and the British ship began to fall rapidly astern. It was no contest. He had listened to every sound of what was happening. As the sails filled completely and the *Mary* leaped ahead, he sighed and wiped his eyes on his sleeve.

Johnson saw what he was doing in the faint moonlight. "Something in your eyes, Captain?"

"Yes, dammit. And I don't mind admitting it's tears. This may be the last time I will ever take this lady through that dance."

"Cheer up, Captain. You have two more days to sail her on the bay."

"Yes, but it will be simple. No opposition. No big winds. Maybe thunderstorms."

Johnson shook his head as he turned the helm back to the helmsman. "Yes, Captain, I could swear she flipped her skirts at that poor bastard astern."

After an hour the ship decided she could not catch the *Mary* and gave up. Matthew came back to a course for the entrance. At dawn the Bailey was in sight ahead, and the *Mary* quickly passed her.

A day and a half later they turned up the Severn River toward the familiar outlines of Annapolis. Matthew had been away only four months, and he hoped his wife would be happy to find out he was home early.

Chapter 38

As the two ships sailed up the Chesapeake Bay, Matthew stood by the binnacle, savoring the green of the banks of the low coastline of the bay. He thought he might never sail past it again, except on a pleasure or fast packet boat. The wind was moderate, churning up small wavelets that passed discreetly along the smooth waterline, disturbing the small tufts of green sea grass that were beginning to grow in spite of the copper sheathing that peeked above the waterline. The sound was almost minimal, and Matthew concentrated on listening to it to impress it on his memory. Never going to sea again would have its rewards, but he knew he would miss the sounds of the wind and water and the crying of the birds. Even now the bay seagulls were following the ship, searching for discarded scraps.

As he watched, Johnson came to the side and heaved a tub of scraps overboard. Then he stood and watched the gulls fighting over the swirling refuse. He turned toward Matthew and laughed. "Ain't going to do this any more."

An occasional bay gull swooped into the fight. Then a tern came by and joined in on the argument, only to be out-manuvered by smaller, more agile bay gulls.

The color of the water in the Chesapeake Bay was not the clear blue of the ocean. The bay water was diluted by millions of gallons of fresh water bearing with it tons of brown and black silt. The result was a dark green, changing with each new storm as it added more tons of silt.

As they neared the anchorage off Annapolis, Matthew could not resist one last Jones-type dash. "Hoist all sail!" he shouted to the boatswain.

The boatswain looked at him oddly. "Sir, we have only a mile to go to the anchorage."

"I know, but it's going to be a very fast mile. Get with it, now!"

The extra sails went up, hoisted by a grinning crew, watching the byplay between their captain and boatswain.

The *Mary* leaped ahead, seemingly sensing the end of the voyage and a rest at the anchorage.

Christopher concentrated on judging the remaining distance to the anchorage. When he thought it was just right, he shouted, "Down all sails. Stand by the anchor!"

The boatswain carefully checked the anchor releasing gear. "All ready!" he shouted. Then he grinned. "I hope we don't run up on the beach."

Christopher, still concentrating, ignored him. When he judged they were just the right distance short of the anchorage, he took a deep breath and shouted, "Let go!"

The boatswain pulled the wooden pins out of the hempen stops holding the anchor up. The anchor hesitated for a split moment and then plunged into the green water.

The anchor cable whipped out after it, running around a set of bitts. When he judged the speed of the outgoing cable was about right, he yelled, "Snub her!"

The seamen slowed the speed of the cable, and soon it stopped.

"Hold her!" the boatswain ordered. He leaned over the vibrating cable and felt the tension. The catenary of the strong cable rose to almost a straight line, tending aft toward the straining anchor on the bottom. Beads of bay water were wrenched from it and fell back into the bay.

The boatswain said, more quietly now, "The anchor is holding, Captain. Request permission to secure the cable."

"Permission granted," Matthew said in a resigned voice.

MacIntosh soon brought the lagging *Bailey* to an anchorage nearby. A crowd of people slowly gathered on the waterfront opposite the two ships.

Matthew recognized his father, and a boat soon brought him to the sea ladder of the *Mary*. Eric Christopher climbed up swiftly and paused on the quarterdeck.

Matthew said, "Sir, I give your ship back to you. She's a nimble and fast miracle."

Eric said, "Son, I'm glad you're back. I've had word that you have been sending in prizes all up and down the northeastern coast. Are you all right?"

"I'm fine, Pa, and there's no damage to the ship. I brought you a special prize over there. Do you recognize her?"

Eric looked over the frigate carefully. She was now straining at her anchor nearby. Then he said, "Well, I'll be dammned! It's the *Bailey*. She licked us a year or so ago in Delaware Bay."

"No, Pa, she didn't lick us. We put our ship aground ourselves without a shot in her. Let's get back in your boat. I want you to go over and see something."

The boat was called alongside, they embarked, and were rowed to the *Bailey*. Scotty MacIntosh, standing proudly on the quarter-deck, saluted when the two Christophers came aboard. "Sir," he said, "this prize is yours."

Eric Christopher looked around at the battered but partially re-paired ship and the grinning prize crew. "I can hardly believe this."

MacIntosh said, "There's more." He turned to his crew. "Bring Captain Nottingham out here."

Two men went below and soon came up escorting Captain Nottingham, still wearing his torn uniform and a bandage over the cut on his forehead. One of the men carried his sword and handed it to MacIntosh.

MacIntosh held it out toward Eric Christopher and said, "Sir, I present you with this sword. You deserve it."

Eric Christopher took it gingerly, but said nothing as he fought back the tears.

Captain Nottingham drew himself up. "Well, as soon as you send me ashore and I am exchanged for another prisoner, they'll give my sword back to me."

Eric Christopher turned livid. "Well, you bastard, you'll never get this one back." He turned and threw it well out in the river. It turned end over end and splashed into the water.

After Matthew made arrangements to turn the prisoners over to the Continental Navy, and had given the *Bailey* to the prize court sitting in Annapolis, he strode quickly up the brick sidewalks of Annapolis. At his house he leaped up the front stoop and banged on the familiar door.

Inside he could hear the gentle but strong voice of his wife remonstrating with two lively young children with equally strong but less gentle voices. He was home, and he would never leave again.

Chapter 39

For a week Matthew and Martha re-lived their honeymoon. Leisurely days in the garden followed passionate nights.

On the morning of the seventh day, Martha playfully shoved Matthew out of bed. "Go to work, lazy one. I've got much to do around here, and you'll get in the way."

Gradually Matthew worked himself into the routine of the shipyard. Ryan Buchanan was doing well as its head, but frequently Matthew's expertise was needed.

Once a week Eric Christropher drove into town behind a team of prancing thoroughbreds hitched to a gleaming carriage.

Matthew shook his head watching his father tie the team to a hitching post with a clove hitch. "Are there more horses out there on your farm?"

"Oh, yes, about one hundred when I last counted. By the way, you are all invited out for a picnic dinner next Sunday. You'll eat food you never knew existed before."

"Wonderful! I know my little ones will like it."

"They've been out there many times before when you were at sea and are getting to be good little riders. Martha and Theresa are getting to be close friends. By the way, wear your old boots."

"Why so? Yours are clean and polished."

"They are. They get worked on every night by an expert."

"I don't see why."

"Well, you know how we sailors are. We walk around looking up at the sky, the sails, the sun, or even the water. Out in the fields, I haven't learned to look down yet, and the next moment I've stepped in something. Believe me, the damned horses have been everywhere, and as I said, there are about one hundred. I can't walk fifty fathoms without getting my boots in a mess, and Theresa won't let me in the house until I take them off."

"You're not happy together?"

"Oh, yes, we are, and don't mistake me. Theresa is wonderful, but sometimes I think she needs something to occupy her time.

We have twenty servants. Some just take care of each other. There is a groom or maid behind every bush."

"You must have a plan. You always do."

"Oh, yes. I'm working on it. I figure she'll be pregnant in a couple of months. That will keep her so busy that I'll be able to sneak off to the shipyard a few days a week."

"But you have Ryan Buchanan."

"He is in love, and until he gets married he won't be worth a piece of frapping line."

"When will that happen?"

"About a month if he can hold out."

Matthew grinned. "I'm very happy for Elizabeth Scranton."

Three months later Matthew was firmly in command of the ship-yard, and Buchanan was back from his honeymoon. One day about 8 A.M., his father charged up to the hitching rack on horse-back astride a skittering chestnut horse. "Belay!" he shouted. "Drop anchor!"

The horse seemed to figure it out by himself and came to a halt in front of the hitching post. He knew from past experience that a nice lady would come out, take off his bridle, and put on a nose-bag full of oats.

Eric Christopher ambled into the office, poured a cup of coffee from the pot tended by the new Mrs. Buchanan, and sat down at the desk, now kept for him.

Before the group could get into their usual deep discussion of the day's plans, a young man carrying a briefcase walked in, looked around, and fixed his gaze on Matthew. "Former Lieutenant Christopher?" he said confidently.

Matthew frowned. "Yes, I am. And who, may I ask, are you?"

"Lieutenant Graves Marion. I'm a confidential messenger for the Congressional Marine Committee. I have a very important let-ter for you. May I deliver it in private?"

"You may, but I'll still read it with my colleagues present, so you might just as well give it to me here."

The young officer grinned. "They told me you would do this, so I have permission to give it to you any way you want it." Lieutenant Marion opened his briefcase and took out a bulging envelope. "This is from Captain John Paul Jones. After you read it and give me your decision, I have several other documents to deliver to you from the Marine Committee."

Matthew took the envelope and read the address. "It's from Captain John Paul Jones, all right. I've seen the handwriting often enough."

He picked up a small knife and slit the top of the envelope. He began to read silently. He frowned frequently and occasionally muttered. Finally he tossed it to his father. "Pa, read this and then give it to Ryan."

Matthew got up and strode up and down impatiently as his father read the letter. When Eric Christopher finished it, he frowned just as deeply as his son had, and tossed the letter to Buchanan, who picked it up as if it were a poisonous snake. He shook his head. "From the way you two are acting, I don't think I want to read this."

Matthew sat down. "Go ahead. You may be involved, too. While you read it I'll send for some coffee for Lieutenant Marion."

Matthew turned to his father, "Pa, what do you think?"

Eric Christopher shrugged. "It's up to you, son, and if you want to go to sea, Ryan Buchanan and I can handle the business. The key is your wife. I suggest you go home and let her read the letter right away."

The young officer broke in. "You will have to make a decision soon. I will be here all day visiting relatives. I am to take the fast packet back to Philadelphia the morning after that. If you choose to come back to active duty, I will deliver your commission to you. It will have the same date as the original commission you had. The Marine Committee will make arrangements to send you to L'Orient, France, on a fast Dutch sloop. You will go incognito with a Dutch passport as a Dutch merchant. Even if the Dutch ship is stopped, you will be safe. I am sure you will be back with Captain Jones within three weeks, and the letter you have explains why he wants you. Obviously the Marine Committee is strongly behind him."

Matthew nodded. "I understand. There's no need to talk about this now. I'll go to see my wife right away. I'll see you on the packet pier at 7 A.M. with my answer one way or the other."

"Very well, good luck. Captain Jones, your navy, and your country need you."

The young officer left. Christopher suspected that there might be a young lady of some interest among the relatives he was to visit.

Eric Christopher grinned. "I'd hate to be there when Martha reads that letter."

Matthew shook his head slowly. "Pa, what shall I do?"

Eric Christopher pursed his lips. "I can't help you. Your conscience must guide you, and your wife must agree with what you choose to do. She has given enough to her country already by sending you off twice."

～

Matthew trudged up the streets toward his home. The letter seemed to be burning a hole in his pocket. He opened the door and was greeted by the laughter of his children.

Martha, following close behind them, said in alarm. "Are you sick? It's only 10 o'clock."

Matthew shook his head. "Just a little. Can Mammy sit with the children? I have to talk with you."

"Of course. Let's go out into the garden. The day is beautiful."

Matthew sighed. "Maybe it won't be so nice after you read this letter."

When they reached the summer house, Matthew sat down next to Martha and handed her the letter. "This says it all," he said.

Martha looked at him hesitantly and took the letter out of the foreign-looking envelope She began to read. After the second page she stopped. "I can tell this is from Captain John Paul Jones, but I have trouble reading his continental writing and I don't know any of the people he is talking about. Maybe you ought to read it aloud and explain it to me. I'll stop you when I don't understand something."

Matthew took the letter and began to read:

"*Dear Lieutenant Christopher:*

I address you thus because I hope with all my heart you will soon become a lieutenant again.

I need your services most urgently, as does my new ship, the Bon Homme Richard, *and our navy. I would not petition you if I knew anyone else who could carry out this task for me. I know you have already done this before and should not be asked again, but I must. I know how it is, the patriotic and capable ones are always turned to again and again.*

I will be as brief as possible and will fill you in when I see you. As I predicted, I had continuing troubles with the Ranger *and Lieutenant Simpson. At one time I had him incarcerated awaiting court martial. Just as I was about to be able to order the necessary number of senior officers to conduct his trial, one of the Lee brothers, those scoundrels, who were in league with Simpson's relatives, deliberately held up the orders of one of the captains so that the trial could not take place, and Simpson was released from detention and parole and allowed to take command of the* Ranger *and bring her back to America. I can't tell you in a letter about the two Adams' traitors and the three Lee crooks. I will tell you in person later.*"

Martha broke in. "Who are these men? I thought they were patriots who had started the revolution."

Matthew shook his head. "Some day the truth will come out. John Adams and Samuel Adams did take part in the start of the revolution but turned badly when they went to France to represent their new country. What they and the Lees have done in France is reprehensible, bordering on treason and theft. The three Lee brothers, William, Arthur, and Richard Henry, have so dishonored the name of Lee that several decades will be required to cleanse it."

"This is too much for me. Go ahead."

Matthew cleared his throat and went on reading:

> "*So much for the poor* Ranger. *The crew left in rags and had not received a single sou of their pay or prize money. The Adams' and Lees apparently got it all, or at least prevented it from being paid to the crew. I could not even get enough to pay for provisions for them.*
>
> *When the* Ranger *sailed, I concentrated on getting a new command from the French. I fought the Americans and the French for six months without success. Finally I went over their heads to the King, and he generously ordered that I be given a suitable ship to command and that it be accompanied by a number of French warships on projects His Majesty had in mind. Now the Marquis de Lafayette is considering bringing five hundred troops with him for a foray around the coast of England.*
>
> *This sounds interesting, but I will not mislead you. The politics in France are fierce, and I cannot predict what will happen.*
>
> *My new ship, which I took over yesterday, used to be the* Arras, *and I have re-named her the* Bon Homme Richard. *Of course the King is pleased. Frankly, she is a floating cheese box. She has no sails, guns, crew, or provisions. It is with all this that you must help me.*
>
> *I need you badly. The lieutenant bringing this will explain how you will join me.*
>
> *One last time I beseech you to exercise your patriotism. I promise to return you to your wife as soon as possible, probably in nine months.*
>
> *Your admiring shipmate,*
> *John Paul Jones.*"

Martha tried to laugh but could not. "Just enough time to bear a baby."

Matthew started, "Are you pregnant?"

Martha sighed, "Thank God, no. But when you come back I won't waste any time again."

"Then you won't object if I go?"

"Of course I object, but I know you'll never forgive me if I don't let you go. When will you leave?"

"Tomorrow morning."

"My God! That man is in a hurry to begin."

"Always, but he finishes in a hurry, too. I will be home as soon as possible, and this time I promise never to leave you again."

Chapter 40

Promptly at 7 A.M. the next morning, Matthew appeared in his office at the shipyard. His father and Ryan Buchanan were there, idly drinking coffee while waiting for him.

Christopher said, "I turn over my keys to you. I expect to be back in nine months."

"That should do it," Eric Christopher said. "I expect you'll have a younger brother by then. In the meantime we'll keep the yard going."

"What? Your new wife is pregnant?"

Eric Christopher grinned. "Just the way I planned. That's why I'm here. She won't want me to infect the nursery."

Soon the young officer showed up on his way to the packet landing. "Well, Matthew Christopher, are you to be a lieutenant again?"

Matthew sighed. "Yes. Give me the damned paper and I'll sign it."

He read and signed the commission and gave it to his father. "Pa, give this to Martha and ask her to frame it and hang it somewhere."

He hoisted his seabag over his shoulder and he and the young officer walked to the packet landing, Matthew explaining points of interest as they went.

When they got underway, Matthew looked back at the Annapolis steeples. Graves Marion looked at them, too. "I've never seen them before. They're very impressive, and there are a great many of them."

"They look a damned sight better on the way home." Matthew said.

～

Two days later the packet landed at Philadelphia. Matthew made his way with the young Marion to Continental Navy Headquarters. "You are to call on the head of the Continental Navy, and he will take you to see the senior members of the Marine Committee. I believe they will have some oral instructions for you to relay to Captain Jones and several letters and dispatches to take to Mister Franklin. Some of them seem to remember you from a previous visit."

Christopher grinned. "I should think so. I delivered a lot of choice rum to them."

"Why don't they write to Captain Jones, too?"

"They don't trust the diplomatic mails and those who have accesss to them. They know the Lee brothers and the Adams will open the mail."

"So? The treachery is well known, isn't it?"

"Yes, and the Adams' or the Lees might delay the delivery of the mail or destroy it. Captain Jones will explain this to you."

After Matthew had carried out the calls, the young officer took him down to the waterfront and pointed out the Dutch ship waiting at the pier. "This is as far as I can go," he said. "I don't want them to see me. Here is your ticket and Dutch passport. Good luck."

Christopher boarded the ship and was given a small stateroom. The trip was unusually boring because none of the officers or crew spoke English. Matthew spent the time exercising, trying to regain his physical condition. He knew that it was the first thing Jones would notice.

Three weeks later the Dutch ship entered the port of L'Orient, picked up a pilot, and headed for a small landing. Matthew walked over to the quarterdeck and stood near the pilot. He was still wearing civilian clothes. The pilot asked in passable English, "Good voyage, sir?"

Matthew grinned. "Yes, Captain, and a quick one. I haven't been able to talk to anyone for three weeks. Can you tell me if the large ship over there is the *Bon Homme Richard*?"

The pilot shrugged. "I understand she is now known by that name. A Captain Jones took her over, hoisted the American flag, and changed her name from *Arras*. The old name is still faintly visible on her stern."

Matthew nodded, "She looks a little like a New England barn, but I'll bet she is fast and maneuverable like all French-built ships."

The pilot put his finger alongside his nose. "Ah, young man, you are not like most Americans. You recognize nautical skill in my countrymen." Then he shook his head. "But what am I saying? That one over there is an exception and is as slow as American molasses flows. Are you headed for her?"

"Yes, Captain. I am to be one of her lieutenants."

The pilot shook his head. "Poor peasant. No guns. No sails. No supplies. You will have a very big job."

"Yes, Captain, and I am eager to get at it."

The pilot fingered his mustache and shook his head doubtfully. "You Americans never cease to amaze me as to what you want to do. Personally I wouldn't want to go aboard her for any purpose. Too many passengers."

"Too many? I thought you said she had only a few men on board."

"Not many men, but plenty of passengers."

"I don't understand?"

"You will soon. Not many men aboard but plenty of rats."

Matthew swung down the brow of the Dutch ship after the pilot. He threw a salute at the captain of the Dutch ship, and went over to a nearby rowboat to negotiate passage to the *Bon Homme Richard*.

The pilot took pity on his minimal French, walked down the pier, and talked the rowboat skipper into a reasonable fee for the passage out.

After half an hour of vigorous effort by two oarsmen, the boat was pulled alongside. There were no men visible topside, but Mattew climbed up the sea ladder and had his seabag hoisted to him by the boatmen.

On deck a lone man in a marine uniform was leaning against the bulwark. Matthew asked, "Are you on watch?"

"I guess so, sir."

Matthew fumed. "I'm Lieutenant Christopher. I'm going below to change into uniform. When I get back, I will expect you to be squared away and keeping a proper watch. If you ever let another boat come alongside and discharge a passenger without a challenge, I'll have you in irons."

Christopher turned on his heel and headed below, half expecting to run into a platoon of rats, but saw only a few bright eyes in the darkness. He found a vacant stateroom, appropriated it, and unpacked his seabag. He hung up his clothing and changed into uniform. When he thought he was reasonably togged out, he went in search of Captain Jones' cabin.

Chapter 41

Just aft of the quarterdeck in the after deck structure, he found a door he thought would lead to the captain's cabin. There was no sentry on watch. A small calling card was tacked to the door. It read "Captain John Paul Jones." He knocked firmly on the door. A voice said, "Who is it?"

"Lieutenant Christopher, reporting for duty."

There was a bustle inside, the noise of the sliding of a door bolt, and the door was flung open. A beaming Captain Jones flung his arms around Christopher. "My God! Am I glad to see you! I was afraid you might not come."

Matthew said, "I would have gone anywhere in the world if you needed me. Where is your orderly and why is your door bolted?"

"We don't have enough men aboard yet to permit such a luxury. As for the bolt, I need protection from my enemies, internal as well as external. France is a forest of villains, and some of them, unfortunately, are Americans."

"I'll do what I can to protect you, but I need to find the armory so I can draw a cutlass and a pistol. Then I need to know what you want done first."

"You are looking at the only person who can do that now. Let's take a tour and then we'll rustle up some lunch, as the American westerners say. Strangely enough, my chef is superb. He was sent by the King. Cooking lunch is the best thing he does. Then, he samples more and more of the cooking wine as the day goes on. The supper falls off, or sometimes he falls into the supper. Now let's go topside. I assume you did not travel with a sword, so I will take you by the armory first and issue you a cutlass and two pistols. As you can guess, I keep the keys on my belt. Please use the cutlass on the rats, both animal and human, to save ammunition. We have very little powder and no guns yet, but I have prospects. As a matter of fact, we have only enough powder to make up a half dozen pistol charges."

"What will be our armament?"

"If we could get them somewhere, you will see that we have prepared positions for twenty-eight twelve-pounders on the gun deck, twelve eighteen-pounders on the lower deck, and eight nine-pounders on the weather deck at the forecastle, quarterdeck, and gangways."

Now they were passing down the center of the main deck. Jones shook his head, "I will be lucky to find old second-hand twelve-pounders for this deck. Either the gunner, if I can find one, or you will have to scour the countryside for old guns left in unused fortifications. Now let's go below."

Below, in the gloom, Matthew could see six ports on either side, now tightly closed. What little light there was reflected in the eyes of several expectant rats.

Jones, who was wearing his sword, drew it and flailed away at the twinkling eyes. "Good exercise," he said. "I recommend it. I kill a dozen a day, but you have to remember to assign a man to throw the corpses over the side. When we get more officers and more marines aboard I expect to make this ship a living hell for the rest of the rats. I will declare a bounty for each dead rat of a gill of rum to be paid by the purser."

"What about the twelve eighteen-pounders you planned for this deck?"

"I have made arrangements for the King's foundry to cast six of them. We will move them from side to side as needed. They should be first class."

Matthew frowned. "French ships are good sailers, but I have heard that their guns are awful, even if the King's foundry makes them. Are you sure we can't get English guns?"

Jones shrugged, "I have no choice here. I would like them if I could get them. I will be lucky if these are finished before we sail. Let's go up to my cabin and see if our lunch is ready."

As they passed aft along the weather deck, Matthew noted that the ship had the traditional three masts of a frigate, but had no sails rigged yet. She seemed to be larger than a British frigate. The structure aft was awkwardly placed, and he wondered what he could do to increase the ship's speed and maneuverability.

Jones sensed what he was thinking about. "Don't bother at this time to think about making major changes in the ship's structure. I have neither the money nor the time to do it. Perhaps changes in the arrangements of the sails and shifting of the ballast might give us a knot. Let's face it, this is a French barn that happens to be at sea. We'll make up for its shortcomings with courage, zeal, and intelligence. With just two of those qualities, we'll beat the damned English any time."

As Jones had predicted, lunch was superb. Matthew felt his spirits rising. After dessert, he said, "Captain, I can see we have a lot to do. Just where do you want me to start?"

"Recruiting is our biggest problem. We are not allowed to approach skilled French personnel. There may be some peasants still available. We will literally have to beat the bushes for a few English prisoners at large who might join us. There are some Americans who may join our cause to serve their nation. We want foreigners of any kind, Swedes, Germans, Lascars, and even Irish."

"If we are successful we will have quite a collection."

"That won't matter if I can convince them to fight, and I think I can."

"You always have."

"There is another hope. The Marquis de Lafayette is behind us, and at one time he hoped to take a substantial land force with us, but a few treasonous Americans have been at work to spoil this plan, and now Lafayette has been ordered to take a small land force on some minor expedition. His help has been cancelled for now, but the mere rumor that he might join us has has encouraged several marine officers to bring about one hundred marines with them to join us. They think we can land a force on the shores of England, and they want part of the action."

"Will we?"

Jones grinned. "No comment just now. Even the rats have ears on this ship."

"Do you want me to travel around and recruit?"

"No. I have just signed on a purser named Mease. He will join a Lieutenant Amial and two Lunt brothers on trips throughout France. I have also signed on a Lieutenant Richard Dale. He will be our first lieutenant in view of his extensive experience. Your seniority makes you next in line, athough I still consider you my aide with complete access to me at any time. I hope to add another lieutenant, a boatswain, and a gunner. I have one midshipman, Nathaniel Fanning, and I have prospects for others. They will be very useful in commanding prizes. I think the recruiting problem, although serious, is going on apace. I want you to concentrate on getting the ship in shape. Your skills will be taxed. If you can add some speed in tacking, I will be happy. Also make sure the magazines are safe and designed to supply the guns properly without blowing us all up."

"I'll try, sir."

"Well, we've done all we can to enjoy this lunch. Now let's get on with it. I leave tomorrow to see Mister Franklin and will take the dispatches and letters you brought this far. You will be in command until I get back. Don't let a rat named Captain Landais aboard. We have enough already. Oh, by the way, I may send you up to Paris for subsequent matters." Jones raised his eyebrows. "Would you like to go and perhaps find a few interesting companions?"

Matthew laughed. "I don't think so. I've got all I can handle at home."

Jones beamed. "Ah, yes, I remember that lovely lass of yours at home. I only wish I had met one as charming in my youth."

Chapter 42

For the next weeks, until early June, 1779, Christopher worked night and day, sometimes supervising French carpenters by the light of lanterns. Slowly the main faults of the ship and her equipment were corrected. As he walked about the ship, Christopher shook his head in frustration. "Can't change many of these faults. The hull is just built wrong. The French designer must have been habitually drunk."

Guns arrived by barge almost daily. Christopher had the guns hoisted aboard and emplaced in carriages made by local carpenters and fitted with the restraining rigging. He spent hours making the magazines and the powder transport system as safe as possible, remembering the tragedy of the *Randolph*.

The guns cast by the King's foundry finally arrived and were loaded. Christopher inspected them carefully, now assisted by a recently recruited gunner named Aristo. Aristo sniffed in disgust. "I don't like this," he said. "Typical French junk. The metal smells cheap. We'll test these with reduced charges when we get to sea, but I don't want to be down here when they are fired in anger with full charges."

Gradually boatloads of sailors of many nationalities arrived. Lieutenant Dale, now permanently aboard, received them and did his best to parcel them out to the various departments vying for them. By the end of June, over three hundred men were aboard, of whom over one hundred were marines. These were quickly dressed in uniforms designed by Captain Jones to resemble the British marine uniform. Jones glowed with pride at their appearance and told them he wanted to make them experts at fighting from the fore tops and ratlines.

On the last day of June, four French ships to be placed under Jones' command slipped into port. The *Pallas, Cerf, Monsieur,* and the *Vengeance* were converted from prizes and carried various numbers and weights of guns, but none was as well armed as the *Bon Homme Richard*.

The *Alliance*, also recently added, was new and trim, carried thirty-six twelve- and nine-pounders and was as fast as she looked. Jones stood one day on the top deck with Christopher. "Look at that beautiful ship! She could be very valuable, but I fear she will be wasted."

"Why so?"

"She is now under the command of one of the sorriest naval officers I've ever seen. Even worse than Simpson."

"How did he get to command her?"

"He was a terrible failure as a French naval officer. After he was fired, Landais went to America and ingratiated himself with several members of the Marine Committee, by telling awful lies. He used the influence of the Adams' and the Lee brothers. Landais was given the command of the *Alliance* over the heads of several American naval officers as a gesture of friendship toward the French."

"Hasn't he been found out?"

"Mostly by me. His officers and men have petitioned several times for his relief, but Adams and the Lees keep interfering. His crew is near to mutiny."

"Can't you get rid of him?"

"I could challenge him to a duel in light of the false statements he has made about me. I could run him through easily, but the French would not like it and my project would collapse."

"Now he is under my command, but I am sure he will continue to do whatever he wants to do. Always keep an eye on him. I am sure he will shoot us in the back some day. That is just the kind of lowlife he is."

"Well, all Frenchmen aren't bad. Your cook is all right."

Jones laughed. "He can cook all right, but I never tell him what to cook."

"Who are these men, Adams and Lee?"

"John Adams was well known as a patriot who led those who started the revolution. He deserves credit for those actions, but later, as commissioner to France, he changed completely. He took every opportunity to act against Mister Franklin and me.

"Samuel Adams, a cousin, was also an early patriot and he later acted in concert with John Adams.

"The Lee brothers were worse. They used their positions as congressmen to send each other to important positions in our diplomatic mission in France. There they diverted funds sent by the American Congress to our officials in France, protecting the money intended for paying, clothing, and feeding our crews.

"Some day Franklin will get the upper hand and dispose of them, but we will all suffer until he does it. It will not be an easy task."

Ten days later, Lieutenant Richard Dale, accompanied by Christopher, reported that the *Bon Homme Richard* was ready for sea.

"Good," Jones said. "Are we missing any important equipment?"

Dale cleared his throat. "This may sound trivial, but we don't have any manacles for prisoners."

"Why not? I thought we ordered some."

"We did, but the French minister of Marine, De Chaumont, turned down the request."

Jones laughed. "I believe he thinks I am toying with his wife."

Christopher, ever ready to speak up, asked, "Are you, sir?"

Jones guffawed. "Not by the rules of our country. All I did was write several letters."

"Are you sure that's all, sir?"

Jones sighed. "Well maybe one did contain a poem of slight passion, but it was not directed at her specifically. Maybe she left it lying around."

"Monsieur De Chaumont challenged you about it?"

Jones shook his head. "Of course not. But he has been a little stiff and cold in his correspondence lately."

Christopher nodded. "Maybe you should send me on the next trip to Paris."

Jones beamed. "Of course. Capital! But we won't have to do that before we get underway."

"I see, sir."

Jones smiled. "Maybe Monsieur De Chaumont is jealous of my skill as a poet."

~

On 19th of June, Jones ordered the four accompanying ships to get underway on a practice cruise. The flotilla settled down for the night, but the peace did not last long. Just before midnight, as the watch was changing, the *Bon Homme Richard*, sailing downwind, crashed into the *Alliance*. She was lying to for some strange reason. Captain Jones was in his cabin, but Captain Landais was on deck. Later it was learned that he had failed to take any action to avoid or ease the collision. He left the young officer on deck without any instructions. He dashed below to get his pistols, believing his wildly shouting crew was mutinying. Fortunately no one was injured and the damage was minimal.

Jones kept the ships at sea for a few days, testing their capabilities. Then he signalled a return to port.

As they sailed slowly along, Jones said to Christopher, "Look at those other ships. All have reefs in their sails or have struck sails to slow down so they won't over take us. At the same time, I've ordered every scrap of canvas we have to be set. Let's face it. This ship really is as slow as a barn."

Christopher fumed. "I can add another half a knot."

Jones shook his head, "Don't bother. It will still be too little."

The ships entered L'Orient and anchored in an atmosphere of gloom. Jones looked at the surrounding ships. "Well, Christopher, all is not lost. One or two of our ships are fast. I will have to use them well to make up for our lack of speed."

"What will you do with her?"

"Hope the enemy is stupid enough to let us close, throw over grapnels, and board her."

Chapter 43

The following days in L'Orient were confusing, as the French government dithered and repeatedly changed their rules regarding the taking of prizes. The word from Paris would deprive the Americans of most of the proceeds from prizes.

Then the participation, long in doubt, of the Marquis de Lafayette, was cancelled for good.

A note from Mister Franklin indicated that the French were inadvertently, and maybe even deliberately, leaking to the English the forthcoming plans for Jones' venture.

Jones crumpled the note and threw it over the side. "Damn! We're fighting everybody! Here we are in a rotten ship with second hand guns, a cobbled-together crew. We're saddled with four ships of doubtful loyalty and the *Alliance* that may shoot us. To top it all, my best ship is commanded by a captain who is hostile to me. Frankly, when the battles start, we'll be fighting alone."

Christopher laughed. "So what? You always fight best against those odds."

At midnight on the 13th, Jones finished writing letters, sent them ashore, and announced that they would get underway at 4 A.M. "That way," he said, "none of the captains will have more than four hours notice, nobody ashore will see them weighing anchor, and no spies will have time to do anything."

The ships slipped quietly out of the harbor with Jones pacing the quarterdeck slowly. The sortie was smooth.

Still dissension arose quickly after they were out of harbor. The captain of the *Monsieur* tried to take a prize and plunder it by himself rather than take it as part of the flotilla. Jones quickly brought him up, and he left the formation for France.

Landais, in the *Alliance*, continued to ignore Jones' orders, refusing to take positions assigned, and frequently moving off in various directions. Sometimes he returned that evening. Other times he remained absent overnight.

The *Cerf* and *Grenville* captains soon made the same mistake as the *Monsieur*. Jones sent them packing, too.

As the ships cruised up the coast of France in dangerously shallow waters, the wind died into one of the rare calms in the Atlantic. Jones looked out over the smooth sea. "You'll only see this once every five years. The Atlantic Ocean in the eastern side of Great Britain is wild and cold, rarely smooth like this."

Christopher said, "I've never been here before. The Atlantic Ocean off the coast of Ireland is quite different. Bits of sargasso weed and kelp float in it and there are more birds. I would judge the temperature in that area is twenty degrees warmer."

Jones nodded. "Every large body of water has its own appearance. This is a darker blue, almost metallic. The seas off Ireland are greener. The Mediterranean is azure blue, as is the Caribbean. The southern seas are said to be unique, although I have not seen much of them."

Jones became nervous waiting for a breeze and sent the barge ahead to take a tow line and swing the ship free from the expected rush of the tide peculiar to that coast. The barge's crew, mostly ex-English prisoners-of-war, cut the towline and fled to the nearby shore.

Jones sent Third Lieutenant Cutting Lunt to retrieve the barge, but his inexperience caused him to go too far toward the shore, and a sudden dense fog hid the boat. In spite of a prolonged wait for its return, Jones concluded that the boat had been captured.

Captain Landais came aboard to remonstrate with Jones over the lost boat. He was wild-eyed, his color alternating between red and white.

Christopher moved close to the two officers, expecting trouble.

Jones tried to answer Landais' arguments, but they were impossible to counter. Before Jones could answer one point, Landais was off on another tack without waiting for Jones to answer.

Christopher shook his head, "This is worse than Jones told me," he muttered. He remembered reading the letter to Jones from Sam Adams describing Landais as "jealous of everything and everybody. He is constantly bewildered and is near to insanity." Christopher wondered how Adams could write this while still championing Landais before Congress.

Landais got even louder and put a hand on Jones' arm, speaking right into his face. Christopher moved rapidly toward the pair to avert a crisis.

Jones waved him away, but Christopher, sensing trouble, remained close by. When Landais' sneering, loud voice again got out of hand, Christopher grabbed his arm and propelled him toward the gangway. Fortunately his gig was still below, or as Christopher said later, "I would have heaved the bastard into the water."

As the flotilla cruised northward, Landais showed alternating impudence and cowardice, sometimes dropping out of sight for days. Now only the *Pallas* and *Vengeance* remained in constant company. On September 18th, Jones called the commanding officers aboard the flagship for a conference to outline the plans for the future.

After the conference, Jones' instructions were carried back by the two captains, who grumbled as they left.

"What's wrong with them?" Christopher asked.

Jones shrugged. "Just Frenchmen. They don't want to do something different or what they're not familiar with."

"And what did you tell them?"

"I said we were going to take the port of Leith."

Christopher laughed. "No wonder you frightened them. How are you going to do it?"

"I will put my good Colonel of Marines Chamillard and his hundred and forty men in my boats. I will tow them close to Leith and send them ashore with a letter demanding a substantial ransom. I will tell them in the letter that I will burn their miserable city if they do not pay up. But of course I would not harm the poor citizens."

Christopher sighed. "I hope it works, and I'm sure you have arranged for signals between you and the colonel in case of bad weather or some other unexpected event."

"Of course. You know how I play the game. With initiative, but with enough care to be able to retreat."

Just as the *Bon Homme Richard* was in position off Leith, the citizens of that city were headed for the hills, and the marines were being loaded in the boats, a squall struck them. On signal, the men were hastily returned to the ship, and the boats were hoisted. The *Bon Homme Richard* was able to claw offshore. The squalls turned into a full fledged storm. Jones shivered. "This is more like the usual weather in the Atlantic. That calm didn't last long."

For several days the ships beat back and forth, well offshore, but in sight of the population, now streaming back into town.

As the storm subsided, Jones decided to attack Edinburgh rather than Leith, and the approach of his ships created an even worse crisis ashore as the word was sent from Leith to beware of the crazy Americans. The results could be seen as the populace gathered on the shore with ancient swords and other weapons.

Jones changed his objective to Kirkuddy, but the sturdy Scots stood on the shore laughing and brandishing claymores and fowling pieces.

Jones laughed. "We don't want to confront the good Scots. They might spill some blood rather than run away."

The continuing bad weather forced Jones to change his objective to Tyne, where Jones declared, "I can stop the movement of half the coal coming into England if I take Tyne."

That evening they captured a small fishing boat that had come out to challenge the weather and take advantage of high prices of fish in Tyne that had resulted from the inability of the fishermen to get out through the weather into their usual fishing grounds.

Jones had the skipper brought to his cabin and gave him a double shot of rum. "How is it over there?" he asked.

The fisherman downed the drink and grinned. "Well, Captain, you done a right proper job of confusing people. They don't know where you're going to land, and the few troops they had are exhausted from trying to follow you."

Jones laughed. "I don't know where I'm going to land either. Will I find much opposition?"

"Not until yesterday. Before that there would have been only a few old gaffers too slow to run away, and who would have had a few fowling pieces. Now several hundred troops have moved into Tyne and will try to follow you wherever you go. There are some small sloops that will shadow you and send the word ashore to the troops."

Jones sent the fishing vessel skipper ashore with a jug of rum and a small sum of money for the catch of fish he bought from him.

Jones called Christopher into his cabin. "I think we've confused the authorities enough. We'll have some of the fish for lunch and send the rest to the galley for the crew. Then we'll be off for our next rendezvous at Flamborough Head. That will be the 23rd of September and then by the schedule I set, I must be in Texel, Holland, for the scheduled end of the cruise."

"What do you intend to do at Flamborough Head?"

"That will be our final battle ground. We should be able to intercept and destroy a good portion of the English merchant fleet bound there from the Baltic."

"Why did you choose that location?"

Jones walked over to a chart on the table. He pointed to Flamborough Head. "This prominent point on the English coast is a vital navigational point for ships coming from the Baltic and headed for English ports. The English escort will come close to the English coast to establish where they are after crossing the Baltic Sea. They come down in convoy from the Baltic several times a year. Without the cargoes of these ships, the English would be hard pressed to feed their citizens."

"I see."

Jones went on, "I intend to be there before the English. My spies in Paris have given me the information I need. If we can capture a large part of the merchant fleet, we triumph. If we don't, we must at least destroy the escorting warships. Either event will resonate around the world. We must prevail if our country's cause is to be advanced."

"But you may have to pay a heavy price."

"Of course. I will give my life for my country of I have to do so."

Christopher sighed. "I don't think you will have to go that far. I believe you will win."

Chapter 44

Jones' flotilla arrived one week before the expected arrival time of the English fleet from the Baltic. The *Pallas* and *Vengeance* were firmly committed to fighting with her, but the *Alliance*, as usual, dashed about with no apparent aim. Jones paid little attention to Landais.

Jones sailed up and down the coast off Flamborough Head awaiting the English fleet. Ashore he could see hundreds of civilians watching him from the safety of the dunes, brandishing antiquated hand weapons as the Englishmen and Scots had done at Leith and Edinburgh.

Jones laughed, "We've stirred those poor people up over there. At least they'll have a good view of the upcoming battle and a long time will pass before they stop fearing the dastardly Americans."

On the 23rd of September, Jones was sailing just south of Flamborough Head, taking small prizes. As the *Bon Homme Richard* rounded the prominent head, chasing a prospective prize, the lookouts began to shout, "Many sails ahead!"

Jones ran aloft with his long glass. He was ebullient and fairly flew up the ratlines, the coattails of his jacket flying out behind him to leeward. When he got down, he shouted, "The whole damned fleet is out there! Let's after them! Beat to quarters!"

Christopher asked, "Did you recognize any warships when you were up there?"

"Certainly. They are the ones my spy said would escort the convoy. Captain Pearson commands the convoy from the fifty-six gun ship Serapis and she is accompanied by the *Countess of Scarborough* of twenty guns.

"Damn!" Christopher said. "We are badly out-gunned and out numbered."

"Never!" Jones said. "What are a few guns? And they may have more sailors and marines than we have, but that doesn't mean they out-man us. That's a matter of the fighting qualities of the men. We'll have the advantage there. They may have a new ship, a lot more speed, and other advantages, but I aim to make it all even in the end. We are Americans and therefore better than any English-men."

"Better?"

"Yes. We know what we are going to do. They don't. We'll take them."

The Serapis moved to the eastward, trying to give added pro-tection to the panicked convoy. Her speed advantage was obvious, and Jones expected her to close them, but she soon headed back, apparently for the protection of the coast at Flamborough Head. This reversal of course was wasted and let the *Bon Homme Richard* get closer. Jones followed her with every scrap of canvas he could pile on.

The dark was coming on, and a full moon was expected.

Christopher said anxiously, "Do you really want to fight at night, or shall we wait until dawn?"

Jones laughed. "The dark will be our best ally. The Serapis won't be able to see how weak we really are, and Landais will have a hard time shooting at us in the dark."

"You want to be close to the *Serapis*?"

"As close as a newlyweds in bed."

The moon rose as the *Bon Homme Richard* bore down on the *Serapis*, keeping her bow toward the enemy.

The ships narrowed the distance rapidly, and the officers and crew grew tense. Only Jones appeared to be calm as he strolled the deck, occasionally looking toward the *Serapis* through his night glass.

"Soon," he said.

Lieutenant Dale came to him and murmured in Jones' ear. "We are ready, sir."

Jones grinned, "Oh, yes, we are."

The ships were now on approximately opposite courses and were passing at pistol range, so near the officers on the quarter-deck could hear the flapping of canvas and the rustle of the light wind through the rigging of the other ship.

Jones was coldly silent, but Pearson, the captain of the *Serapis*, became anxious. Finally he shouted, "What ship is that?"

Jones said to Dale, "Say something, but don't give them our name."

Dale shouted some unintelligible answer.

Jones poked Dale in the ribs. "Shout louder."

Dale repeated the message.

Jones grinned. "Good perfomance. You should be on the boards."

Captain Pearson challenged them again.

Jones laughed. "Tell him the 'Princess Royal.'"

Dale was now getting into the game and shouted the name loudly and with feeling.

Pearson shouted back, "Answer truly or I'll fire."

Jones shook his head, "He's pretty dense. Answer him with a broadside. Maybe it will clear his ears."

Christopher moved nearer to the bulwark to get a better look.

The guns detonated and the battle was on. It would have to be to the end. Neither opponent would leave the convoy.

On the first broadside, tragedy struck the lower deck of the *Bon Homme Richard*. Gunner Aristo's worst fears came true about the ability of the guns. Two of the eighteen-pounders cast by the French King's foundry burst, killing their crews and many who stood nearby.

The *Bon Homme Richard* had suffered a grievous loss of gun and manpower before the battle had fairly started, but Captain Pearson would not know it for some time because of the covering darkness.

Above the bloody deck, the guns on the top decks continued to fire as the *Serapis* continued to punish her crippled opponent. Both ships traded unequal broadsides with the *Countess of Scarborough* adding several rounds. The *Pallas* and *Vengeance* failed to fire. The *Alliance* stayed aloof, sails aback, their whiteness flashing occasionally in the moonlight.

Christopher looked over his shoulder wondering how much the *Alliance* could contribute to their success if she would only join in.

By now Jones was sure the *Serapis* would soon overpower the *Bon Homme Richard* by her sheer weight of metal, and he decided to execute his plan to grapple with her. They had circled to come on parallel courses. He backed his sails, attempting to come astern of her, but could not attain the position he wanted. Now neither ship could fire a broadside. Jones waited tensely, but appeared calm. The men on the *Bon Homme Richard* behind the bulwarks and in the tops cradled grenades and pistols and were ready to board instantly at Jones' command.

Then the *Bon Homme Richard* drew clear as the vagaries of the light winds favored her. Captain Pearson, peering through the darkness, apparently over-confident, shouted, "Have you struck your colors?"

Jones, intent on maneuvering his ship, did not hear the question and therefore did not answer it, even though it was warranted. It was clear that the *Bon Homme Richard* had suffered serious and possibly fatal damage, easily twice as much as the other ship.

Then Jones got his second wind, knowing at last he could take the offensive if only he could close the *Serapis*. He ordered all canvas spread, and the *Bon Homme Richard* drew up to the side of the slowing *Serapis*. "Get your grapnels ready!" he shouted.

Captain Pearson, mistaking the intent of the *Bon Homme Richard* and her ability to continue to sail, backed his sails, and the *Bon Homme Richard* drew slightly ahead and then crossed her bows.

Jones shouted, "Now we've got her! Come to port while we put her in our grasp."

The ship swung rapidly to port toward the *Serapis* using the ability to turn quickly put in her by the shifting of ballast by Christopher.

Grapnels went over, but the lines were cut. Christopher, from his position, could see what was happening. "More grapnels!" He shouted.

The crew of the *Serapis* continued to cut the lines as fast as they came over, but Christopher organized a group of marines waiting behind the bulwark who soon shot down the *Serapis* sailors.

The marines aloft began to shoot at the men on the deck of the *Serapis*, killing any man who showed his head.

Jones sent Stacy, the sailing master, to find a large hawser to lash the ships together. He returned with two men dragging the huge line. As soon as it was wrapped around the ratlines above the two buwarks they appeared to be in a grim embrace.

Pearson struggled to direct his operations on his top side under the withering fire from aloft. But he managed to order his boatswain to drop an anchor, apparently hoping the strong current would scrape off the *Bon Homme Richard*.

The anchor dropped with a loud splash, but had little effect on the way of the ships.

By now the ships were side by side, so close the gunners had to lean out into the opposite ships and turn around to man their rammers.

The *Serapis* began to pound mercilessly the side of the *Bon Homme Richard*. The balls of her guns easily penetrated both sides of the hull and many of the internal braces were carried away.

On the other side, the *Bon Homme Richard* crew in the tops, particularly the marine sharpshooters, completely cleared the men topside on the *Serapis*. Some of the more agile sailors walked across the yards to the yards of the *Serapis* and threw grenades down on the men below trying to hide behind deck structures. Soon the deck of the *Serapis* was covered with wounded and dying men.

Christopher, concerned about the safety of the ship, came running up from below. "Sir, the internal bracing below has been destroyed, the deck may fall in at any moment."

"I suspect so, but we'll have the *Serapis* by then."

"The damage below is terrible, and almost all the men in the gun crews are dead. A few have run down to the cable tiers and the orlop deck."

"They should stay there until the fighting topside is over. We won't need them."

Suddenly the sound of grapeshot was evident as it spattered on the sails and topside. It alerted Jones, and he looked over his shoulder. "My God! That madman Landais is shooting grape at us!"

The *Alliance* could be plainly seen in the bright moonlight as it cruised slowly by them.

Jones said, "She can certainly make us out in the moonlight and the light of the fires."

Christopher gritted his teeth. "This is terrible. He can't have made a mistake."

The guns of the *Alliance* flashed again. "Get down behind the bulwarks!" Jones shouted.

The grape sounded like a swarm of large bees as it spread all over the ship. Christopher swore, picking a small piece of metal out of his jacket. "I'll challenge him this time, even if you don't want me to."

Jones laughed. "I have something planned for him worse than the sword."

After two more broadsides the *Alliance* passed out of range. Jones stood up. "Anybody hurt?"

The marines got up and were mustered by a nearby sergeant. "All present," he said. "We're ready."

Jones grinned in the moonlight. "Looks like as long as the Alliance stays out of range and the topside of the *Serapis* stays clear, our quarterdeck is the safest place to be. Let's get back to our guns."

Now fire broke out in a dozen places on both ships and many of the remaining crews had to leave their stations to fight the spreading flames. The *Serapis* crew was having more trouble fighting the fires and keeping them from spreading upwind because the *Bon Homme Richard* could prevent their movement in the open.

Christopher said, "Shall I continue to concentrate our guns on their topsides or fire at their men coming out to fight the fires?"

Jones shook his head. "Leave then to their tasks. If the fire on the *Serapis* gets out of hand she won't be of any use to us if we sink."

One of the marine officers, having just come up from below, said to Jones, "Sir, for God's sake, strike your colors or surrender!"

Jones shook his head. "No, I will sink, but I will not strike."

Below, the broadsides of the *Serapis* continued to blow enormous holes in the *Bon Homme Richard*'s sides. The carpenter and gunner came topside, both in a state of near panic. They thought the ship was sinking from the narrow view of the fight they had below. A passing man shouted, "The captain and Mister Dale are dead." Unfortunately neither warrant offcer tried to confirm the rumor.

The two warrant officers tried to send word to Captain Pearson that the *Bon Homme Richard* was striking, but the captain was wise enough not to take the word of a warrant officer and asked if Captain Jones had struck. Jones heard the conversation and saw the gunner at the top of the hatch. He swore, snatched two pistols from his belt, and not realizing that it would leave him unarmed, heaved them at the gunner. "Get below, you cowardly bastard!"

One pistol struck the carpenter in the forehead and bowled him over backwards and down the hatch.

Jones turned to Pearson, anxiously hanging over the bulwark. "No, sir. I don't ever dream of surrendering, and am determined never to strike."

Dale heard the reply, but the gunfire was so loud he could not hear it exactly. Later he would approximate it as, "I have not yet begun to fight," and it remained recorded in history that way. Jones was aware of the importance of such things to morale and never denied having made the statement in that form.

In the meantime the gunner, the recovered carpenter, and master-at-arms were at it again. Despite repeated instructions from Jones to the contrary, the master-at-arms released the prisoners whom he could not control without manacles. They promptly fled back to the *Serapis* by jumping through the gun ports.

The *Bon Homme Richard* still had her guns on the topside in commission. Christopher took charge of this battery, concentrating fire on the masts and rigging of the *Serapis*. Then a fire on the Serapis reached a cache of powder on the main deck outside the magazine, blowing up several guns and their crews.

There was not much more damage that could be done to the *Bon Homme Richard*. With the crew of the *Serapis* unable to stir from below, they could not get at the crew of the *Bon Homme Richard* gathered on the quarterdeck and in the tops. The topside of the *Serapis* was a shambles. The continuous fire from the tops wore Captain Pearson down as men on the open decks continued to fall. Jones could sense his change in fortune, and shouted to Pearson, crouched behind the bulwark, "Do you strike?"

Pearson replied in subdued but loud tones that he did, but said he could not lower the colors. "They were nailed to the mast," he said.

"You'll have to get them down yourself," Jones said.

Pearson climbed shakily aloft, afraid of men still unaware of the situation and who might want to take a free shot at him, but he made it and released the colors. Soon he was back on deck and the battle was over.

Christopher shouted to his gun crews, "Cease firing. It's over." Then he shouted aloft, "Come on down."

A marine aloft shouted back. "Sir, can I slide down one of the shrouds like the sailors do? I always wanted to."

Christopher grinned. "Come on down any way you want to. You men up there have earned anything you want."

Chapter 45

Dale was on the quarterdeck when he heard the *Serapis* had struck. He asked Captain Jones if he could board the ship. Jones gave his consent and ordered Christopher to follow to assess the condition of the stricken vessel. Midshipman Mayrant followed with a platoon of men. Just as he jumped down from the bulwark, an English sailor, hiding behind the bulwark, jumped up and thrust a pike into his thigh.

Christopher heard his cry of pain, turned around, and dispatched the English sailor with his cutlass.

The first lieutenant of the *Serapis* came out to the quarterdeck now that the firing from aloft had ceased. He asked Captain Pearson, "Have you struck, sir?"

"I have."

The lieutenant was distraught, and Dale was afraid he might cause trouble, so Dale ordered him to accompany his captain over to the *Bon Homme Richard*.

The scene on the two quarterdecks was one of terrible carnage. Pieces of bodies lay about. Blood soaked the decks and pieces of broken equipment littered the decks. Christopher looked about and shook his head, wriggling his nostrils at the stench of blood, burned gunpowder, and charred wood.

Pearson stepped aboard the smoking *Bon Homme Richard*, carefully avoiding the bodies, followed by his first lieutenant, and offered his sword to Jones. Jones took it momentarily, caressed it slowly, and gave it back to Pearson. "You fought a gallant fight," he said. "This was a battle of historic proportions, and your courage will be talked about for years."

Pearson muttered something about not wanting to surrender to a man with a rope around his neck, apparently referring to some troubles Jones had encountered in the Caribbean, but Jones was in an expansive mood and chose to ignore whatever he had said.

Christopher bristled and started to say something.

Jones interrupted him. "Nevermind. He's got a right to be upset."

Jones turned to the *Serapis* and yelled over to Dale, "Cut the lashings and follow me."

As the *Serapis* broke loose, Dale realized the anchor was still down, and he ordered the anchor cable cut. As the *Serapis* swung out of the wind, two of the masts at which Christopher had fired so many rounds fell over the side.

Jones, watching from the *Bon Homme Richard*, said, "You can't tell who won. Both ships are so badly battered."

Christopher said, "I don't think the *Bon Homme Richard* will last another day. You should make preparations to shift to the *Serapis*."

As the ships lay to, boatloads of men from the *Vengeance* arrived to help with de-watering, but the pumps had been destroyed, and their efforts were useless. Christopher used them to bring wounded and dead topside and tried to begin a muster. Over two hundred lay dead and many were wounded. From what Christopher had seen on the *Serapis*, their casualties were about the same, although they had started with many more men.

Christopher shuddered at the mounting piles of dead. Blood soaked the decks and was running out of the scuppers. It was the worst battle carnage he had ever seen or heard of.

Late that day, Jones ordered all the wounded transferred to the *Serapis*. When he was sure they were all off, he shifted his flag to the *Serapis*.

That evening he sent Christopher back to the *Bon Homme Richard* to try to salvage his papers and the crews' records. Christopher tried to board the foundering hull a few minutes later, but she was doomed. She rolled over and sank, her colors still flying.

Christopher, hatless, saluted as the colors dipped under the water. He watched the burbling foam for a few minutes, thinking about the ship. "Awful old barn," he muttered. "But Captain Jones made her something special. He could do that with anything."

Christopher sighed and ordered the coxswain back to the *Serapis*.

~

For two days, Christopher, the carpenter, and the boatswain, using the few still able men, managed to rig jury masts and a few sails. Gradually the *Serapis* built up speed and an ability to tack.

Jones followed zigzag courses, aimed to throw off pursuit. The English did not guess he was heading for Texel, and over twenty ships failed to find him.

On October 23rd, the flotilla sailed wearily into Texel Roads and anchored. Jones had spent hours of the voyage in the cabin of the Serapis writing his report of the action.

After they were anchored, Jones called Christopher into his cabin. "Christopher, the time I told you about has come. You have done all I asked. What I have to do now is diplomatic and will take a long time and a lot of useless arguing. You will not be good at it. As a matter of fact you will be a liabilty."

Christopher colored and started to say something. Jones held up his hand. "When I wanted someone to throw Landais off my ship, I depended on you. You are direct, honest, and strong. You take direct action. These people over there don't like that sort of action and I am good at it. You are not, and I'm glad of it. There is something better you can do. I have here a report of our action and a prediction of what will happen to our relations with the Dutch. I want you to take a stage to Paris with these letters and report directly to Mister Franklin. Do not let any of the diplomatic bastards intercept you or ask to see the letters you are carrying. See Franklin directly, and tell him anything he wants to know. He will depend on your oral reports to amplify my writings. After Mister Franklin is through with you, ask him to arrange for your passage on a fast Dutch ship to Philadelphia.

"I trust you still have your passport and civilian clothes. When you get to Philadelphia ask to see the senior members of the Marine Committee and do the same as you did with Franklin.

"When they are through, submit your resignation and take passage to Annapolis. Your duties will be over, and I wish you a happy return to your lovely wife. I look forward to meeting her some day. She is as much of a patriot as you are."

Christopher shook his head sadly. "Captain, I hate to leave you, but my usefulness might not be over. I could help you repair the *Serapis*."

Jones laughed. "She will never be repaired. My way out of here is on the *Alliance*. These letters are only the beginning of a plan to coerce Mister Franklin to bring Landais to book. Franklin will take care of him, but it will take time. Then I will take the *Alliance* and flee through the straits back to L'Orient. You will be long gone, but think of me as I sneak though the waiting English."

Christopher nodded. "They will never catch you."

Jones grinned. "Now pack and get off as soon as you can. I am anxious to get these papers into the right hands."

Chapter 46

That night Matthew took leave of the few shipmates who were not ashore in the hospitals. He gave all his gear and uniforms except for one to Lieutenant Cutting Lunt.

Matthew had a farewell breakfast with Captain Jones, who saw him over the side and watched as he was rowed ashore to the landing in Texel Harbor.

He found the stage office and booked passsage to Paris. "About a week's travel to Paris by fast horses," the agent said in broken English. "You will like the scenery."

Matthew grinned. "Better than that damned gray salt water of the Baltic."

The road was surprisingly good, mostly built on old foundations laid by the Romans. The inns in Holland were clean as were those in Belgium. In France they were dirty, but the food was better. Matthew relaxed and enjoyed the trip as each day brought him closer to home.

On the eighth day the stage clattered over the rough cobblestones into Paris. Matthew booked a room in a small pension, and made his way to Franklin's office. The carriage driver laughed when Matthew asked him if he knew where Franklin's office was. "Everybody knows," he said. "Especially the ladies."

Franklin received Matthew almost immediately and cancelled his day's appointment when he heard who Matthew was. Matthew recognized Frankln as soon as he came into the reception room. His spectacles were unique, and his well-muscled physique was pleasantly overloaded with fat, just as Jones had told him.

Franklin said, "Come into my office, sit down, and count on staying for dinner. We will be talking for a long time. Now have a hot toddy while I read these letters."

Franklin read the letters slowly, now and then nodding or chuckling. When he finished, he looked up. "Remarkable," he said, "I've read all this, but there's more I want to know. Now tell me what happened in your own words."

Matthew talked for an hour and expanded his report to include his early days with Jones and then the troubles with the French and Landais.

When he had finished, Franklin said, "You talk well. I can tell you've read a lot, even though you may lack a formal education."

Matthew nodded. "Correct, sir. I'm going to the college in Annapolis when I get time."

Franklin laughed. "People like you never get time. They'll be after you for political office as soon as you get unpacked."

Franklin asked question after question, each more penetrating than the last. After two hours, he held up his hand, "That's enough for now. Let's have dinner and we'll talk about other things."

The dinner was excellent when compared to what Jones' French chef had produced. Franklin held forth on a dozen subjects. He explained the evolution of the American government operations in France and his difficulties in coping with the scoundrels sent over by Congress to run it.

"You include the four Lee brothers?"

"Oh yes, and the two Adams'. Then there are many French who have helped them."

"And of course Captain Landais."

Franklin laughed uproariously. "That bastard is worth an hour of conversation alone."

"How did he get and keep the *Alliance*?"

"Too long a story for now, but the Adams' and the Lees put him up for it and have been stuck with him, so to speak. I think they'd like to have him go away."

"Will he ever?"

"Don't worry. I'll triumph some day."

Matthew was a good listener, but always contributed to the flow of words. By eight o'clock Matthew was exhilarated, and when Franklin suggested that he see some of the shows in Paris, he was so motivated that he agreed.

They were interesting, but the constant parade of partially naked girls soon palled, and he returned to his pension.

The next day Matthew took the stage to L'Orient, keeping in mind the arrangements Franklin had made for the rest of his trip.

Boarding the Dutch ship with his passport and ticket was easy, and by the next day she was well out in the Atlantic. The next three weeks of the voyage seemed endless. When the debris-filled waters of the gulf stream appeared, Matthew knew the voyage was nearly over.

Two days later the Dutch ship docked at Philadelphia. Matthew booked a hotel room, put on his uniform, and took a carriage to the headquarters of the Continental Navy.

The officer-in-charge greeted him warmly and asked his mission. As soon as he learned where Matthew had come from, he leaped up and made arrangements for a carriage.

"Will it take a long time to get to see the members of the Marine Committee?" Matthew asked.

"They will stop anything they are doing as soon as they know you have reports on the recent battle. We know little about it and the members are very anxious to hear you. I am coming, too. Could I see the letters on our way there?"

Matthew shook his head. "Sorry, sir. I have strict instructions from Captain Jones and Mister Franklin to put these letters directly in the hands of the committee. I would hope you can be present."

At the office of the Marine Committee they immediately gathered, received Matthew, and passed the pages of the reports from person to person. The Head of the Continental Navy positioned himself at the end of the line and also read the letter. After the members of the Committee had questioned Matthew for an hour, the senior member said, "Lieutenant, we are through and you may carry out the rest of your orders. I understand from the letter that you are going to resign and return to Annapolis. Captain Jones speaks in glowing terms of your service. If you ever want any help, please call on us. Also, I would think we would put you in command almost immediately, if you should choose to stay in the navy."

Christopher nodded politely. "Thank you, sir, but I only want to command my own shipyard again. I will call on you if we can do mutual business in the future."

Christopher left and made reservations to leave on the next packet for Annapolis. Two days later he was eagerly waiting to land in Annapolis.

He trotted up the street, carrying his much lighter seabag. He knocked loudly on his door, and a voice inside said, "Don't knock so loud. I'm coming."

The door flew open, and it was Mammy Sarah. Her frown changed to a broad smile. "Mister Matthew! I'm so glad to see you!" She flung her arms around him and then let him go. "Your family is in the study. Go."

Matthew flung aside the seabag and ran to the study. Martha gasped when she saw him and ran into his arms. She held him tightly for several minutes before the children realized who was there. Then they ran over and grabbed at his trousers, trying to get his attention.

When he could disengage himself, he said, "I'm here for good, and this time I mean it. Where's that commission I left with you?"

Martha pointed to the wall, and walked over and took it down. She held it out to him. He noticed that a large black cross had been made across the face of it. "Why did you do this?"

"You asked me to hang it. I did. I wanted to save it for your children, but with the markings it's no good if anybody comes after you again."

"You're right. Put it back up to remind me that I'm permanently out of the navy. Now I belong to you only, and there's no date on that."

Matthew leaned down and hoisted his son. Martha picked up their daughter. Matthew laughed and swept the three of them into his powerful arms.

Martha's smile was happy, but her eyes were filled with tears. She held them all a more tightly, as realization spread in her heart that happiness was stretching far ahead now and her lonely months were over. Now she and her children could enjoy the life she had longed for over the many years.